MW00639531

GOODBYE
Birdie Greenwing

www.penguin.co.uk

Also by Ericka Waller

Dog Days

GOODBYE Birdie Greenwing

ERICKA WALLER

doubleday

TRANSWORLD PUBLISHERS
Penguin Random House, One Embassy Gardens,
8 Viaduct Gardens, London SW11 7BW
www.penguin.co.uk

Transworld is part of the Penguin Random House group of companies
whose addresses can be found at global.penguinrandomhouse.com

First published in Great Britain in 2024 by Doubleday
an imprint of Transworld Publishers

A CIP catalogue record for this book
is available from the British Library.

ISBNs 9780857527257 (hb)
9780857527264 (tpb)

Typeset in 11.75/16pt Fairfield LT Std by Jouve (UK), Milton Keynes
Printed and bound in Great Britain by Clays Ltd, Elcograf S.p.A.

The authorized representative in the EEA is Penguin Random House Ireland,
Morrison Chambers, 32 Nassau Street, Dublin D02 YH68.

Penguin Random House is committed to a sustainable future
for our business, our readers and our planet. This book is made
from Forest Stewardship Council® certified paper.

1

For Aunt, for ever

So Eden sank to grief,
So dawn goes down to day.
Nothing gold can stay.

Robert Frost

Prologue

BRIGHTON IS AN ADVENT calendar; we are counting down the days. Behind each door, cardboard people are sleeping, unaware of how fragile their lives are, of what is coming. Birdie and Audrey snooze at number six Shrublands Road. Audrey's snores are loud, but to Birdie, they are musical. Birdie dreams of Rose and Arthur, of days that have already passed and things that have already happened. Birdie has an appointment tomorrow that will kick her back into the present.

Next door, at number eight, Jane and Frankie Brown are doing the washing-up. Jane has one eye on her phone in case her sister, Suki, texts her. Her fingers, in the bowl, are crossed in hope. Frankie doesn't want to go to school tomorrow. She is planning to stay up all night and watch documentaries about taxidermy. She misses her grandmother, Min, but doesn't say so. There is dried porridge on the rim of the saucepan Jane hands her. Frankie hands it back.

Up in Bristol, Min Brown is awake too, clearing out her cupboard. It's been on her mind. She wonders how Frankie and Jane are doing. She gave them her best milk pan and her second sharpest knife. She worries about their fridge, how full it is, when their bathroom was last bleached. Did the landlord make it nice for them? Min finishes polishing the doors and moves on to the sink. Maybe if she scrubs hard enough, she can clean the pipes all the way down to Brighton. A secret tunnel from her house to her daughter's. If Min could, if Jane asked, she'd crawl down and scour the sewers all the way too. But she hasn't been invited. All she can do is wait. They'll need her soon enough.

At number twenty-two, Ada is reading a medical journal, scanning for the latest developments. Her white coat is on a hanger by the door, neatly ironed and ready for the next day. Ada is always ready, of course. Sometimes she looks out of her window and longs for someone to call for help, so that she can run outside, into the street, stethoscope round her neck, so that she can save the day.

Outside, the moon is on the move, the stars are all aligned. A breeze whispers through the leaves on the trees. Under their feet the Earth is turning. Sands are shifting in the deepest abyss beneath the sea. A change is coming. None of the people on Shrublands Road have any idea that tomorrow is hurtling towards them like a comet. Best let them get some rest while they still can.

I

Birdie

BIRDIE'S MOUTH IS COBWEB dry and her throat hurts. A crawling sense of fear, like spotting spiders in the corners of a garden shed, coats her tongue. She automatically reaches for Rose's hand, but Rose is not beside her.

'Did you hear what I said, Mrs Greenwing?'

Tears load like bullets behind Birdie's eyes.

'Yes,' she croaks, blinking hard.

The doctor pushes a box of tissues across the desk towards her and says nothing.

Birdie holds her own hands tightly under the desk, an impossible knot of knuckles, focuses on her breathing. Her lungs are two rusty saws, cutting the air so it comes in jagged fragments. Her vision blurs, violet dots dance across the room, but Birdie refuses to pass out. She forces in a breath, thin as a straw, then out, then another and another, until she can no longer feel her heartbeat pounding in her chest. Until the fingers of panic remove themselves from her eyes. The world comes back, slowly colouring itself in.

And then Birdie can hear everything. The clock ticking,

rubber-soled shoes squeaking in the corridor outside. The over-watered plant in the waiting room photosynthesizing.

Just for a single second, Birdie is aware of the whole world. Newborn babies on the top floor opening little mouths, like purse clasps, in the second before their first cry. The flop of a heavy breast as it is hoicked out of a flannel nightgown, leaking colostrum, like butter.

Birdie can feel the needles in the phlebotomy department, that sharp scratch inside the elbow, stormy-blue veins releasing an indecent shade of red. The pain of the amputees' phantom limbs down in Skylark Ward. Birdie can sense arms she never had burning. The sole of someone else's foot itching through her nylon pop-sock. The breathing apparatus in the critical-care ward, pumping like pistons. The crinkle of the prescription bags in the pharmacy, as they are handed over the counter. The release of a catheter being removed, the intrusion of the enema. Birdie's body, a collection of stigmata. As if she's not just been given her news, but the news of everybody else. Every wince, every cautious step on crutches. Each X-ray showing her bones. The hole where her sister should be.

'I'm afraid there are no treatment options available.'

The oncologist, Dr Ada Kowalska, had laid out each word carefully, alongside a leaflet, like a garnish on a tray of sandwiches. Time ticks loudly in this quiet room. One second gone, and then another.

'How long do I have left?' Birdie asks finally. Her voice wobbles only slightly as she speaks, like a well-set trifle carried by steady hands. Meanwhile, underneath the table, bone-white fingers clutch the strap of her handbag.

'Take as much time as you need,' Dr Kowalska says, in her clipped accent, neatly sidestepping what Birdie is asking her. 'You must have lots of questions. Would you like me to repeat anything?'

Birdie opens her beak, but nothing comes out, so she closes it again. When she used to take her sister Rose to the doctor, Birdie always brought along a list. What will these pills do and what side effects might they cause? What should we expect? How soon might they make a difference?

'Do you have someone with you?' Ada asks.

'Yes, Audrey. My dog. Well, she's at home waiting for me,' Birdie babbles, as she does when she's nervous. Rose would pinch her arm to make her stop.

She sees the doctor frown, a wrinkle sliding across her perfect forehead like a crease in silk.

'Do you have anyone else at home, Mrs Greenwing?'

Birdie shakes her head hard, like a horse does when flies have settled on its eyelashes. Birdie's flies are sadness, fear, the fact that she lives alone. She cannot make them leave. 'How long?' she asks again. 'Tell me, please.'

The doctor shuffles a stack of papers. Clicks her mouse. She's biding her time, but what about Birdie's?

They are on the fifteenth floor of the hospital. Outside the window, the rusted green turrets of crumbling buildings pierce an Earl Grey sky smudged with clouds. Someone has wedged their attic window open with a shopping trolley. Unmatched trainers hang by their laces from sagging phone lines. Chimneys stripe the air with black smoke. Birdie sees the tops of red buses, of glass bus stops, seagull-splattered white vans. She sees tiny people scurrying busily, spreading through the city like spilled ink. Birdie flies above it all, as though she's already left.

'I really don't—' the doctor starts to say.

'Three months? Six?' Birdie interrupts.

The oncologist looks at her notes again and blinks. What a horrible question to know the answer to, Birdie thinks.

'Well, we never know for sure, but . . . four months, maybe six,' Dr Kowalska says finally. 'But . . .'

Birdie nods. She understands. No promises are being made. What do you do when your life has been given an expiry date?

'Just think what Princess Margaret would do,' Rose would suggest, if she were here. Birdie and Rose adored Queen Elizabeth's sister, were convinced that they were directly related to her. 'We have her nose, her *je ne sais quoi*!' Rose scoured the society pages for her heroine's latest scandal, hooting in staunch approval at every turn. If Princess Margaret were sentenced to death in six months, she'd demand someone else die for her, then waltz out smelling of Chanel and fur coats. She'd buy herself a delightful new hat and wear it to the Ritz for a vodka pick-me-up.

The thought raises Birdie on to shaking legs. She belts her wool coat tightly, as though binding herself together. 'Thank you for your time, Doctor.'

'Mrs Greenwing, we have more things to go through. Please—'

But Birdie has heard enough. What else is there to say? Shutting the door behind her, Birdie keeps her head down as she passes back through the waiting room. She doesn't want to see the expressions on expectant faces, as if she's been in some exam and they can tell how hard it has been from looking at her. I failed, she thinks. Or passed, I suppose, depending on how you look at it.

As she walks on, Birdie wonders how many people have made this same stunned exit from the oncologist's room, their lives forever altered from just half an hour earlier, everything in their existence boiled down to the result of a scan. Pearly ribs in grey soup. No extra points for good behaviour. For not speeding, for separating the recycling or washing clothes at thirty degrees.

I'm *dying*, Birdie thinks, wondering why she's so surprised. Her body has always let her down, after all. In her mother's womb it took too much, leaving her twin, Rose, with less. Then her own womb failed to reproduce. Now it's eating itself. She should be happier about this outcome, surely. Birdie had *wanted* to die after Arthur and Rose were gone. She'd tried to lure Death round for a nightcap, seduce it with her indecent dressing-gown. And now Death has finally RSVP'd, so why isn't Birdie feeling better about the news?

'Well, hello again, Birdie Greenwing.' The voice comes from a barely visible head, topped with a whip of white candyfloss hair. Both hair and voice belong to Connie, who runs the WRVS café in the centre of the hospital. 'Long time no see.'

'Connie!' Birdie says. 'You remember me?'

Connie is tiny. Even smaller than the last time Birdie saw her. She barely reaches above the high counter. Her black skin is paper thin, her arms are like twigs, but her eyes are bright, her gums pink when she smiles.

'Of course I do,' Connie says. 'You and your sister – Rose, was it? – used to come here all the time.'

Connie makes the place sound like a restaurant, not a hospital. Birdie wants to answer but finds she can only nod.

'Well,' Connie says, 'you look like you need a nice cup of tea. Go and sit down. I'll bring it over to you.'

Birdie is in no rush to go home and tell Audrey the news. She slumps gratefully into a plastic seat at the back of the café by the window that overlooks the optimistically named 'pleasure garden'. Seagulls peck at empty crisps packets. A man in a dressing-gown smokes a cigarette with one hand and holds his IV drip stand with the other. His gown is gaping open, like theatre curtains, and sagging nipples and a fluff-covered gut take a bow when he bends down to pick up his coffee. The bushes are bare and brown, the paths cracked and faded. Birdie struggles to spot any pleasure.

When Connie finally shuffles over, there is also a scone on the tray. 'Fresh out of the oven,' she says. 'Tuck in.'

Rose and Birdie used to love scones, but were dreadful at making them. 'How can such nice ingredients turn into something so horrible?' Rose used to marvel, looking at their hard, bulbous creations, the raisins bitter and burned. 'They could be served as a punishment,' she said. 'I sentence thee to four homemade scones and no water to wash them down with.'

'No! I beg you, Your Honour, anything but death by scone!'

Birdie takes a small bite. It is warm, buttery, soft. Is this the last scone she's ever going to eat? She loads on more butter, just in case. Another dollop of jam. It's not a Princess Margaret level of debauchery, but she's trying.

Plate empty, Birdie goes to take a sip of tea. As she swallows, she notices that the mug is emblazoned with the words

'Cheer up! It might never happen.' Birdie chokes. Raisins fly from her mouth and she sprays tea across the wonky tin table on to her hands, on to her wool coat. Her coughing fit is so loud that it scares off the seagulls outside in the pleasure garden. When the tears finally come, Birdie is not sure if she's laughing or crying.

2

Jane

Jane's alarm clock vibrates itself across the nightstand, as though it's coming for her. She reaches blindly to turn it off, knocking over a framed picture of her and her sister Suki. Both have their mouths open in mock horror. The ghost train broke down halfway through the ride. A teenager who, like someone from a Dire Straits song, smelt like leather and diesel led them out through the back of the ride, shuffling past plastic skeletons missing limbs, a Frankenstein's monster faded from green to puce. Suki has a copy of the photo, too, or did have. Jane sighs and gets up, her spine clicking into place. She pulls on her uniform, then plumps up her pillow. Just once, Jane would like someone else to make her bed for her.

'Morning,' Jane says, when she makes her way into the living room.

Her twelve-year-old daughter, Frankie, nods but doesn't look up. Jane glances at the screen, where two women – Pat and Janet – stand in white coats and yellow gloves, trying to decide where to start de-cluttering a hoarder's house. Collecting old hamster bedding is undoubtedly troubling, but even more so, surely, are people like Pat and Janet, who happily go into strangers' homes and clean them for free. Is this what Pat and Janet dreamed of in their childhood beds? Jane wonders. Being on morning TV wearing a hairnet, armed with bleach and poking at old grey underpants with kitchen tongs?

'Morning, Pat, howya, Janet,' Jane says, giving the screen a wave with one hand as she twists up her long hair with the other. 'Love that seashell necklace, Pat. Is it new?'

'She can't hear you,' Frankie says flatly.

Jane notices Frankie has the phone to her ear. 'Morning, Min!' Jane says.

'Min says shush,' Frankie says. 'We're trying to watch Pat and Janet.'

Jane tries very hard not to picture her mother, alone in her spotless house in Bristol, her granddaughter reduced to a voice down the phone.

'We'll always have *Britain's Biggest Hoarders*,' Frankie had told Min as she was leaving, as though she were Humphrey Bogart telling Ingrid Bergman, 'We'll always have Paris.' Bogart and Bergman's romance had ended abruptly at the beginning of the Second World War with the Nazi invasion of France.

Jane had felt like a stormtrooper herself as she marshalled Frankie out of the house, the two of them laden with suitcases, Min's happiness crammed into one, alongside Jane's old knickers losing their elastic and Frankie's retainer brace.

'Right! Let's tackle that kitchen!' Pat cries on screen, rubbing her Marigolds together enthusiastically.

'No, let's get to the bathroom,' says Janet, brandishing a plunger. 'I can smell it from here.'

'Hallway,' Frankie says into the phone. 'Start with the hallway – right, Min, clear a path first?'

Jane had hoped Frankie would make some actual friends when they moved to Brighton, but so far she just has Pat and Janet from the telly and phone calls to Min. That said, Jane is doing no better herself. She clicks on the kettle, pulls down a mug. Milk in first, two teabags and two big sugars added quickly before Frankie sees. Frankie calls salt and sugar 'the deadly whites'. Jane imagines them like the Kray twins, a pair of gangsters. She spots a Tupperware box and knows that inside it she will find perfectly measured amounts of protein, carbs, grains and veg. Frankie's focus is on calories and nutrition; flavour and variety are secondary.

Frankie is a worrier. She frets about Jane getting tired in the afternoons. Worries that she'll forget to cling to the pole on the bus when it stops. That Jane's cheap shoes will be slippery in wet weather. Life is an accident waiting to happen, according to Frankie. She wants her mother to live like an egg, padded in cotton wool, lest she crack. Jane secretly googles sky-diving and wing-walking with the furtiveness other people have when they search for porn.

Since leaving Min, Jane and Frankie have each wanted to mother the other. They argue over who pushes the shopping trolley, who opens the post, who pours the boiling pasta water down the drain, who takes out the bins, who answers the phone, and which one calls the final goodnight. Back in Bristol, Min used to do all these things. Without her around, their roles in the relationship, in anything, feel uncertain. Jane wants Frankie to be a happy, carefree child. Frankie wants Jane to take atmospheric pressure more seriously. Back in Bristol, Min calls and calls and calls.

'Once more unto the breach,' Jane says, as they zip up coats, check pockets for tissues and lip balms, and head out into the windy morning.

'Don't forget to drink plenty of water,' Frankie says. 'You don't want another dehydration headache.'

'Don't eat your boiled eggs in class.'

'Why not?' Frankie pulls one from each pocket. 'They serve a dual purpose. Excellent hand warmers until ten a.m. and then a healthy snack.'

'But they smell,' Jane says.

Frankie stops to look at her mother, a frown scrunching her eyebrows together. Jane wants to smooth them down, stroke them like two tiny shrews, but Frankie cannot be touched.

'So what?' Frankie says.

As a child, Jane tried to blend into the background, to fly under the radar. She dreaded being asked to read aloud in class, would stumble over the words, the book trembling in her hands. You could have fried an egg on her blushing cheeks when she was called on to answer a question. Getting changed for PE was her worst nightmare. She still remembers her padded crop top, the high-waisted knickers Min ordered in bulk. All Jane wants to do is prevent Frankie from being picked on or singled out. She cannot go to school for her, but she can try to soften the blows.

'They are the most perfect form of protein available,' Frankie continues. 'The sulphur in the boiled egg white creates hydrogen sulphide gas when it reacts with the iron in the egg yolk. That's what the smell is. A chemical reaction.'

Frankie didn't speak, didn't say a word, until she was almost four years old. When she finally found her voice, buried deep inside her, it was as though everything she'd noticed since birth needed excavating. As though she'd finally crowbarred open the tomb of her mind. All of it, the good, the bad and the ugly, spilled out. Frankie raced through language learning. Dog, bird. Red shoe. Black-and-white zebra. Butter comes from cows that eat green grass. I don't like that person's hair. This fabric is too itchy. This place smells. That person has a rotten tooth. I don't like the sound of birdsong. Frankie defaced princess stories and fairy tales. Talking animals on the television made her furious. Frankie wanted facts, and more facts. 'But is it true?' she would demand when told anything. 'Is it real?'

Frankie didn't cry often, but when she did, she really went for it. The only thing that calmed her was covering her head with a cellular blanket that Min named Charlie Cloth. Underneath squares of soft cotton, Frankie's world became pixilated, muffled, manageable. 'I'm not happy,' Frankie would mutter. 'I'm not happy. I'm not happy. I'm not happy.' Jane would rock her daughter, a sad little ghost in her arms, shamefully enjoying the way Frankie clung to her like a limpet. How needed Jane was, how only she would do.

Min would whip Charlie Cloth off Frankie's head as soon as she'd calmed down and put it straight on a hot wash, as though sadness, feeling different or unhappy could be boiled away, bleached out with sunshine on a windy washing line. Once, Jane came home from work to find Min wedged under Charlie Cloth alongside a sobbing Frankie.

'Well, I'm not happy either,' she heard Min say. 'They've put up the price of long-life milk. Shouldn't be allowed. Took me ten minutes to find the bleddy stuff because they keep moving things around for no reason other than to waste my blinking time. Loo rolls where the boil-in-the-bag fish used to be. Bananas in the cleaning aisle. Then your man over the road has got himself a bike and keeps appearing out in some sort of skin-tight costume doing his stretches. Enough to put me off my porridge. Her at number four had a party last night. Did you hear it? Eight thirty p.m. and what happens? They only start doing some sort of bleddy line dance up and down the road. Singing about pushing pineapples and shaking trees. I called the police. Noise pollution, I said. What's that, Frankie? You feel better now?'

Jane had crept back out, sweet and sour tears trickling down her face.

Now, as she turns to shut the front gate, Jane spots their next-door neighbour setting out to walk her dog. If you could call it a dog, that is. It looks more like a hairy orange-and-white tank. The woman seems to be about Min's age, but Min would never wear a yellow raincoat like that. Nor would Min leave the house without a headscarf knotted under her chin. 'Hair thievery on the up again, is it, Min?' Suki used to say, as Min checked her scarf was securely tied in place.

'Look, Frankie, there's our neighbour,' Jane says. She waves, but the woman doesn't notice. 'We must go round and introduce ourselves later.'

'Hmm,' is all Frankie says, walking ahead. Frankie is not a fan of meeting new people, exchanging pleasantries or making eye contact. That is not to say she doesn't notice everything with her hidden third eye. Frankie knows the names of most of the people on their street already and, more often than not, what they do for a living.

'Tony and Bill at number ten both work for the council,' Frankie says, as they pass their shining black and green bins, bedecked with stickers. 'That's how they got those extra recycling bins.'

'How do you know all this?' Jane once asked, when Frankie had commented that Adrian Holmes at number three must be off to do his shift at the blood bank.

'I asked Ivy Dell, the Neighbourhood Watch woman, when she came round,' Frankie said, as if it were obvious.

'Quite the open book, wasn't she? Let's hope Ivy Dell cares more about the security of the street than she does about confidentiality,' Jane said.

'Min said you'd say that,' Frankie replied.

'Yes, well, Min wouldn't know privacy if it tap-danced in front of her.'

They carry on down the road towards Frankie's school. Every time Jane leaves Frankie at breakfast club, she feels a small candle being snuffed out inside her, guilt like oily smoke in her guts. If Jane had stayed in Bristol, Min could have carried on dropping Frankie at school at eight forty, not seven thirty. *Bad mother*. A bell clangs in Jane's head. *Shame, shame, shame.*

'I hate breakfast club,' Frankie says, as she does every morning.

'I know. I'm sorry,' Jane always says in reply. Around her, other mothers are apologizing to their sons and daughters. For having to work, for wanting to. Jane hears bribes of pizza and sweets. Of weekend treats and cinema trips as the parents look at their watches, frowning at the time, already at work in their minds.

When Frankie and Jane say goodbye, they do not say, 'I love you.' The words carry no weight for Frankie. Instead, they nod solemnly at one another – two comrades on a mission.

'See you later,' Jane says.

'Unless something terrible happens,' Frankie says.

On the bus, Jane thinks of how Brighton is not quite the same place she remembered. When she planned her move, she imagined sunshine and sea-swimming. She forgot that it rains here too. That the wind blows right through you. Today the clouds are the colour of brains and the sea is a sickly green. A yellow scum of foam has washed up on to the beach. Seventeen-year-old Jane used to love the graffiti and the traffic, the smell of brine and petrol. Thirty-two-year-old Jane notices the litter on the streets, the homeless people propped up in doorways, their clothes-horse bones draped in rags. Jane notices the cost of fish and heating bills. She'd been unprepared for so much disappointment. Is it her age? Has Brighton changed, or is it because Suki is not at her side?

Her phone rings as she is digging in her bag for her pass.

'My pipes are frozen.'

'Good morning to you too, Min. Have you called the local plumber?' Jane asks.

'I don't trust him. Karen says he's a peeping Tom.'

'Karen is not a reliable source of information.'

Guilt and Annoyance see-saw inside Jane, jockeying for position. You should not have moved away from your mother, says Guilt. Your mother could at least try to understand your decision, says Annoyance. I hate breakfast club, comes Frankie's voice from somewhere inside Jane's cracked heart.

'I'll have a look later and find you someone else,' Jane says.

'And what about my microwave? It's playing silly buggers.'

'Have you made sure the glass tray is in properly? Turning round as it should?' Jane says.

Min's silence speaks volumes.

'Min, I've got to go. I'll call you as soon as I can, okay?'

Min mutters something along the lines of no one caring whether she lives or dies, then rings off. There is no time to call her back. A team member is off sick. Jane's morning is a blur of catheter checks and blood-pressure cuffs, cups of tea and picking up dropped dressing-gowns, checking for bladder infections and dishing out compression stockings, noting pulse rates and passing out tiny paper cups of pills.

When she checks her phone at break, there's a text from Frankie complaining about the book they're studying in English. *A boy is washed up on an island in the Pacific after falling from his parents' yacht. Impossible for the following reasons.* Frankie goes on to list them.

There is also a text from Suki: *Have you spoken to Min? She's having problems with her plumbing. Obvs I can't do anything from here.*

Jane feels the hairs on the back of her neck prickle. She fights the urge to text back that Suki *could* move home from Japan, or wherever it is she's working these days, and share the responsibility, instead of burdening Jane with everything while she gallivants about, living the life of Riley. Jane is aware how much like Min she sounds as she thinks this, which annoys her even more. 'What is a gallivant, Min?' Frankie once asked. 'What does it do?'

'Never you mind,' Min had said.

Jane stabs out *Yes, will sort* and then, unable to help herself, adds *How are you?* before pressing send. She worries at a piece of loose skin round her nail as she waits for a response. She should just rip it off and be done with it. Suki doesn't reply and Jane leaves the tag of skin, red and sore.

Behind her on the ward, a patient presses her call bell and the phone rings on the desk. A visitor cannot find her mother. Jane is sucked back into the here and now, each task all-consuming, leaving no time for thought. She doesn't check her phone again until she's on the bus home. Frankie has given her a running commentary of her day. In summary, nothing good has happened. Suki hasn't replied. Suki, who used to write 'from the cradle to the grave' in all of Jane's birthday cards. Suki, who held her hand when she had period pains and wiped away her tears when Min's mean streak left a wound. Suki, who went first down flights of stairs so that if Jane fell she'd be there to cushion the fall.

How did it come to this? Jane thinks. Could one decision really have undone so much?

'I hate after-school club,' Frankie says, when Jane walks into the cold room. It smells of stale lunchboxes and PE kits left to fester in the bottom of bags. 'The teacher smells of soup.'

'Sorry,' Jane says. 'Let's get you home.'

'Ms Brown?'

Jane feels every vertebra in her back stiffen at the sound of the teacher's voice.

'Do you have time for a quick word?'

Jane pastes on a papier-mâché smile. It is made from sheets of words that Frankie has called people. From opinions on what is wrong with her daughter. It's old news. Jane pulls her lips into a lemon shape, lets them dry hard and firm. 'Not today, sorry,' she says stiffly, through the glue. 'We have to go to the dentist. Come on, Frankie, or we'll be late.'

'We do not have the—' Frankie says, as Jane pulls her out of the door.

'—dentist?' Frankie finishes, when they are outside. Jane looks at her. 'Oh,' Frankie says, after a moment. 'You lied.'

'I did. I assume you, on the other hand, told some of your hard home truths.'

'Some people should not be allowed to sing,' Frankie says, 'or use scissors. Min says it's best to let people know when they're wasting their time.'

On cue, Jane's phone rings. She pulls it out of her bag and hands it over to Frankie.

'Hi, Min!' Frankie says. 'Guess what happened today . . .'

3

Ada

ADA THINKS OF BIRDIE Greenwing as she heads towards the *Polski sklep* on London Road. It is hidden between a row of other corner shops that are not on corners (one of many English idioms Ada has come to learn), and sells fruit and veg and imported produce to the xenophobic and the homesick. Ada's white coat is folded over her arm, and she's changed from her work heels into her old boots. She wishes she could swap her oncologist's head as easily. It had been a shock to realize she lived on the same road as Birdie. Not that Ada knows many of her neighbours. She nods at them if one passes by, picks up their recycling bins if they have fallen over. Once, a woman called Ivy knocked on her door asking Ada if she'd like to watch the neighbourhood. Ada pretended not to speak very good English.

Ada wishes she hadn't noticed the quiver in Birdie's voice, the way she shook her head when Ada asked her if she had anyone at home. Ada's mother, Janina, would have taken Birdie round a basket of homemade goodies as soon as she heard the news. A bottle of homemade cordial. She would have sent Ada's father, Marek, round with eggs, and Ada with a stew. 'We look after our neighbours, Ada,' she would say. 'That is what we do.'

Ada tells herself to stop. She's not in Poland now. She doesn't live in a village any more and her neighbours are not her friends. They share a postcode, nothing more. Ada steps off the pavement and crosses the road, as if she can leave her thoughts on the other side. She skips through the row of cars that snake along the seafront in a solid line of hot traffic, tail-lights like red eyes, exhausts coughing out smoke. Inside, impatient drivers tap steering wheels, pick noses, beep horns. Refuse to let anyone in.

Ada thinks of their farm back home, the field where their horses gathered beneath overhanging trees. In spring, the branches reached out like hands and sprouted sticky leaves that autumn discarded. No matter the weather, the mares would stamp their hoofs when they saw Ada approaching. Would shamble over, flanks swaying slowly, plumes of white breath streaming from their noses. The warm, musty smell of sweat and leather, the softness of their muzzles in her out-stretched palm. Silence lay like a blanket over everything, warm and safe. Now Ada rounds a discarded sofa on the pavement, dodges a man walking six miniature dachshunds, ignores the two students busking, saucepans for drums, wooden spoons for sticks.

The *Polski sklep* isn't much to look at from the outside. The red paint on the shutter is peeling like sunburn. A stand of free magazines, pages flapping, like gummy mouths talking. The window display is dusty and faded, labels now illegible. Inside, the shelves are overfilled, the aisles narrow and cluttered. Ada has to press herself into a shelf of ketchup to let someone pass.

'*Wybaczcie mi.*'

'*Bez problem.*'

Ada loads up a basket with beetroot, plum jam, white cheese and smoked mackerel, frozen *pierogi*, thick red sausage, sweet paprika crisps and doughnuts filled with rose jelly. The freezer at the far end hums angrily. The door to the storage room is ajar. Ada can see a bucket and mop, the same packs of toilet roll her mother buys. Polish Radio London plays through a tinny speaker. At the counter, the owner, Lech, argues with his son, Aleksey, about stock. Aleksey spots Ada, winks and rolls his eyes at his father. 'Ada, my saviour. Have you finally come to agree to our marriage?' he asks. Beside him, Lech snorts.

'Hello, Aleksey. Do you have any *ćwikła*?' Ada says.

'No, but I have a lump I need you to check out,' Aleksey says, grinning at her.

'There is nothing wrong with you,' Ada says firmly.

'Oh, there is,' Lech says, as he hands Ada some homemade horseradish sauce.

'Just come for dinner,' Aleksey implores. 'One dinner. You'll fall in love with me after you've tasted my sausage stew.'

Ada sighs but her mouth twitches. It's impossible not to like Aleksey with his buzzcut and tight T-shirts, the twinkle in his eye and the way he bickers with his father but never loses his patience. He's been asking Ada out ever since she first stepped into his shop eight years ago. He doesn't ever mean it.

She heads to the cleaning aisle. A smashed jar of sauerkraut has been swept into a corner and abandoned. Ada can smell the vinegar. She unscrews the top of a bottle of laundry detergent, closes her eyes briefly and smells her mother's tea-towels, drying on the washing line. She is surrounded by familiar spices, people murmuring in her mother tongue. Ada hides inside the moment, missing her own *matka*.

'Got you a little something,' Lech says, handing over a brown parcel when Ada goes to pay.

She's always being given extras. 'You've already given me something,' Ada says, pulling out her purse again.

'Put that away.' Lech tuts. 'I scratch your back . . .'

In return she examines Lech's mole for him in the store cupboard, wedged among the cleaning supplies. 'Looks fine, no bigger or darker. You should still go to your GP about it, though,' Ada says.

'I don't need him. I have you,' Lech says simply.

'It's not my area,' Ada argues.

There's a pounding on the door.

'Get out, old man. It's my turn in the cupboard with Dr Ada.'

'Go out with Aleksey, just once,' Lech says quietly, buttoning up his shirt.

'Yes, what he said,' Aleksey calls through the door.

'You have the ears of an elephant,' Lech says.

'That's not the only big thing about me . . .' Aleksey calls back.

Ada laughs, swears at him in Polish. Feels a brief sense of kinship, but the moment is popped, like a balloon, when she remembers Birdie Greenwing. Ada wonders what Birdie did when she got home and there was no one to share her news with, to press a cup of tea and a tissue into her hands. What will happen to Birdie now? There are procedures in place for this sort of thing, for people who live alone, services and charities, but even so . . . Birdie left too soon. Ada feels their meeting was incomplete. Not that there was anything more to say, really. Birdie's cancer was and is inoperable. It's a case of managing her pain, but Birdie left before Ada could ask her about that. There is more that Ada wants to say to Birdie Greenwing, but she's not sure what it is.

'Stay for dinner,' Lech implores.

'I can't,' Ada says, and means it. She can smell something wonderful, is tempted to cave in and accept, but then she'd have to return the favour and she can't. She mustn't take too much without being able to give back the same. She stays for a shot of cherry vodka, though.

'To the best doctor in England,' Lech says. 'Shame for Poland, really.'

When Ada first qualified (top of her class), she had taken a job as a GP near her village. Shined up her name plaque daily and ordered her reference books neatly. Fervently cleaned her stethoscope, keenness oozing from every pore. To start with, she had enjoyed it. Children with coughs and colds. Pregnant mothers. Men with bad backs, farmers with infected wounds, animal bites and sciatica. Then one day her mother's friend, Magda, had walked into her consulting room.

'Please don't tell anyone I'm here,' Magda had whispered.

'Of course not,' Ada said. 'Anything you tell me is confidential.'

Magda stood, looking awkward.

'Please, have a seat,' Ada said, trying not to feel like a child again at the sight of her.

Magda used to look after Ada when she was little, while her mother ran her monthly market stall. Magda and her mother were the same age, born the same month. Janina would always make Magda a poppy-seed cake. Magda would make Janina an apple and sour cream crumble. When Magda looked after Ada, she'd stew pears for her with cinnamon and sing her a broken nursery rhyme, '*A-a-a, kotki dwa*'. Magda used to call Ada her little kitten, pour her a glass of cold milk, let her roll out and pat warm dough. Magda went to church every Sunday, was always collecting donations for some cause or another.

'I'm bleeding,' Magda said to Ada, a blush staining her cheeks.

'Okay,' Ada said, trying to sound calm. She knew Magda had already been through the menopause. 'How long has this been happening?'

'A long time,' Magda said. Then, after a pause, 'I hoped it would stop.'

Ada has heard that sentence many times since. 'I prayed it might go away on its own'; 'I thought it was nothing.'

People put faith in luck as though cancer is a bet placed on a roulette wheel. When Marie Curie's mother died from tuberculosis, Marie renounced Catholicism, vowed that she would never again believe in the benevolence of God. Ada hadn't really understood what Marie meant until Magda died only a few months after her visit to Ada. No one knew the real reason why. Ada never told her mother, who wept over the stove as she made a stew for Magda's widowed husband. Ada realized then that if she stayed at home others would come. That one day her mother might come, ask Ada to have a quick look at something. Or, worse, her mother wouldn't ask, would think she was putting Ada out, wasting her time. Ada felt like a plague doctor, still part of her village but separated by a mask. By knowledge.

Her decision was made. Ada applied to extend her training in England, specializing in oncology. She'd treat faceless people in a foreign land, strangers who wouldn't remember her when she was small and scared of snails and thunderstorms. Ada would treat people she didn't carry home with her in her heart. Or, at least, that was the idea.

'See you soon, Aleksey,' Ada says.

'All of you, I hope.'

'You are a pig, Aleksey. Go and clean out the bins,' Lech says.

Ada leaves, swinging her bulging bags of shopping.

Her bungalow is cold and dark when she walks in. Turning on the lights makes no difference. The empty walls throw up shadows. Ada did try. She went to IKEA. Bought everything needed to make a living room. The *gronlid* sofa, the *besta* TV stand. Even the *svartnora* side lamps and pictures of white beaches. The vase she saw in the showroom, plastic flowers, battery-lit candles. It all went into the trolley, and back at home Ada arranged it exactly the same as it was shown in the brochure. None of it made the place come alive, though. None of it made the house feel lived in. Ada goes into her white *knoxhult* kitchen, complete with knife racks and *skruvshult* cupboard handles. Unpacks her shopping into her smart blue fridge. Eats what doesn't need chopping or heating. She wonders what Birdie Greenwing is having for dinner. What her mother is cooking. She can still smell Lech and Aleksey's stew, imagine the flavour of it on her tongue, how it would taste like home.

4

Birdie

BIRDIE IS LOST IN the past. She and Rose are ten years old. They are playing hide and seek. Birdie is hiding behind the curtain in the living room that smells of dust. Birdie holds in her breath, a sneeze, a giggle, a tiny little fart. She can hear Rose asking the cat if she's seen Birdie anywhere.

'Is she under the kitchen table? No, she is not. Where could she be, I wonder?'

Birdie's knees tremble with the effort of standing still, of keeping quiet. She knows she's about to be discovered at any second. She always hides here, and Rose knows it. When the sitting-room door is pushed open, Birdie closes her eyes in delicious anticipation. Seconds later, the curtain is pulled back with a *whoosh!*

'Aha! Found you.'

Creeping past their mother, who is ironing fussy frocks in the dining room, the twins make jam-and-cheese sandwiches, mugs of strong cordial, then climb out of their broken bedroom window to sit on the flat roof, which they are absolutely forbidden to do.

Rose swings her bruised legs over the ledge. Birdie tosses

tacky crusts to the seagulls in the garden below. It is a damp squib of a summer. The children in their class are all going camping. One has a chalet booked on the Isle of Wight. It sounds impossibly glamorous. Birdie and Rose, fatherless and poor, have only each other and dreams of their future selves to keep them occupied for six long weeks.

'Violet's eldest sister is getting married, and Violet says she's allowed to pick whatever dress she likes for the wedding,' says Birdie. Rose and Birdie dislike Violet with a passion.

'I bet she picks something awful,' says Rose.

'I bet it's not even true anyway,' Birdie says. 'Remember when she said she was getting a horse?'

'Or when she said she was moving to Paris?' Rose says.

'I'm never going to marry,' Birdie announces grandly. 'It sounds so boring.'

'You don't know. I think it might be fun,' Rose says, wiping a sticky ring of cordial from her mouth with the back of her hand.

'I'm going to be a jockey,' Birdie declares.

'Now *you* sound like Violet. You've never even been on a horse,' Rose argues.

'Dad will teach me,' Birdie says confidently. 'Horses are in our blood.'

Rose and Birdie have never met their father. Their mother never talks about him, but something very bad must have happened, because their grandparents live in a big house in Hassocks with a swimming-pool and tennis court, while they live in a tiny terrace house full of damp. Their mother works as a seamstress and never gets a break, will still be ironing in her grave, according to her. Asking about their father does not go down well, so they have stopped trying. It's easier to make things up. Their favourite explanation for his absence is that he's secretly royal. He fell in love with their mother – who was a bit more fun back then and said things like 'terrific' – and wanted to renounce his place in line to the throne, give up the crown and all the gold ingots, to live in a small hut with their mother surrounded by trees and raise goats, but their mother refused. Told him his duty was to his country and it was too important. They had a tearful, passionate goodbye, their mother vowing never to tell a soul about the true identity of the twins' father. Sometimes Birdie and Rose would act out this tumultuous adieu wearing outfits stolen from the ironing pile.

'Don't ask me to walk away from you, Eunice!' Birdie wailed, hands clasped together. 'You must know you have my whole heart. All the riches in the seven seas are incomparable to your beauty.'

'You must go,' Rose cried back. 'I cannot be responsible for mutiny on the *Bounty*!'

Birdie and Rose followed the royals with the devotion of small-town football fans.

'If you do become a jockey,' Rose had said thoughtfully that day, 'I suppose I could help you look after the horse in the royal stables.'

'Thank you,' Birdie replied. 'If you get married, I'll be nice to your husband.'

'Well, maybe I won't get married. Maybe you and me will live together instead.' Rose paused. 'I'll never leave you, Birdie,' she had promised her then, 'like Dad did to Mum.'

'I'll never leave you either, Rose, no matter what,' Birdie had vowed, meaning every word.

But Rose lied, left Birdie first, although maybe Rose hadn't seen it like that.

Birdie is pulled back to the present by someone ringing the doorbell. This is rare. She used to put a plaster over the buzzer when Rose was having a bad day, would stick a note to the door that read, 'Rose asleep, please come around the back,' so Arthur would know to take off his shoes and tiptoe down the hallway, which he did, like a comedy villain. Before Rose moved in with them, he'd slung open the front door loudly, so it banged on its hinges.

'Where is my wifelet?' Arthur would shout. 'Why is she not waiting with a pipe and hot toddy?'

'Because she's been at work all day too!' Birdie would reply, laughing, and Arthur would come and find her in the kitchen, swing her up into his arms and carry her into the living room for an Old Fashioned and debrief. Best bit, worst bit. Funniest bit. His knuckle in the arch of her foot, massaging away the tension of the day.

Birdie used to be a legal secretary. Clipped along the pavement in conker-coloured shoes feeling very important indeed. She had worked for a very nice man called Mr Dickens, who was old enough to be her father. Even so, Arthur was convinced he was in love with Birdie. ('And why would he not be? The man has eyes, does he not?') Birdie had liked her job, and the people she worked with, but they never got her jokes the way Rose and Arthur did. Her colleagues would be rude to the waitress when out at lunch, or moan about the Queen.

That's my family you're insulting, Birdie would think. Other people's company always made her miss her sister. It was like buying a knock-off handbag. Fine from far away, but up close it was obviously fake. After she left Dickens's, she didn't stay in touch with her colleagues beyond the odd Christmas card.

Birdie and Rose had never been good at making friends. At school, being the only two without a dad, they'd been cast out. Disapproved of, somehow, as if it were their fault. 'You are weird,' the other kids had told them. 'It's not natural to look so alike.' They'd found out early on that children could be unkind. 'We don't need anyone else anyway,' Birdie and Rose used to tell one another. And Birdie had meant it, until she met Arthur.

The doorbell rings again. Audrey finally notices and breaks into a series of yaps and barks, ending on a strangled yodel.

'An excellent guard dog,' Birdie says, getting to her feet. It's probably Ivy from the Neighbourhood Watch, delivering the local newsletter. She'll no doubt lurk about for gossip, asking ridiculous questions like 'And how are you in yourself, Birdie?' as if Birdie could be anyone else. Ivy would like Birdie to take a more active role in watching Shrublands Road. 'You *are* at home a lot . . .' Ivy always said. Birdie goes to as few meetings as possible, just enough to keep Ivy at bay. She has no desire to stand in the road with a pretend speed camera or dob in a neighbour for mixing their recycling. Birdie doesn't want to campaign about potholes or streetlamps. She just wants to be alone with her dog, her memories and the odd gin and tonic.

Birdie considers ignoring the door, but her porch light is on, Audrey is barking madly and it's obvious that Birdie is at home. Plus Ivy won't give up easily. She has a new project: replacing the glass in the bus stop. Birdie doesn't see the point – it will only get smashed again. Sighing, she opens the door.

'Hello! I'm Jane Brown and this is my daughter, Frankie.'

Birdie stares blankly at the two people outside her door. She's never seen them before, but they're looking at her expectantly, as if they have something in common. As if Birdie should know why they're here, on her doorstep, at seven p.m. Ah, Birdie thinks, Jehovah's Witnesses. Rose would keep them talking for ages. Ask them a million questions. Birdie just wants them to go. 'Sorry, I'm not interested in your religion,' she says. She's taken two painkillers on an empty stomach. The edges of her vision and voice are blurred.

'We are your neighbours,' the shorter one says.

The last thing Birdie needs, today of all days, is a sermon about God. She'd laugh if she had the energy for it.

'I'm an atheist,' she says, tugging at Audrey's collar.

'No. We really *are* your neighbours. We've moved in next door to you,' the one called Jane says. 'We just wanted to say hello.'

Birdie pauses. She had noticed a large white van on the drive next to hers recently.

A slim bunch of closed daffodils, held together by a plastic band, is thrust at her through the Audrey-sized gap in the door.

'I'm an atheist too!' Frankie says. 'The Bible is full of impossibilities from start to finish. It claims Adam was nine hundred years old when he died, and the River Nile ran with blood. At one point Moses grew actual horns, and then there's the talking donkey. My grandmother Min says whoever wrote it must have been smoking something funny.'

Birdie longs to shut the door, put several inches of wood between her and these smiling, friendly people. They are so bright, so shiny and fresh, like a bowl of waxy lemons, it hurts her eyes to look at them. Birdie is on the other side of all that. She is an old, forgotten Christmas nut, drying out at the bottom of the bowl. Even looking at them makes her feel tired.

'Come on, Birdie,' she hears Rose mutter. 'Rouse yourself. What would Princess Margaret do?'

Girding her loins, Birdie pats her hair, hopes there is no trace of cancer about her, like lipstick smeared on teeth. It shouldn't be embarrassing to be dying, but it is. 'Forgive me,' she says, letting go of Audrey's collar to accept the flowers.

Audrey gives a grunt of delight at being free and barrels towards Frankie, who steps back in horror. 'Dogs can have up to three hundred fleas living on them at any one time,' she says in alarm. 'Dogs lick their bums and then your face. Dogs lick *other* dogs' bums and then lick your face. Mum, don't stroke it!'

'Audrey is spotlessly clean. I just wormed her, and she won't hurt you,' Birdie says. 'She has breathing problems, which is why she makes that terrible racket. Look, her little stump is wagging at you.'

It was the wriggling nub that had done it for Birdie. When she had seen Audrey at the rescue centre, the dog was nothing but bones and bald patches, and she emitted an awful yeasty smell, yet she still shook her rump. 'Well,' Birdie had said, 'that's that then,' and the three wonky teeth at the bottom of the bulldog's mouth had poked out over her upper jaw. There was something so brave about their smallness. That such a muscly dog could own such minuscule incisors.

'Thank you for the flowers. You really shouldn't have,' Birdie says. 'Sorry about before. I've had a bit of a bad day.'

'Oh dear, are you okay?' Jane asks, gazing up at Birdie with what looks like genuine concern. 'Sorry, I don't know your name?'

'I'm Birdie Greenwing,' Birdie says, trying desperately to swallow the lump in her throat, 'and, yes, I'm fine. Nothing too serious.'

'Well, if there's anything we can do,' the woman says, 'we're only next door.'

'That's very kind,' Birdie croaks. Knowing she is too far gone to stop the tears, she mutters something about a quiche burning in the oven and says a hasty goodbye. Hopes they cannot hear her choked sobbing in the hallway, which she tries to muffle with her fist.

When she's finally got herself back under control, Birdie wipes her eyes, straightens her blouse and heads towards the fridge. She can hear the oncologist's clipped accent in her ears as she drops ice into a glass.

'Do you understand what I'm saying, Mrs Greenwing?'

Birdie pulls out cheese and piccalilli. Once, she and Rose made a jar of it themselves. It's hard to mess up pickled cauliflower and mustard, but they managed. It's probably still at the back of the cupboard somewhere, intact. How can a jar of fermented vegetables survive indefinitely when people die? Birdie wonders.

'Stage-four cancer.'

Birdie spreads butter on a cracker, slices an apple into four.

'Do you have anyone at home?'

As she carries her tray into the living room, Birdie wonders what the doctor is doing now. Is she out with her handsome husband in one of those fancy wine bars along the seafront? Or is she at home, reading books about lost umbrellas and ballet shoes to tucked-in children smelling of honey and milk? Maybe she's at a yoga class. Birdie has always wondered about it, but Princess Margaret would not be caught dead doing yoga, so neither would Birdie.

Crying has always made Birdie oddly hungry, like swimming used to. She eases herself down on to the sofa, Audrey hoovering up the crumbs she drops. As she chews, Birdie closes her eyes, imagines her living room as it used to be. Arthur reading the newspaper after long minutes of snapping and folding the pages *just so*. Birdie and Rose watching something daft on the box. Arthur's occasional tuts at their giggles and constant commentary. Rose's swollen feet in Birdie's lap.

Birdie does not want to open her eyes and see those empty armchairs. Does not want to sleep alone in an empty bed. She wants to stay here with her eyes closed and imagine Rose coming in to find her, Arthur locking the doors and drawing the curtains. But Audrey needs to be let out before bedtime and Birdie's days of falling asleep, drunk, on the sofa are behind her. She drags herself to her feet and opens the back door.

'Be quick,' she tells her dog, who proceeds to do the exact opposite, making no less than four slow turns about the garden before finally committing to a spot. She comes back in, very pleased with herself, muddy paws on the hallway carpet. Birdie goes to tell her off and then thinks, Really, does it matter any more?

She carries Audrey upstairs, both of them panting. Birdie has a quick wash at the sink, a swipe of toothpaste around her gums – cavities, be damned! – before covering her bones in thick flannel, her face in thick cream, and then she crawls into bed, where sleep comes in an instant. Dying, it seems, can be exhausting.

5

Jane

ON HER FIRST DAY at work, Jane made the grave error of getting a coffee from one of the chains situated near the main entrance, as opposed to the Women's Royal Voluntary Service (WRVS) by the X-ray department. She didn't know the little café was there at the time, but she has never been allowed to forget her mistake. When she walked into the ward bearing a burgundy cup with its famous logo, her teammates looked at her as though she'd come bearing a cup of excrement. Now Jane knows better.

'Morning, Connie,' she says, to the tiny, wizened old lady behind the counter. Connie is one of the good ones. An utter star. Never off sick, makes rock cakes the size of fists, studded with cherries and sultanas, dipped in sugar. The softest scones ever. She is also the slowest person Jane has ever met. Jane swears she once saw Connie nodding off to sleep while she was in the middle of ringing up a customer's order.

'Cup of coffee for you, is it, Jane?' Connie asks, creeping her way over to the urn.

'Yes, please.'

'And one for me while you're there, please, Connie.'

Jane looks round to see Helen, a nurse on her team, smiling at her. 'No rush,' Helen adds. 'You take your time.' Wait, what? Jane thinks. Is she bloody joking?

Helen winks at Jane. Jane, who can't wink, blushes.

'Right you are, Helen,' Connie says, her hand quivering its way over to a pile of mugs. Another impressive thing about Connie is that she serves drinks in proper mugs. She never seems to read what is printed on them first, however. Or maybe she does.

'Wherever does she find them?' Helen asks, holding up a black mug emblazoned with the words 'Pizza Slut'.

'Car-boot sales? Recently deceased friends?' Jane suggests. Her mug says, 'Jesus loves you' on one side and 'Everyone else thinks you're a twat' on the other.

Helen laughs. Jane thinks about sending a photo to Suki, but she's probably sipping a cocktail from a glass slipper in some chic new rooftop bar, surrounded by friends who laugh like horses.

'Perhaps you should give your mug to Sadie,' Helen muses, as they walk back to the ward. Sadie is their team leader, and no one likes her. Jane's laughter feels like a glow, like a lamp being turned on inside her.

'I'm not sure even Jesus wants Sadie for a sunbeam,' Jane comments. Now it's Helen's turn to laugh, loudly and unselfconsciously. It's been a long time since people found Jane funny. Frankie doesn't do jokes (waste of time) and Min always says, 'And that's what you call humour, is it, Jane?'

It wasn't always that way. Min stopped laughing when Jane and Suki's dad died. Jane was eleven and Suki was twelve. He'd developed lung cancer from working with asbestos – nothing new, nothing other people hadn't suffered from before, but that didn't make it any easier. He spent a long time in bed towards the end. Jane and Suki were told never to go into his room. Min could often be found standing on sentry duty outside it, hissing like a snake when they went past. Jane and Suki crept about the house like burglars, learned which steps squeaked, how to open cupboards as quietly as possible. It was as if Min thought their dad could be mended by silence.

'Shush, your father is trying to sleep. Shush! You're louder than a herd of bleddy elephants. Don't you want him to get better?'

That was all Jane wanted. Her dad, whistling as he opened the front door, the sound of his boots hitting the kitchen wall when he kicked them off after a long day. His rough hand patting her head. Jane was convinced he'd feel better if she were allowed to go in and see him, to tend him, but Min wouldn't let her, no matter how much she begged.

'No, you'll knock something over. You'll wear him out.'

What Min meant was 'I don't want you to see behind this door,' but it had taken Jane a long time to realize that.

One day Jane heard her dad coughing, a dry bark that went on and on. She'd promised Min she'd never enter, but her dad needed help and Min was downstairs bleaching something. Jane tiptoed towards the door. Inside, the room was dark. The closed curtains trapped in a thick smell that Jane didn't want to think about. When she got to the bed, her dad was not there. In his place was a tiny skeletal man. A prune under the covers. His arms had been replaced with knobbly walking sticks.

'Hi, Dad.' Jane poured him a glass of water with a shaking hand and held it up to his dry lips as he struggled to get into a sitting position.

He glugged at it noisily, uselessly. Jane had the angle wrong. Water sloshed down his pyjama shirt, soaking him.

'Sorry. I'm so sorry.' She started to take the glass away, but he grabbed her wrist with surprising strength and carried on trying to drink, his eyes locked on hers. All these years later, Jane is still not sure what she saw in them. Shame, gratitude, love?

At the sound of her mother coming up the stairs, Jane had snatched the glass back and fled.

Her dad's heart had come to a stop that evening. Jane can't remember how Min told them. Can't remember her face, her grief. If they had dinner that night, if it had been Jane's fault her father died. If she'd killed him with her clumsy help. She can't remember who came and took her dad away. Jane's first clear memory after holding the water glass was being at the funeral. Shiny black shoes that pinched her feet. Suki crying. Min looking like a cardboard cut-out of a person.

That was the day when Jane decided she would become a nurse. Never have to leave the room again. She couldn't bring her father back, but with each person she tends, something inside her eases. The band of guilt slackens slightly. A hair shirt she has made for herself, a pilgrim pebble in her shoe.

That said, Jane also loves her job. She smiles as she takes blood, helps people into the shower, measures out Oramorph. Apologizes as she inserts suppositories up bottoms, changes pads and checks stitches. She watches patients pink up like prawns under thin waffle blankets when they come back from theatre. Hers is the arm that guides shaky first steps post-operation, washbag under arm. Hospital gown stamped all over with 'Property of NHS' and, very briefly, the property of Jane Brown. She holds hands with strangers, comforts patients as they wait, vulnerable in itchy gowns and paper knickers, to be put under and sliced open. Their dignity in the hands of overworked staff, of surgeons who hold their future in their hands. Each time a patient is wheeled down to theatre, Jane thinks of Frankie *in utero*, an ovum, a whisper, a half-formed thing, and silently begs the specialists to be careful.

Inside her ward, with its warm orange walls, it is as though Jane is hidden inside a clementine, the way all the women roll on to their left-hand sides, a row of curved spines, with Jane and the other nurses their pith, their peel. When the surgeons come to do their post-operative checks, Jane looks at their fingers. Simple digits that do up buttons, send texts and tilt bottles to lips. Hands that roam over skin, their own and other people's. How incredible it is to Jane that fingers capable of such mundanity can also be capable of holding the universe that lies inside a woman. No matter what she does, her own hands feel useless in comparison.

Jane's favourite patient of the day is an eighty-year-old called Doris. Still groggy from her anaesthetic, she clutches Jane's hand and says, 'Don't leave me, Annie.'

Jane carries out her observations as discreetly as she can, all the while assuring Doris that she'll explain what's going on to the cat and get the milk in from the doorstep. 'You are such a good daughter,' Doris says, rheumy eyes watering.

Jane thinks of Min, of their last phone call. 'Suki's had another promotion, you know.'

'Has she?' Jane had said lightly, stung that Suki hadn't told her.

'Annie. Annie? Check on my neighbour, Cath, won't you, while I'm in here? We normally have tea at two p.m. She'll be so worried.'

'Of course I will,' Jane says, making a note to check Doris's chart and see who's coming to collect her. Jane has a horrible feeling that the name on it will not be Annie. There is something frantic in Doris's confused gaze. She keeps asking for her handbag, searching through it fruitlessly, tutting as she pulls out the same handkerchief again and again. 'I know it's in here,' she keeps telling Jane. 'I know it is.'

Jane is reminded of her and Frankie's visit to their neighbour, Birdie. She'd had a strange look in her eye – a look that Jane had seen before but couldn't put her finger on.

Jane checks Doris's chart. The number listed is for Morelands residential home. Jane tells the care assistant in charge of Doris's 'corridor' that her operation was a success. It was only a small cyst, easy to get to.

'Good, good,' the assistant says, sounding distracted.

Jane can hear a commotion in the background. She imagines a house full of lonely pensioners all ringing bells at once. For some reason, Jane pictures Birdie there, Min too. Alone in rooms, pressing buttons, hoping someone might come.

'What time will I tell Transportation to collect her?' the care assistant asks. 'Dinner is at five here. Will she be ready before then? I'll need to order her meal. Not sure what'll be left. It's pork chops today. They all go bananas for them.'

'No!' Jane says quickly. 'She won't be back that soon.'

'Okay. That's fine.' The assistant sounds relieved. One less person to care for, Jane supposes.

'What's your name, please?' Jane blurts out.

'Annie,' the girl says, sounding suspicious. 'Annie West. Why?'

The doctor agrees that Doris could benefit from a night of observation, due to her confusion and low blood pressure.

'Did you sort out the milk?' Doris asks, as Jane brings her another pillow and a blanket at the end of her shift.

'I did. Don't you worry about a thing,' Jane says, tucking the thin blue cover over Doris's tiny feet and giving them a squeeze. If feet could talk, what would Doris's tell her? Jane can see from the gold ring on her finger, dull and loose, that they had once walked her down an aisle.

'Cath will be wondering where I am,' Doris says, eyes growing heavy. 'I'm such a silly goose. All this fuss.'

'I'll explain it to her,' Jane murmurs, making sure the call button is within reach. 'I have to go home now, Doris,' she says, 'but I'll be back in the morning, okay?'

'Okay,' Doris says, then asks in a small voice, 'Can I please come home with you?'

Jane can still hear Doris's question as she walks up the hill from the bus stop. She could never imagine Min behaving like that. Some people revert to childlike behaviour as they get older. Some, like Min, have been pickled by life. Her mother is a sour gherkin in a glass jar. She could outlive locusts and cockroaches. She probably will.

Going back to check on Doris has made Jane late and the playground is empty when she arrives. Late is bad enough, but late to late club? Not cool.

'Miss Brown?' the teacher calls, but Frankie is already sprinting towards Jane.

'Go!' Frankie orders, heading for the gate.

'Good day?' Jane pants, as they run along the pavement as if they're being chased.

'No,' Frankie replies, 'and I don't want to talk about it.'

*

At home, Frankie heads straight to her room, firmly shutting the door behind her. Jane looks at it for a moment, wanting to go in, but knows it won't help. Sighing, she heads to the kitchen to make dinner. The phone rings as she is slicing carrots into batons. Unlike Frankie, Min is very keen to talk about her day.

'Bleddy next-door neighbour's cat shat on my doorstep, again. That awful MP was on the radio this morning, making my ears bleed with his lies. Myrtle was in the post office, being her nosy old self. If I wanted her to know what was in my bleddy parcel I'd have shown it to her. It's just some bits for Frankie and some new knickers for you, by the way . . . the state of your old ones. What if you got run over by a bus? Then I walked home in the rain. Now my knee is twice the size it should be. Each step is agony. I think it's dropsy.'

'You mean oedema.'

'They are *my* knees, Jane. I think I know what's wrong with them.'

'Of course. Sorry.'

Jane thinks of Suki's text. Of Frankie's bad day. Of Doris. 'I was going to ask if you fancied coming down this weekend, see our new place. But if your knee is—'

'I'll manage somehow,' Min cuts in. 'I'll book a train tomorrow – well, a seat on one, not the whole bleddy thing. Be with you Friday. Meet me at the station. I'll let you know the times.'

Jane smiles as she puts the phone down. 'Frankie,' she calls, 'I have some news that might cheer you up . . .'

6

Ada

'Morning, Ada.'

'Connie.' Ada nods as she pulls out her wallet. Struggles to keep her foot from tapping as Constance shuffles over to the silver machine, pats it before pressing the button. Ada's dad pats his cows like that. An affectionate tap on the rump. Sometimes he does it to her mother, who rears round to waggle her finger at him, but laughs as she does so.

'Black coffee and a bacon butty?' Connie asks.

'Yup,' Ada says, trying to speed Connie up by the power of her mind. The café at the front is much quicker, but Ada was brought up to shop local. Plus Connie's sandwiches are like doorsteps. Ada is still licking ketchup off her fingers when she turns the corner to her office. She assumes the man sitting outside her door is a patient. He stands up when he sees her. He looks too healthy for cancer, but Ada knows better.

'Have you checked in with my receptionist? I'll come and call you for your appointment,' she says. Even cancer has to form an orderly queue.

'I'm not a patient, I'm Wilbur Smith,' he says.

Ada looks at him blankly.

'Your intern? I . . . Didn't you know?' He runs a hand through his thick brown hair. It sits in a wave on his head. Ada tries not to picture him bald.

'Yes, of course I did. I know everything that happens here.' This bit is said loudly and aimed at her secretary, Denise, who is sitting at her desk, pretending to type something very quickly. 'Come in.'

Ada unlocks her door and pushes it open. Apart from a cactus, a box of tissues and sanitizing spray (Ada is meticulous about not spreading germs to immunosuppressed patients), there is not much to see. A row of books she knows off by heart. No calendar (crass), no paintings (patronizing: 'Hey, I know you just got diagnosed with stage-four cancer but look at this cheap reproduction of Monet's *Japanese Bridge*').

Ada makes a note to ask Denise why she was not informed about Wilbur Smith. Every time she is offered an intern, she says no. Ada is busy. She hasn't time to explain every decision she makes to a student. Plus she works best alone. Denise should know this by now.

'Well,' Ada says, not knowing what is supposed to happen next. Rattled at being caught off guard, she tidies the papers on her desk, moves her pen.

'Perhaps I should tell you a bit about myself?' Wilbur asks politely, as if sensing that Ada is not sure what to say.

Ada nods. She wants to put on her white coat, but it feels wrong to do it while Wilbur is in the room. As intimate as undressing somehow.

'Can I have a seat?' he asks.

Ada nods again. '*Proszę*.' She reverts to Polish, her lizard brain, when she's uncomfortable.

'Polish?' Wilbur says.

'*Tak*,' Ada says, refusing to be impressed.

'I had a Polish friend in the army,' Wilbur says, taking a seat. Ada notices he pulls up the fabric of his trousers before he sits down. 'I was a medic.'

His throat bobs as he speaks. Ada has a sense he's made this speech many times before and doesn't find it any easier. She can relate.

'I did three tours, lost four mates,' he tries to shrug but the gesture falls flat, 'so I thought I'd try a different way to help people.'

There are holes in his story. Ada wants to poke her fingers into them and pull them apart. Why did he give up? Why choose cancer work when it's another kind of war? He got out alive, why go and work as one of Death's henchmen?

'This job is hard,' is all she says. She doesn't mean it to come out as a challenge, but it does. She's still pacing the room.

'I know,' Wilbur replies, looking up to meet her eyes, 'but hard doesn't scare me.' There is no ego in his voice. He is not bragging. Wilbur doesn't sit with his legs spread, as a lot of big men do. Ada, tiny even in heels, does not feel small in comparison.

'People die here too,' Ada says, pressing the point, wanting him to understand.

'Yes, but not people I've trained with. Not people I've got to know or slept next to. No one I've got drunk with or eaten three meals a day with. Not . . . friends,' Wilbur says, looking down at his hands. 'I won't have to deliver a dog tag to my best mate's wife and tell her how sorry I am. That I couldn't . . .' Wilbur trails off.

Birdie Greenwing's face appears in Ada's mind, there one moment, then gone. A watch-face reflecting a ray of sun, temporarily blinding her. Something about the woman has snagged on Ada, like that sticky weed boys used to chase girls with at school. So, Wilbur wants to help strangers without getting attached to them. Well, who is she to tell him that's impossible?

'So, new city, new job, new start,' Wilbur says. He has long fingers, clean nails. Beata Górska, an old woman in Ada's village, used to read palms. Ada would hide hers in her pockets whenever she passed Beata's house. It's all nonsense, her father used to tell Ada, but her mother said nothing. Janina must have gone to see her, Ada realizes now, must have asked Beata about babies. Ada feels a lump in her throat. When she looks at Wilbur, his smile seems slightly sad, despite his declarations about making a new start.

Ada should tell him there's been a mistake, she's too busy. That she does not take interns. That he will only get sadder. That she cannot save anyone, him, most of her patients, or even herself . . .

There is a long beat of silence. Wilbur does nothing to break it. He has an air of calm about him, a quiet confidence. Ada is reminded of her father's vet, Darek. How he'd wait until the horse sniffed his palm, learned his scent, made sure the animal was settled before picking up a hoof. Even drenched in the winter rain, Darek never rushed, and always explained what he was going to do first, as if the horse or cow could understand him. Could give consent.

'Well,' Ada says finally, 'I suppose the best place to start is by reading the patients' notes.' She nods at the stack of bloated orange files on her desk.

The morning passes quickly. Wilbur doesn't dominate the space, doesn't interrupt her when she speaks or try to take over. She was expecting him to start explaining how she should use her computer, like her first – and last – intern did. Even so, when he goes across the road to the phlebotomy department, Ada calls Denise in and asks her why she hadn't been informed about Wilbur.

'Oh, didn't I tell you?' Denise says, looking at her electric-blue shoes, sounding overly innocent.

'You know you didn't,' Ada says.

'Fine,' Denise admits. 'He came in to ask if there were any placements here, said you'd been recommended as the best of the best.'

Ada lets the compliment slide over her – she is used to Denise's tricks. 'And you didn't tell him I don't take interns because . . . ?'

'Um, hello? Have you seen him? Because he's bloody gorgeous!' Denise says, laughing. 'And you deserve something pretty to look at all day.'

'Denise . . .' Ada pinches the bridge of her nose.

'Sorry, call coming in, got to go.' Denise skips out, winking at Ada as she goes.

Ada normally works through lunch, but doing so might mean Wilbur feels he has to as well. She doesn't want to have to consider another person's needs. 'Go take a break,' she snaps at him, at one o'clock. 'See you back here in an hour.'

'Know anywhere I can get decent food?' Wilbur asks, standing up.

'The WRVS is good, if you don't mind spending your whole lunch hour in a queue.'

'Waiting isn't a problem,' Wilbur says easily, pulling a battered paperback out of his bag and heading for the door. Ada refuses to find the fact that he reads fiction sexy.

He comes back forty-five minutes later, holding two mugs of coffee. 'Hope this is okay?' he says. 'I asked Connie and she said you take it . . .' He turns a mug towards her. 'Strong and steamy' is written on one side of the mug and 'I like my coffee like I like my men' on the other.

'Connie is almost blind,' Ada says, blushing as she takes it from him.

'Hey, could be worse,' Wilbur says, holding up a pink mug that says 'I put the Hot in Psychotic'.

Ada snorts and Wilbur grins. Time, for a moment, seems to get stuck, like the needle on a record player. 'Well,' Ada says, after a beat. She takes a sip of too-hot coffee and burns the roof of her mouth. Later, she will put her tongue there and think of Wilbur for no reason.

The streetlights are on when Ada walks out of the hospital. She can see her breath, white, like cigarette smoke, in the frigid air. At home, her father puts down extra hay on nights like this. Leaves the heat lamp on in the barn. Lets Jess the sheepdog sleep inside.

Ada peers through open curtains as she goes past, sees snatches of other lives. She is a thief, stealing secrets. Crowded rooms, TVs with dancing images, fairy lights. A teenager playing on his computer. A woman painting in the window. An old man asleep in a chair. The smell of chicken roasting and wood fires burning. Ada passes a family sitting round a laden dining table. Parents, children. A big brown dog. One in two people born after 1960 will be diagnosed with cancer in their lifetime. The thought comes to Ada out of nowhere. Who will it be? Ada spies lovers entwined on a sofa and wonders which one will become sick. Will one stay to care for the other, or will they run away? The couple washing up, side by side at the sink. The sisters playing cards. The two men trying to put up a shelf. She thinks of her mother and father. One in two. One in two.

Unable to face her sterile kitchen, Ada gets a takeaway. She wraps her cold hands around a paper cup of miso soup and thinks of her mother's cream-cheese *pierogi*. Of piping hot blueberries in sour cream. Ada could never wait until her food had cooled before cramming it into her mouth, as if her plate was about to be taken away. Her mother would smack her hand lightly. 'Always in such a hurry, Ada,' she'd say. 'Slow down. Enjoy it.' If her mother could see her now, drinking broth and stuffing in rice balls as she walks along the street, her mouth full, cheeks bulging. Right now, her father will be locking gates, mixing feed for the morning. Her mother will be starting another batch of *bigos*. The whole of Ada's tiny village will be dense with darkness by nine p.m., whereas here in Brighton, everything shines. Cars, restaurant windows. Buses. The lights on the pier. Ada finds herself walking towards them, through the thick black iron gates, across the old wooden planks that creak beneath her feet.

Sitting on a damp wooden bench, Ada watches people

brave the cold to clamber into the waltzer cars. Dance music plays over the sound of slot machines in the arcade, the wind whistling through the metal joists. Ada tries to look at everyone as people, not potential patients. One in two. One in two. Ada once came here with Ania. The rides were rubbish and overpriced, the doughnuts nothing like the ones at home. They went and got drunk on cheap beer instead, ate too-hot chips and pitta at two a.m., laughing puffs of steam into their hands. So very different from home. Ada walks back out of the gate, tossing her empty soup container into the bin. She wipes her hands on her skirt. Ada's mother would tell her off. Ada's mother would say you should sit down after a meal. Ada's mother would do more to help Birdie Greenwing.

Back on her own street, Ada's feet carry her past her bungalow towards Birdie's. She hovers on the pavement outside, unsure what to do next. There is a light on in what looks like the living room, and another on the landing. Birdie's recycling bin has been placed at the bottom of the drive for collection the next morning. Ada takes a quick peek. It is full of tins and empty milk cartons. Sachets of dog food. She is coping then, Ada thinks. She is managing – for now.

7

Birdie

It's odd to wake up knowing you're one day closer to dying. Birdie's vision is blurry in a not altogether unpleasant way, as though she's wearing swimming goggles. She feels herself surface slowly. Checks all her faculties – rusty but operative. Imagines a bomb inside her ticking away slowly, too quiet to hear. She feels like Dorian Gray. Each morning, she wakes up preparing for pain. For the end to feel closer. But she feels no different than she did yesterday, or the day before that.

Arthur used to bring her coffee in bed. Birdie would wake to the sound of a cup tinkling on a saucer, his ugly house slippers slapping along the hallway towards her. He'd slip back between the sheets and talk to her as she drank it. Sometimes he'd tell her he didn't have to hurry to work that morning, would take Birdie's half-empty cup from her and place it on the bedside table.

That was before Rose moved in. Then Birdie was the one who got up first. Serving Arthur his tea with an arrowroot biscuit, before tiptoeing into her sister's room with a tray.

'Get in,' Rose would say. 'Warm me up.'

Rose always seemed to feel cold, no matter how many blankets Birdie piled on her. When she died, Birdie lost four pounds three ounces, the exact weight of her twin sister when she was born. It was not the entire sum of her grief, but Birdie has never put the weight back on in the years since. It wasn't much, nothing more than two little bags of sugar, but Birdie felt lighter without those pounds, less stable. Colder. After Rose died, every time Birdie went out of the house, she felt as if she'd forgotten something. Her coat, her purse, her hat, the left ventricle of her heart.

Back then, newly alone, Birdie had feared that a strong gust of wind might sweep her away. Her nest felt unstable too, badly built, as if it were in danger of toppling out of its tree. It took a long time for Birdie to adjust. She still found herself talking to Rose and Arthur, making dinner for three. The seagulls came to know her garden, the bird tables piled with uneaten food. They nested on her roof and waited for leftovers.

Getting slowly out of bed, Birdie makes her way to the window, pulls back the heavy velvet curtain. Outside, the sky is a tangled duvet of white, the sun no more than a dubious stain in one corner, a yellow smudge, like something spilled there long ago. Birdie's breath mists the glass. Through it, her back garden is a study in flat browns and oily dark greens. It reminds Birdie of a Turner landscape.

What do you do with your days when you know they are numbered? Arthur and Rose were not afforded the tarot card of cancer. They had no idea. Grief is a fish hook; it has caught Birdie's heart and tugs, wanting to reel her in. Her ribcage aches with the effort of holding herself together, and she squirms to free herself from the metal spike of loneliness. Lord knows she's had enough practice at it.

Birdie has been on her own for eight years. The first couple passed in a blur of gin and sleeping tablets. She is not pleased, or proud of her actions, though in her occasional lucid moments she did feel that she was channelling *pure* Princess Margaret. Birdie was pretty sure most of the Neighbourhood Watch meetings were about her for a while. She got a lot of letters she did not read and her recycling bin caused more than one person to pause as they passed. For two Christmases, Birdie did not decorate her house or bake mince pies or wrap parcels to put beneath a tree. For two autumns she did not collect the tart apples that fell in her garden with muffled thuds. She did not wash her hair weekly or make fat balls for the birds.

Then, finally, she accepted that Arthur and Rose were never coming back. That drinking herself to death would be a long and painful process. She wrote out the Dorothy Parker quote – 'Guns aren't lawful; Nooses give; Gas smells awful; You might as well live' – and pinned it to her fridge. But Birdie did need something to live for. To get up for. And that something turned out to be a lumpy old bulldog with selective hearing and a yodel for a bark.

The life she has built post Arthur and Rose is a small one. Walks in the park because the sea is too big for Audrey, its waves like teeth. Plus the pebbles are painful on her cracked little paws. Birdie's days are filled with shopping and laundry and documentaries. Films she's seen before. The odd chat at the post office or bus stop. Handing back library books with a brief review. Afternoon naps that carry her back into the past, where she and Rose are playing hide and seek in the garden, or Arthur is snoring gently beside her, her hand on his heart, that big old bass drum.

The phone rings as Birdie is shoving clothes into a bin bag. She doesn't know how long she'll feel well enough to stand on stools or climb ladders, and she doesn't want strangers going through her things after she's gone. Her and Arthur's and Rose's things, because Birdie never got rid of any of them. Her husband's old shirts have turned into octopuses, they keep trying to crawl back out of the bag, and Birdie is feeling hot and sore and itchy. Audrey hides beneath a pile of Rose's summer dresses. At first, Birdie had folded each item neatly, smoothed collars and tucked in cuffs, but now she just wants to get the job finished. It hurts to smell Arthur but not be able to see him. To feel the soft cotton of his shirts, the scratchy wool of his jumpers without the bulk of him inside them. Even the bulge in the side of his leather shoe, made by his ugly old broken toe, makes her sad. Her lovely husband, who drove her mad and was rubbish at party tricks but never gave up trying. 'Watch this,' he'd say. 'I'm going to set my wallet alight. Oh, damn, hang on. I actually have.'

If Arthur had been in the room with Birdie when she got the cancer news, he'd have put his big hand on her knee, given her leg a squeeze, would have told her that everything was going to be all right, even though it wasn't. And Birdie would have believed him. She allows herself a brief, snotty sob into his golfing shirt. The phone finally stops ringing, but minutes later, it trills again. And again.

'Hello? Mrs Greenwing? It's Fleur Williams here? From the Macmillan nurses?'

Birdie should have been expecting this, of course. She imagines her name on a long list. How did they sum her up? Birdie wonders. Are there any other B. Greenwings flying solo, like she is?

'Just phoning to arrange a time to pop round?' Fleur says. All her sentences sound like questions.

'Pop round?' Birdie says, falling into the pattern.

'Yes. To assess your house and your needs?'

Birdie thinks about the gin bottles – far fewer than in the past, but still . . . The bathroom, where empty blister packets of pills adorn each surface. Her embarrassingly empty fridge. The mark round the bathtub she can't scrub off. Audrey's paw prints all over the place.

'I have a slot at three thirty today, if that's any good for you?'

Fleur's voice is bright and friendly but no-nonsense. She has no doubt been into countless homes and seen all sorts of things. She is probably unshockable. Birdie is nothing special, nothing new or different. Birdie has paid her taxes all her life, donated to charities. Even went on a march once, for something or other. She may be entitled to support, but she doesn't feel she deserves it. Rose never asked for help, even when she really needed it. Rose's smile was always the widest when she was in the most pain.

'I'm a bit busy today,' Birdie says, rubbing a sore spot on her spine.

'Okay. No problem,' Fleur says easily. 'I can come on Friday? Same time?'

'I think I might be busy then too.'

There is a pause at the other end of the phone. Birdie wonders if she is being written about in a book. Maybe her name is being crossed off, as though she were already dead.

'Birdie? Is it okay to call you Birdie?' Fleur asks slowly. 'My notes say you live on your own. If you have someone helping you that's wonderful, but we can still get involved.'

The frank words crack something inside Birdie. She is a brittle pot, over-baked in the sun.

'We offer support in various ways,' Fleur continues. 'We can organize shopping, trips to the hospital, help with dressing, cleaning . . .'

A tear falls down Birdie's cheek, silent and salty. She catches it with her tongue. Tastes her own sadness. 'That's very decent of you,' she says, her voice as steady as a poorly made table. She clears her throat and tries again. 'But I'm fine, honestly. Lots of help on hand!' She tries to channel Rose's voice, bright and determined. Princess Margaret's vim. 'Sorry, must dash. I have an engagement this afternoon!'

There is another long pause.

'Okay, Birdie. I'm going to make a note to call you back in a couple of weeks,' Fleur says slowly. 'Meanwhile, you take care now, okay? And call me if you need anything. You have the number.'

Birdie clatters the receiver back into its cradle and sags into the nearest chair. She'd planned to finish packing up Rose's things this afternoon, but she hasn't got it in her any more.

She sits for a moment, then gets down her yellow coat, clips on Audrey's red lead and they go out walking through the mulch of late January, treacle-brown leaves and grass slick with mud. The sun is trying to break through, but the glow is dim. Birdie knows how it feels. She wipes the old wooden bench in the park with her gloved hand before sitting down. Even so, her bottom is damp within seconds. It's hard to be happy with a cold derrière. As Audrey makes her rounds, Birdie looks out for the other people walking alone. Once she saw an old man holding an empty collar and lead. It dangled by his side as he walked in circles round the park. It was as if he'd forgotten what he was doing, that there was no need to do this any more. Birdie almost went up to him, felt that she knew him by that lead, that ghost dog, by the way his head hung low.

Audrey spots a squirrel and breaks into a frantic, yodelling gallop across the grass. When Birdie finally finds her, she is sitting at the bottom of a tall tree, gazing up into the branches. There is no way that Audrey will ever catch a squirrel and she should have learned that by now. They always outrun her. Some even stop to turn back and snicker at Audrey's lopsided gait, but Audrey never stops trying and, truth be told, Birdie has nothing better to do with her diminishing time. She's in no rush to pack her sister and husband into bags and boxes. She tells Audrey to return at leisure, and goes back to her damp bench to continue people-watching. To look for the broken ones, like her, and give them a tiny little wave.

8

Jane

MIN MARCHES DOWN PLATFORM three at Brighton station like a soldier heading towards the front line. Back straight, eyes focused, a massive kit-bag on her back. Her mission is clear. Total world domination. Jane notices, as Min wields her stick to get to the front of the ticket barrier, that there is no sign of her sore knee.

'Miraculous,' Jane mutters to Frankie, but she's relieved to see her mother in such rude health. Min was not made to limp: she was made to conquer.

'Jane, Frankie. Where are your coats?'

Min knows better than to expect a hug from her granddaughter. She gives Frankie's shoulder a quick squeeze.

'Min!' Frankie says happily. 'You made it!'

'Only just. The train was loud, full of punks. The tables were sticky with I don't want to know what. This platform stinks – everyone needs a good wash.'

'Thar she blows,' Jane says to Frankie, then turns to her mother. 'Good to see you, Min,' she says, leaning in to kiss Min's ruddy cheek, to press one hand into the stegosaurus spikes on her mother's spine.

'No one offered me a seat. We waited for ever to set off. Why can't trains run on time?'

Jane breathes in her mother's perfume – Stardrops and Pears soap and sheer dauntlessness. She leads Min, still raving, out of the station exit.

'Look at all the bleddy seagull plop. It's like pebbledash. And the state of the pavements!'

Jane spots a hen party coming towards them and tries to distract her mother by pointing out a war memorial, but it's too late and the party are too pink and pissed not to be noticed. One of them is wearing a glittery top with the words 'Honk here if horny' across her ample chest.

'Well.' Min sniffs.

'It's just a bit of fun,' Jane says, hoping Min won't say anything as the hens pass by. She never knows how far her mother will go. When Jane finally admitted that her lunch was routinely being stolen by a girl in her class, Min had marched into assembly, unannounced, and had addressed the whole school. 'Which one of you dirty urchins is stealing lunch from my Jane? Stand up and show yourself, or I'll check every bleddy lunchbox in the school until I find her egg sandwich.'

'Just a bit of fun, eh? Well, look where that got you,' Min scoffs, nodding at Frankie.

Jane has never made a secret of the fact that Frankie was a surprise. Nor has she lied about where Frankie's father is – Jane doesn't know. She and Suki met him in Laos. He left behind his sunglasses and his seed, both by mistake. There is no need to remind Frankie of this all the time, however.

'You are the best thing that has ever happened to me,' Jane whispers to Frankie.

'I know,' Frankie says, and Min pats her arm in agreement.

Min manages to keep her mouth zipped as they pass through the crowded Lanes, but her eyes are huge and all-seeing. Jane can tell she's soon going to burst. Around them, people smoke and laugh, jostle pints, make toasts. Music blares from windows and doorways. The streets smell of pizza and burgers, of weed and badly washed clothes. Her longing for her sister winds her. Jane rubs her right-hand side, where Suki should be.

Jane chose to move from Bristol to Brighton after she and Suki came for an epic weekend visit as teenagers. It took six months of saving and squirrelling away every penny. To them, the trip was an adventure, a quest. The sisters had watched the film *Quadrophenia* until they knew each word by heart. It had driven Min mad at the time. 'Never mind them rods and mockers, make yer bleddy beds or you'll be going nowhere.'

At eighteen and nineteen, Jane and Suki had been well past the age of needing their mother's consent to do anything, but it was always easier to go along with her.

On the train heading south, Jane had made a half-hearted attempt to study, until Suki tossed the book aside and pulled out her heaving makeup bag. 'You are not plain Jane this weekend,' she said, coming at her with a pot of blusher.

'Who am I, then?' Jane had asked, with a laugh.

'Anyone you want to be. With this brush, I anoint thee.'

Jane had sat patiently while her sister ceremoniously painted her face, filling in the blanks, and the beige, with colour and sparkle. The sisters looked alike, but Suki had always been the glamorous one. It was in the name, Jane was sure. Once, she'd made the mistake of asking Min why she had chosen *Suki* for her firstborn.

'I knew a fluffy white cat called Suki once,' Min said, stopping her scrubbing of the hob long enough to push her steamed-up glasses back up her nose. 'It had nice pink paws. Big swishy tail.'

How a newborn baby could look anything like such a creature was anyone's guess. Jane had foolishly pressed on. 'And, um, my name?' she'd asked hopefully. 'Where did the inspiration come from for *Jane*?' Even said with a flourish, the moniker fell flat. It was not a name, it was a noise. A sigh. The sound of something deflating.

'The what?' Min had said crossly, furiously going at a spot on the stove.

'The inspiration for my name,' Jane repeated, feeling tears prickle, hating herself for not walking away. For not letting it go. 'Me, Min. Why did you call me Jane?'

'Oh, I don't bleddy know, do I?' Min had snapped. 'It's a good, solid name. What should I have called you? Queen bleddy Nefertiti?'

'Don't worry,' Suki had whispered. 'I was named after a hairy pussy.'

Jane did worry, though. It was as if her mother had dictated her whole future with her dull name. I christen thee Jane. Plain and solid, like a boiled potato.

Min had tried to make up for it, still does at times. 'I named you after Jane of Arch,' she said once. 'I named you after Jane of Green Gables.' It has become a sort of joke, sticking plaster over a wound.

That day, when Jane and Suki had first walked out into the

Brighton sunshine, Suki had grabbed Jane's hand and they ran, heavy rucksacks clanging against their backs, feet slapping down the steep hill to where the sea sparkled and winked in invitation. Trainers were pulled off, bags dumped, clothes shed and abandoned. The water was so cold Jane couldn't breathe. Suki had waded straight in, of course, bold and fearless. 'Come on, Jane,' she'd said, through clenched teeth, 'to the buoy and back. Sea water has healing properties.'

Jane took a deep breath, dunked her shoulders under and imagined being better, cured from her mundanity. 'Wash away plain Jane,' she had whispered to the waves. 'Make me anew.'

Afterwards they had wrung themselves out on the pebbles, picked seaweed from each other's hair in the queue for fish and chips – golden grease that coated salt-swollen lips and pruned blue fingers, warming them up from the inside out.

The youth hostel they checked into would have made Min drop down dead on the spot. The carpets had never seen a Hoover, nor the windowsills a squirt of Stardrops. The whole place smelt of unwashed hair and stale sheets.

'I can't get into that bed until I am very drunk,' Suki had announced, when she saw their bunks. And so, minidresses on, makeup reapplied, hair sprayed to within an inch of its life, they had stumbled on new heels along dirty old pavements.

The night was a blur. Loud music, bright lights, a shot of something vile, the smell of too many bodies mingling together in sweat. In sweet reckless abandon. In joy. Song after song that they simply *had* to dance to, because when Debbie Harry is singing that your hair is beautiful and the lights are falling like shooting stars, you can almost believe it.

Suki had gyrated enthusiastically against a topless boy with a shaved head and a nipple piercing. An insistent hand tugged at Jane's arm, leading her towards a dark corner for a slow, open-mouthed kiss. The bass had moved through Jane's body and, just for a moment, she was extraordinary.

Neither of the Brown sisters remembered getting home that night. Suki lost a shoe. Jane stole someone's lighter. They collapsed in the filthy bunks, were late for the train.

When the doors had opened back in Bristol, Brighton already seemed light years away. A bit of Jane had been left behind. Her hairs on the hostel pillow, her first kiss against a wall. I'll come back and get you one day, Jane had promised herself. Wait for me.

''Scuse me, love, have you got any spare change?' The voice is weak and muffled by a blanket.

'Spare change? What's that when it's at home?' Min erupts, pulling Jane from her memories.

'Min!' Jane gives her mother a pleading look and scrabbles in her purse for some coins. 'Sorry. So sorry,' she says to the man leaning against the newsagent's window.

'Why are *you* sorry, Jane?' Min snipes. 'It's not your fault.'

'It might not be his fault either,' Frankie says objectively. 'Perhaps he has something wrong with him.'

'Lazyitis, that's what's wrong with him!' Min honks. 'Why don't you cut your hair and get a job?'

Jane drops a fistful of change into his paper cup. He doesn't say thank you.

'Manners cost nothing!' Min tells him, then turns to Jane. 'And you wonder why you have no money? You wouldn't catch your sister throwing away her hard-earned cash on any Tom, Dick or Harry.'

Jane doesn't wonder why she has no money. She knows why. She works for the NHS. Also, she remembers Suki shoving handfuls of cash down an oily stripper's thong in Thailand as he thrust his crotch into her face. Jane should've taken a photo as proof.

Min turns to Frankie and says, 'Well, then, Frankie, how are you getting on down here? Still mad on taxidermy? Want to stuff every dead animal you find?'

'Yes,' Frankie says. 'Very much.'

'Well, there are enough bleddy gulls about,' Min remarks. 'Start with them.'

'They are protected,' Frankie says.

'Against what?' Min asks, watching one strut into the bakery, looking like it's about to stage a hold-up. 'It's us who need protecting. Look at the bleddy beak on it. Bigger than your aunt Irene's nose.'

'I've been reading up on embalming,' Frankie says. 'That's the process of preserving a body by delaying the natural effects of death.'

To her credit, Min does her best to look interested. 'Oh, aye?'

'It's done by introducing a special solution into the corpse, which helps to give it a more peaceful appearance.'

'I wonder if that's what Suki has done to her cheeks,' Min remarks.

Jane snorts, but the comment also hurts. Did Suki get work done? They swore they would never do that. Vowed to age naturally and beautifully.

Did you get fillers or something? she texts Suki. *Min says you've had embalming solution injected into your cheeks.*

Her phone dings seconds later. *No, I haven't. Who is she saying that to?*

Jane grins. So, Suki can reply quickly when it suits her. *Oh, just everyone*, she texts back.

Frankie spends the journey home explaining how embalmers sew people's mouths shut and put caps over their eyelids. Min interrupts with critical commentary about her surroundings. 'Look at all the graffiti, it's like a slum. Vegetarian shoes? Whatever next?'

'Garlic bread?' Jane asks innocently.

'Shouldn't be allowed,' Min says, grimacing.

'I agree,' Frankie says.

'Well, at least I raised one of you properly,' Min says.

Jane and Frankie have done the best they could with the bungalow. Removed the last of the cardboard boxes, and picked up some winter pansies for either side of the front door, planted hastily in some of Frankie's old boots. It still looks like what it is, though – a half-furnished bungalow that badly needs renovating.

Min takes it all in, making a slow circle of the living room, eyes narrowed. Jane hates how much she wants her mother's seal of approval.

'Decent fireplace, I suppose,' Min says eventually.

This is as good as Jane is going to get, so she takes it. 'Make yourself at home, I'll get dinner started,' she says.

Min's way of making herself at home is to put on a housecoat over her blouse, pull a bottle of disinfectant from her bag and start cleaning. Jane makes spaghetti Bolognese, which Min looks at with suspicion, as if it had crawled in under the door and up on to her plate. 'I'm not sure about the meat down here. Is this that *tofunk* nonsense?'

'It's beef, Min, just like you get back at home,' Jane says, but Min remains sceptical, holding bits of orange mince up to the light and frowning. Jane, in turn, eats as if she's dining on lobster, rolling her eyes in feigned delight, sucking in strands of spaghetti with gusto. In truth, the meat is tasteless and gritty, the sauce vinegary and the onion chunks too large. Frankie just eats the spaghetti.

'Sensible,' Min says to her granddaughter.

Later, dishes washed up, dining table scrubbed as though it had sworn at Min and needed its mouth washed out with carbolic soap, they sit down in the living room.

'Oof! This sofa is low,' Min says.

'Sorry,' Jane responds automatically.

Min sniffs. 'Pass me my knitting, then.'

Jane has never seen her mother doing nothing. Min cannot sit unless she is also ironing, or making a blanket, or writing a stern letter of complaint. As children, Jane and Suki used to think she was a robot. The thought of her lying down, not moaning or polishing, was alien to them. They'd try to stay awake so they could creep into her bedroom to see if she ever slept. To find the flap of skin that hid her batteries and take them out. They never managed it. Min was like Margaret Thatcher: she only needed four hours' sleep, and she got them in when no one was watching.

The sound of her mother's knitting needles is comforting, though. Jane feels something in her unclench at the clicking noise. She casts round for something to talk about that won't start an argument, but it's Min who speaks first.

'It would've been our wedding anniversary today. Mine and your father's,' she says.

'Oh?' Jane is surprised. Min never talks about their dad.

'He'd have been almost eighty by now,' Min adds, knitting even quicker, as if it's the needles saying the words, not her.

Jane finds herself sitting still, holding her breath, scared to say anything that might make Min stop talking.

'Always said he wanted to retire at seventy. Move to the sea.' *Clack, clack, clack.* 'Never made it, of course. That bleddy, bleddy asbestos.'

Min's needles are going like the clappers. She's making a jumper of grief. Jane will wear it, will hang it on the back of her bedroom door.

Min did not meet their father, Tom, until she was forty, which was *ancient* back then. She had given up on love and taken over running her father's cobbler's shop. Jane imagined it would be hard to meet someone when you were as short as you were round. When you marched everywhere like you'd just been wound up. Min was scary even then, but Tom was brave. He'd come in to have his boots resoled and left with Min's number. And that was that, apparently.

'None of your bleddy beeswax,' Min would say, if Jane and Suki ever asked about their courting days, and their dad would just smile and tap the side of his nose. They were left to study the few photos Min owned, write a script to fill in the rest. They never could work out how it had happened, Tom entering the shop and being struck down by passion.

'You must allow me to tell you how ardently I admire you, Min.'

'You can admire me all you like, Billy Shakespeare, but you still owe me money.'

'Min, your face is like a poem. I simply must have you in that brown pinny.'

'Go and wash your mouth out with Stardrops.'

'Min, would you do me the honour of holding my . . .'

It used to make them cry with laughter, and then their dad died, and that only made them cry. They'd always been so focused on Min's experience, and now they would never know his side of the story.

Jane thinks about her parents' wedding photo back in Bristol. In the picture, her father is looking directly into the camera, awkward and proud in equal measure, but Min is looking at Tom's profile. She's staring up at him, her expression that of a child who has opened a gift and found the thing they most wanted for Christmas. 'Me?' her expression seems to say. 'Does he really belong to me?'

Jane's early childhood had been happy. Tom made Min giggle, as if he'd found her 'on' button. She didn't clean all the time back then. She cooked pies and walked the girls to school and back, stopping to buy them fizzy strawberries from the post office and lace up their shoes while singing a silly rhyme about a fox going into a hole.

But then their father had developed a cough. He'd tried to laugh it off, would take himself into the pantry to hack and wheeze. Claim he was not the one making all the noise. It was the dog next door barking. Eventually he went to the doctor. Eventually he got too tired to work. The more he faded, the brighter Min got. Grief made her almost fluorescent. Her cheeks aflame, her hair turned white. Then all she ever said was no. No to Suki getting her ears pierced, to her going out. No to Jane joining the basketball team. Min had become obsessed with germs. The house smelt of bleach and pine and resentment.

'Well, then . . .' Min sniffs, tugging at a ball of brown wool, and Jane knows the conversation is over. They sit in a semi-peaceable quiet, save for Min's tutting needles. Absently, Jane picks up the wool and unravels it for her mother. The bungalow is cold, and the sofa is cheap. It sags in the middle, forcing Jane and Min into one another. Jane marvels that she came from the body next to her. That she was inside such a strong woman, yet slid out Plasticine-weak. Pale and boring. Maybe Suki took all the good stuff when she was *in utero*, leaving Jane with the remnants.

Jane closes her eyes and thinks about her gentle, kind dad – the fragments of him that she can remember. Of Min back then, when she still wore bright colours. Jane tries to arrange the past like a jigsaw, to make something solid from the little pieces. Just as she is falling into sleep, she feels fingers briefly brush across her forehead, her mother's calloused hand, there and gone so fast that perhaps it never happened.

When she wakes, it is six a.m. The seagulls are shrieking as though they've been wronged. Min must have fetched a blanket at some point and Jane is tucked in tight, like a sausage roll. Min is already on her hands and knees in the kitchen, scrubbing the oven.

9

Ada

ADA DOESN'T ENJOY SHOPPING. Around her, clusters of teenage girls sniff moisturizers and dab eye-shadow on the back of their hands. She didn't own any eye-shadow until she was fourteen and her mother and father took her and Ania to Kraków for the weekend. Gave them both a crumpled handful of notes. At the time, Ada never considered how much more it would have cost them – paying someone to mind the farm, the travel. How much Ada's mother disliked busy places. She'd tugged at her plait, stayed close to her father's side. Flinched at all the noise, her fingers constantly gripping her bag. It had annoyed Ada. She wanted Janina to see the city through her eyes, to breathe in the crowds and smoke and blood and life. To feel the rush from the fried sugar doughnuts. The heat from the charred meat on skewers. It was all beautiful to Ada. She didn't even mind the rotting food in metal bins, or the sourness of dark alleys. There was always the brief respite of a flower stand, of coffee being brewed to cleanse the palate.

Everywhere Ada looked there were people. Old and bent over, like question marks; teens arranged in spiky poses outside bars and cheap cafés; toddlers with red cheeks wearing mittens. Dogs and bikes and prams. Kraków thrummed, and Ada felt it running through her, like a thumb down a fretboard. All those smells, all those hearts beating. Ada could taste the city on her tongue, fizzing and popping.

After much deliberation, Ania had spent her money on lip gloss and mascara, and Ada had spent hers on a hardback book about anatomy.

Now Ada's shopping basket is more than half empty. Deodorant and face cream. Still no lip gloss or mascara, just Vaseline and cocoa butter. Ada's gaze snags on a tiny bottle of baby shampoo. It is teetering on the top shelf like an abandoned nesting doll, taken from its babushka mother. Again Ada thinks of her mother. Of how much she'd love to have a grandchild to use it on.

A memory comes over Ada, like a song playing on the radio . . . young Ada and her mother visiting Lidka, who had just had a baby. Lidka's husband, Franciszek, was working away in the nearest city. This was their first child. All the neighbours in Ada's tiny village would make the same pilgrimage, bearing bread, cheese and *pierogi*, in place of gold, frankincense and myrrh. To nine-year-old Ada it seemed a silly thing to do, but she was at that age where things were just as they were.

Ada's mother had made pork stew and apple-crumble cake. Ada's father had carved the baby a round wooden disc for teething, the same as he'd made for Ada when she was born. Lidka's house smelt strongly of something Ada could not place. A rich, fecund smell. It seemed to be coming from the baby's head. Ada had gone to touch it but her mother told her to be careful.

'That's her fontanelle. It's soft,' Lidka had explained. 'Her skull bones haven't grown together yet.'

Ada was fascinated. She'd thought babies came out like cows did, small but fully formed. She had wanted to put her finger in the cleft of the baby's head and measure the space, feel the bones, like an open mouth, like lift doors trying to close. But Lidka told her that babies were quite different from cows. That, for example, babies' kneecaps didn't form for the first couple of years, although they were born with more bones than adults.

Ada had looked at the baby, flopped over Lidka's arm like a rag doll, and frowned.

'It's true,' Lidka had said, smiling. 'Bones are made up of living tissue and calcium. It's always being built up and discarded throughout your life.'

Ada thought about teeth falling out, the way another tooth was always ready to take its place. She wondered where her discarded bones would go, or if they were just floating about inside her, like knobbly ghosts.

'How do you know all this stuff?' Ada had asked.

'I used to be a midwife,' Lidka said, carefully moving an arm from under the baby to accept the cup of tea Ada's mother passed over.

'How come you're not any more?'

Lidka had laughed as she opened her blouse to feed the baby, who rootled with an open mouth for its mother's pink nipple.

'Won't it bite you? Does it hurt? Why is the milk that colour?' Ada asked. 'Milk is supposed to be white.'

Lidka had explained about colostrum, how it was full of

antibodies that helped build an immune system. 'It's called liquid gold.'

Ada wanted to know what antibodies were. Were they the opposite of normal ones? How could they fit in milk?

'Ada, stop crowding her,' her mother said. 'Give Lidka some room to breathe. And stop asking so many questions.'

'I don't mind,' Lidka had said, nodding to her baby. 'This one's not much of a talker. I miss chatting.'

Lidka told Ada to put a finger under the baby's toes. 'See how they try to curl round it? That's called the Babinski reflex.'

Ada was enchanted. 'What else can it do?' she asked. She wants to take the baby apart like a Mr. Potato Head toy.

Lidka smiled, then yawned.

'We'd best get on and let you rest,' her mother said. 'Ada has worn you out!'

Before they left, though, her mother had gone into the kitchen, washed the plates that were piled up in the sink and swept cake crumbs from the floor. When Lidka got up to show them out, Ada noticed that her hair was wild, as though she'd not brushed it in days, and her skirt was on back to front.

'I might get my head down for half an hour,' Lidka said, through another yawn. 'Thank you so much for coming to see me.'

She had given Ada a book about Marie Curie ('I think you might like this woman'), and Janina two hard kisses. Her mother ran a finger gently across the baby's chubby cheek. She didn't accept Lidka's offer to hold her and Ada had wondered why, when it was obvious she wanted to.

'You'll make a wonderful mother when your time comes, little Ada,' Lidka said.

Walking home, Ada scuffed her shoes in the frozen leaves, thinking hard.

'You're quiet,' her mother said lightly.

'Why didn't you have any more babies?' Ada asked.

'Well,' her mother said, looking up at the sky, 'to start with, we just wanted you.' She had turned to smile at Ada, but there was a smudge of sadness on her face, like ash from when she cleaned out the grate, 'and then it turned out we couldn't have another.'

'Why not?' Ada asks.

'I don't know,' her mother replied. 'Sometimes things don't work out like you want them to, no matter how hard you try.'

'Hmm,' Ada said, but privately, she disagreed. If her mother could have one baby, why couldn't she have another? The cows did it, the sheep too. The rabbits were always at it.

'Why don't you try again? Maybe you're doing it wrong?' she'd offered.

Her mother had laughed, then pulled Ada into the warmth of her wool coat. 'Maybe, little Ada,' she said. They had walked in silence for a minute more.

Eventually her mother spoke again. 'I'm tired of trying, my little *pieroge*. And what do I need another baby for anyway? I have you. I'm the luckiest Minka in all the world.'

Ada had rolled her eyes but squeezed her mother's hand.

'Plus one day you'll have a baby of your own and I'll get to do it all over again with you.'

Ada had realized three things that day. The first was that she wanted to know more about the inside of bodies. She wanted to know what could go wrong and how to fix it. The second was that she didn't want to have a baby and stop being something else and have messy hair and wear dirty clothes. The third thing Ada realized, young as she was, was that one day she was going to break her mother's heart.

Ada picks up the bottle, tests the weight of it in her palm for a moment, then puts it back. She picks up toothpaste and cotton buds instead. Her only indulgence is bubble bath. She buys bottles that promise far more than they could ever possibly deliver, bearing statements such as '*Moonlight skies in white cashmere*' or '*Enchanted escape in the midnight orchard*'.

'Sorry, can I just . . .' An arm reaches out and grapples in the plastic dispenser of dental floss in front of Ada.

'*Przepraszam*. I mean, sorry.'

In the queue, Ada adds tissues and hand sanitizer. Studies the baskets of the people around her. Nail varnish. Tooth-whitening paste. Super-sized tampons. Corn plasters. Cystitis-relief sachets. Anusol. Vaginal wipes. Condoms. It's as if the whole queue is standing naked. Ada wonders what her basket says about her. Do they see an oncologist, a successful woman with letters after her name, or do they see a fraud with nothing better to do at the weekend than spend money? Ada blinks the thought away. A tall man with wide shoulders brushes past her, and Ada thinks of Wilbur. Of his honesty when he told her why he'd left the army. He wears his past, his failings, like a badge of honour, while Ada shoves hers down so far inside her that it makes her feet drag. Wilbur is brave or stupid.

Outside, the wind is blowing the rain sideways. Umbrellas go up, heads go down. Ada likes inclement weather, when her father is with her. Back home, they'd camp out in one of their sheds, safe and dry with the pigs and chickens while rain thundered down on the tin roof.

'Got any spare change, love?' an exaggeratedly forlorn voice asks from the pile of blankets beside her. Ada hands the man a note.

'Wow, thanks,' he says, staggering to his feet and looking at the money in surprise. His nails are long and black.

Ada waves him away. She is paid well. Too well, she often thinks. She keeps enough to cover her mortgage, bills and food. Everything else she sends to her parents. They don't want it, of course. They want the things money cannot buy. But she cannot give them that. All she can give them is *zloty*. Money they hate taking from her and never spend.

'On your way home, are you, pet?' the homeless man says. The woe-is-me voice has gone. He's jauntily gathering his stuff together. Rolling up his sleeping bag, shoving T-shirts into a backpack. 'I'm going straight to the hostel, now, thanks to you.'

'Good,' Ada replies. 'There's a place on St James's Street.'

'I'll check it out. Russian, are you? Never been myself. Love to go, though.'

'Polish,' Ada replies.

'Ah, how long have you been in England?'

Why do people always want to know this and is there a right or wrong answer? Ada has been in the country for eight years and only gone back to Poland once in that time, after her father had a fall, which she found out about only because Ania had phoned her.

'We didn't want to bother you,' her mother said, when Ada had arrived in a fluster. 'We know how busy you are.'

Busy looking after other people, not her own. Guilt had hit Ada like a slap in the face. She wasn't a surgeon. She couldn't fix her father's broken leg, but she could ask the person who was going to operate on him a million questions. Ada's fascination with bones had never wavered. She'd researched the procedure, demanded to see the X-rays, tried to explain everything to her parents.

'We trust them, love,' her mother had said, patting Ada's hand. 'Let them do their job.'

Ada had wanted to shout at her. To tell her that mistakes still happen. That doctors and surgeons are not gods.

The operation had gone smoothly. Her father was home two days later, leg propped up on a stool. Ada had done everything she could to help. Pegged out washing, carried buckets of water, fed and milked the animals. Cleaned out the pigs, collected the eggs.

'You don't need to do all that,' her mother had said, seeing Ada on her knees in the barn. 'You'll ruin all your lovely clothes.'

'I don't mind, Minka,' Ada said, but her mother did. Ada had somehow changed from being a family member to a posh guest. Her mother had put the best towels on the end of Ada's bed. A bar of her precious rose-petal soap. Kept telling her to sit down.

'I don't want to sit down. I've come to help,' Ada kept saying. She wasn't helping, though, she could tell. Her brief unannounced visit, arriving in her smart work suit, arms full of English food and fussy flowers, had not helped at all. It had done the opposite. 'I don't think I'm better than you,' Ada had wanted to tell her mother. 'I'm still your daughter, little Ada. I still belong here too.'

When she was leaving, her mother had told Ada to give them a bit more warning next time, 'so we can make it nice for you'.

'It was nice, it is nice,' Ada had said, her voice full of tears, but there were clouds in her mother's eyes again, and her father said he was sorry he couldn't get up to see her out, to drive his daughter to the airport in the car he borrowed from his friend.

Ada hasn't been back since. She has become a stranger at home, and she is a stranger here in England too.

The *Polski sklep* is empty. The fridge at the back hums loudly and strip lights flicker in the gloom. The lino floor has been poorly mopped, then walked over while still wet. Ada follows the footprints round to the counter.

'Idiot English, scared they'll melt if they get wet,' Lech says, when he sees Ada. 'Come and have a drink.' He is sitting on a box of tinned tomatoes in an unironed blue shirt. Around him are piles of unopened stock.

'Where is Aleksey?' Ada asks.

'On the sofa, drinking gherkin juice. Too much vodka for him last night. Heh, heh, heh.' Lech gives a little laugh.

'Doctor, doctor. Come attend to me,' croons a croaking voice from upstairs. 'I am very sick and need nursing.'

'He tried to out-drink the boys from the Albanian shop,' Lech says.

The rivalry between the two stores is a long-standing one. No one can remember how it started, but it seems to be never-ending.

'Did he win?' Ada asks.

'Yes,' croaks Aleksey.

'I found him on the doorstop, cuddling a stuffed toy,' Lech says.

'It was not a stuffed toy, it was a beautiful lady,' Aleksey shouts brokenly, 'but not as beautiful as you, Ada,' he adds.

Lech rolls his eyes, pours Ada a black tea.

'Want some help?' she asks, casting a glance around the shop. 'Unpacking?'

'Ah, I'll get to it,' Lech says, waving an arm. Ada looks at him again, checks his face for signs of illness. The whites of his eyes, the capillaries on his cheeks. She wants to ask him to stick out his tongue, to go and get a blood test.

'Stop it. I'm fine, just tired from being up all night with my idiot son who should know better. He did win, though. They didn't open their shop till twelve o'clock today. We were open at seven thirty as always.'

He sounds so proud, and Ada feels so small. Do her parents talk about her with that tone in their voice, that hint of wonder?

She jumps off the crate of peppers she is sitting on, turns round and picks it up. 'Tell me where it goes,' she demands.

'You don't need to . . .' Lech says. Then, 'Aisle two.'

And that is how Ada spends the rest of her day off, restocking and cleaning the *Polski sklep* while Lech sits on a stool and points at things. By the time Aleksey has finally made it downstairs, Ada is wiping the counter and the shop is sparkling, labels facing the right way, floor mopped with hot water and bleach.

'You look horrible,' Ada tells Aleksey. 'You're green.'

'It's all the gherkin juice,' he tells her, coming towards her. 'You, however, are a beautiful rose.'

Ada takes his pulse, pinches his skin to check for dehydration and tells him to drink some more water. 'You'll live,' she assures him, patting his shoulder.

'Stay for dinner,' Lech says. 'I owe you.'

'No, you don't,' Ada says. 'This is what we do.'

Outside, the wind has died down and the rain is petering out. Ada is reluctant to leave, but knows it's time to go. The pavements are the colour of liquorice under the streetlights. She walks slowly, her hands smelling of Poland. She will wash it off when she gets home, with a bubble bath that promises *'a tropical paradise'* but which will probably smell of chemicals. Ada takes the long way round, stopping briefly outside Birdie Greenwing's house, as has become her habit. Ada wonders if she goes out to the shops in weather like this. If she is okay. If she has bread, butter, milk. She sees the recycling bin is no longer at the bottom of the drive and a different pattern of lights is on. Bathroom, perhaps, or the kitchen? It's like Morse code. I – am – okay, the lights say. Ada nods and heads towards her own bungalow, hands in pockets, trying not to think how one day she might end up just like Birdie.

10

Birdie

BIRDIE WAKES EARLY AND can immediately tell that today is going to be a pain-free day. The last couple were exhausting, as if she was trying to pull a reluctant carthorse along behind her. Every small task felt elephantine – brushing her hair, getting dressed. Was that how Rose felt most days? she wonders. Today, however, is a piece of cake. Literally. Birdie finds some still in date in the back of the cupboard, warms a slice of the fruit loaf under the clonking grill. Audrey barks at the noise, then hides under the table. Birdie feels zesty, freshly squeezed, like a glass of orange juice.

That said, she still doesn't feel up to the task of clearing out the rest of Rose's wardrobe, so she decides to have a look around the garden shed instead. She might still have four to six months left to live, but she's not been in the shed for the last eight years.

It rained through the night and the lawn is wet and boggy. Birdie's boots sink into the mulch with an unpleasant squelch. Audrey watches her from the back door, not one for getting her paws damp. The shed, when Birdie finally reaches it, smells of compost and bike tyres. Of creosote and stale coffee grounds and moth-eaten sunshades. Birdie spots a wicker basket full of hideous china cups and saucers that had belonged to her mother, Eunice. Both she and Rose felt guilty for not displaying them, but they were truly awful. ('They are so ugly they put me off my coffee,' Rose said. 'Pink and green should never be seen.')

'You mean blue and green.'

'I mean, specifically, that crockery.'

Perhaps some part of Birdie has come here hoping to find her sister. To pretend the last few years were really just a long game of hide and seek and Rose will appear at any minute. Perhaps Birdie has nothing else to do and is looking for something to waste moments on. The idea almost made her laugh because the hours, for so many years, were never long enough. Not when Arthur wanted to take her out for dinner while Rose wanted Birdie to watch a film. When Arthur wanted to go away for the weekend with his wife, but Rose was having a flare-up. Birdie's arms used to feel too long from being constantly pulled in two directions. Every choice she made meant letting down someone she loved. Sometimes she almost envied Rose, even with her illness. She only needed Birdie to make her happy, but Birdie was greedy: she needed Rose *and* Arthur. A sister *and* a husband.

Birdie had never planned to fall in love with Arthur, but it was like falling down the stairs – by the time you'd realized what was happening, it was already too late to stop it. Birdie tried to fight the attraction between them, to keep him at arm's length, but Arthur made that as difficult as possible.

They had met in a dance hall the spring before the twins turned twenty. For the first couple of weeks, Arthur did no more than smile in Birdie's direction, which Birdie couldn't help but return. Rose got tired early and worried about people stamping on her feet. Arthur noticed this when they first started chatting, and he'd make sure she had space to twirl in without being trampled. Then one night he offered Birdie his jacket, then another to drive them home. He turned up the heating in his car for Rose and never minded his evening being cut short. He filled the space with chatter and the smell of lime cologne. They would stop for hot chocolate at the late-night café. Try to stretch the night out to its furthest point. Birdie didn't know what came next, how to turn Arthur into a daytime thing.

'For God's sake, Bird, when are you going to invite him in?' Rose hissed one night, as she got out of the car. 'If you don't do it soon, I will.'

Birdie and Rose were identical, but from day one, the relationship between Rose and Arthur was different, more like that of slightly competitive siblings. They got on, but there were moments of tension. Occasional bouts of friction. Silent dinners punctuated by forks scraping on plates, the atmosphere thick and taut, before either Arthur or Rose would break into slightly forced laughter, and the subject would be changed. The kettle put on. Click. The moment gone.

'Whatever I do, wherever I go, she'll be coming with me,' Birdie had told Arthur. He'd taken her for a drive to see the sun set over the Downs. Spring had turned into summer and Birdie's love was in bloom.

'Of course,' Arthur said easily, looking into the rear-view mirror as he indicated.

'I can't leave her, Arthur,' Birdie had insisted, turning in her seat to look at his handsome face. 'It would be like leaving half of myself.'

'Birdie,' Arthur had replied, putting a hand on her knee, warm and reassuring. 'I understand. You come with a spare button. I get it.'

Birdie had laughed. Suddenly everything felt possible and nothing more was said. He proposed. Birdie said, yes, please. Rose wore a bridesmaid's dress, modelled on an outfit she'd seen Princess Margaret wear. Yellow and ruffled, with a matching hat. 'I either look wonderful, or I look like a duck,' Rose had said, peering into the mirror. 'I can't decide which one.'

'You look like the princess of all ducks,' Birdie said.

When Birdie said, 'I do,' she looked first at Arthur and then at her sister, as if she could bind the three of them together with her vows. Her mother was crying in the front row, an empty space next to her where their father should have been. 'Busy in battle,' Rose had said, though he would have been far too old by then, just as they were for such nonsense. But sometimes the idea of a father is better than no father at all – even if he's a made-up royal.

In the shed, behind the wicker basket, Birdie finds a stack of vinyl soundtracks. An old memory plays out in her mind. Herself and Rose, giggling like children as they watched *Some Like It Hot*, wedged together on the sofa, a box of chocolates melting on their laps. Birdie had felt so happy, so contented, until Rose had turned to her and said, 'Shush, don't laugh so loud or Arthur will come and take you away.'

'What?' Birdie had said, sobering up immediately. 'What do you mean?'

Rose had said nothing more, but moments later, Arthur had appeared in the doorway and asked Birdie if she could help him find a pair of cufflinks.

'I'm tired anyway, Bird,' Rose had said, getting slowly to her feet. 'Going to turn in now.'

Arthur did not need help finding his cufflinks. 'Sorry, Bird, I was just feeling a bit left out,' he admitted, and Birdie's heart hurt with love and remorse in equal measure.

When she comes out of the shed, Birdie is wearing a helmet of cobwebs, there is dust all over her cardigan and she is holding the record collection, which will make her horribly lugubrious, but she can't resist. Some days she will do whatever it takes to feel close to Arthur and Rose again, even if it's just shuffling round the living room with their ghosts.

It's as she is turning to shut the latch on the shed that she slips on a patch of mud. Twisting her ankle on the way down, she lands heavily on her side, catches her temple on the corner of a paving slab, and then there is nothing but blackness.

When she comes to, her head feels as though it's been kicked by a horse. When she tries to move, her ankle shrieks in protest and a string of nausea pulls tight inside her. She feels dizzy, old and scared.

What would Princess Margaret do? Birdie thinks, the thought coming with a sob. She remembers one of Rose's stories. Margaret dropping her coat at a function, someone offering to pick it up. Margaret saying, no, to leave it there. That she'd never remember where it was if they moved it. Birdie feels like that dropped jacket. She wonders if anyone will remember her if she doesn't move.

Birdie tries again and again to get up, to drag herself towards the back door, but her strength has gone. All she can do is lie there, prawn-like, on her side, as the hours pass and the sky starts to darken. The stars seem to appear all at once, as if switched on by some unseen hand. She and Rose used to love sky-gazing, the ground damp beneath them as they made up names for the constellations. Watched clouds move across the moon. Scared each other silly with stories of crows and ghosts. Attempts at camping always ended up with a hot bath at ten p.m., their beds, flannel nightgowns and a hot-water bottle. All of that had stopped after Rose became ill, when getting damp meant a week in bed to recover.

When Rose was thirteen, she began to complain of sore hands and feet. Growing pains, the doctors had said. It will pass. But Rose's joints swelled beyond recognition and were hot to the touch. The skin beneath her eyes became bruised with exhaustion. Even picking up her spoon seemed to hurt, to take all her energy. Birdie dunked bread in soup, fed Rose like she was a baby. Back and forth their small family hobbled to hospital. At first their mother had tried to prevent Birdie going with them, but she'd insisted. Finally they got their diagnosis – a 'blood disease', the specialist said. Birdie shivered at the words, as though Rose had been cursed somehow. If this were a story, Birdie would discover a cure, go on a quest to find some flower that only came out at midnight. But there was no remedy for rheumatoid arthritis.

They clung to the hope it was something she'd grow out of. Instead, it was something that Rose grew into. Twisted fingers and bunched-up toes. Elbows and knees that did not bend. Meanwhile, Birdie blossomed like her sister's namesake, with long stem-like legs and narrow ankles, thick hair and clear skin.

'Sorry,' Birdie said, a million times a day.

'Don't be silly, Birdie!' Rose would say. 'It's not your fault.'

But to Birdie, it was. She'd overheard her mother on the phone once, saying how Rose had been the smaller, weaker twin. How Birdie must have taken up more than her fair share in the womb. Birdie had come out pink and squawking, while Rose had been born silent and blue. Had to be put in an incubator, laid under a sunlamp, like a rejected chick, as Birdie kicked her chubby legs in their cot at home. Birdie never knew until then that she and her sister had ever been apart. That conversation stayed with her, rewording itself, like whispered rumours, as the years rolled past. 'All Birdie's fault, took too much. Poor Rose.'

Lying in the garden, Birdie thinks perhaps she should just give in and let sleep claim her. Death, even. This is not how she'd planned to go, knickers on display and blood dripping down her forehead. She'd known the end would be ugly, but not this sort of ugly. Does it really matter, though? Dead is dead.

The garden starts to glow gold. Heaven, Birdie thinks. So soon? Then she realizes it's her neighbour's kitchen light being switched on. They must have just got home. She lies in the orange beam, feeling alien and strange. A light rain starts to fall. Her hair clings limply to her scalp. Birdie tastes her own blood, her own fear. I'm not as brave as you, Rose, she thinks. I can't hold it all in like you did.

'Help!' she cries weakly. 'Can anyone hear me? Please. Please. Help me.'

11

Jane

THE NURSING TEAM ARE having a morning 'huddle'. A lovely word, suggesting a circle of bodies, keeping one another warm. Emperor penguins braving the Antarctic winds together. What a shame it is being left out of the group. It's like there is a Book of Jane that she has never seen but everyone else has read. Her teammates must all have been given a copy because Jane has already, without audition or a trial period, somehow failed. Her nose tingles and her eyes burn. Don't do it, Jane, she tells herself. Do not let them see you cry.

The team leader, Sadie, really likes the sound of her own voice. Everything she is telling them has been written up on the whiteboard she is standing in front of. Frankie would point this out. Add that they can read. Frankie would calculate how much time and productivity Sadie is wasting as patients ring bells and ask for water as though they've been parched all night. Jane thinks of how Suki is probably leading a meeting in a big glass-walled conference room too, her voice ringing out clear and confident. Saying things like 'Take a thought shower' and 'Let's toss it in the ideas wok.'

Meanwhile, Min will be scrubbing something back in Bristol. She took the early train, looking less fierce than when she'd arrived, her gait slightly lopsided. Maybe she does have a bad knee after all. For all her hot air, Jane rarely saw her mother looking tired. Her cheeks were always like two polished apples, her hands warm. She chugged out heat like a generator. Was forever flapping at her cardigan, tugging at her scarf. 'Here I go,' she used to say. 'Here it bleddy comes.'

When they were teenagers, Min's hot flushes were the stuff of legend. Once, she'd almost ripped the buttons off her blouse in the middle of the freezer aisle at their local supermarket.

'What are you all looking at?' she'd told everyone around them. 'I am too hot, and I don't bleddy care who sees it!'

She'd bent over the frozen peas, leaned into the cod fillets, the steam rising off her.

'You have no idea,' she hissed at a man who was trying his best to shuffle past unseen, pointing at him with a crooked finger, 'no idea what us women suffer.'

That was just after their father had died, when white-hot grief bubbled out of Min like a volcano.

'Just give me a minute, girls,' she'd said, holding some broccoli florets against the back of her neck, 'I just need a minute.'

Poor, poor Min.

Seeing her mother looking lame has made everything else feel off kilter. It makes Jane want to ring Suki. Interrupt her fancy meeting and say, 'I saw Min yawn. A proper actual yawn, not the fake one she does when people are boring her. She's starting to fade, Suki. You need to come home now. You need to do something.' Because I'm a bit scared, and you are my older sister and you always used to hold my hand, when I was feeling shy, when the plane took off.

'Right,' says Sadie, with a loud hand-clap, which makes one of the patients shout, 'Gun!' Jane imagines her trying to get out of bed to hide under it, catheter intact. 'Enough chit-chat. Let's get to work.'

Helen looks at Jane, rolls her eyes. 'It's a no from me' is printed in block capitals on her coffee mug. Jane smiles. 'How many cats do you think Sadie has at home?' Helen whispers.

'Five at least,' Jane says.

'What do you think she does when she's not at work?'

'Writes letters of complaint,' Jane says.

'Tells people off for using the "five items or less" queue at the shops when they have six,' Helen says.

'Circles dog poo on the pavement with chalk.'

'Takes things back to the pound shop and demands a refund. Has strong opinions on the weather reporter's makeup. Gets cross with her when it rains without fair warning.'

Helen doesn't wear any makeup, Jane notices. Her face is clear, bright and freshly scrubbed, and her hair is the colour of wheat. She makes Jane think of peaches and cream and country walks through fields of corn. Harvest festivals and pumpkins.

'Helen, Jane? Something you want to share with the group?' Sadie asks loudly.

Helen holds up her mug. Jane laughs and the conversation keeps her feeling cheerful all morning, until Min calls to piss in her cornflakes.

'How's your knee?' Jane asks brightly.

'Never mind that!' Min says. 'You should see the ganglion on my wrist. It's as big as your head.'

'Hit it with a Bible.'

'Pah, that's medical advice, is it? Honestly, Jane.'

'Well, any big book will do. It breaks the ganglion down, so the synovial fluid disperses into the surrounding area. It won't get rid of the cyst shell, though. The fluid will re-accumulate.'

Min humphs again. Nothing annoys her more than sound logic.

'Have you been to the doctor about your knee, though, Min?'

'The doctor? What would I want to bother him for?'

When Frankie was living with her, Min would spend hours on the floor doing jigsaws. Would bend at the waist to put Frankie's socks on for her, button up her coat. Would probably have brushed Frankie's teeth for her had she been allowed. Never once had Min complained about aching joints or antiquated-sounding ailments such as milk leg or quinsy. Her mother has aged ten years in the few months since Jane and Frankie moved away.

'It's those bleddy stairs, they get steeper each day. Not like your bungalow,' Min says down the phone.

'It's not mine, I rent it,' Jane says, but her heart speeds up. Is that what Min wants? Is this what she's angling for, to move to Brighton? Jane's dream of finding that eighteen-year-old girl who swam in the freezing waves and kissed strangers is fading more and more by the day. 'Got to go, Min, call you back soon.' Jane hangs up, her palms sweating.

All day, guilt takes little nips inside her, a hole punch to her resolve. She rushes from patient to patient, tries not to think about Min, limping home alone. Doing her washing for one. Does she even bother to cook herself dinner any more?

Jane can't shake the feeling that she's in the wrong place. She's distracted as Frankie tells her about her day on their walk home. Minute by minute. Min used to make the same absent hmming noises Jane is making now. That 'I'm not really listening, because this is not interesting, is not important to me' noise. Jane remembers how much it hurt when Min did it to her. All she wanted was for Min to *look* at her. To put down her sewing or her mop and give Jane all her attention, just for five minutes. Just once, Jane wanted to be more important than Suki, than cleaning, than the news. It's harder than she thought, she realizes now. When you grow up and have a million cards to keep close to your chest, and your worries won't stay where you put them, but keep reappearing, like bindweed.

At their front gate, Jane spots a fox creeping across their garden, long nose to the ground, white-tipped tail in the air. When it looks up and meets her eye, Jane feels her breath catch in her throat. Foxes do whatever they like. Take what they want, leave a mess for someone else to clean up. They have always scared her. A childish fear, but real nonetheless. The smell they leave, the way they come out at night to rearrange the garden. They should come with a cartoon soundtrack, something sinister to warn people.

'How cool is that?' Frankie whispers.

'Mmm,' Jane says, digging in her bag for her keys, keen to get inside.

As Frankie goes back to dissecting her science lesson, explaining how the teacher was wrong, how Frankie knows more about photosynthesis than he does, Jane can't stop thinking about Min's comment. Min would hate Brighton; she *did* hate Brighton. She said it was filthy, full of ne'er-do-wells and thieves. Bristol was hardly any better, but there was no point in arguing.

When Jane had texted Suki to say she was moving, her sister had replied with three words, 'What about Min?', not 'Love Brighton, good for you', not 'I'll come visit', not 'About time you lived your own life.' What about Min? What about *me*? Jane had wanted to shout. I exist too.

Inside, Frankie goes round switching on lights, starting their evening routine. Jane watches her retrieve a giant cabbage from the fridge and sighs. Jane wants a takeaway, pizza and wings, cookies and ice cream. Kate Moss once said that nothing tastes as good as skinny feels. Jane wonders if Kate Moss has ever tried a stuffed crust. She's just putting together her argument for a treat day, although it isn't a Friday, a leap year or anyone's birthday, when Frankie races over to the kitchen window.

'Mum, I think Mrs Greenwing has fallen over in her garden. I can hear her calling.'

Jane drops the takeaway menu and runs outside.

'Help,' comes a weak voice from the other side of the fence.

The fox is still in the garden, skulking in the corner. It doesn't run at the sound of Jane's footsteps or Birdie Greenwing's panicked cry, but pauses to watch Jane go past, green eyes like night-vision goggles. Jane feels that sense of fear again, curdling in her guts.

12

Ada

WILBUR HAS BEEN CHANGING the shape of Ada's day. She has begun to notice when he is not around, a bit like a draught, except it makes her want to open doors. That morning she found him in the WRVS café chatting away to Connie. She should have warned him it was a bad idea. Connie could not do more than one thing at a time, not even talking, but Wilbur was listening, rapt.

'He would have been fifty-six,' Connie intoned slowly, 'would've made someone a lovely husband. Always asked to carry my bag for me, even as a child. My lovely boy. God needed another angel, I suppose.' One very small tear rolled down her puckered cheek and plopped into Wilbur's mug. 'Sorry,' Connie said, 'I'll make you another.'

'Nonsense! It won't need any sugar now,' Wilbur said, and winked.

Connie laughed like the cartoon dog Muttley, one hand over her mouth, a wheezy snigger that lifted her shoulders up to her ears. The kind of laugh that made everyone else around join in, even if they didn't know what was funny.

'Morning, Ada!' Connie called. 'The usual?'

'Just coffee, please.' Ada was hungry but felt awkward about cramming a huge bacon sandwich into her mouth in front of Wilbur. She didn't want to examine the reasons why.

The mug Connie passes her said, 'I licked it, so it's mine.' Ada found herself glancing at Wilbur.

'Want to see what I got?' he said. There was an odd moment of tension between them, eye contact that felt like a challenge, and then he turned his mug round. Written in brown bubble letters were the words 'Coffee Makes Me Poo'. 'Accurate,' he told her ruefully.

Ada's burst of laughter shocked her. Should an oncologist be seen giggling in the middle of the hospital? The thought was a sobering one. Ada pulled herself together as she and Wilbur headed towards their department, her high heels tapping along the corridor.

'Morning, Grace,' Wilbur said to the girl in the X-ray department. 'Hi, Mickey,' he waved to the lift porter, shared some ludicrous handshake with the Latvian cleaner.

'How do you know everyone's names?' Ada asked. 'You've only been here five minutes.'

'It's on their name tags.' He shrugged, biting into a muffin.

Ada never looked at name tags. She didn't stop to say hello to porters or the cleaning staff. The underbelly of the hospital.

'I've been invited to join the PALS badminton team,' Wilbur said, brushing crumbs off his shirt. 'Are you in it?'

'No.' Ada hadn't even known such a thing existed.

'Do you play?' he asked.

At home, Ada and Ania's idea of competitive sport was to

spit sour cherry stones into a bucket that they moved further and further away. The first one to twenty won. Ada carried on long after her guts began to ache from the bitter fruit. 'No,' she said now, 'it's a pointless game.'

'Well, that's fighting talk. Badminton, or "badders" to people in the know, is a game of skill and endurance.'

Ada rolled her eyes.

'I'll ask if you can come along, if you like,' he offered.

Ada noticed that he didn't allow her to go first into her office but opened the door slowly and made a quick inspection of the room, as though someone might be hiding in the corner. Old habits die hard, she supposed. The only thing lurking in her office were documents in recycled cardboard folders confirming the presence of cancer.

'No, thank you,' she said coolly.

Ada thought she heard him mutter, 'Chicken,' under his breath as he opened the blinds. I am not a chicken, Ada wanted to say, her competitive spirit sparking to life. I'll prove it. But she couldn't. And not just because she'd never played badminton, but because then her faceless co-workers might start to form features, personalities. And then they might get sick.

Cancer is not contagious, Ada knows this, yet she puts her white coat into a hot wash each evening, steams it to within an inch of its life. Scrubs her skin under the shower. Ada's hands are chafed and sore from washing them so many times.

For a while, Ada had felt appropriately detached from her patients in England. Could deliver bad news in her clipped accent easily, factually. But then she had met Francis Albright, young, strong and about to become a father.

'Blast me,' he told Ada. 'Hit with me with everything you've got. Both barrels. I can take it.'

The treatment had worked, initially. Ada really thought she had saved him. Top of the class, Ada, getting everything right. She had glowed as his tumours shrank. His bloods were good; he never lost his eyelashes. Ada buzzed. Francis smiled at her with chapped lips, called her his hero. Ada put her hand on his shoulder as he left her office, squeezed his almost cancer-free bones. 'I'll be back,' he told her each time he closed her door. He died during his last round of chemo. Ada was out drinking with Ania at the time. Dancing away to 'Don't Stop Believing'.

Ada cried when she heard the news. Ugly sobs that hurt. Ada knew the statistics, had known what the job entailed, yet she couldn't stop herself going over and over Francis's file, wondering what she could have done differently. She still pulls it out now and again, whenever a new drug shows some success, and wonders if it might have saved him.

Cancer is not a game that Ada can win. She cannot outsmart it, run faster than it, or arm-wrestle it into submission. She knows this, yet every time a new patient walks through her door she thinks, You are not having this one. Please, don't take them. She has no idea who she is talking to.

'I can teach you how to play badminton, if you like,' Wilbur said.

'I know how to play . . .' Ada was scared to say the word. It was a tricky one to pronounce '. . . that silly game.'

'Ah,' Wilbur said, looking at her over his coffee cup, 'I understand.'

'There is nothing to understand,' Ada snapped, getting annoyed. 'I'm too busy to skip about hitting a ball.'

'Shuttlecock,' Wilbur coughed into his fist.

'Shuttle . . .' Ada paused on the second syllable, then told herself to grow up, and ended up almost shouting it '. . . cock! Over a fence.'

'Net,' Wilbur amended quietly.

'In Poland we play a different version,' Ada said, 'a better one.'

'I see,' Wilbur said, trying not to smile.

'Just drink your coffee and go for your poo,' Ada said, straightening the files on her desk. 'We have work to do.'

Denise had called Ada's office phone while Wilbur was out at lunch.

'So, how's it going with Wilbur?' she asked. 'Are you getting on?' Ada could hear her typing in the background.

'I've no idea what you mean,' Ada said. 'Wilbur is my intern. Not that I even wanted him.'

'I think he goes to the gym at lunch,' Denise said, as though Ada hadn't spoken. 'You should see his legs in his shorts . . .'

Ada pinched the bridge of her nose, where her self-control lived.

'Mother, may I?' Denise said, with a laugh.

'No, you may not,' Ada said. 'You are married, remember? You moan about your husband to anyone who'll listen.'

Ada had told her secretary time and time again that she did not work in a school office or a youth hostel. The people who come here are nervous. They need calm, peace, sobriety. They do not need the latest instalment of Denise's tumultuous relationship. (He introduces her to his friends as his current wife. What more does Denise need to know about the man?)

Maybe Ada was wrong, though. Maybe her patients needed people like Wilbur, learning their names. Perhaps they welcomed Denise's overly familiar tone, her deep-purple mascara, orange fish swimming in coral-coloured tanks. Connie's cartoon laugh. Maybe Ada was the one getting it all wrong. Maybe she *was* a chicken.

'He likes you,' Denise said, 'I can tell he does.'

'I am his boss, he has to like me.'

'Not really,' Denise argued. 'Why don't you invite him out to lunch?'

'Why would I do that?'

'To get to know him.'

'I don't want to know him,' Ada said.

'Liar.'

'Go and do some work,' Ada said, putting the phone down.

At home now, the day repeats itself in her head. Ada paces from room to room, restless and irritated. Wilbur has upset her pH balance and she doesn't like it. She blames him for not being able to concentrate on the documentary about serial killers. For having washed her hair with conditioner instead of shampoo. When her doorbell rings, she is relieved. Even though it will probably only be Ivy, again.

But it is not Ivy. It's a girl with red cheeks and matching hair. 'You're a doctor, right?' she asks.

Ada goes to correct her, then notices the girl's hands are balled into fists.

'My neighbour has fallen in her garden. Her head is bleeding, and her leg . . . We need your help.'

Ada's pulse thrums, her boredom, her sense of helplessness gone in an instant. This strange girl had said Ada's magic words. *We need you.* Ada grabs the medical bag she keeps in the hallway, shuts her door and chases the girl back down the street, her shoes slapping on the wet pavement.

13

Birdie

IF THIS IS HOW Birdie is going out, she wants to remember her best bits before the end, like a murderer on Death Row being served their favourite meal. Birdie rootles through her memory, tossing years aside as though searching for her favourite silk scarf: Arthur and her in their greenhouse. Muddy handprints up her thighs, Arthur gasping half in delight, half in panic, 'Careful, Birdie! You're crushing my "Cardinal Farges"!' Birdie shivers violently, sending sparks of pain shooting down her arms and legs. She needs another memory, quick. Something to warm her up. She is so cold. Her teeth are chattering. Talking to themselves. They sound like a typewriter. Yes, Birdie, think about typewriters! Her fingers flying over the keyboard. The potential of a fresh sheet of paper, like newly fallen snow. The whirr of the knob as she pulled out a letter. The satisfying ping of the carriage return. Her low heels clacking across the tiled floor as she made coffee for clients, collected the post. The neatness of the files, the appointment book with its red leather cover. The way everything worked as it should. 'Sign in, please,' she'd say. 'Mr Dickens will see you now.'

When their mother died, she and Rose were in their forties, and much as Rose insisted otherwise, she couldn't live alone. Birdie demanded she move in with her and Arthur. When Rose finally conceded, Birdie went part-time so she could take Rose to her appointments, could be there in the mornings when Rose's joints made her walk like the Tin Man from *The Wizard of Oz*. 'Let's oil you up,' she'd say, passing over pills, massaging Rose's sore hands. Soon Birdie's beloved job became another hand pulling at her, demanding attention. She felt like a Stretch Armstrong toy, elastic limbs being tugged out of shape. At the end of the day, she loved her job, but she loved her sister more, so she had let go of Mr Dickens, of her career.

These memories are not helping Birdie at all. They hurt more than the cut on her forehead, than her throbbing ankle. Can't she just die quickly? Forget the four to six months. She has nothing left to live for anyway, only Audrey who, Birdie is well aware, is anyone's for a piece of cheese. She scrunches her eyes closed. Wills it to be over quickly. Come on, Death, she thinks. Find me.

'Mrs Greenwing!'

And then cool fingers are on her wrist, checking her pulse. A quiet voice in her ear.

'Birdie, it's me, your neighbour, Jane. I have a doctor with me.'

'Hello again, Mrs Greenwing.'

Birdie knows she's heard that voice before, but she's not sure when. Her pain is as big as a whale. She is stuck behind its teeth. Slipping on its foetid tongue. She hears people muttering about her in technical terms. A hand pulls down her skirt. Another smooths the hair from her face, warm fingers on her temple. A gentle tut.

'Call an ambulance,' the clipped voice says. 'Fetch a blanket.'

Birdie feels something warm being laid over her.

'It's okay,' Jane tells her, 'everything is going to be fine.'

'It isn't,' Birdie says. 'I fell.'

'Help is on its way,' Jane says. 'Won't be long now.'

Birdie feels herself shifting in and out of consciousness.

'My dog,' Birdie moans, as she is lifted on to a stretcher, carried towards the bright lights of the ambulance, not Heaven.

'We'll look after your dog,' Jane promises.

The siren makes Birdie jump with its high-pitched wail, cutting into the night, slicing through her aching skull. The sound dislodges a memory. Birdie aged thirteen, running along the pavement, chasing the ice-cream van with its jingling tune. Suddenly she tripped, falling hard on to her hands and knees. Shock and pain and blood. An overwhelming desire for her mother. But when she hobbled home, she'd found her mother busy helping Rose. Birdie had watched, unseen, from the doorway, blood trickling into her socks, as though her knees were crying. Quietly, she had turned and gone into the bathroom. Mopped at her hands, picked out the gravel, applied the antiseptic and plasters herself. They were wonky, but she pulled fresh socks up and her sleeves down and never said a word.

'Not long now, my lovely,' a voice says absently, as the blanket under her chin is adjusted. 'You just have a nice rest.'

The crew talk about traffic, about the diversion on the seafront. About the new takeaway opening on Middle Street.

At the hospital Birdie is inspected, prodded and poked, like a specimen in a jar. Her ankle is X-rayed in a machine. Broken, apparently. She wonders what a scan of her heart would look like. A doctor tells her she has a lot of bruising but nothing too serious. The cut on her forehead is glued together with something that stings. Finally, she is wheeled on to a ward by two orderlies who talk over her head as if she is not there. Football scores and betting odds. She is just falling asleep when a doctor comes, draws the blue curtains around her bed and pulls up a chair.

'Mrs Greenwing?'

Birdie doesn't answer. Her name is on a board above her bed, on a piece of plastic around her wrist. Her power of speech must have disappeared along with her clothes. She has been dressed in the standard NHS uniform of thin gown that gapes at the back and long blue compression socks. Birdie has become part of a flock of supposedly bovine old ladies who nod, dumb as cows. Who open mouths for tablets without asking what they are for. Who lie back and think of England.

'I've noticed in your file that you have . . .' The doctor pauses.

She knew this was coming. Could tell by the tone in his voice. 'Cancer,' Birdie mouths, turning her head away.

'Is there someone we can call for you?'

Birdie didn't think she had any more tears left to cry, but one trickles down her cheek. She lets it speak for her.

'You're tired,' the doctor says, standing up, 'get some sleep. We'll talk again tomorrow.'

All night long, nurses come and go, checking her blood pressure, her temperature. A red glowing thing is put on her finger. She is given fluids through a drip in her arm. It hurts to bend her elbow. How can she sleep with all the beeping and groaning and snoring around her? How can she sleep without her gin and her dog and her flannel nightgown?

'She's very unsettled,' the nurse tells the doctor at three a.m., 'can you give her something to help her sleep?'

Birdie opens her little beak willingly. All she wants is oblivion. I don't want to wake up, she thinks, as the sleeping tablet starts working and everything fades away. Please don't let me wake up.

14

Jane

'GANNETS ARE THE LARGEST birds in the northern hemisphere.'

'Are they?' Jane tries to look interested in what Frankie is saying. They are at the Booth Museum. Jane is trying to make up for being distant all week, is determined to be fully present for her daughter. Frankie is not making it easy.

'One of the earliest examples of a large animal used for taxidermy occurred in 1771, when Captain Cook brought a kangaroo skin back to England.'

'Is that so?' Jane says. 'What about the rest of the kangaroo?'

Frankie ignores her. 'In early taxidermy, the most common type of preservative used was arsenic. Now dermestid beetles are used. Their larvae love animal flesh. They are only millimetres long but will eat until only the bare bones are left.'

'Lovely.' Jane feels itchy just thinking about it.

They have been at the museum for three hours already, and it doesn't look like Frankie is going to want to leave any time soon. Jane is keen to be off. The stuffed-animal museum is not the reason Jane moved to Brighton. She wants to go to the open market, wander round the Lanes. Try all the free samples being handed out. Pakoras and elderflower sorbet. Earl Grey Creme leaf tea from Bird & Blend and cubes of cheese on cocktail sticks from the stall by the station. Jane wants to go swimming at the Prince Regent pool, with its old-fashioned blue tiles and the smell of damp towels that always sends her spinning back to childhood. The rusting sign proclaiming 'No Bobbing! Shouting! Running! Heavy petting!' Jane thought that meant taking your dog swimming until Suki explained it to her. Jane wants to bob along in a lane divided by floats and ropes, her arms cycling her through the water, calmed by the bubbling sound of her own breath. Maybe somewhere on the bottom of the pool, among the kicking feet and dropped hairbands, she might find that feeling again, that child-on-Christmas-Eve excitement she felt the first time she came to Brighton.

'No way. Not again,' Frankie said when she suggested it. Frankie thought public swimming baths were hotbeds of infection. 'You are ingesting so many diseases,' she told Jane loudly, the first and only time they went. Instead of getting into the water, Frankie had stood by the side with blue plastic covers over her shoes, pointing out floating plasters and men with hairy backs. 'That person just sneezed. That one has an open wound. I think you should get out.'

Jane has considered a dip in the sea, but she's not the brave girl she was. She remembers Suki wading straight in, throwing her shoulders under the waves without pause. Min says Suki runs now. Jane can tell that her mother is not sure of the context. 'Suki's been at it again today,' she tells Jane. 'Maybe she was late for the bus.'

Jane and Suki once tried to do a park run together. Jane

tripped on a tree root early on, taking Suki down with her. They landed in a pile of mud. Other runners, serious runners, with T-shirts about other runs they'd done, galloped past frowning. Jane got the giggles. Min tutted when she saw them limping towards the finish line, covered with leaves and twigs.

'I named you after the film,' Min said, later that night, '*Calamity Jane*.' But she also polished their cheap medals weekly and hung them from a nail on the mantelpiece, in pride of place.

'Mum! Are you listening? I said, Edward Booth's ambition was to capture an example of every single British bird. When he died, he was about fifty birds short of his target,' Frankie recites, reading from a leaflet.

'Was he?' Jane says, zoning back in. 'So only fifty species escaped this fate?' She looks at the bird behind the glass in front of her. It's like something from an Alfred Hitchcock film, two huge black eyes silently screaming and a yellow hooked beak.

'Booth gassed the smaller birds. He caught them in a net first, of course. A rifle would have blown them to pieces,' Frankie says cheerfully 'Oh, look, there's his punt gun!'

Frankie goes off to examine the weapon in great detail while Jane walks to the end of the aisle, thousands of glassy eyes on her as she goes. Let me out, she imagines each bird trying to cry through its glued-together beak. Let me out!

In a large diorama on the far wall, a hawk is turning away from a sheep. Something in the way the animal is lying reminds Jane of their neighbour when they found her. Like she'd been dropped or discarded. Admittedly, Mrs Greenwing's eyes had not been pecked out, Jane thinks, leaning closer, but still, the helpless angle of her body was the same. Something about it felt so exposed.

The doctor that Frankie fetched had been amazing. Jane hadn't seen her before. 'Oncology,' was all she'd said, when Jane asked if she worked at the hospital. She was gone the moment the ambulance arrived. Didn't even say goodbye. A cold fish, as Min would say, but kind and gentle with Birdie. Which version of her was the real one? Jane wondered.

Jane had asked one of the ambulance men to let her know how Birdie was getting on. A text at ten p.m. confirmed that Birdie had a broken ankle but nothing else too serious. She was spending the night in hospital for observation and rehydration. Jane hoped Birdie would be on her ward tomorrow.

It had felt wrong, going into Mrs Greenwing's house when she was so clearly uncomfortable about having visitors, but they'd promised to get Audrey. Jane had worried about what they might find there, but aside from too much furniture and piles of old magazines, the house felt strangely empty, and echoed with loneliness. It smelt of long-closed-up rooms, of cold that had been allowed to spread, to move in and take over. No radiator could remove that sort of chill. It was a house that used to feel like it was lived in and enjoyed, and now it was not. Mould creeping round windows, the floor tiles curling up. A tiny pint of milk that made Jane want to call her mother for no good reason.

They found Audrey cowering under the table, next to a puddle of wee. She is now at their bungalow, has been walked, fed a tin of dog food, which she initially scowled at, and is currently watching a David Attenborough documentary, or at least she was when Jane and Frankie left her.

Jane gazes at the sheep again. Its black eye sockets look like the end of a rifle. It has stopped looking like Birdie and has morphed into her mother.

Frankie had called Min to inform her that she was looking after her next-door neighbour's dog after she'd tripped and fallen in the garden. The old lady, not the dog. Mrs Greenwing was there for hours, Frankie said, bleeding out slowly.

Min had crowed in delight. 'It'll be me next, lying there dead in the garden, no one coming to save me. Both my daughters miles away.'

'She wasn't dead, Min. She had a broken ankle, and you don't even have a back garden,' Jane said, having wrestled the phone off Frankie. 'How's your knee?'

'Huge,' Min said. 'Like a lump of ham.'

Passing the 'exotic' display cage, Jane stops to take a photo of a small bird with a curved red beak. It has huge pink plumage and an electric-blue crest. The rest of its body is covered with fluffy apricot down. Its eyes are huge and surrounded by a deep purple ring. She sends the photo to Suki with the caption 'Found Min's spirit animal.' She doesn't mention Min's knee. What's the point? Suki sends back a thumbs-up.

'Mum!' Frankie comes to find her, eyes glowing with excitement. 'Mum! Mum! Up there!' She points to a row of metal stairs. 'There's an albatross chick!'

'Cool,' says Jane, trying to mean it, 'and interesting.'

'And a three-headed cat, and foxes and squirrels playing cards.'

'What?' Jane says.

'But they won't show them any more,' Frankie laments.

'I wonder why?'

'Because people are stupid,' Frankie says.

'Cheer up. I'll buy you a pencil from the gift shop.'

It has become a joke between the two of them – finding the cheapest, which is often also the most boring, item in a gift shop.

'I don't want a pencil. I want a dog,' Frankie says. 'A live one,' she adds.

While Jane is pleased her daughter is finally showing an interest in an animal that is not already dead, a dog is the last thing Jane needs. 'Frankie, we can't have a dog because I work all day. You're at school. It wouldn't be fair . . .'

Frankie rifles through the stationery on display, pretending not to hear.

'Plus the cost. I'm not even sure we'd be allowed a dog in a rented bungalow . . . Franks?'

But Frankie has walked over to the postcards, her back to Jane. She eventually picks one, a photo of the diorama by the door. A whooper swan, wings outstretched, white tips pressed up against the glass. It looks like it could still kill you if it wanted to. 'Even cheaper than a pencil,' Frankie says brightly. 'More money for a dog-sitter!'

15

Ada

ADA'S WEEKENDS HAVE STARTED to seem longer. Normally she idles them away easily enough, reading, sleeping, catching up with Aleksey and Lech. Suddenly Saturday and Sunday have doubled in length. Ada's days off feel like a colouring book, and all she has is a black crayon.

She thinks again of the knock on her door on Friday night. Of Frankie, of Birdie Greenwing in her back garden. For one horrible second, Ada thought she was too late. Birdie had looked half the size she was in Ada's consulting room.

'That's Jane with her, my mum. She is a nurse,' Frankie had told Ada.

Ada saw the ugly twist of Birdie's ankle, the pale colour of her cheeks. Blood, pink and watery, was running down her neck. A far cry from the dignified woman who had walked out of the hospital, head high, eyes dry, so recently. Ada had sunk to her knees in the muddy garden alongside Jane. 'Tachycardia, I suspect a broken ankle. Not sure about the cut to her temple, it doesn't look too deep, but she's confused,' Jane told Ada. 'I think that's the worst of it.' Ada could not tell the woman about Birdie's cancer. The knowledge sat like a rock in her chest.

Frankie was fretting on the side-lines. Ada saw her trying to put her coat around her mother's shoulders as she stooped over Birdie. 'I'm fine,' Jane said to her. 'Don't worry about me.' Frankie had offered to make them tea, but Ada refused. As soon as the ambulance came, she had left. Birdie's body print in the flat grass was too sad to bear, her death somehow horribly close. Fight, Ada thought, please fight it. But it was not Birdie she saw in her dreams that night, lying in her garden, bent at odd angles, it was her own mother, and Ada was not just down the road, she was miles away.

Saturday passes in the usual solitary way – shopping, walking, wandering around. People-watching alone, missing Ania's razor-sharp commentary. She wakes on Sunday early, spends the morning doing housework that does not really need doing. Thinks of Wilbur playing badminton as she folds her washing, snapping the sheets quickly, angrily. Ada has been in Brighton for eight years and never once has she been invited to join the badminton club, the quiz night, the book club, or any of the other hospital socials. She's only been out with her colleagues a handful of times – Christmas, leaving dos, that sort of thing. It's one thing to drink shots of vodka with Lech and Aleksey, but another to let herself get drunk with the people she works with. Drunk Ada can be a bit loud, or a bit tearful. Drunk Ada is unpredictable. Drunk Ada once tried to steal a tractor and drive to Warsaw. Her father found her, in the bottom field, going round in circles. But sober Ada comes across as rude. Brief. Curt. Like a full stop in the middle of a sentence. Tipsy Ada would be ideal, but not very professional.

'Such a pretty face. Try smiling a bit more often, dear,' Connie had once said. It was not the first time Ada had been told this. As if she should be happy, grateful that she's beautiful. Beauty is not a shield. Beautiful people still fail, still bleed, still get cancer. Beautiful people still let other people down.

Ada is best on her own. Which is just as well, because when you look like a Russian gymnast, but can eat whatever you want, other women don't like you. And then there's her personality. Ada is not like Connie, or Denise, or Wilbur, who find small-talk easy – for Ada there is nothing small or easy about it. Denise says the first thing that comes to mind. Ada likes to examine her answers before she shares them. She wasn't brought up to drop her opinions all over the place, like dog hair. Her mother and father are hardworking, reserved people who speak with their hands. Show love by making food, helping their neighbours mend leaking roofs, repairing fence panels. Ada is not afraid to get her hands dirty, but her heart is another matter. Her thoughts, her fears, are hers alone.

Ada looks around at her pristine, from-the-catalogue bungalow, her neatly ironed clothes, her well-stocked fridge. It's Sunday lunchtime, and she has run out of things to do. This would not have been possible on the farm. Weekends at home still started at dawn, her mother reaching for the flour and salt as her father headed out to the barns. Their little house always had extra people in it at the weekend. If you could open up the roof, like a doll's house, you'd find Pavel from three doors down, hiding in the kitchen with the morning paper, avoiding his wife. You'd spot the butcher in the living room. He'd pop in at lunchtime with a cut of meat, bones in a bag. He liked a quick nap on the hard sofa before heading back to his shop. You'd notice the widow from number seven, dressed in black, wedged by the stove, sewing fussy handkerchiefs that never sold at the market. Ada would be hidden in her little attic bedroom, hung-over from a night out with Ania, drinking gherkin juice, and trying to sleep through the noise below. People were drawn to Ada's parents. They were the lighthouse of their village, beaming out warmth to those who needed it. Ada, in comparison, is an Arctic wind. People put up hoods and umbrellas as she walks by.

Ada contemplates trying to cook something after she finishes sorting out her underwear drawer. A batch of her mother's *pierogi*, perhaps. Little Ada perched on the kitchen stool as Janina rolled out dumpling dough until it was almost transparent, so thin that Ada was sure it would break. She was always wrong. Ada's job was to dollop on a spoonful of mushrooms, or minced pork, or blueberries soaked in lemon and sugar. To lick the spoon.

'Now press the edges together, Ada,' her mother would say, 'like two lips kissing.' Ada's lips make a sad little *moue* in memory.

'Your problem, Ada,' Ania told her once, 'is that you want too much. You want to have a career here in England, but you also want to be a good little Polish farmer's daughter. You want to be two different people.'

They'd come to Brighton together, but Ania had moved back to Poland four years ago. 'That's me done,' she'd announced one Friday night, as though she'd just come off the dance floor, feet too sore from heels to carry on jiving. 'Time to settle down and have babies,' she added.

'You can't be serious?' Ada replied, remembering her mother's friend, Lidka, who'd stopped being a midwife to become a mother. All that studying, all that learning, given up. Why?

'I want a new adventure,' Ania told her. 'Maybe I'll go back to work in a few years, but right now I want to meet a man and breed. And I want to be near my parents as they get older.' Her voice was without accusation, but Ada prickled in defence.

'So I'm selfish, am I?' Ada challenged. 'I should go running back home too? Fire out babies like cherry pips?'

'No,' Ania said calmly. 'You are you, and I am me. I choose to go. You choose to stay.'

Ada has replayed that conversation many times since Ania left. She's still trying to work out which of them was in the wrong. Ada had felt oddly abandoned as she watched Ania's plane take off. The thought that this was how Janina must have felt when Ada left home put more distance between Ania and Ada than the miles on a map ever could.

They stay in touch, loosely. Usually more of a check-in than a proper catch-up and Ania is always the one to phone. Ada sometimes ignores her calls. She doesn't want a false conversation with someone who taught her how to use a tampon.

'How are your babies, Ania?'

'Wonderful, thank you, Ada, and how is your career?'

'Wonderful, so rewarding, thank you, Ania.'

Now Ada looks at her phone, thinks about calling her mother, but what would she say? I miss you, I'm lonely. Her mother would ask her to come home for a visit, then treat her like a stranger and she'd feel even lonelier.

Ada no longer fancies trying to cook. She picks up a magazine instead, sits down on her pristine sofa with the throw arranged just as it was in the photo. Normally she pores over her medical journals for hours. Loses herself inside the human body, the million miracles that take place each second. Today she scans the same line three times and still can't remember what it says. She thinks about going to see Lech and Aleksey. They say she's always welcome any time, but Lech likes to go for a nap in the afternoon while pretending he's doing paperwork, and Aleksey loves to watch English football while pretending he thinks it's stupid.

Ada thinks about Wilbur again, going for post-badminton drinks, packed into a booth in a big pub that overlooks the sea, toasting new friends with cold beers. A log fire, pie and mash. The thought fills her mind with bees. And the need to get out, to do *something*.

She decides she'll go for a run. That will blow the cobwebs away, as the English love to say. She pulls on leggings and laces up her old trainers before she can change her mind. It's not a good day for running. The wind is in her face, whipping away her breath. The sky is dark and ominous, the sea brown and green. Ada struggles along the seafront, trying not to notice all the couples holding hands, the mums pushing prams, the groups of friends laughing as the spray washes up over the railings and catches them. She's out of shape, which makes her cross, makes her push herself harder, forcing her legs to break into a stiff sprint for the last kilometre. She has to bend over when she finishes, hold her shaking knees and pant out hot breaths, like a dog. Her face is numb with cold and her nose is running. She feels awful. She feels wonderfully, pleasantly alive.

On Monday morning, she wakes up with blisters on her heels and aching buttocks. Less wonderful then, more like she's been kicked by a herd of cows. When Wilbur asks her what she did at the weekend that is making her limp, she tells him she's training for a marathon. She doesn't know why she says it. Must have been the pity on his face. Her father used to look at some of their newborn calves like that, or the silent piglet in the litter, too tired, too small to make a noise. Ada hadn't noticed anything was wrong until she caught her father's look.

'Can't you do something, Dad?' she'd asked.

'It's not up to me, it's up to nature,' her dad had said. Ada has never felt comforted by that answer.

'Which marathon?' Wilbur asks.

'The Brighton one,' Ada says, looking at her computer screen, which is not switched on.

'The one in April?' Wilbur persists.

'Yes,' Ada nods, 'that one.'

'I'm doing that too!' Wilbur says.

Gówno, Ada thinks.

'What time are you aiming for?' Wilbur asks. 'I'm hoping for a sub four hours.'

'Mm,' Ada says, an exquisite twinge of sciatic pain shooting from her left buttock down her leg. 'Same.' She wants to take some very strong painkillers, but can't do that in front of Wilbur, especially not now.

'Wow! Amazing. What are your splits like?' he asks.

'Very good,' Ada replies, wondering what he's on about. 'Can you go and get the first patient in, please?'

She quickly swallows two ibuprofen while he is out of the room, glugs down a bottle of water and makes a note to look into the marathon.

'I train at lunchtimes, if you'd like to join me,' Wilbur says that evening, as they are packing up. 'I didn't today because I had an appointment, but I'll be running tomorrow.'

'I run alone,' Ada says. It comes out sounding slightly sinister.

'Okay. Well, if you change your mind, let me know.' He raps on the door frame with his knuckles as he leaves.

Denise comes racing in the second he is out of sight. '*You* are doing the Brighton marathon?'

'How did you hear that?' Ada asks. 'Do you stand outside the door all day listening?'

'I didn't know you were a runner,' Denise persists. She looks at Ada suspiciously.

'That's because, unlike you, I don't share my private life with anyone and everyone.'

Unperturbed, Denise carries on. 'Are you going to run it with Wilbur? I think you should. I'll come and cheer you on. I can get a T-shirt printed!'

Ada's mind is blanking out how far a marathon actually is. She'd only gone for a run because she had nothing else to do. She wants to put her head down on the desk, have a good cry, eat an entire cheesecake, then sleep. She wants Wilbur to massage her sore thighs and run her a hot bath. What? Wait. No. Where did that thought come from? Pain has obviously made her lightheaded.

'Anyway, good for you, putting yourself out there,' Denise says. 'I can't think of anything worse. Twenty-six miles, round our hilly city? You must be mad!' She laughs.

So that's how long a marathon is – over forty kilometres! Ada's calf muscles cower in fear.

'A lot of people walk it,' Denise says kindly.

'I will not be walking the marathon,' Ada says, her competitive spirit waking up.

'You'll be joining our badminton team next.' Denise slips into her large fuchsia-pink coat.

'Since when have you played badminton?' Ada asks. As far as she knew, the closest thing Denise did to exercise was lifting her giant handbag.

'Since your man Wilbur joined,' Denise says, making a pretend serve in the air. 'He can send his shuttle—'

'Do not finish that sentence,' Ada says, and Denise giggles her way to the door.

Ada waits until everyone has gone, then hobbles to the lift. At the shop, she buys a very large bar of chocolate, a bag of ice and a copy of *Running Weekly*.

16

Birdie

'WHEN CAN I GO home, please, Doctor?'

The doctor frowns at Birdie, who is perched on the end of the bed, legs dangling over the edge like a child, a giant cast on one foot. 'Well, your blood pressure is still very low, and you've not had much practice on those crutches. You *were* outside for quite a while, Mrs Greenwing. There's no hurry. Take some time to warm up.' He pats her hand with his big warm paw.

Birdie had thought she'd be unplugged and sent on her way within hours of waking, but it seems not. Whatever happened to the shortage of hospital beds? In truth, Birdie wants nothing more than to lie down, be tucked under the blue waffle blankets for a nap and made another cup of tea when she wakes, but at some point she has to go home. Has to go back to looking after herself, being on her own. Someone else is waiting for the bed she is lying in. Birdie needs to vacate it before she gets possessive, like Audrey does about a certain lamppost along the road.

Whatever was in the IV drip was good. Birdie's pain has been reduced to a dull ache. She wishes she could take the

IV stand home, wheel it round her bungalow like a friend. She imagines Audrey barking at it, jealous and scared, and feels more tears looming. 'I'm ready to go now,' she says.

She can sense the doctor watching her. She wonders what he sees. A lonely old pensioner being awkward, or does he spot her shaking? Does he notice that she is scared?

'The thing is, Mrs Greenwing,' he says, rubbing his chin, 'I can't make you stay here, but I don't feel comfortable sending you home. Your file . . .'

Don't say it, Birdie thinks. Don't read out my file.

'I'd really like to keep you in for another night,' he says finally, 'and you're going to need some proper lessons on those crutches before we send you packing, so lie down. Doctor's orders!' Another pat of his paw. Birdie wants to grab it, close her eyes and pretend he's Arthur. Cling to his hand and refuse to let go.

Instead, she crawls back under the covers. Her eyes click closed, like those of a doll she used to own, the second she tips her head back. She's used to the noises on the ward now. Rather likes the sound of the doctor's footsteps, the trolley wheels, the curtains swishing open. The buzz of the main doors and the hiss of the blood-pressure cuff. Likes, too, the drip and the little pills she is given that take the sharp edges off the world.

'Mrs Greenwing?'

Birdie must have fallen asleep again. For a moment, she forgets where she is, then remembers the fall in the garden. Her broken ankle. Her cancer. A little three-car pile-up in her head.

Her neighbour, Jane, is standing by her bed. 'Sorry to wake you.'

Birdie struggles to sit up.

'No, don't get up,' Jane says. 'How are you feeling?'

Birdie is not used to being asked how she is all the time. After Arthur and Rose, people sent her cards, saying they were thinking of her, but no one asked what Birdie was thinking. How she was doing. They all just told her how awful it was, as if she didn't already know that.

'I'm fine,' she says now, feeling as if she's been dropped into a foreign land with only a handful of phrases to get by on: I'm fine; no, thank you; I'd like to go home. She's going to wear out the 'fine' if she keeps using it, but she doesn't have the words for what she really wants to say.

'You're on my ward today,' Jane says. 'I've come to help you have a wash. Get that mud off. But if you don't feel comfortable with me, I can ask one of the other nurses.'

Birdie blushes. She doesn't want Jane to wash her; nor does she want to be difficult. She wants Rose to be here to launder her lady bits, but that is impossible. 'Well, you've already seen my buttocks,' Birdie announces, louder than she planned to, and Jane smiles widely.

'And very nice they are too,' she says, as she helps Birdie out of bed and leads her, clonking, down the ward to a large shower room. 'I brought you a couple of bits from home,' she says. 'I hope you don't mind. Your clothes were wet from the rain.'

Birdie sees Jane has packed her a nightgown, cardigan, cold cream and flannel. They blur in her vision. Oh, where do the tears keep bloody coming from? Why is she crying about a flannel? It's not even a nice one.

'Right, then,' Jane says, nurse voice on. 'You're going to hold on to this bar for me, please.' She bends down and ties a big blue bag over Birdie's ankle to stop the cast getting wet, then carefully washes the mud and blood from Birdie's hair with gentle fingers. The cut stings when she gets soap in it. Birdie winces. 'Sorry, almost finished, Mrs Greenwing.'

Jane wraps a towel around Birdie when she is done, helps her into the nightgown, which smells of home.

'I think you can call me Birdie now,' Birdie says, when she's decent.

Jane smiles again and gives her arm a squeeze. 'I hoped you'd be on my ward,' she says, as she tucks Birdie back into bed.

Birdie cannot think why. There is something almost too nice about Jane and Birdie is feeling too exposed right now. Too weak. All her secrets are on her tongue. She pulls the cover up over her lips.

'I'll go and get your medicines,' Jane says. 'You rest.'

Around her, patients sit up in bed, knitting, doing puzzles, making phone calls, complaining about the food, asking after family at home. Birdie thinks of Audrey. Wonders what she's doing. In the afternoon, visitors flock in through the ward door like homing pigeons. They land on mothers and grandmothers with kisses and chocolates. Pecks on cheeks and hand squeezes. False cheery waves and cries of 'There she is!' as though the person could have been anywhere else. As though the patients could have unplugged all their wires and tubes and escaped out of the window trailing catheters behind them.

Birdie feels embarrassed in her little bed at the end, with

no flowers, no magazines, no one coming to see her. Princess Margaret, she thinks. Channel Princess Margaret. She forces herself to sit up, pat her freshly washed hair, adjust her clean nightgown as though it were a taffeta tea dress and pretends to enjoy her lunch, though she's never liked tinned peaches. She and Rose ate too many of them during their poor childhood.

'When Dad comes to get us, we'll have fresh mango and lychees,' Rose had said.

'I thought that was an illness?' Birdie replied.

Rose feels so close to Birdie right now, the veil between them gossamer thin, as though Birdie could pluck her sister out of the ether. Maybe it's just the morphine talking. Birdie decides not to think too much about it, just enjoy the trip.

Jane reappears in the afternoon and Birdie can tell from the look on her face that she's read Birdie's file. 'Birdie,' Jane says gently.

'I'm fine,' Birdie says, 'much better. When do you think the physio will come? I need to get some practice on those crutches before I go home.' She tries to keep her voice light, lemon-posset positive. She's not an injured deer lying in the road. She's fine. She's angora, silk, velvet. 'Please,' Birdie adds, when Jane says nothing. How she hates this. Being beholden to people. Being pitied. Having her history, her sad little life, documented in a folder for strangers to read. 'The only thing wrong with me is a sore ankle and the fact that I miss my dog,' she says.

It's a lie and they both know it. Birdie's file will say that she has breast cancer. That it has spread into her lymph glands and beyond, like spilled milk between the floorboards, seeping everywhere, souring everything. She is soaked in the stuff. Jane frowns like the doctor did. Birdie feels like a child, asking for permission to go to the park. To stay out past curfew. Her longing for Rose is like sunburn.

'I'll see what I can do,' Jane says finally.

The discharge coordinator arrives an hour later.

'Ah, Birdie Greenwing, is it? Not a wing you hurt, though, but a claw, eh? Now then, did you have a nice lunch?' The coordinator drags a chair along the floor. The noise makes Birdie's teeth clench. 'Can I call you Mrs Greenwing?'

'Yes?' Birdie says, confused.

'Excellent. Thank you. My name is Cathy. You can call me Cathy. We have to say that now. You can call me whatever you like, to be honest. I can assure you I'll have been called worse! Anyway, it says here that you live alone.' Cathy scans the file in front of her. 'Lucky you! I'd love a break from my kids and husband! Right, then, it looks like we'll need to get some support systems put in place before we send you packing.'

'There's no need,' Jane says. 'I'll be looking after her. I'm her neighbour.'

Birdie hadn't noticed Jane appear beside the bed. Birdie looks at her and frowns. Jane winks.

'Oh that's lovely,' Cathy says, as though Jane had just announced they were engaged. 'What a lucky duck you are to have a nurse living next door, eh?'

'Very lucky,' Birdie says, wondering why Jane has offered to help.

Cathy spends forty minutes asking Birdie increasingly

personal questions, some of which, Birdie is sure, are not on the form and are just her being nosy. Rose would ask Cathy to answer them too: 'And how about you, Cathy? Are you managing to pass gas, soft stools?'

Finally, after learning all there is to know about Birdie's bodily functions, Cathy leaves. Her glasses steam up when she stands. 'Menopause,' she explains, wiping them on her blouse. 'Awful. Must have been invented by a man. Ha ha ha! Nice to meet you, Mrs Greenwing!'

Birdie is taken off the drip that afternoon and told she can go home the following day as long as she's eating and drinking and feeling herself. An odd thing to say, she's always thought. She'd prefer to be feeling someone else, preferably Arthur.

In her hospital bed that night, Birdie wonders how soon she'll be back here. She doesn't like the thought of a thin blue curtain being the only thing between her and someone else's death. Between someone else's and her own. No visitors, no hand holding hers, just quiet whispers and the sound of the porter's trolley.

Sleep is hard to find, and by morning, Birdie is exhausted. When Jane comes to collect her, she is ready and waiting, her muddy possessions in a plastic bag by her side. 'Hello, Birdie,' Jane says, with a smile. 'Let's get you home.'

The crutches hurt Birdie's hands. The boot on her foot is like a block of cement. The corridor feels endless.

'Take your time,' Jane says. 'There's no rush.'

Birdie can feel the breeze coming in through the automatic doors and, for a second, she pauses. Can she really do this? Go home and cope on her own? She feels a sudden urge to get back into the hospital bed with her call bell and her extra blanket. To stay there till the end.

'Okay?' Jane asks.

'Fine,' Birdie says. 'I'm fine.'

17

Jane

JANE IS NOT SURE why she persuaded the doctor to let Birdie go home. Helping her neighbour will not offer Jane atonement for having left her mother alone in Bristol, for taking Frankie away from her. Life doesn't work that way. But there was something about Birdie's face. Something in the way she knew her chin was wobbling but tried to pretend it wasn't. In the way she used the word 'fine' when she was clearly anything but. Having read her file, Jane now knows that Birdie is seventy-five, the same age as Min. That she had a twin but now has no next of kin. Jane can relate to this. She knows a bit about feeling sisterless. Lost. Suki wouldn't have offered to help Birdie, but Suki has the enviable ability to put herself first without feeling selfish or guilty about it. As children, when Min told them to do something, Suki would ask, 'What, right now, this second? Is it life or death, Min, do or die?' then stall for time in the toilet, while Jane raced off to get whatever it was done as quickly as possible. Jane lived for praise, for pats on the head and 'Well done, you.'

'You are such a bottom,' Suki told her once.

Suki was always very good at saying no. Still is. At staring people down, at standing up for herself. Once upon a time, she used to stand up for Jane too.

'Can my sister come with?' Suki used to ask when she got invited out. 'Because I'm not coming without her.' And grateful Jane would traipse along in her sister's high-heeled shoes, smile widely and pretend she was having fun, that she was a part of it all. But Jane never knew the words to the songs, the people they were talking about. She hung about like peeling wallpaper as couples paired off, and never knew what to do with her hands.

'Loosen up a bit,' Suki used to say, handing her a bottle of beer, but Jane didn't know how. The real Jane was locked up inside her somewhere, desperate to get out, but she had no idea where the key was. The last time she'd seen her was in Brighton.

Her fingers reach for her phone, type out the text: *Hey, remember that news article about a woman who went missing in Iceland and accidentally joined her own search party?*

What is it that Jane wants back? A laughing-face emoji? For Suki to read through the ambiguity and see that Jane is lost? And then what? Suki is not coming to her rescue any more.

There was a time when Jane didn't need to think for herself. Didn't need to look up. She could just follow her sister's lead, live in her shadow. Bold, fearless Suki, who always knew, right from the day she was born, exactly who she was. The world was a spinning top and Suki held the crown that spun it like a globe. Suki made all their plans, arranged their social lives, knew which records to buy.

It was Suki who suggested they go travelling. Suki who made the plan, who told Min.

'Go on, go and see the bleddy world then,' Min had said crossly, after two days of saying no they were not allowed, of slamming pans and doors and hissing. She handed them both envelopes of cash that smelt of Stardrops. 'Take this, spend it, and then come back home, you hear me? With all your arms and legs intact.'

'We promise, Min,' they'd said, throwing themselves at their little Weeble of a mother, who wobbled but never fell down. 'We'll be back before you know it.'

They'd meant it too, back then.

Far away from Bristol and Min, Jane had felt herself pressing up against some internal prison door, so close to the person she wanted to become. She wore a pair of very short shorts, wriggled out of them under the light of the moon and went skinny-dipping. Ate fried insects on sticks. Jumped off a cliff, holding her nose with one hand and her boobs with the other, breaking the surface of the blue lake like she was smashing glass. Came up, gasping for air, feeling so alive it hurt. By day, she and Suki hiked through humid jungles, descended into dripping wet caves. Climbed snowy mountains and swam in pools under waterfalls. At night, Suki charmed the pair of them into nightclubs for free, persuaded people to buy them drinks with her smile alone. 'Come on,' she'd say to Jane. 'A load of lads are going to this amazing island to see the sunset and they said there's space for both of us.'

There is a photo in Jane's wallet: Suki's face in profile, kissing Jane's cheek. Jane is staring at the camera like it's challenged her to a fight, her chin tilted up towards the lens. How close she got to unlocking the cellar of herself. Would she have discovered who she was, an archaeologist unearthing exquisite treasure, had Frankie not happened? Jane hates this thought. It makes her feel sick with shame. Hates how much she misses her sister, when Suki clearly doesn't miss her at all.

Jane was supposed to start her first year of nursing when they finished travelling. Suki was due to begin an internship, something in marketing. Jane never really understood what. But then Frankie happened, and Suki never went home, breaking her promise to Min. Frankie took her place instead.

I'm not selfish, Jane tells herself, as she looks out of her own kitchen window into Birdie's garden. She'd set Birdie up on the sofa, remote control, drinks and painkillers at hand, Audrey on her knees. It didn't seem enough, but Birdie practically begged her to leave.

'You have been so kind. Please go home,' she'd insisted.

'I'll come back tomorrow, first thing,' Jane had promised. 'My number is right here on this pad. Call me if you need anything.'

'I am not a bad person. Min is not my responsibility,' Jane whispers to her reflection in the glass. If only saying things made them real. If only Jane had the courage to ring her sister and tell her as much, to tell Min the truth about everything.

Instead, she goes to check on Frankie, who is fast asleep, her eyes and mouth scrunched up tight, chest rising and falling under her neat little sheets. Jane watches her daughter's face shift in dreams, the way she twitches, serious even in slumber. Jane wonders what Frankie dreams about. Determines she will find a way to make them come true. Jane vows she will never be a burden. A barrier to her daughter's happiness. Finally, she crawls into her bed, where she curls into a ball and cries for everyone. For her mother, her father, for Suki and Birdie. For the girl she never got a chance to be.

18

Ada

For some reason, every morning at five thirty, Ada gets up in the cold, spongy darkness and goes running. She has no idea why she keeps doing it. Why she went and bought eye-wateringly expensive trainers and special socks as per the *Running Weekly* recommendation. She could picture her dad's face if she told him how much they cost. 'Do you know how many cows that would buy?' he'd ask. Cows would possibly have been a better investment. Running is a form of torture. Ada drips and sweats translucent pearls of herself along the seafront, something like emotion, running down her arms and legs, licked off by the wind. She secretes her suffering in tiny piles of silt that scatter themselves into the sea. And then she finishes and feels clean. Empty in a pleasant way, like a heavy bag that has just been unpacked.

Things are simple when Ada is running. Life is reduced to two thoughts: stop or carry on. That's it. Ada chooses to carry on. Her gait is still slightly off kilter and her shoulders are up by her ears. She has to concentrate on her breathing, like she's copying a complex dance sequence. Sometimes, she falters, but never stops. Other runners have begun to recognize her. They wave at her, raise an arm, give her a thumbs-up. Ada nods back, scared to break her stride. They think I'm one of them, she muses. It is like stepping into a patch of sunlight.

In other news, it turns out that you can't just show up on the day of a marathon and join in. Who knew? When Ada went to book her place, all the normal entries were taken. Ada has to raise three hundred pounds for a charity before she can run twenty-six miles for no reason other than to prove to Wilbur that she is not a chicken.

'I'll sponsor you,' Denise says. 'What charity are you running for?'

'Well, a cancer one, obviously.'

'Oh. I'd run for those tiny rescued donkeys. They always look so sad. What charity are you running for, Wilbur?' Denise asks, using the moment to put a hand lovingly on his arm.

'Veterans,' Wilbur says.

'I bet you've raised loads of money already,' Denise says, gazing at him with big eyes.

He smiles, looking slightly awkward, then turns to Ada. 'How's your fundraising going?'

'Excellently,' Ada says. She has three signatures and twenty-five pounds, which she donated herself.

'A marathon?' Lech said when she told him. 'What on earth are you doing that for?'

'You will need a massage before and after,' Aleksey said. 'Please allow me to offer my services.'

'I'd prefer your cash,' Ada said.

'Look at these hands,' Aleksey said. 'They were made for giving pleasure.'

'You have your grandmother's hands,' Lech interrupted. 'Now go and make me a drink with them, and fetch the ingredients for *babka* cake.'

'You will win, Ada,' Lech announced, as he mixed dough on the counter.

'Win it? I'll do well to finish,' Ada replied.

'No, don't touch the dough!' Lech said. 'Just stand near it and think happy thoughts.'

Lech stuffed the dough with cinnamon filling, made poppy-seed streusel, thick apple cake with yogurt. Ada was allowed to dollop on the icing and lick the spoon. Aleksey watched, transfixed.

The smell of nutmeg and warm honey wafted out into Kemptown from the open windows, like Christmas Eve on a rainy afternoon. Within minutes of the cakes coming out of the oven, people start shuffling in, sniffing the air.

'I didn't know you sold cakes,' someone said, admiring the display on the counter. 'Can I have a slice of the apple cake?'

'I don't have any apple cake,' Lech said, covering it with a cloth.

'But I just saw it?'

'Lech,' Ada says, 'sell the people the cake.'

She'd planned to take them into the WRVS café, ask Connie if she wouldn't mind shifting a few, but within an hour, they were all gone, and Ada was well on her way to reaching her charity target.

'How can I thank you?' Ada said, as they washed up.

'I have dreamed of you asking me this,' Aleksey said. 'Let me get my notebook.'

'You don't need to thank me,' Lech said. 'This is what we do.'

Ada wants to tell her parents she's running a marathon, but they won't understand. To them, it would seem a waste of time. It would be showing off. 'But why?' her dad would say. 'What is the point? What happens at the end?' Ada was brought up to be proud, but also humble. She was not raised to go around asking people for money. Charity began at home.

'Why don't you auction yourself? The person who bids the most gets to take you on a date?' Denise suggests.

'I think that's called prostitution, Denise,' Ada says, her ears going red.

'Just trying to help.'

'You could come along to badminton,' Wilbur says, 'and ask them to sponsor you.'

'I don't need sponsors,' Ada says. 'And your phone is ringing.'

Connie offers a pound. 'I'd love to give you more, but I've sponsored eight people already this morning alone.'

'Don't worry about it,' Ada replies, feeling guilty, Connie's warm coin in her palm. 'This is very generous. Thank you.'

Connie beams. 'Don't forget these,' she says, nodding to two coffees that Ada did not ask for. 'That'll be two pounds, please.'

Ada spends the walk back to her office trying to decide

which mug to give to Wilbur: 'Blow me, I'm hot' or 'Kayaking gets me wet.'

'I feel trapped between a rock and a hard place here,' he says, looking from one mug to the other.

'Just close your eyes and pick one.' Wilbur's smile is slow and beautiful. Just when you think he's finished, up go the edges of his lips a little more. Ada does *not* want to climb inside that smile and swing in it like a hammock. She does *not* want to make him do it again.

'Why don't you pick for me?' Wilbur says. Is he flirting? The idea that she might be making a fool of herself comes out of nowhere, smacks her over the back of the head. She hastily passes him a mug without looking at it, burning her hand in the process, then dashes behind the safety of her desk.

'Busy day today,' she says, trying to sound professional. If Wilbur notices the change in her attitude, he doesn't mention it. So bloody adaptable, like a multi-tool pocket knife. Ada scrolls through the morning appointments, opens folders and makes notes. Tries her hardest not to notice how nice her office smells since Wilbur came to work with her. Like moss and wood and tobacco without the smoke.

'I'll go and get the first patient,' he says.

'Thank you.' Ada looks up to see that she has given him the 'Kayaking gets me wet' mug. 'Amazing work, Ada,' she tells herself. Denise is going to love this.

Wilbur probably doesn't get wet when he goes kayaking anyway, because he seems to be good at everything. A real Boy Scout. When a patient enters the room, Wilbur sits without fidgeting, listens without intruding, all the while chugging out heat like a radiator. Ada swears he makes the harsh fluorescent lights glow yellow instead of white. He doesn't comment on Ada's awful handwriting or criticize her working methods. When they go to meetings together, he shakes hands firmly then takes notes. He is always kind to Denise. Lets her sound off about her awful husband. Tells her how nice her hair looks, and makes Connie do her cartoon laugh every time he sees her.

He is too good to be true, Ada thinks. It's annoying. He must be hiding something. Everyone is always hiding something. His calmness makes her irritable. A little storm brews inside her as the days go by. Heavy black clouds gather low in her belly. Spikes of electricity flash and spark. Ada makes a playlist of angry music to run to. Aggressive guitars, a bassline that she feels in her toes. Outraged youths and long-dead rock stars shout in her ears about life not being fair. She takes their energy and expends her own.

Ada still pauses at Birdie's gate each evening, checks to see if the lights are on. Once, Birdie was in the window and she waved at Ada through a gap in the curtains as though she was just about to walk out on stage. Ada considered going to knock on the door, but what was there to say? Birdie Greenwing had been discharged. Jane is her neighbour and her nurse. Ada had done her bit. Now she is superfluous. She could not cure her cancer. All she could do was knock on the door and ask Birdie how she was getting on, and what help was that to anyone?

Feeling useless makes Ada faster, powers her up hills and into the next mile. She keeps her head down as she goes, looks at her feet, and tries not to think at all. Falls into bed at nine p.m., passes out in a heap of limbs, face down on the pillow. Each sleep is more like a small death.

19

Birdie

Birdie is having a pig of a day trying to get anything done with her cumbersome boot and the crutches that hurt her hands and make her shoulders ache. She swears her furniture had a meeting while she was asleep and decided it would all move around a little bit, to get in her way. She has tripped, slipped and staggered, and that was just getting dressed. At one point, to her horror, she even kicked Audrey. 'I'm so sorry. It was an accident,' she said, but Audrey backed away, trembling, yapping at the boot like it was the cat from over the road.

Birdie can't get comfortable. She can't sleep. Her cast makes her back ache, but when Jane popped by to see how she was getting on, Birdie said she was fine, good. Feeling better. Tip-top! She couldn't bring herself to ask Jane to wash her hair again, to send her to the shop with a list. She is just thinking of caving in and calling Fleur Williams from Macmillan, cap in hand, when Frankie knocks on the door.

'Hello, Mrs Greenwing. I've come to see Audrey, if that's okay?' Frankie says. At the sound of her voice, Audrey hurls herself through the door. She is so excited a little trail of wee comes out.

Birdie tries to bend down to wipe it with her hankie but catches her crutch on the hall table.

'I'll clean it,' Frankie says, walking past Birdie to get a cloth, too fast for Birdie to protest.

When she goes to put the cleaning spray back in the hall cupboard, Birdie hears the clatter of cups being washed. It should feel like an invasion, but the sound of the water, the tinkle of the china, is oddly pleasant. It could be Arthur in there, his shirt sleeves rolled up, singing about being a modern man. 'You don't need to do that,' Birdie calls.

'It's okay,' Frankie calls back, 'and you don't have anyone else to help you.'

She doesn't say it cruelly, but Birdie's nose starts tingling nonetheless.

'I noticed your fridge is empty,' Frankie says, walking into the living room. 'I can go to the shop for you if you give me some money. I am allowed,' she adds, almost defiantly, hands on her hips, a ray of morning sun throwing a slice of light across her earnest face. 'I don't mind. I have nothing better to do. I don't have any friends either. My grandmother, Min, says they're overrated.'

When Birdie looks into Frankie's green eyes, she finds no sadness in them. She is very Princess Margaret indeed, Birdie thinks. Rose would adore her.

Birdie picks up the pad and pen Jane left out for her. The list ends up being quite long. Birdie is out of more or less everything. Painkillers, soap, cheese for Audrey.

'What's this?' Frankie says, when Birdie hands it over.

'Sorry,' Birdie says, reaching to take it back, 'it's shorthand.' Birdie is so used to writing lists only she needs to read.

'Is it some sort of code?' Frankie looks delighted.

'It's a phonetic system. The symbols represent sounds rather than letters.'

'Wow.' Frankie looks at Birdie as if she's just told her she can fly. 'Will you teach me how to write it, please?'

'Well, yes, I suppose I can. If you'd like,' Birdie finds herself saying.

'Deadly!' Frankie says.

Birdie might well be dead before she finishes teaching Frankie Pitman shorthand. It takes a while to grasp, and Birdie doesn't have long. She pushes the thought away. Hides it in a box in her mind.

'Are you sure you're allowed to go to the shop on your own?' Birdie asks.

'Yes. I'm twelve and very responsible,' Frankie says. Even so, Birdie finds herself watching out of the window as Frankie struts up the road, shopping list in hand.

Birdie and Arthur had decided against children. Well, sort of. They hadn't ever actually discussed it. Birdie had just assumed that it would happen after they got married, as did Arthur. The getting-married bit happened soon after they began courting. In fact, Arthur had proposed in the back of his car one evening when things were getting particularly steamy.

'We'll have to wed!' he'd said, pulling away from Birdie's enthusiastic kiss with a gasp. His normally slicked-back hair had fallen messily over his forehead. Birdie's skirt was up round her thighs. She had one foot on the gearstick and the other pressed up against the passenger window.

'Shush, don't stop. We'll be fine,' she'd cajoled, arching her spine. She didn't want to think about weddings, about the fact that Rose had no one to say 'I do' to. She just wanted Arthur to keep doing what he was doing. Something wonderful happened to Birdie when Arthur touched her. The whole world fell away. She forgot about her sister, her mother. Her head was pleasantly empty of all thought, while her heartbeat speeded up until she could feel it in the tip of every finger and toe. She felt outrageously, indecently alive with Arthur. A bee leaking honey, thrumming with life. It was inebriating, and addictive.

'Do that thing again!' she'd demanded.

'Birdie! You'll end up in the family way if we carry on!' Arthur had panted.

When Birdie told Rose about the engagement, she'd watched a shifting cloud of emotions pass over her twin's face – joy, yes, but there was a dropped stitch in her sister's smile. A small hole of sadness, and Birdie's happiness lost some of its sheen.

While the wedding was short and sedate, the consummation was anything but. It was as though they'd invented the sport. Birdie was sure she'd fall pregnant immediately, but nothing happened. Month after month, Birdie prayed for a miracle. Marked hopeful days on a secret chart, then cursed her foolishness when she felt that deep internal twinge. Birdie could not find words to explain what it felt like in the second that she realized she was not pregnant, yet again. That it had not worked. She held her breath for twenty-eight days at a time. Her underwear became her enemy, that single drop of blood like a gunshot, shattering her into a million little pieces. How lonely Birdie felt. For the first time she was going through something she couldn't share with Rose. It would be too selfish. So she hid her sadness inside a smile, and avoided the baby-equipment aisles in shops.

'Cheer up, duck,' Arthur would say, bringing her a hot-water bottle.

'Do you think we should go to the doctor?' Birdie had asked, when a year had passed, and she was no more pregnant than she'd been in the back of his Morris Minor.

'I don't think so. Best to let nature take its course,' Arthur had said, sounding slightly guarded.

Maybe he was the one who couldn't have children. The truth would humiliate him. Birdie couldn't bear the thought of Arthur hating his own body. She knew all too well what that felt like. So she took the blame and the shame instead. When people at work asked why she wasn't pregnant yet, she joked that she must be doing it wrong. When her and Arthur's mothers called to 'see how it was all going' she told them she was trying her best.

One day, Rose had come over and found Birdie crying, saw the sheets balled up by the washing-machine.

'I'm so sorry, Bird,' Rose said.

'No, I am. I don't deserve a baby. It's selfish to want so much,' Birdie had sobbed into Rose's hair.

'No, it isn't. It's natural. To want is to be alive,' Rose had said, stroking her hair. She'd wiped away Birdie's tears, led her to the sitting room, sat her down and hobbled off to make tea. Later, Birdie found a note in her sister's faint handwriting, hidden under a sofa cushion. Birdie knew how difficult Rose found writing. How the pen shook in her swollen fingers.

Bluebird,

I know it's not easy, adjusting your dreams. I am so sorry you might not become a mother. That you might not pace the floor at night with a fretful baby in your arms. We do not always get what we deserve. But. Remember there is always a but in life, sister of mine.

But: you can go out in the rain until your skin gets goosebumps. You can drink hot toddies and warm up by the fire, naked on a fur rug. You can get up late like Princess Margaret, eat toast in bed, listen to the radio and scatter the newspapers all over the floor. But: you can chain-smoke, take a two-hour bath, go out for a twelve-thirty vodka pick-me-up. Eat a four-course meal with five different types of cheese. You can eat trifle for breakfast and wave at strangers from steamed-up bus windows while wearing an outlandish hat. You can wear jelly shoes with socks just to make yourself laugh.

Remember when Princess Margaret told her guests that dinner was at eight thirty, which was actually the time her hairdresser was due to arrive? And everyone had to wait for hours, hungry and bored, while he concocted her coiffure? Princess Margaret would not wait for a baby to enjoy her life and live it to the full. Never forget her motto: 'Disobedience is my joy.'

Love, Posy

PS You may not have a baby, but you'll always have me. I will never leave you.

Frankie rings the doorbell, summoning Birdie back from Memory Lane.

'There's far more here than I wrote on the list,' Birdie says, as Frankie starts unpacking bags on the kitchen table.

'You didn't ask for a single vegetable other than potatoes, which can actually be poisonous. When exposed to light, they produce a toxin called solanine. Good protection from insects and bacteria, but toxic to humans.'

'Oh . . .' Birdie says.

Frankie lays bananas, frozen peas and a box of clementines on the table. She also pulls out some cartons of mousse. 'Min likes these,' she says, 'and you're about the same age. Maybe you'd get along. Min doesn't have any friends either, except for me. Anyway, she has one after dinner when she's feeling *extravagant*.'

Birdie doesn't know what to say. She's not used to children. Do they all talk like this, so, well . . . frankly? Would Birdie's daughter have had friends? Would she have been a twin? Stop it, Birdie, she thinks. Why hurt yourself like this? But Frankie's little hand, still slightly chubby in the last of childhood, passes her a sandwich and Birdie wants to fold it in her own. Wants to feel the soft skin, wrinkle and arthritis free. Miles of life ahead of her, of things still to come.

'Sit down. You need to elevate your foot for half an hour. The discharge letter says so,' Frankie orders.

Birdie sits quietly in her chair, foot propped up on a stool, watching as Frankie fills Audrey's bowl and puts the shopping away. Places Birdie's painkillers on the table with a big glass of water. 'Need anything else before I go?' she asks.

'No, you've done enough. So much. Thank you. I . . .' Birdie trails off, unsure what else she can say.

''S all right,' Frankie says awkwardly. 'I'll come back tomorrow then, shall I?' she asks, bending down to stroke Audrey. Frankie has a double crown, Birdie notices, just like her and Rose. It used to drive Rose mad. She was forever trying to get her hair to lie flat on her head. Birdie has to resist the urge to lick her hand and press it against Frankie's scalp, like she used to do for her sister. Like she would have done for her daughter.

It is not until Frankie has gone that Birdie wonders if she was supposed to pay her. She looks at the space where Frankie stood just moments ago, missing her already.

20

Jane

Jane can tell something is different the second she opens the doors to the ward. The light inside feels warmer, and the windows are open, dispersing the smell of antiseptic and porridge and lavender hand cream. Music is playing. Jane looks round in confusion. Has she fallen into an alternative reality? Is this one of her fever dreams?

'Sadie's off,' Helen says, in explanation, walking towards her. 'Dentist.'

'Must be all those skulls she eats for breakfast,' Jane says, and Helen laughs.

'So I'm going to sit on my bottom all day and do nothing,' Helen says. 'There's an empty bed at the end of the ward, might get a nap in. Do you know what the lunch menu options are?'

Jane looks up sharply.

'Ha, your face!'

'Funny,' Jane says, shoulders dropping in relief.

'Seriously, though, Kim and Stella will try it on because Sadie's off, so don't pick up their slack.'

Jane nods with gusto but her stomach tightens. When

Jane tries to say, 'No,' the word 'okay' comes out instead. Which is why, an hour later, having checked on all her patients, Helen finds her changing sheets alone. 'What happened to you not picking up the slack?'

I'm pathetic, Jane wants to say. I have the resolve of a packet of bath salts. I can't help it. Saying no makes me feel sick, like I'm breaking the law.

'I don't mind,' she says instead, sliding a case on to a pillow and plumping it up.

Helen sighs and flicks a fresh white sheet over the plastic mattress Jane has just sprayed down. 'Well, you *should* mind,' Helen says, 'always pleasing everyone else all the time. Do you ever please yourself?'

Jane blushes. 'Um, I, well . . .'

Helen laughs, a lovely sound, bright and uncensored. She puts a hand on Jane's arm. 'All I'm saying is, I used to try to make other people happy at my own expense. It took a long time, but I managed to stop.'

'By finally giving in and killing them all?'

Helen smiles, pauses, and then says, 'Permission to be awkwardly vulnerable and overshare?'

'Permission granted,' Jane says, smiling back.

'Thank you. Let's talk turkey as the Yanks like to call it,' Helen says. 'Imagine your standard poor-me childhood story. Distracted parents, all-night drinking. Unstable environment. No school trips. Mouldy bread for the packed lunch. Yada-yada. Point is, I needed to make my parents happy in order to feel safe. I had to be an adult instead of a child, so my parents could be children instead of adults.'

Jane thinks of Min, of how Jane will always be a child in

her eyes, how Jane was never allowed to pour away the chip oil in case she burned herself. Jane was raised to believe that shielding from pain was a parent's job and Helen's childhood makes her feel oddly tearful. Helen smiles widely as she talks, though, her mouth a slice of watermelon. 'It took me a lot of time and money spent on counselling to understand that. Even more to realize I don't need to do it any more. I don't need to please my parents or anyone else. And you don't either. It's okay to not always do what other people expect of you.'

Jane nods but the lump in her throat is still there. For Helen's honesty. For the fact that Jane is still going to call Min as soon as this conversation is over. Will text Suki and hope for a reply. Will go and see Birdie, check her vitals. Will probably even go to the latest bloody Neighbourhood Watch meeting that she got a letter *and* a phone call about. 'I'll write it on a mug,' Jane says weakly.

'Which you'll probably hand to someone else. Was it like this at your last job, too, you doing everything?'

'I worked in A and E before here,' Jane says, 'so it was different. Too busy for anyone to slack off.'

'I used to work in A and E too. Still miss it sometimes,' Helen says.

'Me too,' Jane says. The excitement of not knowing what was going to happen next. One minute she'd be tending a stab wound, the next she'd be telling someone, after a thorough investigation, that sadly the mango was properly stuck up their bottom and would need to be surgically removed. Min would wait up for Jane to get home, then make her a full English breakfast, and demand to know everything about her night as she served her tea and a second round of toast. Tut her way around the kitchen, eyes on stalks. A mango! 'Yes, best part was, he came in with his mother who kept saying, "I was going to use that mango for a trifle. Why couldn't you have used a pear?"'

'So how come you moved to this sort of work?' Helen asks, folding over the top of the white sheet.

'That was back in Bristol, so my mum was able to look after my daughter, Frankie,' Jane explains. 'Since we moved here, I have to rely on school clubs for childcare, so I can't do long shifts or evening work.'

They move on to the next bed and start stripping the sheets, balling them up and tossing them into a bag, like a four-armed machine.

'How about you?' Jane asks. 'What made you stop?'

'I did ten years in A and E. Loved it too, at first, but Brighton Accident and Emergency is full on. It can get pretty abusive at times, and it was only going to get worse with all the cuts and lack of funding. I was never paid enough to compensate for the insults and the threats,' Helen says, pushing the trolley to the next bed.

'True.' It had been the same in Bristol. Jane understood that people were in pain and worried, but she saw a distinct change in the way patients spoke to her as the effects of the budget trickled down from a news update on the TV, to the service they received in hospital, when they discovered the cuts actually affected them.

'Only so many times I could be called a fat bitch before the novelty wore off!' Helen says loudly, not seeming to care if people hear her.

'You are not,' Jane says immediately.

'Oh, I know I'm not,' Helen says.

'If it makes you feel better, I got called a ginger . . .' Jane trails off.

'Ginger what?' Helen whispers, leaning in, and for a second, Jane feels the way she used to with Suki, like they were inside a bubble that no one else could penetrate.

'I'm sure it must be written on one of Connie's mugs,' she says primly, and Helen gives that big laugh again.

'Anyway,' Jane says, 'it's nice to be able to see patients for more than half an hour. To get to know them.'

'True, less likely to get called a fucking imbecile by this lot as well.' Helen nods towards the end of the bay where their patients lie prone, snoring loudly on their backs, mouths slack. Noses whistling.

'Or be asked if there is a male doctor available,' Helen adds.

They high-five at that, and Jane can feel Helen's hand print against hers for the rest of the day.

When the porters arrive at 1 p.m. to take the patients down to afternoon surgery, Helen tells Jane to take her break.

'I'm okay, honestly,' Jane says.

'It's not optional. Get out of here for half an hour.'

Jane feels a little light come on inside her as she leaves the ward, a tiny orange flame, brightening her corners. She normally works straight through her shift, filling in paperwork as she eats her bland packed lunch. Jane decides to treat herself to one of Connie's corking doorsteps.

'Hello, Connie.'

'Hello, Jane, love.' Connie's head pops up from under the counter.

'Coronation chicken sandwich, please.'

'Right you are. Sit down, I'll bring it over.'

Hopefully before the next coronation, Jane thinks.

Choosing a seat in the corner, Jane checks her phone. Frankie has texted, reminding her that she is walking Audrey again later. Jane was the one who promised to help Birdie, but Frankie seems to have taken it on. 'I like the dog and I don't have anything else to do.' She shrugged. 'It's a bit like being with Min.'

Frankie's words had made Jane feel like the worst mother and daughter in the world, but Frankie wasn't trying to make her feel guilty. If Frankie said she didn't mind, she didn't. She'd soon let you know if she did mind something. Frankie has the wonderful capacity to accept people for who they are, unlike Jane who can't stop wishing they'll change. Herself included. Can't stop sending Suki messages, photos of Frankie. Rants about Min. It's a unique form of self-harm.

'Hello, Connie.'

'Hello, Ada, the usual?'

'Please.'

Jane looks up to see the doctor who helped them when Birdie fell. She's wearing a white coat, black high heels, and sounds like a villain from a Marvel film. In the daylight, Jane can see she is beautiful, with high cheekbones and a straight nose. That she oozes importance. Jane remembers the way Ada left as soon as Birdie was put into the ambulance. Didn't hang around like a bad smell, as Jane did. Ada would never chase after her older sister, but then, Ada's older sister would never not want to spend time with Jane.

'How's the sponsorship for the marathon going?' Connie asks.

Of course, this doctor also runs marathons, Jane thinks.

'Excellently,' the woman says, in her clipped accent.

'Will I make a coffee for Wilbur?' Connie asks.

'No. He can get his own,' Ada says.

Imagine being that cool, that in control of life, Jane thinks. Ada wouldn't spend her evenings on the phone to her mother or watching programmes about taxidermy. She probably only goes home to get changed before another fabulous night out. Jane watches her until she's out of sight, heels clicking along the corridor, and sniffs the air for a trace of her perfume. Perhaps Jane can buy Ada's confidence in a little bottle, spray it on her wrists.

She spends the afternoon removing IV lines, changing pads and leading ladies to the shower where she soaps them gently, positions them discreetly and dries them with care. Jane has seen a million naked bodies. Imelda Northey, in bed three, is no different. She has a papery pouch on her lower belly from carrying her babies. Tiger-striped stretch marks on her hips, like we have to fight our way into becoming a woman, Jane always thinks when she sees them, like it's a battle. Imelda has dimpled buttocks and thin turkey skin under her biceps. None of these things give Jane pause. It's her feet. As she's putting powder between Imelda's toes, she realizes they are exact replicas of her mother's. That bunion.

The way the second toe has bent, like a tree in the wind, and is leaning against the one next to it for support. Jane's fingers pause in their application. She has powder on her hands. The smell also reminds her of Frankie. Of the first time Min met her. The way her mother reached out automatically as if she was not in control of her limbs. The way Frankie's head fitted into Min's cupped hand as though she'd grown to exactly that size for that very reason.

'Are you okay, dear?' Imelda asks, peering down. 'I think they're dry enough now.'

'Sorry,' Jane says, standing up. She doesn't look at Imelda's toes again as she slides pop socks over them. Doesn't want to think about Min needing help to take a shower one day. Doesn't want to think about her daughter helping Birdie when it should be Jane doing it. When it should be Min next door.

At three p.m. Helen comes to find her.

'We're quiet today. I can manage. Go and get your daughter from school, save her from Late Club.'

'Really?'

'Yes, really. Go!'

Jane hasn't done a normal school pick-up in a long time. Min always used to do them, when they were living in Bristol. Jane wants to be an independent working mum, set an example to her daughter, but she also wants to volunteer to be the classroom assistant. To work in the school library, do lunchtime shifts in the cafeteria. Serve Frankie the best slice of cake and steal cherries from the children who call her daughter odd. The ones who say that Frankie Brown should get a bus out of town. That she is a weirdo who never makes eye contact and is scared of the sound of a pencil case unzipping.

But even if she did every drop-off and pick-up, Jane would never be in the coffee-gang. The mothers who cluster round a table to talk about the people who couldn't make it, or who didn't get the invite. Jane would be welcomed with that well-practised 'You're not welcome' smile. What does Jane have to offer them, after all? She has nothing to bring to the party. She can't go on nights out; she has no money or good connections. Maybe she could curry favour with free condoms and morning-after pills? Offer smear tests at the next school fête? Maybe she might find someone like her, someone else slightly out of time, singing in the wrong key. But if her own sister can't find time for her, why would anyone else?

'Get out of here!' Helen repeats loudly.

'Right, yes! Thank you. Thank you. I owe you one,' Jane says, gushing gratitude like a leaking tap as she pulls on her coat and grabs her rucksack.

'I'll hold you to that,' Helen calls after her.

'Mum? Is everything okay?' Frankie asks, when she sees Jane waiting in the playground. She was on her way to the classroom in the far corner. Before she noticed her mother, the look on her face was that of a prisoner being led to their cell.

'Everything's fine. I just managed to get off early, thought I'd surprise you.'

Frankie's smile is a rare but beautiful thing. 'I don't have to go to club?'

'Nope.'

'Deadly. You are the best mum ever!' Frankie says loudly.

Heads turn to look at them. Tired mums, made-up mums, mums in leggings, mums in skirts and boots and beanie hats. Mums standing alone, mums standing in the middle of a circle. If children are coats, then mothers are the mittens on string through the armholes. For a second, Jane feels like she is a part of that bunting. That she belongs.

21

Ada

'DO YOU THINK WILBUR will ask you out?' Denise asks, hopping on to Ada's desk. 'He's single. I asked him. And you're single . . .'

'How do you know?' Ada replies. 'And get off my desk.'

'You work every hour under the sun.' Denise ticks the reasons off on a list. 'You never say yes to anything. You never check your phone or put lipstick on before you leave the office.'

'Okay, okay, I get it,' Ada says, shoving Denise away just as Wilbur appears in the corridor. 'Go and do some work.'

'How long has it been since you last had sex?' Denise hisses.

'Goodbye, Denise,' Ada says.

Denise would laugh at Ada if she knew the truth. That Ada was a virgin when she booked her flight to Brighton. Ada's tiny town was full of relatives or the kind of people who would kiss and tell her relatives. People who would assume you were going to marry them if you had sex with them. Cook their dinner and wash their boots. Become a Lidka.

Ania had lost her virginity when she was sixteen to a

farmhand who was staying with her parents for the summer. She'd said it was 'painful but quick, like getting the flu jab'. Ada didn't feel she was missing out on much, so concentrated on her education instead. Before she knew it, she was in her twenties, about to leave for the UK, and still hadn't gone to bed with anyone. Her maidenhead, as Ania called it, felt like an unwanted party guest, not realizing no one wanted it there.

'I can't leave Poland still a virgin,' Ada declared. It made her feel like a child, innocent, ignorant.

'Let's get you laid, girl,' Ania said.

So they went out in Bydgoszcz on a mission. The town, famous for rowing, was full of athletic types. Clusters of boys for girls to take their pick. Ada downed three shots of cherry vodka for courage. The last one was paid for by a good-looking boy with dark hair and a square jaw, who told Ada she was funny, although she hadn't made any jokes, and sexy, although she hadn't even stood up or unzipped her leather jacket.

His place wasn't far, but her silence made him talk too much, mostly about rowing. Ada nodded politely, nerves coiled in her stomach. She hoped his sex talk was more interesting than his rowing talk. He made his move the second they got inside. Too much tongue and enthusiasm, her body backed against the door, the handle poking into her spine.

'Are you sure?' he'd said, more out of duty than interest.

'*Tak*,' she said. 'Yes.'

The sex was painful, quick and messy. Ania had missed that bit out. Ada felt like a snail had crawled over her skin.

'Is it good?' he asked, moaning and panting.

Is this it? Ada thought. 'So good,' she said. 'Truly.'

With a final grunt, he slumped against her for a moment, then eased out and went to the bathroom. Ada lay in his small bed and imagined her hymen being flushed away with the condom, another piece of her history that she was leaving behind.

When he came back, he was carrying two cans of Coke. He reached for his cigarettes, lighting two and passing her one. The Coke fizzed up over Ada's hand and on to the sheets when she opened it. They both said sorry at the same time, then laughed awkwardly. Ada lay next to him smoking, contemplating the ceiling for a while as his sweat cooled on her body, and realized she felt the same as she had before. She'd thought having sex would change her, but all it had done was tick a box.

Ada has been asked out a few times since she moved to Brighton, but she always says no. There was nothing about her experience with the rower (Ada is ashamed that she can't remember his name) that she is in a hurry to repeat. Ada only likes doing things she is good at, and sex doesn't feel like one of those things.

Denise would fall off her high heels if she knew Ada had done it only once. Wilbur, she imagines, has done it many, many times. He's probably very good at it. His sex talk is probably just the right—

'I'd give up this white chocolate chip brownie to know what you're thinking right now,' Wilbur says.

'Running,' Ada snaps. 'I'm thinking about running.'

Ada might not be good at sex, but she's getting better at sprints. She even overtook someone the other day. The wind was at her back, and they were old, but still. Her legs no longer hurt all the time, and she's sleeping better than she has in years. She just needs to raise the charity money and then she's all set. But she can't get her head around asking. She wasn't raised that way. Ada's parents were poor people in a poor village. No one talked about money. People gave what they could, be it bread, meat or milk. A hand to push a tractor stuck in mud. Ada wishes she could raise the entrance money by manual work. By mending fences and cutting logs. Digging mud out of the horses' hoofs.

If only her parents could see that under her white coat, Ada is the same girl who rode their farm horses bareback, who slept with the sheep during lambing season. That just because she left home does not mean she has left them. If only Ada could tell her father how much she misses the sound of his voice. As a child, she'd step inside the prints his big boots left when she followed him through the muddy fields. If she could find the words, she would tell her mother how she misses the smell of her long hair. She always kept it off her face, one thick long plait that hung down her back. Her father would tug it occasionally and her mother would swipe him away with a tea-towel. Ada saw her mother's hair loose only if Ada woke in the night and called her. Her mother would come, kinky waves falling to the bottom of her spine. She seemed like someone else in her white nightdress and bare feet. Ethereal. Angelic. Fragile. A different woman entirely.

Ada thinks again of Birdie Greenwing at her appointment, smartly composed with her neat coat, shiny shoes and curled hair. Then Birdie in her back garden, rain on her face, shrivelled little rump exposed. How shameful it must have felt, how mortifying. To a doctor, bodies are nothing to be embarrassed about. They are regarded as something separate to the self, abstract. They are cars, photocopiers, machines that need dismantling. Doctors are technicians, mechanics. Puzzle-solvers. As a daughter, though, seeing a mother's body prone and powerless? It is incomprehensible. It's terrifying and no amount of money can change that.

'Here,' Wilbur says, 'you can have the last bite,' and hands over the remains of his brownie. His teeth marks are the shape of his smile.

22

Birdie

HER SCALP ITCHES TERRIBLY. Birdie was hoping she'd be able to last until the boot came off before attempting to wash her hair. She'd tried to scrub at it over the sink, but it was impossible to get her head under the tap.

'Why don't you just go to the hairdresser?' Frankie asked, seeing Birdie scratching away. Jane offered to help, but Birdie refused. Her neighbour had done so much for her, more than Birdie could ever repay. Frankie had offered as well, but Birdie didn't like the thought of Frankie's little hands touching her dirty old scalp. She hasn't been to the hairdresser in a long while, has taken to trimming her ends herself, become expert in controlling her curls. She hadn't been able to cope with the hairdresser after Rose went, and who was Birdie trying to look nice for with Arthur gone? Their questions only served to highlight her aloneness: 'Going anywhere nice on holiday?', 'Any plans for the weekend?', 'Getting your hair done for a special occasion?' No, no and no.

Finally, she relents but Frankie insists on accompanying her.

'I need to have my hair washed, please,' Birdie tells the

woman on reception, when they arrive at Hair Today (Gone tomorrow? Birdie wonders). Her cumbersome boot clunks loudly on the marble floor. 'Sorry about the state of it,' she adds, feeling embarrassed and shabby in the shiny salon, with its huge brass mirrors and pink velvet chairs.

'No problem, ducky,' the receptionist trills. Her eyebrows are so big, Birdie is reminded of the pet ferret a boy at school kept up his jumper. Nigel, his name was. The ferret, not the boy. His name was . . . Oh, what was his name, and why does it matter? The painkillers the hospital doctor prescribed scatter her brain, like birdseed. Birdie keeps slipping down snakes into the past, her thoughts snagging on nails of memories.

'I'll just finish off my other lady. Do take a seat. Would you like a nice cup of tea while you're waiting?' the hairdresser asks.

'Why do people ask that?' Frankie comments, as they sit by the window. 'If you want a nice cup of tea. As if you'd prefer a nasty one.'

Rose used to say the same: 'I'm off to put the kettle on. Dreadful cup of tea, anyone?'

'Ha!' Birdie says.

'And she should think about what she's saying,' Frankie carries on. 'She can't really mean we can take a seat because that would get very expensive.'

Princess Margaret would definitely take the seat, Birdie thinks, picking up a magazine full of people she doesn't know. Body shapes have changed dramatically since she was young. She's pleased to see larger derrières are coming back, but what about the giant lips?

'Plastic surgery,' Frankie says, looking over her shoulder. 'Botulinum. It's an anaerobic bacterium. The most toxic substance known. The amount put in lips isn't dangerous, but even so. Why would you pay to have something deadly injected into you?' She tuts.

The tea, when they finally get it, is not nice. It's cold and there is no fresh milk, only those fiddly little pots of long-life substitute. Birdie is reminded of her honeymoon. Of the morning after that first night with Arthur. Him muttering, 'Oh, Christ, oh, hell's bells, Birdie,' then laughing in joy and saying, 'Well, hello there, wifey,' into her neck. The curtains blowing in their modest guest room in the New Forest. He'd brought her tea in bed, spilling the first tiny pot of milk on the tray. 'Sorry,' he'd said, looking down at the dubious lukewarm brew, 'but we do have posh shortbread.'

They'd spent the morning dozing and reading. Gone down to a lunch of ham and pea pie and buttery mashed potato. Strawberry and cream cake that they walked off across the moors. Birdie fed the wild ponies mints from her pocket. Arthur took photos with his new camera: Birdie with her little bunch of heather, sitting on a log. Arthur had stopped a passing hiker and asked her to take a shot of him and his new bride. The breeze lifting Birdie's scarf. Her low-heeled wellies, Arthur's arm around her, the smell of them together still clinging to his neck.

Their smiles in the photo were so wide it hurt. Birdie and Arthur, looking like they'd won some sort of competition, caught a prize-winning fish. They were champions – they were solid gold. Being in love had been as easy as pie, as easy as tipping overboard in the rowing boat Arthur took her out in. Reeds in her hair, cold pond water in her mouth. Mud on her legs, frogs leaping in her heart.

Rose, meanwhile, was at home with their mother. Birdie brought her back a packet of vanilla fudge, some shortbread in a patterned box. She had wanted to bring Rose a slice of the moor, the feeling of being so in love you could die, but they didn't sell that in any of the shops.

'Now, you just lie back and relax,' the hairdresser coos. Birdie hears the squirt of a shampoo bottle, then feels soft hands on her neck, warm water running over her head. Fingers massage her scalp, cradle her cranium. It feels so nice that Birdie has to close her eyes and bite the inside of her cheek to stop herself making a noise. There is something oddly vulnerable about tipping your neck back for someone, trusting them to hold you without hurting you, not get soap in your eyes. The hairdresser rubs at the skin behind Birdie's ears, smooths bubbles off her forehead, runs a comb through her hair. Birdie wants to stay there for ever.

'There. All finished.'

Birdie must have nodded off because she wakes with a snort.

'Come on over,' the hairdresser says, smiling. She must be used to daft old ladies, Birdie thinks.

In the chair facing the mirror, a black towel wound into a turban on her head, Birdie is shocked by her appearance. When did she get so thin and drawn? Her cheeks are two screwed-up paper bags, hanging off the bones. Her lips are dry, and her eyelids have sunk into themselves. She should have put on some lipstick before coming out. Princess Margaret would be appalled.

'So, are you and your granddaughter off to do something nice after this?' the hairdresser asks, when she has finished snipping Birdie's tatty ends and is blow-drying her hair.

'She is not my grandmother,' Frankie says. 'She is my friend.' And there go Birdie's tear-ducts again. She puts her head into her handbag under the pretence of looking for her purse so no one can see her eyes.

'Would you like your hair cut too?' the hairdresser asks Frankie. 'I could sort out those curls a bit.'

'No,' Frankie half shouts, and clamps her hands over her head.

'Only Min is allowed to cut my hair,' she tells Birdie, as they make their way back along the road towards home.

Birdie notices she pauses to look in the window of the YMCA. 'What do you want in there?' she says, peering through the glass. The shop is full of old-fashioned walnut cabinets, dining- and side-tables. Soon Birdie's furniture will join them. Odd to think of the bed she and Arthur made love in being put in the window on display, like John Lennon and Yoko Ono protesting for peace.

'I need a bed,' Frankie says. 'I'm sleeping on a futon. Min says second-hand is dirty, but I'm all right with dead people's things.'

They peer through the glass again. Half-folded sheets lie in heaps. Chairs with missing legs are stockpiled in one corner. The boy behind the counter has one finger up his nose and the other hand holding the spine of a book.

'I know where we can find some good furniture,' Birdie says suddenly, walking on.

She'd never planned to give away Rose's bed. Still often goes to look at it, pulls back the sheet, where the imprint of her sister's sleeping body is still faintly visible, a fossil of her twin. Birdie fits that sarcophagus perfectly. When Rose first died, Birdie spent a long time lying there. Days would pass, Birdie going from her sister's single bed to Arthur's side of hers. Sleep was her only respite, a break from herself. From the pain and the guilt and the monotony of living without truly having a life.

Giving Rose's bed to Frankie is a way of thanking her and Jane for their help. Birdie cannot offer much, but she can offer this.

'Where are we going?' Frankie asks, falling into step beside her.

'Back home,' Birdie says. 'I have a spare room full of furniture. All it needs is a good clean. No germs, just dust. What do you say?'

'I say I hope there are spiders.'

'You like spiders?'

'Oh, Mrs Greenwing, spiders are *brilliant*.'

Birdie thinks of how she used to shriek whenever she spotted one, call for Arthur to hurry in with some ridiculous humane contraption he'd sent off for from a magazine. 'Get it, Arthur!' she'd shout, cheering him on as though he were a bullfighter in the ring. Arthur, sweating as he chased the critter up walls and behind the sofa.

Ever since Arthur died, Birdie has avoided the corners of her bungalow, has stopped looking up. Doesn't want to see what's there. 'Spiders I can offer too,' she says.

23

Jane

'MS BROWN? IT'S MR Lister here, Frankie's teacher. I wonder if you have a minute to chat?'

Jane had known this phone call was coming. There are only so many times you can run away, pretending you have not heard your name being called.

'Ideally I'd ask you to come in, but Frankie says you work long shifts.'

'Yes. I'm a nurse,' Jane says, hoping this might appeal to his better nature.

'Well, the thing is,' Mr Lister continues, 'there's been a bit of a situation with another girl in class.'

'Oh?' Jane tries to sound surprised. 'How odd. Frankie is normally so easy-going.'

There is a long pause before Mr Lister says, 'Yes, well . . . Frankie is refusing to work with her because, and I quote, "She always has bits of green stuff in her braces, and it makes me feel sick."'

'A silly misunderstanding,' Jane says, attempting a light laugh. It collapses like a half-baked cake.

'That is not all Frankie said.' Mr Lister carries on, citing a host of other complaints Frankie has made against her 'desk-mate'. She's really taken the kid apart. Min would be proud. Jane is horrified.

'I'm so sorry, Mr Lister. I don't know what's come over her. I'll have a stern word,' Jane promises.

'The mother has complained to the head teacher. He wants a meeting. Can you come in after school today?'

Jane feels a rare primal urge for her mother. Min always dealt with this stuff. Marched in, wielding her stick, guns blazing, and strutted back out with a slight swagger. 'How about if Frankie writes a letter of apology?' Jane suggests.

'I don't think a letter is going to cut it. The poor girl is refusing to come back to school, to leave her bedroom, since Frankie's comments.'

Never mind poor Frankie, thinks Jane, who can't help her reaction to things like bad breath, bits in teeth and high-pitched noises. Tables not in rows. Textbooks not lining up, spines out of order. At some point Braces Girl is going to lose the metal mouth, learn some personal hygiene and put all of this behind her. Frankie will have to continue to fight, every day, to keep control of herself, not rock back and forth or flap her hands. As well as trying to listen to the teacher, Frankie has to block out a million sounds, like ants crawling over her skin. The squeak of a chair leg. Someone chewing gum. The buzz of the overhead lights. Frankie can have a full-blown panic attack over fabric. Who gets to decide who's right and who's crazy? Jane thinks. Why is Frankie always the one in the wrong?

For a long time, Jane thought Frankie's outspokenness, her inability to keep her opinions to herself, was due to her spending so much time with Min. When the school suggested having Frankie diagnosed, Min wouldn't hear of it. 'Diagnosed with what? There's nothing wrong with her,' Min said. 'It's everyone else that's the problem.'

Min never blushed when Frankie told a stranger they smelt, or had a meltdown in a shop because things were not in the order Frankie needed them to be. 'I agree,' Min would say loudly. 'Too right, Frankie. You tell them.'

Jane will never forget the look on Min's face when she told her she'd accepted a job in Brighton. That she and Frankie were leaving. All the bones in her mother's face seemed to crumble. The very scaffolding of her collapsed. Min's whole body deflated, as though Jane had put a pin into her. Oh, my God, I've killed her, Jane thought, and then Min's chin had gone back up. 'No,' she said, 'you're not allowed. Go to your room.'

'Min—'

'I said no!' Min cried, her voice breaking.

Jane had been wrong to think Min might understand, or Suki. Her family were all so unapologetically awkward, unwilling to bend or adapt. If life were a game of Monopoly, they were the stubborn and proud pieces to play, leaving Jane to be the thimble that no one else wanted. With her family so inflexible, Jane was left with no choice but to be elastic. It was Jane who had to breathe in, had to mould herself to fit into the tiny gaps left in between.

'I really am sorry to hear this, Mr Lister. It is truly out of character, and I'll speak to Frankie when she gets home. Now I must go,' Jane says. 'I have a code blue.' She hangs up hurriedly, her palms sweating.

'You okay?' Helen asks, coming past her with a trolley of pills.

'Fine.' Jane tries to smile. 'The school, my daughter's teacher . . . Sometimes, I'm just crap at being a mum.'

'Want a diazepam?' Helen offers, picking up a tiny cup.

'I'd love one, but I don't think it's the best idea,' Jane says.

'Just as well. These are for constipation,' Helen replies, with a wink.

Jane thinks about calling Min, telling her what's happened. But then what? Min will tell her what she should do. What Min would have done. What Jane cannot manage to do herself. Grow a bloody backbone. Jane is sick of other people dictating her life. Making her feel wrong. Helen is right. Jane isn't going to get into trouble for displeasing someone, so why does the thought of it scare her so much? Jane wants to rip off her own face. For good old plain Jane, reliable and beige, to be a mask that she can remove. Find someone better, braver, underneath.

When Jane goes to get Frankie that afternoon, her daughter is in the corner of the classroom, curled up like a woodlouse under her coat. The teacher is asking her something, but Jane can't work out what it is. All she can hear is Frankie saying, 'I am under no obligation to make sense to you,' over and over again. The words are like bullets through rotten fruit, stabs straight into Jane's heart. She copied out that quote for Frankie the day before she started primary school, drew the Mad Hatter in the corner, cups of tea and White Rabbits, pinned it to her bedroom wall. Frankie always said she didn't believe in fairy tales. Now here she is reciting the words from one.

She needs her Charlie Cloth, Jane thinks. She needs her mother and her cup with stars on. She needs Min.

'Mr Lister, sorry I'm late. Can we talk outside?' Jane says. Frankie pokes her head out from under her coat like a mole. Jane gives her a wobbly smile.

In the corridor, Mr Lister repeats everything he said on the phone and Jane nods, trying to look suitably apologetic without actually admitting to anything. It's a skill she and Suki learned when Min was laying into them. 'Who broke this? Who moved that? Who ate all the custard creams?'

'I'm not sorry,' Frankie says, as they walk out of the year-seven classroom, which is lined with posters about saving trees. Saving endangered animals. Saving energy, the environment. The whole bloody world, but not the people in it. Where is the poster about saving kids like Frankie? With 'did you know' boxes and 'how you can help'.

'I only told the truth. Why is the truth wrong?' Frankie asks.

Why indeed? Jane wonders, thinking about what happened with Suki. 'You know what, Frankie?' Jane says, as they make their way home. 'I think you're brave. I wish I had an ounce of your courage.'

24

Ada

'YOU WANT US TO come to your bungalow for dinner?' Lech says, frowning. 'Why don't you come here instead? I will make us a nice meal. Good, solid Polish food.'

'Because I want to make *you* a nice meal,' Ada says firmly. She has come to the *Polski sklep* with a long list of ingredients.

'Quite the ambitious menu you're planning,' Lech says, scanning it. 'Is it just us coming, or will Pope John Paul II be there also, or Frédéric Chopin?'

'Shut up. I need to practise on you,' Ada says, snatching the list back, 'for my marathon fundraising sale.'

'What is wrong with you, Ada?' Lech says, advancing from behind the counter to feel her forehead. 'Are you coming down with a dose of English, going round asking people for money! What next? Queueing all day for no reason. Moaning about the cold? Wearing those funny plastic shoe things? I can just bake you more cakes, ones that people will actually pay money for.'

'What my rude father means to say is that we'd love to. Thank you for your gracious invitation. What shall I bring?

Vodka, a toothbrush?' Aleksey says, appearing from the storeroom.

'Just vodka is fine,' Ada says, passing him the list. 'Now help me find these, please. Come hungry.'

'I'll come however you like,' Aleksey says, picking up a basket.

In the end, Ada has to call and tell them to come an hour later than planned, and then an hour later still. By the time they arrive, Ada has every ingredient from her fridge smeared through her hair, and her clothes have been Jackson Pollocked with nefarious-looking stains. The smell coming from her kitchen is not one of home-cooked comfort. It smells like very bad things have taken place in there that should never be spoken about.

'I am very hungry,' Lech says, when she opens the door. He looks grumpy.

'Hungry enough to eat anything?' Ada asks.

'Well, we'll soon see, won't we?' he says, stepping into the hall and passing Ada his jacket.

'I think it smells excellent,' Aleksey says. 'I don't feel at all like I have walked into a true crime documentary.'

'Did you cook an animal with all its fur still on?' Lech asks.

'Welcome to my home. Do come in, have a seat,' Ada says.

The food is terrible. The gravy is thin, the potatoes like bullets. The meat is tough. Her dumplings look like a child's drawing of dinosaurs. Her entrées were too burned to serve. Ada tossed them out into the back garden, where the seagulls shrieked at them then flew away in fright.

'This one looks like an ear,' Lech says, biting into a *pieroge*, 'but it tastes like feet.'

'It's supposed to be cream cheese,' Ada says, sighing.

She wonders if Wilbur can cook. Ada bets he can whip up something delicious out of three ingredients that don't even go together. He could probably make Ada enjoy avocado and she hates avocado. Unwanted thoughts about Wilbur keep popping up like weeds between the paving slabs of her mind. Ada tramples on them internally.

'Well, my stegosaurus is wonderful,' Aleksey groans, 'so good.'

'You've been chewing the same mouthful for the last five minutes.'

'I'm savouring it,' Aleksey replies, grimacing.

'Liar,' Ada says.

'If I swallow this mouthful of evil, will you kiss me?' Aleksey asks.

'Ada,' Lech announces, wiping his lips with a napkin and indiscreetly spitting his mouthful into it. 'You must never attempt to cook again.'

'Rude,' Ada says crossly. 'My mother showed me how to make these dishes.'

'Were you watching?' Lech asks.

'Ada, your mother may be able to make better *pierogi* than this,' Aleksey says, poking at a ridge of bloated dough, and cringing, as though something might fly out of it and bite him, 'but she cannot mend bones, or save a man from death with nothing but her bare hands and her bra wire.'

Wilbur's face flares in her mind, white and hot like a flame coming to life. Him in a dusty street, screaming into a radio.

Men and blood and guns. Wilbur going back into a burning building. 'Aleksey,' Ada says, 'what is it you think I do?'

'Heal people,' he says assuredly, looking at her with a proud smile.

Ada specialized in oncology thinking she could do just that. Heal people. She thought cancer was a mountain she was going to climb and stick a flag in the top of it. I got here first. Now she knows better. She'll never reach the summit. Cancer is the South Pole, and she is Shackleton.

Ada fell in love with Marie Curie after reading the book Lidka gave her, as she'd predicted. Demanded to be taken to Warsaw, to stand in front of the house Marie had grown up in. To touch the door that Marie had closed each day had opened something inside Ada. That Marie Curie died because her bone marrow stopped producing white blood cells after too much exposure to radiation only made Ada admire her more.

'Isn't it ironic?' Ania used to say, whenever Ada mentioned her.

'Isn't what ironic?' Ada would ask.

'That trying to save other people meant Curie slowly killed herself.'

'The word is heroic, not ironic,' Ada would reply.

Lech and Aleksey insist on doing the washing-up. Ada can hear them muttering in the kitchen about the burned food crusted on her new *kavalkad* pans as she wipes her *tarsele* extendable table. Lech mentions a blowtorch, and how Ada's fingers must be made of knives because she's butchered everything she touched. Aleksey tells him that's his future wife he's talking about.

'Are you sure you still want her after this?' Lech says. Then, 'I see, flick water at an old man, very grown-up.'

They leave late, laden with leftovers that Ada knows will be put into the bin.

'Let me help you, Ada,' Lech says. 'This is what we do, yes?' He holds her face in his old, calloused hands and squeezes it until she nods. Then he tells her that she tried and that is better than nothing. Ada doesn't think trying counts for much if you don't win, but keeps quiet.

Aleksey tells her he will still marry her, even though she would not be a very good wife.

'Thank you,' she says, 'that's a very kind offer.'

'I am all heart,' he says, 'and penis.'

On her run the next morning, Ada tries to picture how a phone call with her mother would go. Ada only rings on birthdays, or special dates such as Easter, when she knows that her mother is about to leave for market. Any time she can say, 'Just a quick one, Śmigus-Dyngus Day, or Happy Easter as they say in England.'

When they talk, her mother asks her question after question and Ada's answers always feel wrong. Should Ada say she's happy, or should she say she's lonely and let her mother talk her into coming home? Ada sends gifts in place of herself. Subscriptions for farming magazines that her father would never pay for himself. Slippers for her mother, made from sheepskin. A long cashmere cardigan, made from the finest Gobi Desert goat's underbelly hair, a hug that Ada can send through the post. She knows these gifts will not be welcome. Sometimes good intentions can be as damaging as bad ones. Her father will think she's telling him he's out of touch by sending magazines full of new methods, better equipment. Her mother, who sells every part of a sheep she can, will find the slippers incongruous. Will keep them tucked away in their tissue-lined box like two sleeping babies. The cardigan will scare her with its indulgent softness. All Ada is doing is separating herself from her family even more, but what else is there to do? How do you show love from far away?

If she were to go home to see them, she'd give herself back over to that old life, start plaiting her hair again and wearing her dad's tartan shirt. She'd never leave. Ada would be sucked backwards. There isn't enough to hold her here, not enough tent pegs pinning her in place. But going home would feel a lot like giving up and Ada promised herself she would never do that. She and her parents had worked too hard, sacrificed too much to get Ada to where she is now. She should have realized that it would carry on being hard. That it would only get harder still. Ada misses her mum like a lost tooth, worries at the foreign hole where she should be. Misses, too, the sound of animals waking her up, of wind through the long grass. The thick silence of a forest and the colour of the sun when it shines through the linden leaves, with their clusters of yellow blossoms. Ada misses wide-open spaces, miles of fields stitched together by her father's crude wooden posts.

She runs past people curled up in sleeping bags under rusted bus stops, through snatches of conversation, perfumes and dinner plans being made. Ada feels like smoke, like vapour. When she's out of her white coat, people move through her as though she's invisible. If Ada trips on the seafront, but no one knows who she is, did it happen? Can it still hurt?

Shake it off, Ada, she thinks. She diagnosed a twenty-two-year-old boy this week. Told him and his family the worst news a person can hear. The words fell like dropped scalpels from her hands, slicing their world in half. Wilbur, she noticed, didn't look at her patient as she told him, but at Ada, the concern on his face for her.

Ada may not have much, but she has her health. That in itself is a miracle and never to be taken for granted. So Ada pushes on, tells her body to do what her mind demands of it. Sprints like she's being chased, swings her arms as if she's cutting through the air. On and on she goes, past the ice-cream shop on Hove seafront with its red and white awning. Past the big celebrity houses with their direct access to a private beach. Past the Lagoon where kids try and fail to windsurf and wakeboard. Ada runs past it all, as though she's fast-forwarding a TV show. She knows she's going too far, too fast, too soon. That she's going to have to turn around at some point and go all the way back. That this is going to hurt. Tomorrow and tomorrow and tomorrow. But she cannot stop. Her feet keep lifting and landing, her calves burn but carry on. Her heart bangs like a drum and the rest of her moves to its steady beat. Maybe this is still about Wilbur, about trying to prove something to him, or maybe Ada is just trying to outrun herself.

25

Birdie

HALF ASLEEP, BIRDIE CAN hear shoes crunching on the gravel path, the jangle of keys. The lock is stiff – it always takes a couple of goes. Finally, Birdie hears the click of the mechanism giving way, the yawn of the front door opening. Footsteps in the hallway. They are back – Rose and Arthur are back at last!

'Birdie?'

Rose's voice is higher, and her legs are shorter. Her face is smooth, and her fingers are straight. She's wearing a black coat, which is unlike her.

'Birdie, are you okay?'

Birdie opens her eyes. Of course it isn't Rose. Birdie has not fallen into some Lewis Carroll adventure full of magic keys and shrinking potions. She is not Alice in Wonderland, she is Birdie and she is lying on her bed, with Frankie looking at her, frowning. 'Sorry, I must have fallen asleep,' she says, struggling to sit up.

'We've come to take you to the hospital. You get your boot off today, remember?' Frankie says. 'Then you can wash your own hair like you want to.'

'Oh, yes, lovely.'

But ever since the visit to the hairdresser, Birdie can't stop thinking about how nice it had felt to be touched. How comforting it was to have her scalp cradled delicately in a pair of strong hands, someone taking the weight of all her grey matter, just for a little while. She wants to go back again. Wants to do it weekly for whatever weeks she has left. Why not? Rose says in her ear. Why not, says Princess Margaret, make death wait while you get a bloody perm?

Frankie goes down the hall to visit Audrey, and Birdie forces herself off the bed, one limb at a time. She's beginning to feel hollow, unsure her body will stay all in one piece or move as it is supposed to. Birdie is reminded of the skeleton that lived in the corner of her school room, held together by metal clips. It was called Mr Chips and its arms and legs were always falling off. Boys used to chase one another around with femurs and forearms, making the girls squeal. Birdie feels cold all the way through, like a piece of cod in the freezer. Her chattering teeth remind her of the one and only time she and Arthur went camping. 'This is the life, eh, my bird of paradise?' Arthur had said, once the infernal tent was finally up, folding chairs forced into submission and the cheap stove temporarily lit. A breeze had come along the second Arthur got his matches out, as though God was laughing at them.

'Yes, indeed,' Birdie said, wondering where on earth she was supposed to go to the toilet, and where to put the loo roll afterwards. There was nothing romantic about smelling of pee.

After a walk along the riverbank where all the wildlife, except the thunder flies, had obviously got wind they were coming and therefore left, Birdie and Arthur had returned to the empty campsite for a supper of sausages that refused to cook. 'They're actually getting paler. How is that possible?'

Once inside the tent for the night ('You go in first. I'm not sure we'll both fit. Perhaps crawl in backwards? Mind the zip!'), the rain found the gaps in the ground sheet where Arthur had got fed up and not pegged it down properly. Before long, the wind built to a constant howl and the inflatable mattress deflated as fast as Birdie's enjoyment of the trip.

'Oh, sod this for a game of soldiers, Birdie,' Arthur said, at one a.m., fumbling for his torch. 'Let's go home. To the city. For we are city folk.'

They'd abandoned the tent in the field – it was too much trouble to take it down in the gale – and the rest of the gear was crammed hurriedly into the car. Arthur drove them back along the coast, with the heater on full blast, all the while moaning about being wet and cold. When Birdie spotted her reflection in the rear-view mirror, she laughed. Her neat bob was poking up like she'd been electrocuted, and there was a stripe of mud across her cheek. Then Arthur started laughing too, and the pair of them chortled all the way home, as if they were powering the car along with it.

What would Arthur say if he could see her now? Thin and grey. Tatty and worn down. Would he laugh at her boot, call her Clonky? Would he lift her up and help her bathe, bring her hot whisky to help her sleep? You know he would, Birdie.

'Come on. We'll be late. Mum will be here any minute.'

Birdie thinks that the last thing Jane should be doing is returning to the hospital on her day off, but she had insisted on going with them.

'Thank you so much for the furniture,' Jane had said awkwardly, and Birdie saw that Jane found charity as hard to accept as she did.

'You are welcome,' Birdie said, and meant it.

At the hospital, in a white room full of metal tools, the nurse takes her time sawing off Birdie's cast. It finally falls open like a chrysalis, and Birdie's white bony foot is exposed, smelling sour and looking shrivelled.

'What do you do with the old casts?' Frankie asks the nurse. 'If people have cut off a finger or a toe and you can't sew them back on, what do you do with them?'

The nurse ignores Frankie, turns to Birdie and says, 'You'll need to do some exercises to get your strength back up.'

She must not have seen Birdie's medical file. Birdie's strength is seeping out of her, a finger poked in a bag of flour; Birdie is being frittered away on the breeze.

'Well, *she* wasn't very friendly,' Frankie says loudly, as they leave, cross that she was not allowed to keep Birdie's fibreglass cast or 'have a quick go on the saw'.

Birdie should feel lighter without the plaster, but a heavy wave of tiredness hits her instead. Silly to think it was the cast weighing her down.

Sensing her slump, Jane suggests they stop at the WRVS café. 'Birdie! Nice to see you again,' Connie says, shuffling over to the counter, her spun-sugar hair glowing.

'You know Connie?' Jane asks.

'Yes. I used to bring my sister, Rose, here for appointments.'

'She was your twin, is that right?' Jane asks.

'Rose,' Connie says, 'took her coffee white with one sugar and always had a toasted tea-cake.'

'You had a twin?' Frankie asks. 'Deadly! Were you identical? Which one was older? Did you have a telepathic connection? If she felt ill, did you feel ill too?'

'Yes, me, and no,' Birdie says. If she could have taken some of Rose's pain, her illness, she would've done so gladly, but even on Rose's worst days, Birdie always felt fine. Rushed about, bashing into chairs and table ends in her haste to fetch Rose drinks or tablets. Would go to bed covered with bruises she had never felt happen. 'Don't apologize for being well,' Rose used to say to her, but how could she not?

Rose's favourite yearly outing was to the circus. 'Breathe it in, Birdie,' she'd say. 'Pure magic.' All Birdie smelt was burned popcorn and stale tents. Hotdogs, petrol and greasy face paint, but Rose smelt adventure. Another life. She was enthralled by the glittery hats and the sequined bodysuits. Birdie had thought it might be hard for Rose to see the clowns tumble as though they were made of elastic, the girls on the high wire who tiptoed across the sky. Acrobats, with legs that could twist like sticks of liquorice, and arms that could hold another person aloft in the air while Rose struggled with a hairbrush. Because, before she got ill, Rose Clarke could run like the wind and swim like a fish, cut through the tide with hands like blades. Birdie would kick like a mule in her wake, trying to keep up.

As children, the twins would spend summers with seawater up their noses. Underwater, the real world was nothing but a blur of blue above them. They stayed in, perfecting their strokes, until their skin puckered. Until their mother was forced to come to the water's edge, hands on hips. Only then would they emerge, monsters from the deep, their hair covered with dark strands of seaweed and knees scuffed from the rock pools. Costumes full of sand and the occasional crab claw. Hopping on one leg, as their mother briskly towelled them off. Once dry, they were given lemon barley squash and banana sandwiches. They could never get enough of the water, of that cheap white bread, of those long summer evenings that felt as if they would never end. But then Rose got sick, and the sea visits stopped. The costumes and caps went into the back of the cupboard, and they never talked about swimming again. What was there to say? 'Hey, Rose, I'm sorry you're not going to be an Olympic diver.' Maybe Birdie should have encouraged Rose to open up more about her pain. Poked holes in the stoicism her sister wore like a second skin.

'Do you like swimming?' she asks Frankie suddenly.

'No, it's unhygienic.'

'I'm trying to persuade Frankie to give sea swimming a go,' Jane says.

'Where various highly infectious diseases—'

'As you can see, she has her reservations,' Jane interrupts.

'Oh,' Birdie says. She and Rose had never stopped to consider what might be in the water. Rose didn't catch her rheumatoid arthritis in the sea. It was inside her the whole time, waiting. Like Birdie's cancer.

'Your mug has a swear word on it,' Frankie remarks.

Birdie turns it around. Jane bursts out laughing. Frankie frowns, stern disapproval on her face. Birdie feels a smile, as thin as a strand of Connie's hair, whisper across her lips.

26

Jane

'SURPRISE!'

Min looks from Jane to Frankie, then back again. She scowls, then smiles, then tuts.

'What the bleddy hell are you two doing here?' she demands, but Jane can tell she's happy to see them.

'We've come to see my lovely mother,' Jane says. 'Is she in?'

'Ha bleddy ha.'

Jane kisses Min's ruddy cheek.

'Hi, Min,' Frankie says.

'Frankie. You've grown. Well done.'

'Thank you,' Frankie says.

For a horrible minute, Jane thinks Min is going to cry. Her little chin wattle wobbles and her eyes go all shiny.

'Well, come on in,' she snaps, pulling herself up to her full height of four foot nine. 'Standing there like a pair of bleddy cough drops. You're letting all the heat out.'

She walks without limping, Jane notices with relief. The smell of home hits hard. Stardrops and burned toast. A cloying pot-pourri in the downstairs loo that Min thinks is posh. The hall is cold, and the TV is blaringly loud. Min never used to have it on during the day. Is the noise a replacement for her and Frankie?

Dropping her bag in the hall, Jane goes into the kitchen, trying not to be bothered by the single mug on the draining board where there used to be three. Four before that.

'Why didn't you say you were coming?' Min asks.

'We wanted to surprise you.'

Jane notices that Min's glasses are a bit smudged, and her blouse is missing a button. Wait – is that a stain on her collar? Min's look is stern beige with neat creases. Heavy material that can withstand a hot wash (none of this fabric-softener nonsense) and a steam iron.

'Are you okay, Min?' Jane asks.

'Of course I am. Why wouldn't I be?' Min says, as she walks to the chest freezer and wrenches the lid up. Bending at the waist, she shoves her head inside and starts rifling. 'I'd have prepared dinner if I'd known you were on your way. Got that chicken in Frankie likes.'

'We can get fish and chips. Save you going to any trouble,' Jane suggests.

Min pokes her head back out. She's tempted, Jane can tell. She needs to snare the rabbit carefully. 'Come on, sit down and catch up with Frankie. Relax! I'll nip out and pick up dinner. We'll put a film on. You can choose.' Jane takes Min's elbow, leads her away from the freezer and into the living room, swallowing her own exhaustion. It had been a mission to get them here, running down the platform at Brighton station because Frankie can only sit at the very front of a train. Changing at Victoria during rush-hour, Frankie struggling on the tube. Jane could see her fighting the urge to flap her hands, to cover her ears. There were no free seats. Jane was forced to hang on to the grab rail. Every time someone passed her to get to the exit, they tripped over her large trainers. 'So sorry,' Jane said. 'I have my father's feet.'

'Well, give them back and get some that fit,' a voice had muttered from somewhere down the carriage. Suki had the same size feet as Jane but wore her shoes a size too small in an effort to shrink them. 'Shoes,' she had told Jane, 'are the mating call of the body. Toe cleavage is the ultimate in sexy.' Even when they were travelling, with no room even for a slim paperback, Suki would buy shoes. Crammed them into her backpack at the expense of more practical things. Suki said, 'Shoes tell you everything you need to know about the state of someone's sex life.'

Now Jane shoves her feet into the sandals that Min keeps by the door for slopping about in and plods up the road.

'Back, are you?' says Justine, when she spots Jane. 'Thought you would be. Brighton not all that good a bag of chips after all?'

'Hello, Justine. Nice to see you too. I'm just up to visit Min,' Jane says, finding a smile at the very back of her mouth and dragging it out through clenched teeth. 'Three cod and chips with mushy peas, please.'

'Min said you wouldn't last down there,' Justine says, shovelling chips into white greaseproof paper. 'Said you'll be back by the summer, tail between your legs.'

Jane's smile is genuine now. Min may be rude to Jane about Jane, but Min would never, ever disparage her daughters to anyone, especially not to Justine from 'The StarChip Enterprise'. Min will have done the exact opposite. She'll have popped in to exaggerate Jane's job and her living quarters. Justine might well have been told that Jane is running the entire Accident and Emergency department and living in the Royal Pavilion, for all she knows.

Jane and Suki have known Justine since pre-school. Justine has a history of making things up, trying to take what is not hers (including, once, a boyfriend of Suki's) and is always spreading lies. She is one of those people who live to see couples break up or things go wrong.

Suki used to love popping in to ask Justine how life was going. 'Justine! Still living at home? What a surprise. Still single too? Never mind, plenty more fish in the freezer. And how's your career? Are you *frying* up the ladder?'

Justine would scowl and say Suki was still a bitch. Suki would laugh and not give a shit. Jane feels a pang for her sister so strong it makes her guts ache. 'Thank you,' she tells Justine, when she slides over the takeaway.

'You look tired,' Justine says back.

'It's all the amazing sex I'm having,' Jane wants to say but doesn't.

'Wooden forks are ten pence each,' Justine adds. Suki would knock the box over. Jane carefully puts back the three she'd picked up.

Annoyingly, the chips are good. Min's rule is that greasy food must be eaten outside, so it doesn't make the house smell. She has no front or back garden so when Jane gets back, Frankie and Min are sitting on the front wall that hides the rubbish bins with a tablecloth laid over it, armed with salt, vinegar and ketchup. Frankie is telling Min about the kids in her class. 'Dirty Berties, the lot of them,' Min says. 'I hope you told them what's what.'

After dinner, they watch *Erin Brockovich*. They always end up watching *Erin Brockovich*. Jane sends Suki a photo of the TV screen with *Guess where I am* written underneath and gets two thumbs-ups in return. Jane replies with *Justine still working at StarChip* and gets a laughing emoji in response. She isn't looking for praise from Suki, or a head pat for going home, but she'd hoped for a bit more than thumbs-ups and a yellow cartoon face. Jane starts typing, *Hey, remember when you got piles from sitting on a cold pavement just like Min said you would, and I had to look at them for you?* but then deletes it.

They round off the evening with a game of cards. Min thinks betting is disgusting ('Should be illegal'), but loves to play Palace for matchsticks. When she turns over a jack, changing the direction of the game, then sheds all her cards in quick succession, she yells 'Palace!' so loudly, with such triumph in her voice, that Jane feels a surge of warmth zinging through her. Min's eyes, bright as berries, her little mouth open wide and, Christ, she's even laughing! Jane wants to film it. Min's hands opening and closing like a pair of little lobster claws, trying to capture the moment. Red, swollen knuckles seizing the seconds.

'Good game, Min.' Frankie nods with approval, and Min pats her head, elation still radiating from her.

'I'll make you losers some hot milk,' she says almost kindly, scooping up her matchsticks.

The next morning, Jane wakes late and disoriented, wondering who killed all the seagulls. Then she remembers. Min has never redecorated Suki and Jane's bedroom. There are neat Hoover lines in the swirly coral carpet, and the smell of polish hangs heavy in the air, but the posters on the walls remain, yellow with age and curled at the edges. She'd thought Min would have had them straight down the moment she left. Jane looks up at the thick cracks in the thin Artex ceiling. Thinks of the hours she and Suki spent together in this small space. In sickness and in health, like an old married couple. Covered with chicken pox and camomile lotion. Sunburned and sore from a day at the beach. Fizzing with excitement on Christmas Eve. Listening to the charts on Sunday evenings after dinner, trying to write down the lyrics.

They'd inspected their growing bodies here on this bed, plucking hairs and comparing knees. Suki used to play the injured patient, sitting while Jane wrapped toilet paper round her head and listened to her heart with the detachable shower hose, as Min clanged about downstairs.

She passes her mother's bedroom door on her way to the kitchen. Even though it's been years, Jane still can't open it. Can't go back in there. She used to wonder how Min could sleep on the bed their dad died in. Maybe, she realizes now, she feels closer to him there. Maybe to Min he has become part of the mattress that takes her weight each night, holding her in her sleep.

Downstairs, Frankie is reading a book on the sofa and Min is making breakfast. Her hair is neat, her blouse clean and ironed. Glasses shiny. 'You look too thin,' she tells Jane, plonking down an over-laden plate. Min still cuts toast into thin strips and scissors the fat off the bacon the way she did for Suki and Jane when they were children.

She smashes the top of Jane's boiled egg with a firm thwack, then decapitates it for her. 'Careful, it's hot.'

For Frankie, Min serves all the different parts of the meal in separate little bowls. If Jane had demanded such a thing when she was a child, she'd have been served her dinner and dessert mixed together in the blender.

After breakfast, Jane walks down the steep hill into town. Roads she knows like the back of her hand. She hoped she'd find the familiarity comforting, like putting on her winter coat for the first time each year, but instead she feels the same sense of claustrophobia that had made her want to leave in the first place. The feeling that she can only be a certain person in this city, and it isn't the real her.

In Accident and Emergency, she receives a hero's welcome. 'Jane! You're back, you idiot. Pass me that cuff, would you? How's Brighton?'

'What are you doing here, you doughnut? You just got out! Wanna go get a drink when I'm done, in . . . ooh, twelve hours?'

Jane passes implements, looks at X-rays, fetches cakes from the café over the road. She even helps remove a needle from the sole of a foot. Makes ten cups of tea in a long line for her exhausted ex-colleagues. Remembers which ones take sugar. It's so easy. Again, part of her wishes she'd never left Bristol. It would have been so much easier to stay. She wouldn't have to worry about Min or feel guilty for taking Frankie away from her. But then she thinks of their little bungalow in Brighton, the sea views, Helen's laughter and Connie's mugs. She thinks about how Suki is out there somewhere, living her best life. I deserve that too, Jane thinks. I must deserve it too – even after what happened.

27

Ada

WHEN SHE HEARS FOOTSTEPS speeding up behind her, Ada's first instinct is to speed up. She's faster now and her legs are used to being pushed out of their comfort zone. Plus she already knows who it is, or her heart does. It was inevitable, she supposes, that they were going to run into one another at some point.

'Ada.'

She glances over her shoulder. Wilbur, in shorts and a long-sleeved top, is making the hill look as if it were flat. She feels a spike in her adrenaline as he sprints to catch up. 'Hi,' she pants. She's not used to running and talking, feels embarrassed by her pale legs in her cheap shorts.

Wilbur easily adjusts his stride to match hers, his breathing deep and even. They run like this for a while, together but apart. Ada wonders what he is thinking about, what music he was listening to. When they hit the next hill, worried that he will go easy on her, Ada pushes herself so hard she thinks for a horrible moment that she might be sick. Then she hears Wilbur mutter something about it not being a race and grins. For a while they do race – short bursts of energy, Wilbur in front, then Ada, laughing, grimacing, swearing. Finally they come to a stop by the kiosk in front of the Palace Pier.

'You are fast,' Wilbur says admiringly, propping a foot on a bench.

For one second Ada is so transfixed by his quads that she forgets how to swallow. Her mouth is bone dry, but she doesn't like to run with a water bottle. She keeps a five-pound note tucked into her sports bra to buy a drink with. She wants to whip it out, toss it at him and tell him to carry on stretching. Slower, deeper. For ever. Instead, she props a foot up next to him, feeling uncomfortable as she bends her head down towards her knee, trying to copy his pose.

At work, Ada does most of the talking. Today it's Wilbur who fills the silence. Asking her how she's feeling. What gels she uses to keep her energy up. He pulls a bag of jelly babies from his pocket and offers it to her. 'These are my weakness,' he confesses. Ada bites into one, taking a little green head clean off.

'Want to do this again?' Wilbur asks. He is looking at her, a half-smile on his face.

Ada should say no. Wilbur is her intern. She runs alone. She has no time, nothing to give. His face glows, his damp shirt is plastered to his body. He is a poster boy for good health. She imagines his insides, two well-oiled pistons for lungs. Two squeaky-clean kidneys and a shining spleen. He probably sweats pure vitamin C. Ada thinks of her own internal organs. Her love of cheese and vodka. One in two, she thinks. One in two. Maybe it'll be me. It will probably be me, not him.

'Okay,' she says, taking another jelly baby.

'Okay,' he says, pulling out his phone. 'Put your number in here.'

She carries on stretching until he's out of sight, then buys a bottle of water, which she drains in one, but she is still thirsty, still full of restless energy although her legs feel almost dead. Instead of going home for a shower, she heads towards the *Polski sklep*. Suddenly ravenous, she cracks into a bag of paprika crisps as she looks round the shelves, wondering if she has ever felt this hungry before. She smells of sweat and her hair is clinging to her neck. Where are the oranges? she thinks. She wants to bite into the flesh of one, suck out the marrow.

'Ada, you look . . . damp,' Aleksey says.

'Been running,' Ada explains.

'Then you need replenishing,' Aleksey says. 'The time has come for my sausage stew.'

'I'll be fine with these,' she says, waving the bag of crisps.

'*Bzdura*. Have some.'

Ada is cold and hungry, so hungry. 'Fine. I'll stay for dinner,' she says. 'After all, you do still owe me for the delicious meal I made you.'

'Really, you will?' Aleksey's face breaks into a grin.

'I'm not going to have sex with you, though,' Ada warns.

'Say it a little louder,' Lech calls, from down the cereal aisle. 'Then we can all dance to it.'

'Of course you won't,' Aleksey says. 'You'll probably want to after you taste my cooking, but I'll remind you that you said no.'

'My son,' Lech comments, 'a true gentleman.'

Walking into their flat upstairs is like entering Narnia, like going through the back of a wardrobe to find Poland on the other side. The walls are covered with olive-green stripes. Her mother has the same paper in her lounge. A similar swirly green carpet and dark wood unit full of blue and white crockery. The air smells of pickled vegetables and cured meat. Lech directs her to an armchair in the cramped living room. She can tell from the oleaginous oval stain on the headrest that it is his special seat. Her father's armchair has the same head-shaped shadow, and he hates having to give it up. Ada declines and takes the sofa. There is stuffing poking out from a hole in the fabric. None of the furniture matches. There are no glass coffee-tables or fancy up-lighters. Ada has not felt so at home, so comfortable, in years.

Aleksey serves them vodka shots in fussy glasses on a tarnished silver tray. '*Na zdrowie!*' he cries.

They toast, though Ada has no idea what they are celebrating, then Aleksey goes into the small kitchen, singing as he slams cupboard doors and rattles about. In the living room, Lech puts on the TV. A Polish commentator fills them in on the news. Ada looks round at the family photos on the wall, but her eyes keep going back to the same one: Lech standing with a pretty but faded woman, too young to be so thin in the face. They are standing on a beach with black sand. Lech had hair back then, while his wife wore a scarf over hers. Little Aleksey is in front of them, grinning at the camera. Was this their last family picture? Ada wonders how Aleksey can admire her so much for being a doctor.

The room is hot and Ada is just drifting off, toes tucked under one of Lech's cardigans, when she remembers a moment like this from her childhood. Ada aged thirteen, falling asleep on Magda's sofa when they went round for lunch. The telling-off she got for being rude. Her mother, red-faced, saying, 'Never ever take without giving, Ada. Always show your appreciation. The world runs on kindness.'

Ada drags herself up from the sofa, folds Lech's cardigan, goes into the kitchen. There are lots of pans all boiling at once, and Aleksey is singing into a wooden spoon. Ada wants to ask him where he gets his happiness from so she can take out a monthly subscription and buy it in bulk. She can imagine the note from the delivery driver: 'Sorry, you were not in to receive your happiness, so we've left it with a neighbour.'

'Can I help?' she asks, going over to one of the pans.

'*Pieprzyć nie!*' he cries, racing over to stand in front of the stove. 'I mean, no. Go and sit down. You made such a lovely meal for us. Now it is my turn.' He puts his hands on her shoulders, steers her back towards the sofa. Ada, feeling she has tried to help and now has full permission from the host not to, allows herself to snooze.

She and Lech jerk awake when Aleksey shouts that dinner is ready. Lech gets up to lay the small round table for the three of them. Cork-bottomed place mats depicting Polish country scenes and matching coasters to protect the cherry wood. Heavy cutlery. Stiff folded napkins. Ada thinks of what she had planned to eat that night, alone, and out of tin foil. Tries not to think about Wilbur's dinner plans. Him dating.

Aleksey serves up a feast. None of it as good as her mother's food, but good enough to make her miss home.

'English can't cook for piss, eh?' Lech says, loading up his plate.

'They don't know which cut of meat to buy,' Aleksey says.

'Queueing hours for little bitty chicken breasts in plastic,' Lech says, shaking his head sadly.

'A whole TV show about baking a cake.'

'One tiny toenail of snow and all the shelves are empty.'

Lech piles more cabbage on to Ada's plate. 'Eat, eat. You are too thin,' he says, pinching her arm. 'Bony.'

'She's perfect,' Aleksey argues, but adds more meat to her plate, 'just a bit pale today.'

'I've been running,' she says again, but clears her plate and holds it up for more.

Aleksey grins.

Lech scoops up the last of his sauce with a spoon.

'You eat like an animal,' Aleksey says.

'I eat the same way you do when the pretty girl is not here,' his father shoots back.

It would be so easy to fall in between these two good, kind men, Ada thinks. Men who open their shop every single day of the year and give credit to people they know can't pay. Ada grew up with men like Lech and Aleksey. She knows if she asked them they'd fix her leaking shower. Would hang shelves in her living room. If she wanted a log-burner fitted (which she does, but can't seem to commit to it), they'd spend their precious free time on their hands and knees, knocking out bricks without a word of complaint. Without accepting a single penny for their time. As far as they are concerned, Ada is family. Ada can picture her own mother here, admiring the fussy thimbles and ornate jugs. The cutlery. Her mother has a thing for spoons. She can't walk past one at the market without stopping to pick it up. Without weighing it in her hand, or pretending to stir a pot. She'd examine it closely for scratches or blemishes then ask, 'How much for this old thing?'

Janina's favourite spoon is the one Ada was weaned on. It has a long handle and a deep bowl. Her mother would load it with poached pears in honey, meat that had been stewing all day. It took her mother a long time to put it away with the rest of the baby things as Ada got older. 'I just like this one,' she'd say. 'It stirs well.' Ada knew that her mother was hoping it might be needed again one day. By packing the spoon away, she was also packing away her hopes of another child.

Ada insists on doing the washing-up. Aleksey comes out with more drinks, then demands they play a game of cards, which he wins because he changes the rules as he goes along.

'You got a six? Oh dear. Now you have to strip, Ada. Rules are rules.'

'I have a six,' Lech says.

'For you, it means put on more clothes,' Aleksey says quickly.

Ada has to force herself to leave. The old sofa with the hole is comfy, and Lech talks to the TV as if it can hear him; Aleksey is there with more cherry vodka and her tummy is full and round and happy.

'Thank you for a lovely evening,' she says, kissing Aleksey's cheek. She'd also kissed a snoring Lech's forehead, his thin strands of dandelion hair soft on her lips.

Aleksey holds his hand to his face, grinning.

'More salt in the stew next time, though,' she calls up to him from the bottom of the stairs.

'And then you'll have the sex with me?' he calls back.

'Never,' she says, smiling.

When Ada reaches her street, she sees that Birdie's house is lit up. She spots someone in the kitchen, the blur of someone else in the living room. Catches a flash of red hair. Ada thinks of the girl who knocked on her door. She wonders if she is there by choice or has been dragged over there by her mother. She thinks of Lech and Aleksey. Of how nice it was not to be alone. She should knock on Birdie's door, do her bit. The next time she passes, Ada promises herself, she will. No need to do so today, but tomorrow, or the next day. Maybe. 'Chicken,' says Wilbur's voice in her head. 'What is it you're scared of?'

Ada stumbles. She is slightly drunker than she thought. Her IKEA house is cold, but she doesn't do anything about it. She goes straight to bed in clothes that smell of cured meat and Polish spices, of home.

28

Birdie

Birdie's eyes don't want to open. Her eyelashes have stitched themselves together in her sleep. She has to prise them apart, like oysters from a shell. When done, her vision is pearly, the room a milky Earl Grey. The hour, too early.

Birdie tries not to think of how Arthur used to pull her body back into his when they woke at this time. Too late to go back to sleep, too early to get up. 'Only one thing for it, Birdie,' he'd say, his fingers dancing over her skin. She'd turn, eager in his arms. Birdie pulls the covers higher, thinks about all the hours she has lain awake in a different life in this bed, listening to her husband's quiet snores. Praying for a miracle to be taking place inside her. She thinks about all the quiet tears she'd shed over the years for a daughter she would never hold. Suddenly she can hear Frankie's voice in her mind, telling her to get up and feed her dog. Birdie's maudlin thoughts can have a lie-in. Birdie needs to get on. 'Stay there,' she tells them.

She moves slowly. Painkillers on an empty stomach make Birdie feel tipsy. Displaced. A little ghost, wafting about in her nightgown, one foot already on the other side. Frankie is back in Bristol visiting her grandmother. Without her daily visits, Birdie floats through the weekend like a hot-air balloon over the Downs. Finds herself in rooms she did not plan to be in, holding items she didn't notice she was reaching for. Arthur's golf club. Rose's summer sandals. A half-hemmed skirt. Birdie had meant to sort it all out. Make neat piles of her past, label it in capitals and have it collected by a charity. But every time she tries, something stops her. An old diary of Rose's. Arthur's gardening secateurs, the ones he always lost. 'I found them,' Birdie calls to no one. The sun comes in through the window, crowns her as she sits listening to the clock on the mantelpiece tick. A stopwatch counting down.

Once upon a time, time used to fly. She and Arthur were forever late to train stations and appointments, chasing clocks like a runaway tissue on the breeze, Birdie's skirt flapping as they ran. 'Where did it go?' they used to say to one another. When Arthur and Rose left, time changed. Birdie has sat through never-ending nights. Days that forgot to draw in. Suns that refused to set and midnights that lingered. Time is all Birdie has had for so long, her hands are sticky with it. Hours and years are clogged up under her wedding band. A whole decade under her thumbnail.

She shuffles to the back door. Outside, the earth is yawning, waking up for spring. Bulbs push at the soil, like Audrey's nose in Birdie's palm, demanding attention, praise. The trees are in bud, pregnant with petals. The grass glows neon in the morning light. The garden mocks Birdie with its beauty, its immortality.

'Did you think I'd expired?' Mother Nature seems to ask her. 'Don't you know that death in nature is reversible? Trees may be stripped of their clothing, the ground may freeze. Green may turn to orange, brown to black. You may see decay and think the world is rotting. But you are wrong. I have fooled you. I have come back to life from nothing. I was only ever sleeping.'

Slightly high on her empty stomach and a morphine patch, Birdie thinks that it's not the sun's warmth that brings back the leaves, the birds and the buds, but human sadness. Grief is love with nowhere to go, after all. How much of it there must be. Lingering in the folds of curtains, under laundry baskets and in the far corners of pantries. Collected, it could easily power the spring, shake the blossoms into summer. It could power entire cities, send a man to the moon.

Does Birdie understand life more now that she is dying? Standing here alone, she can't help but wonder what it was all for. She has accumulated a lot of stuff, but none of it has any worth. She's not leaving anything *good* behind her, no legacy. When Birdie goes, her lineage goes with her. As though she and Rose were never here at all. *Poof* go the Clarke twins. *Poof.*

Birdie thinks in colours. Her white wedding day, the itchy veil, her satin shoes. Rose in yellow, shining like the sun. Arthur's sky-blue tie. Her mother's purple hat. The peach maternity sewing patterns Birdie ordered. She thinks of her black typewriter, whizzing and clicking. Of her conker-brown shoes. The rustle of green tissue paper round freshly cut flowers. 'Ah, the sweet smell of plant genitalia,' Rose would say, just as Birdie lowered her nose inside the bouquet. Birdie thinks of the *And Miss Carter Wore Pink* book that she and Rose loved as children. Read it until the pages disintegrated. Until they wore Miss Carter away.

Birdie thinks in sounds. Rose's laugh, a bell tinkling. Arthur's cufflinks on the bedside table. Leather boots through autumn leaves. Snow falling off shed roofs. Things that Birdie will never hear again.

'I'm ready,' Birdie calls dramatically to no one. 'Take me.'

Frankie finds her on the sofa, cuddling a clay pot that Rose made at school, Arthur's golf hat on her head and Audrey by her feet. 'Are you okay?' Frankie asks uncertainly.

'Fine.' Birdie drags herself into a sitting position. She is embarrassed at being caught in her nightdress, at how very happy she is to see Frankie. 'I was just napping.'

'Min says naps are for babies and idlers,' Frankie says.

'How is your grandmother?'

'Fine. We watched *Crimewatch* and went to the market. Min likes to haggle for her food. Shall I put the kettle on?'

Frankie likes Birdie's kettle. It's an old-fashioned one that goes on the hob and whistles when it's ready.

Birdie wants to tell Frankie that there is no need for her to keep coming over. That she's been fine without her. It's a lie, though. Frankie was away for two days, and Birdie had lain down hoping that death would come and collect her, like a box of recycling.

Frankie goes round turning lights on, filling the bungalow with noise and colour. She turns up the radio, switches on the gas fire. Music spills out from the kitchen, notes dancing in the dusty air. She makes tea and buttery toast. Tells Birdie all about Bristol. Puts on a documentary about killer whales, then talks all the way through it. When she says she has to go home, Birdie looks up and sees that the clocks have started working again, are flying forwards. She wishes she could lift the glass, put her finger on the little hand, wind it back to five p.m. when Frankie appeared. Wind it back by years and years and years.

'Mum is going to the big shop after work tomorrow. Do you need anything?' Frankie asks.

Birdie jots down a list in shorthand. Frankie, who has been studying Pitman, frowns as she reads it out loud. 'Milk,' she says, 'cheese.'

'Good,' Birdie says encouragingly.

'Bread, eggs.'

'Carry on.'

'An entire stuffed swan on a bed of pickled tongue, mousse of game fowl with cream and sweetbreads, a pyramid of rose and apricot jelly, upside-down pineapple cake and four apple soufflés.'

Another sound that Birdie hadn't thought she'd hear again. Her own laugh. Like a clown's nose squeaking, like a dropped horn. Like happiness.

29

Jane

JANE CAN'T STOP PLAYING back the conversation she'd had with Suki in Bristol. Suki hadn't called Jane, of course, she'd called Min. Jane had just got to the phone first.

'Min?' Suki had asked, and Jane's stupid heart did a little cartwheel at the sound of her sister's voice.

'No, it's Jane.'

'Oh,' Suki said, then 'Hi.'

'Hi,' Jane said, hating the stilted awkwardness between them. She could hear music in the background. Wondered where Suki was calling from. A bar, a yacht?

'How's Min?' Suki asked. 'How's her knee?'

'Fine,' Jane said. 'I mended it with Sellotape.'

'Seriously?' Suki asked, where once she would have laughed.

'Min is fine. Her knee is fine,' Jane said, slightly irritably. She wanted to tell Suki about the missing button on their mum's blouse, but she didn't know how. Was scared to in case Suki still did nothing. Still refused to come home for a visit. Jane couldn't bear to think of her sister being that cold, so removed from them.

'How's Frankie?' Suki said, after a beat.

'Frankie,' Jane said, 'is also fine. Amazing, actually. Still into taxidermy. Plans to be an embalmer. She and Min are currently watching *Crimewatch*. Min is convinced she's going to see the local plumber on it soon.'

Suki said nothing, so Jane prattled on. 'She made us eat our fish and chips on the wall outside. Justine said Min said I'd be back home soon.'

'Lying bitch,' Suki said automatically.

'Utter cowpat,' Jane agreed, smiling into the beige handset. 'So, how's the job? Min says you had another promotion.'

'It's amazing,' Suki said, 'really great. I'm so happy!'

When had Suki started talking in exclamation marks?

'Oh, well, good,' Jane said. 'Great!'

A long pause follows. Jane thinks desperately of something to say to fill it.

'An old lady peed on me last week. It went through the holes in my Crocs!' she says.

Once Suki would have laughed. Told her the holes in Crocs are where your dignity seeps through. But all she said now was 'Okay. Well, tell Min I called. I'll ring again soon,' then put the phone down before Jane could say anything else. Jane tried not to cry. Spent the rest of the weekend thinking of all the things she should have said. Kicking herself for being so chatty. Why did she mention being peed on? Why didn't she tell Suki that she was having a great time, meeting loads of cool people? Because Suki didn't ask you, Jane thinks now. Because Suki doesn't care any more. Because she's not your friend.

On the train back to Brighton, Frankie had buried her head in her *Science Weekly*, while Jane looked around her, needing a distraction. She tried to work out the lives of her fellow passengers from the small clues they offered. Wedding rings and shoes. Snack choices and the state of their fingernails. Some people were sitting upright, spine straight while others were oblivious, already back home in their heads, their game faces sliding off into the dirty moquette seats, mouths slack in sleep.

When she and Suki had gone travelling, it was Jane who'd sat up while Suki snored on her shoulder. Jane who'd stayed alert, made sure no one stole their belongings, that they didn't miss their stop.

All those trains carrying them forward. Suki has kept moving on, Jane realizes now, and she needs to do the same. Brighton is just the start. A shiny new life was never going to just fall into Jane's lap. What did she expect? That people would sniff her out, like dogs do in parks? Thanks to Frankie's obsession with Audrey, Jane knows how much dogs learn from smelling another's urine. But Jane is not a bulldog. She can't go and piss up a lamppost and hope it will bring her like-minded friends. She needs to go out and find them, to make things happen. She needs to find a way to feel less lonely. Frankie once told her that bodies emit tiny amounts of light that rise and fall at different times of the day, invisible to the naked eye. Jane pictures Brighton, glowing from the bioluminescence of groups of people, of shoulders connecting, everyone sparking like glow worms. She thinks of how, together, people are briefly, iridescently bigger than themselves alone.

'How would you feel about coming with me to an art class or something one evening, Frankie?' Jane asks, when Frankie gets off the phone to Min.

'No, ta,' Frankie says, picking up a book. 'I'll go to Birdie's instead.'

'I thought it could be something we'd do together.'

'I just said. I don't want to. I like going next door.'

'You do remember that Birdie is poorly, don't you, Frankie?' Jane asks gently.

'Yes, of course,' Frankie snaps, the blinds of her face rolling down as they do every time Jane brings it up. Perhaps trying to talk about it now, so soon after leaving Min, is not the time.

'You really don't mind if I go to an art class, then?' Jane says.

'No,' Frankie says, licking a finger to turn a page, then wiping it on her leggings.

'We should do something together, though. Something fun. How about a roller disco?'

'No.'

'Oh, come on,' Jane cajoles.

'Mum, the potential risks are endless. A broken ankle. A severed finger . . .' Frankie says, voice getting louder.

'That sounds a bit far—'

'The bacteria from shared boots,' Frankie interrupts. 'The germs from the floor, which we will land on all the time because neither of us can skate. Complete strangers reaching out and grabbing me. The lights. The music. The—'

'Okay, okay, I get it. No roller disco,' Jane says, swallowing a sigh. Maybe one of them getting out of their comfort zone is enough. And maybe Birdie isn't a replacement Min. Maybe Frankie has actually managed to do what Jane wants to do so badly: she's made a friend.

30

Ada

WILBUR IS ALREADY AT the bench when Ada arrives. He greets her with a single nod, then breaks into a trot, which turns into a run by the time they reach the sorbet-coloured beach huts. It is five thirty a.m. and Brighton is half asleep. The world is muted by mist. The sky and the sea are asleep in one another's arms. Ada's feet are a blur. She feels herself in motion. Wilbur's tread is light, his breath even beside her. Ada can picture him in the army, steady, strong and brave. She thinks of how he didn't see leaving as giving up and wants to ask him how. If she could talk, she'd tell him that sometimes she wants to hang up her white coat, her cancer-blasting weapons that often misfire, and find a job that hurts less. She wants to tell him about her farm. About the feel of a warm egg in a cold palm. Of seeing a lamb licked clean by its mother. She wants to look at his hands, his spine, the soles of his feet. She has not been as fascinated by another human being since she met Lidka's baby. What else can you do, Wilbur? she thinks.

The balustrades on the promenade are flaking with rust, but the Victorian bandstand gleams with its ornate cream cornices and racing-green trim. In the daytime, it is used for wedding photos. A bride in a white dress smiling on the best day of her life. At night, the homeless come, fill the corners with blue shopping bags full of cans and reclaim the space for themselves. Drink to oblivion. Until they could be anywhere at all. Ada likes the contrast. Loves that Brighton is beautiful and broken at the same time. Sometimes she can't imagine being anywhere else, and sometimes she misses home so much that she has to rub her side as though easing a stitch.

They run all the way to Carats café, where Ada smells bacon, waffles and coffee. Her stomach growls.

'How bad would it be if we stopped for a fried-egg sandwich?' Wilbur asks as he slows, pressing buttons on his big wristwatch.

'Very bad,' Ada pants.

'I'll go and order, shall I?'

Ada watches Wilbur as he walks into the café. She notices how his shirt clings to his spine. How attractive he is. Can he possibly find her attractive too, even like this? She is wearing a pair of shorts she's had since university, odd running socks, because it was dark when she got dressed, and a T-shirt she got for free at a conference. Her hair is pulled back into a knot on the top of her head and sweat pools in every dip and crevice. Wilbur laughs at something the pretty girl on the counter says and Ada feels a pang in her gut that she decides must be hunger.

When Wilbur reappears and puts down her plate, Ada picks up her sandwich and crams in a huge bite. She is cross with him, and herself, is determined not to be too self-conscious, not to be such a *girl* in front of him. She dabs at the spill on her T-shirt with a napkin. The food is almost as good as her mother's. It has nothing to do with Wilbur's company.

Wilbur laughs at her trying to wipe away the stain and says, 'We called them egg banjos in the forces.' When he swallows, his Adam's apple bobs, like a float going under the waves.

'What?' Ada says distractedly, around another bite. Has anything ever tasted better than this?

Wilbur mimics biting into a sandwich, then strums his fingers up and down the top of his shirt. 'Because of the way the egg drips on to your . . .' He looks at Ada's chest, then looks away quickly.

Ada blushes, pulses, glows.

'Why does food always taste better when you eat outside?' Wilbur asks, tucking into his own plateful.

'Or after you've run a half-marathon,' Ada says. She can run half a marathon now. The knowledge gives her a little sizzle, a sense of achievement she's not felt in a long time. On an endorphin high after her first ten-kilometre run, Ada had called Ania to ask her if she'd sponsor her. She didn't over-think it, just picked up her phone and dialled.

'Ada! *Jak się masz?*'

Ania was pleased to hear from her. She asked about Ada's work, talked about her children, but there was no competitive edge to her voice. She drove the conversation eagerly, as though she was the one who'd phoned. As though they were still the best of friends. 'Do you still go down to the beach?' Ania asked.

When Ania lived in Brighton, they used to head towards

the pier after work, with a disposable barbecue, sausages and sauerkraut. Even when it was freezing. After they'd eaten, they'd toss pebbles into an empty gherkin jar. Lie on their backs on the damp stones and look up at the stars, blinking down at them like a thousand cameras capturing the moment. Like paparazzi. Like they were something special. Life wasn't quite real back then. Ada and Ania were still training for it. There was always someone to ask if they were not sure about something. It was like having a parent to go to, a teacher to check your work. And when the day was finished, what had happened was forgotten instantly. The night was theirs alone, the seriousness of their hospital shift shedding itself like snakeskin as Ada changed from scrubs into a skirt. She could morph into more than one version of herself back then.

'Sometimes,' she lied.

'How are Aleksey and Lech?' Ania asked.

'They are good. Same as ever.'

'You agreed to go out with him yet?'

'Never.'

'Oh, Ada, when are you going to settle down?' Ania sighed.

'You sound like my mother,' Ada shot back.

'She misses you,' Ania said.

'How do you know?' Ada asked.

'Because she calls me. To see if I've heard from you. To ask about my girls. She knits these tiny little cardigans for Alina and Kasienka. They're so beautiful. It must take her hours.'

'Let me guess, she delivers them in a basket with home-made soap?' Ada asked.

'Best soap in the world,' Ania replied. 'So, do you think you'll come back home soon for a visit?'

'Maybe,' Ada said.

'After the marathon?' Ania said, as though holding Ada to it.

'Maybe. Yes, listen, Ania, I've got to go. Speak soon.'

'So, what made you want to be an oncologist?' Wilbur asks, when their plates are empty.

Ada takes a sip of water. She has a stock answer for this question, but she's forgotten it, so tells him the truth instead. Wilbur was truthful with her, after all.

'I planned to be a doctor. Was for a while, back in Poland. Loved it too, until my mother's friend came to see me,' Ada says, looking down at her hands. 'She had cancer. It was too late to do anything about it . . .' Ada shrugs. 'But I thought, well . . .' She trails off.

'Thought you'd specialize in it so you could save other people. Stop it happening to them? To your own family?'

It's like he's read her diary. Ada looks up at him and frowns. Wilbur smiles at her. 'We share the same enemies. My dad lost his best friend in a war,' he says. 'I think I thought being a medic could bring him back somehow.'

He traces his finger along the grain of the wood on the bench, traces the whorls. Ada wonders what those fingers would feel like on her skin. How they would light up her bones.

'Dad used to tell me all these stories about him and Zeke. Girls and cars and music. Drunken escapades. Hiding in the bushes from the police. Stealing a milk float. That sort of thing.' Wilbur smiles, then adds, 'The only time Dad was happy was when he was talking about Zeke. About life back then. As though the best years of his life had already been and gone before I came along.'

Ada couldn't imagine how that felt. She knew she was the best thing that had ever happened to her mother. Janina told her so daily. Love was stitched into all her clothes, seasoned all her meals, scented her sheets.

'Zeke died in Iraq. Dad's injuries meant he got early release. Mum was his nurse in the hospital. I don't even know if they'd have stayed together if she hadn't got pregnant with me. I think Zeke was my dad's true love. He didn't seem to want to live without him.' He looks up and laughs hollowly. 'Sorry, why am I telling you this depressing story?'

Because I want to hear it, Ada thinks. I want to know everything about you. 'Go on,' she says.

Wilbur shrugs. 'Not much more to say. I enlisted, soon as I could. Thought I'd make my dad proud. Maybe I did. He died of lung cancer the year before I left the army.'

Ada has heard a lot of sad stories in her life. This one is no different, but it still hurts. She wants to rest her head on Wilbur's shoulder, press herself against him, absorb some of his pain. People never die from not being loved, she thinks, from not being enough or being too much. What a world it would be if they did. 'So now you're trying to bring him back from the dead?' she asks.

'Something like that,' Wilbur says, tidying up the paper sachets of sugar, stacking them neatly just as he does with their patient files.

'When you're not playing badminton, running marathons, or joining quiz teams,' Ada adds.

Wilbur laughs. 'Are you still jealous about that?'

'I'm not jealous,' Ada says, but she is. Not about her lack of invitations, but of Wilbur enjoying them without her.

Wilbur looks at her. His eyes are too green in the sun, his face is too open. Her heart is too wide open right now.

'Ada . . .' he says.

'We should go,' she says, getting up quickly. 'I've got stuff to do.' She busies herself, tying her hair back up, checking her shoelaces.

Ada offers Wilbur cash. He shakes his head and says, 'Let me do this for you, Ada, please.' Ada turns her face towards the harbour, her cheeks hot.

They cannot run back on full stomachs, so they walk instead. The silence is not awkward, despite all they have shared. Ada thinks about what Wilbur said. That they have the same enemies. For so long, Ada has felt alone with so much. When Wilbur says goodbye, he rests his hand briefly on her arm. Ada feels it, warm and reassuring, for the rest of the day.

31

Birdie

THERE IS A BASKET on Birdie's doorstep with her name in messy writing, nothing else, just *Birdie Greenwing*. She looks up and down the street but cannot see anyone. Inside there is no note. Birdie had just opened the door to take the bin outside, and there it was. She lays the items on her kitchen table, frowning. A bunch of dried lavender, a bar of very expensive-looking soap, studded with rose petals. A loaf of bread, so heavy that it falls from Birdie's hand and clonks on to the table with a hollow *thunk*, like the cast she'd had cut from her foot. And last but not least, some oddly shaped parcels that look like elf ears and smell of stewed fruit.

Who could have brought Birdie this? It's not Ivy's doing, Birdie knows that much. Ivy uses the words *Neighbourhood Watch* as an excuse to pry. To judge other people, but never to help. Ivy's latest campaign is a petition demanding Mr Treebus at number nine remove the old caravan from his front garden. Ivy calls it an eyesore, but Birdie doesn't agree. Maybe it's full of treasures Mr Treebus can't bear to part with. Maybe he would love to move the old caravan but has no one to help him.

Nowhere in Ivy's many letters of complaint are there any offers of assistance. There is a lot of 'It has come to our attention that' or 'We write, again, with regard to the mattress on your drive' but never 'We notice your recycling bin is overflowing, the weeds in your garden are waist high and you went to the shop in your slippers yesterday with a banana instead of your wallet. Would you like some help?'

Ivy used to comment on the fact that Arthur lived with two women. Ivy lived alone, of course, in a house that looked like Mr Tidy's from the Mr Men books. Her lawn was cut with razor-like precision. No plants. No weeds. A sign saying 'No cold callers, junk mail, salespeople, canvassers or religious bodies welcome' was laminated and pinned to her front door. Her living-room windows were scrubbed daily with vinegar and newspaper. All the better to peer out of, Rose used to say. Ivy, Birdie realizes, would know who had left this basket, but Birdie would rather die than ask her, literally.

She hacks into the bread. It's still warm and is full of nuts and seeds. Birdie judged it too quickly. With a smear of butter and some jam, it's delicious. But who baked it for her? Who took the time to measure out the ingredients, to sieve and roll and allow it to rise? Birdie wishes she knew who to thank for giving her back her appetite for the first time in days.

Breakfast eaten, plate washed up, Audrey walked and fed, Birdie finds herself at a loose end. She has no pain today, feels oddly fine in fact. On a whim, Birdie dons her coat, and slicks a lick of pearly pink across her lips. 'Back soon,' she tells Audrey. Her dog grunts but goes back to the sitting room and turns in her basket three times. A loud snore soon follows.

*

'I just came in to thank you for my lovely parcel,' Birdie says to Connie half an hour later, 'and bring back your basket.' She places it on the counter.

Connie looks puzzled. 'Sorry, but that isn't my basket,' she says.

'Oh,' Birdie replies. It was a long shot. Connie normally serves scones and cakes, not whatever those odd earlobe things were. Also, there is no way the bread would still have been warm if Connie had had to deliver it. It would be, God bless her, mouldy.

Perhaps Birdie knew this all along, but it has given her an excuse to get out. To sit in the busy little WRVS café, listening to the hiss of bacon frying and feet slapping across the floor in the hospital café. To watch nurses whizz by in their squeaky shoes and doctors in white coats that flap like capes behind them. Birdie likes the way receptionists call out names like a game of bingo, and the phone is always ringing. She likes the friendly porters pushing along sleeping people with masks over their faces and their toes peeking out. This close to death, Birdie can appreciate how much life there is in hospitals.

'Sit down and rest that ankle,' Connie says, slow as molasses. 'I'll bring you a nice cup of tea.'

Birdie wonders about Connie's feet. About how many cups of tea Connie has made in her life, and how many people she has served. If there is anyone to look after her when she gets home from looking after everyone else. 'Are you married, Connie?' Birdie asks.

'I was,' Connie says, wiping her brow with a tissue she pulls from her sleeve. Birdie thinks of Arthur and his magic tricks. It is never the big things that hurt Birdie, adverts for funerals or life insurance. Those old women sitting alone in the Help the Aged adverts. It's men's oversized hankies and the smell of Arthur's deodorant on someone that's not him.

'Love of my life,' Connie says. 'When he died, I wanted to stop the world like I was on a bus, and could just ping the bell and get off, but it wasn't my time.' Connie smiles sadly.

Her teeth are tiny. Birdie can see through the cracks. She imagines heartbreak, coating her molars like plaque.

'So, I had to find something else to do while I waited.' Connie casts a hand back towards her shining urns, her display of cakes and sandwiches. 'I remembered seeing a flier pinned up by the hospital door, asking for volunteers, and I thought, Why not? Best decision I ever made, apart from marrying my Ray.'

Birdie didn't notice anything after Arthur and Rose died, only herself. Only her grief, her pain. She spent her time wishing that Death would realize he'd forgotten something and come back in his carriage like that Emily Dickinson poem. She became a walking coffin. Her vital organs were still working, but the rest of her had turned to wood. Helping other people had been the last thing on her mind. Shame stains her cheeks pink. 'Do you ever have a day off?' Birdie asks.

'I'll sleep when I'm dead,' Connie says, with a laugh. 'Why? You looking for a job?'

Birdie almost laughs too. 'Connie,' she says, 'I've got—'

'I know what you've got, lady.' Connie tuts. 'You think I don't know what cancer looks like? I work alongside it every day. Got some of my own in here somewhere.' She pats her pockets as though looking for a pen. 'Hasn't stopped me. Doesn't have to stop you.'

It's ridiculous, but Birdie lets the idea play out in her head like a film trailer. Could she work here? Would she be able to manage it? Standing up for too long hurts and she gets tired, and there is Audrey to think about, but—

'You could sit there by the till,' Connie tells her, 'on that little stool and take the money. Just take the money. How about that?'

Birdie thinks of her old typewriter, the buzz and ping and whizzing sounds. *Mr Dickens will see you now*. Using a till might feel a bit like that. Birdie feels something fizz inside her.

'You can have a trial right now if you like,' Connie says, 'if you've nothing better to do, that is.'

Birdie looks down at her mug: 'Deeds not Words'. 'I haven't, actually,' she says.

She's not sure where the next three hours go. She's too lost in the sound of loose change, and a card machine that is tricky to use, but when mastered, whirls out a receipt with a most satisfying gurgle. Birdie pulls thin paper from its jagged teeth, hands it over to her customers with a smile. 'Thank you, come again.'

Connie is just asking her if she wants a jacket potato with cheese and beans for lunch when she hears a clipped voice say, 'Mrs Greenwing?' It's the same one she heard in her garden when she fell. Birdie looks up and sees her oncologist, Ada Kowalska, is next in the queue. She looks different from how Birdie remembers her. Her face is glowing, and the bags are gone from under her eyes. She looks younger somehow.

'Hello, Ada,' Connie says. 'The usual?'

'Please,' Ada says, smiling at Connie, then looking back at Birdie. 'Are you working here now?'

'Yep, she's my new assistant,' Connie says, handing Ada a mug that reads 'You are never alone if you have demons', 'and already, I don't know how I coped without her.' Birdie can't help but grin a little and pat her hair a couple of times.

'How are you, Mrs Greenwing?' Ada asks.

'I'm fine,' Birdie says, and means it. 'You came to help me, didn't you? When I fell in the garden.'

'I didn't do much,' Ada says quickly.

'Yes, you did.' Birdie thinks of the warm hand on her scalp. Of Ada's quiet voice in her ear telling her everything was going to be okay. That she was not alone.

'And you're the one who left me that basket?' Birdie says.

Ada blushes. 'I . . .'

'The bread was wonderful. *Is* wonderful. I had some with strawberry conserve.'

'At home,' Ada says, 'in Poland, we have it with rose jam.'

'Sounds wonderful,' Birdie says. 'Do you make that too?' Maybe she could buy some for Jane.

'No, but my mother does,' Ada says, something flashing across her face too quickly for Birdie to name.

'Well,' Birdie says, taking the money Ada hands over, her happy fingers pressing at buttons on the till, 'thank you and please come again.'

Ada stands, looking at the change in her hand for a moment, then back up at Birdie. 'I'm really happy to see you are doing so well, Mrs Greenwing,' she says, in her clipped voice.

'Thank you,' Birdie says. She has the oddest sensation that

the tables have turned. That Ada is the one who needs something from Birdie, but what?

'She's a one, that Ada,' Connie says, watching her walk away. 'You can smell the sadness coming off her. Poor child. Anyway, are you coming back tomorrow, Birdie?'

'Oh, yes, please,' Birdie says, 'if that's okay?'

'It's better than okay. And it looks as though you'll be needing this.' Connie hands Birdie a pinny that says, 'I'm a WRVS volunteer. What's your superpower?'

'Oh,' Birdie says, taking it as though it were made of glass.

'Welcome to the team,' Connie says.

32

Jane

MIN'S BACK IS AS straight as a poker as she walks down the platform. Her suitcase is new, and worryingly large. She's only supposed to be coming for the weekend. When Jane goes to take it, Min slaps her hand away.

'Hello, Min!' Frankie says. 'Is that a new cardigan? It's very . . . snazzy.'

Jane sees her mother's cheeks go pink in delight. 'I got it in the sale. I can get you one if you like. It's not itchy wool. It's the good stuff.'

Jane hadn't meant to invite her mother back so soon. It was that bloody missing button on Min's blouse, the lonely mug on the draining board, blue eyes looking at her as though to say, 'As long as *you* are happy, Jane.'

That image of Min, all alone, pecked at Jane as she tended other people's mothers. As she passed them tablets and helped them sip water, checked pads and adjusted pillows. When she called their worried daughters for them and to say the operation had been a success. That, yes, they could come in for a visit. Each time someone pressed the orange call button, Jane thought of Min. Of her tough-as-teak, hard-as-horn mother. She's a tank, Jane told herself. One of those road-sweeper trucks that don't care who they are holding up or how awkward they're being. She's a bloody honey badger.

'I'm fine,' Min barked, when Jane called her from the toilet cubicle, seized with a sudden panic that Min was lying on a floor somewhere, passed out. 'Why are you whispering?'

'I'm not supposed to be on my phone,' Jane hissed.

'Well, why are you, then?'

'I'm checking on you!'

'It's you who needs a bleddy check!' Min's indignation was a relief. She was as cantankerous as ever. Jane sagged against the cubicle wall. 'What's going on with you, Jane? Have you been smoking those jazz cigarettes? Whole of Brighton reeked to high heaven of the stuff.'

'No, I've not.'

'Well, why can't you check your phone at work? What if Frankie needs you?'

Jane thought of Sadie's rules, of what her mother would say in response to them, and a smile she didn't know she was holding in fell out of the pocket of her mouth. 'I'm fine, Mum, honestly.' There was a silence down the line. Jane never called Min 'Mum'. Neither did Suki, nor even Frankie. As children, the words 'Min' and 'Mum' had sounded so alike that Jane and Suki had just gone with the one their dad used. 'I'd better go,' Jane whispered.

'Don't let them bully you, Jane!' Min roared loudly, as if hoping she might be overheard. 'You always let people walk all over you.'

It was so ironic, coming from Min, that Jane had to stifle a laugh. 'Okay.'

'I mean it. Don't you go doing anyone's dirty work for them.'

This, from the woman who'd cleaned Jane's oven, crusted with grime from the previous tenants. Who had been seen scrubbing the pavement outside her house more than once. Who'd dedicated her life to tidying up after other people as a way of showing love or being useful. 'I'll call you later.' Jane hung up, feeling better. Min was fine. Min was in-mince-able. Then Jane watched an old woman try to eat her dinner without her teeth in, remembered the lonely mug, the loud TV. The greasy glasses and that bloody button.

Sighing, she picked up the phone again. 'Hey, Min. When are you next coming for a visit?'

'I'll book the train now,' her mother said, in a rush.

Now, Jane throws herself at her sturdy mother, into her little arms. Into her carbolic smell, her tightly pinned-back hair. Her tears are wet on Min's warm neck. A wrinkled hand reaches out to pat Jane on the back.

'It's like that bit in *E.T.*,' Frankie says. '"Elllioooot."'

'I'm so pleased you're here, Mum.' Jane snorts.

'Soppy sod,' Min says, squeezing her. 'Let's get out of this bleddy station. Have you looked up at all the seagull plop on the rails?'

'Guano,' Frankie says.

'You say guano, I say—'

'Shit?' Jane suggests.

'Jane Brown! I raised you better than that,' Min says. 'Frankie, cover your ears.'

They walk slowly towards the gate, among commuters and students, suits and uniforms, suitcases and a man in a caftan, selling badly carved wooden toys. An old man is playing the rainbow-painted piano that lives next to the coffee shop, hammering away on the keys.

'Bleddy crowds,' Min says, as they walk out into the late sunshine, 'bunch of beatniks.'

'What's a beatnik?' Frankie asks.

'One of them,' Min says, pointing to a busker who's singing 'Hey Jude'. 'Now, tell me about this girl with bits in her braces, Frankie. Do I need to come to the school?' Min shakes a tiny fist, and Jane wants to stop time for a second. Press this moment into clay and pin it to her wall. Her, Frankie and Min against the world.

All the way to the bus stop, Min comments on the short skirts and the stains on the pavement, but also on a pair of shoes in a shop window that she might like to look at, and when they pass the Taj grocer, she is impressed by the size of the cabbages on display, the reasonable price of red apples.

'See?' Frankie says. 'It's not so bad here, really.'

'I never said it was,' Min says.

'What do you fancy for dinner?' Jane asks.

'Fish and chips,' Min says quickly, pulling out her purse. 'My treat.'

Jane is still smiling when she goes out to get their takeaway. It makes other people smile back at her. Maybe that is what Jane has been doing wrong all this time, walking around with a face like a slapped arse. Suki perfected her resting-bitch face early on, but Jane only ever looked constipated when she tried to look tough.

'Right, out you go, Jane,' Min says, when they've finished their tea, which Min made them eat in the garden. 'Let me spend some time with Frankie alone, so we can talk about you.'

'I'm fine here,' Jane says, flopping on to the sofa and picking up a magazine.

Min flaps her hands at her. 'No, don't sit down there. I want to wash those cushions.'

'I'm tired,' Jane says.

'You are too young to be tired,' Min says. 'Now sling your hook.'

Jane sighs, but showers and brushes her hair. Pulls on her favourite jeans, a vest she stole from Suki years ago.

Spring is in bloom in the Pavilion gardens. The earth is the colour of chocolate, shot through with yellow and purple, like a child's drawing of fireworks. Sticky buds bulge on branches. Everything is fertile, fecund. Jane walks along the winding paths, looks at the dome-shaped rotundas, the minarets and pinnacles. Thinks of when she and Suki saw the Taj Mahal for the first time.

'I thought I'd feel slightly more overwhelmed than this,' Jane had panted. It was hot and she had sunburn. Her backpack was heavy. These thoughts outweighed her wonder.

They had stood for a minute staring. 'Min would have the time of her life dusting it,' Jane added.

'Mm, shall we go back now?' Suki suggested.

'Good idea,' Jane said. 'Quick photo first.'

Jane takes in the blue azalea bushes next to her, the

clusters of buttery daffodils. The red and pink tulips, like a row of upturned lips, hoping to be kissed. She thinks about how impossible things seem possible in the spring. How, for the first time in for ever, it's not Suki she wishes were here with her to share this moment. Jane pulls out her phone, sends the message before she can think twice about it, then waits, her heart in her mouth.

Helen meets her by the waltzer at the back of the pier. She's wearing lipstick. Helen never wears lipstick. The thought that she might have put it on for Jane makes Jane feel as though a fist has reached into her chest and squeezed her heart.

'Hi,' Helen says lightly.

'Hi,' Jane says, scuffing the toe of her trainer along one of the old planks on the pier. Frankie would fill the awkward silence with facts. Suki would not feel awkward at all, but Jane is neither of these people. She is just herself. 'I wondered if you'd like to go on the waltzer with me,' Jane blurts out, forcing herself to meet Helen's eyes.

'About time,' Helen says, her lipsticked mouth curving into a smile. 'I thought you'd never bloody ask.'

Jane's fingers fumble with the seatbelt. Helen is wedged next to her. Elbow in Jane's rib, thigh pressed to thigh. This close up, Helen's face is like a poem that Jane wants to learn by heart. So this is how Tom felt when he first saw Min.

She watches Helen's face, a blur of lips and teeth and shining cheeks, laughing as the attendant spins them faster. This is what I've been waiting for, Jane realizes. What I've been missing. Helen's hand in hers. For Helen to look at Jane like that. To feel her body throb like this.

When Jane finally gets home, gone midnight, and sees the ambulance, her first thought is that it must be for Birdie, but then she realizes it's her own front door that's open. Her house the paramedics have gone into. Her mother on a stretcher, being carried out. Her daughter following, hands in her mouth, trying not to cry.

33

Ada

When Ada told her parents she was leaving Poland, it was like she'd shot her mother. Ada could see the pain on Janina's face as the words went right through her. Could see the bloody hole they left. 'England,' she'd said, 'but why?'

Ada couldn't tell them she was leaving because she was scared that they would die if she stayed. She couldn't tell them that she wanted more, and less at the same time. Instead, she told them what an amazing opportunity it was. 'Opportunity' was not a word often used in their village. Her mother had frowned in confusion, looked to her husband as if he could fix it. Ada couldn't look at her father at all.

That night, he had closed the living-room door, just as he used to do when Ada was a child and they wanted to have an adult conversation. Ada had sat on the stairs, just like she used to, picking at the skin round her nails, listening to her father tell her mother that it would all be okay. That she had to let Ada go.

The next morning, at breakfast, her mother had served Ada blueberry pancakes with sour cream. Her hair, Ada saw, had been plaited back from her face extra tightly, and her smile was slightly too forced.

'So, England,' her mother had said, 'it's exciting.'

'Minka,' Ada said, itchy with guilt. She wanted to tell her mother how scared she was, how much she would miss her. But words like that were weak, and Ada was raised to be strong.

'Lots to organize before you go.' Janina had looked down at the plate in her hands as though reading from a book.

She had helped Ada pack, bought her new nightclothes, and knitted her fingerless gloves, but she didn't go with Ada and her father to the airport. She said goodbye in the kitchen, two hard kisses on each of Ada's cheeks, one quick sniff at Ada's leather jacket, and then she turned back towards her stove. For a moment Ada wanted to change her mind. To tell her mother she wouldn't go. That she'd stay with her. That if only one of them could be happy, it could be Janina, not her.

'Ada,' her dad had said. He was holding her suitcase, his lips set in a thin line. 'It's time.'

He drove her in his friend's old car. The passenger-side window would not close, so Ada sat on damp newspaper. The seat smelt of mould. Her father crunched the gears and muttered about how badly built the car was, turned on the windscreen wipers instead of the lights, pressed the horn when he was reversing. Ada felt as though she was abandoning them to a battle they could not possibly win without her.

Their goodbye was stunted, awkward. Her father, who'd carried her on his shoulders, and slept next to her in the hay barn, who'd whittled her toys and let her tame a pig, looked down at his feet when she kissed him. Shoved money into her hand. Patted her roughly and then pushed her away, like he did to the cows he knew he wasn't going to keep.

She thinks about Wilbur's father. Of what it must have been like to be ignored by the person who was supposed to love you the most. Wilbur had grown up feeling unnecessary while Ada had felt almost too important. She thinks of how her mother would adore Wilbur. Would make him plate after plate of pancakes, kick her father out of the best chair. Nice dream, Ada, she tells herself. Nice dream.

She is in her pyjamas this time when the knock comes on her door. It's Frankie again, her hands balled into fists, face pale underneath her freckles.

'Birdie?' Ada says, hating the tremor in her voice. No, she thinks, please God, not yet. Ada just saw her at the WRVS café. She looked well. She looked great. She was enjoying Ada's bread. You fool, Ada thinks. You bloody fool. What did Marie Curie tell you about hope?

'No,' Frankie says, shaking her head. 'It's not Birdie. It's my grandmother, my Min.'

Ada grabs her medical bag and flies down the street after Frankie, barefoot this time. 'Faster, faster, faster,' Frankie says, 'hurry up.'

Frankie's grandmother is lying crumpled on the living-room floor. She is tiny, the size of a child. She is the size of Ada's own little mother. Ada's hands shake as she bends down to check for a pulse, feels her own slow down slightly when she finds one. Ada murmurs in her ear, checks her vitals. Min's symptoms present so many possible things, none of which Ada can do much about. A heart attack, an infection. All Ada has is her stethoscope and thermometer, an EpiPen and some bandages. She has never felt as scared, as useless.

'I've called an ambulance,' Frankie says. 'Please, Dr Ada, please don't let her die. I really need her. Me and my mum really need her.'

34

Birdie

WHEN FLEUR WILLIAMS FROM the Macmillan nurses phoned back to rearrange her appointment, Birdie had just been heading out of the door. 'Hi, Fleur,' she said breathlessly.

'Mrs Greenwing, are you okay?'

'Yes, I'm fine, just late for the bus to the hospital.'

'We can arrange transport to take you to your appointments, if you'd like?'

'Oh, no, I don't have an appointment. I work there, at the WRVS,' Birdie had said, feeling bubbles of pride rise inside her. 'Must dash! I don't want to be late.'

She stayed in high spirits all day, complimented her customers on their hats and handbags. Asked them about their day. She'd quickly come to realize that people wanted more than just tea and cake. They came to talk, to ask for directions, to avoid going home to an empty house or angry spouse. People told Birdie about their appointments. Some people even showed her their ailments. 'Oh,' Birdie would say, 'that looks painful. Have a tea-cake.'

Birdie liked them all. The dads carrying a giant balloon tied to a teddy, the teenagers who'd had their casts removed just in time for a big match. The sadder stories were harder to hear, but Birdie's pinny was her uniform, and listening was part of her job.

'Thank you,' Birdie said, as she pushed the till closed with one finger. 'Please come again.'

Connie had been making hot cross buns. Birdie told her it was too early on in the year, but Connie said that wouldn't stop people buying them, and she was right. Birdie hoped she'd make it to Easter. 'And if hopes and wishes were loaves and fishes, we'd all swim in riches,' her mother used to say.

Birdie doesn't want to swim in riches, but she does want to see the egg hunt she and Connie planned to hold in the pleasure garden. She wants to buy a big extravagant egg for Frankie. To know who'll end up in the smelly old Easter Bunny costume that no one wants to wear. The porters are going to have to put names in a hat at this rate. Birdie wonders if Arthur would volunteer, were he here.

The wonderful thing about working at the WRVS is that just as you start to feel sad, someone comes along to shake you out of it.

'Can I have a tea? I'm gasping. I had blood tests this morning, could only have a sip of water. Two sugars, please. Oh, is that a hot cross bun? Lovely!'

Sometimes Birdie spotted people like her, sitting at the far table. The bad-news table as she's come to know it. They look out of the window, miles away in their minds. Birdie feels an urge to go and talk to them, to take them tea, just as

Connie had done for her, and a buttered scone that tastes a lot like love. To tell them she's spent a lot of time in chairs looking out of windows, watching the world and not being a part of it. But life is something you have to want for yourself. No one else can live it for you. So Birdie says nothing, just waves from her twirly stool, smiles across the room. I can see you, so you are still here.

'One more week,' she says to the yogurts in her fridge that night. 'I don't want to go off before you do.'

'One more good week, please,' she says, as she applies her anti-ageing cream. Brushes with toothpaste that promises whiter teeth in a month. One more week.

When she hears the ambulance roaring down her street after midnight, she thinks for an awful minute that it must be for her. I don't want to go, Birdie thinks. I don't want to leave the party yet. She gets out of bed and hides behind the curtain, watches as the van skids to a stop by Jane and Frankie's driveway. Jane's mother, Birdie thinks. It must be for her. Frankie runs out of the front door, her mouth open like she's screaming. Birdie can smell death, stale, and foul. She should go and help. Go and see if Frankie is okay. She should be with her. She should be there, not stood here like a lemon. Like a coward. Audrey barks at the siren, then dives under the bed. Birdie draws the curtain back into place, calls to Audrey and hides them both under the covers.

35

Jane

IN THE GLOAMING OF the ward at five a.m., lit only by orange call buttons and the neon green of blood-pressure monitors, Min looks like any other patient. An oxygen mask over her face, hands tucked in. She looks so oblivious, so vulnerable. She could be any small person in a bed, anybody's mother. Jane had always wanted to see what Min looked like asleep, but never like this.

'Min,' she whispers, but Min doesn't answer. Her mother, who always snatches up the phone, and eavesdrops round corners, is somewhere silent and out of reach. Jane wants to shake her, shout at her, demand she wake up.

Accident and Emergency had been full. They'd had to wait in the ambulance for over an hour before Min could be found a bed. What Min would have to say about that, if only she knew.

'Min,' Jane says again, 'can you hear me?'

But Min's mouth doesn't move. It remains slack, as if the elastic of her lips has snapped.

'I'm so sorry I wasn't there,' Jane says, pulling her chair as close as she can to the bed.

She lays her head carefully on the corner of her mother's pillow, tears soaking into the starched cotton. Jane cries until she has nothing left inside her, until her eyes ache. Falls into the scent of Min, the quiet huffs of her breath, clutches her cold little hand.

'Jane?'

Jane opens her eyes, sees the hospital ceiling. Thinks for one dreadful minute that she's fallen asleep at work. But it's not Sadie who has found her, who is calling her name.

'Suki?'

Jane sits up, her neck stiff and sore. She wants to fling herself into her sister's arms, then remembers they don't do that any more.

'How is she? I got on the first flight I could,' Suki says in a rush. 'I was at a conference in Paris, so . . .'

Suki looks thinner and shorter. Nothing like the last time Jane saw her. Suki's hair was long back then, her jeans baggy, wrists lined with bits of string and cheap bracelets. This Suki has a sharp bob and is wearing cropped trousers. They used to laugh about people who wore cropped trousers. Would say, 'Why don't you put some jam on your shoes and invite your trousers down for tea?'

Suki puts down her oversized bag and tiptoes over to her mother. 'It's me, Min, Suki,' her sister says. 'I'm here now.'

All hail Suki, Patron Saint of Daughters, Jane thinks, shock and fear making her angry.

'Everything is going to be okay,' Suki says. 'You just focus on getting better.'

'And at the sound of the Lord's name, Lazarus rose from the bloody dead,' Jane mutters to herself.

'Really, Jane?' Suki says, and Jane notices that her sister's lip is wobbling, that her eyes are red. That she is being horrible.

'Sorry,' Jane mumbles. 'She's been asleep for a while. They had to give her some pretty strong stuff for the pain. We're waiting for her to go down for a CT scan.'

'Okay,' Suki says. 'What will the CT scan show?'

'Hopefully whatever it is that caused her to collapse. Frankie says she clutched her stomach before she . . .' Tears prick at Jane's eyes. She's been waiting so long to see her sister, but she never meant for it to be in these circumstances. Never like this. They gaze down at Min.

'So this is what she looks like when she's asleep,' Suki says, after a minute.

'Yeah.' Jane wants to touch her sister, but there is a barrier between them. 'You look . . . different,' Jane says.

'You don't,' Suki says back.

They sit in awkward silence on either side of Min. Time passes in fractured sentences as they wait.

'So, Paris, how glamorous.'

'It's dirty. You can't look up at Notre-Dame Cathedral for fear of treading on a turd. Were there no signs at all? She went from fine to this?'

'None. Did you cut your hair?'

'No. I had it done by a professional. Don't the doctors have any idea what it might be?'

Finally the porters arrive. Jane's hand creeps towards Suki's as Min is wheeled away. She snatches it back just in time.

'How long will the scan take?' Suki says, pulling out her phone.

'Not too long. Do you want a coffee?'

'I don't drink caffeine. Sorry, need to make some calls,' she adds, her voice distracted.

Jane stops by her ward, needing some normality. It's the same yet different in the dark.

'Hey, what are you doing here?'

Jane is so relieved to see Helen that her knees wobble. 'Min collapsed. While I was out. Frankie had to deal with it alone and . . .'

'Oh, Jane, come here.' Helen puts her arms round her, rubs small circles on her back.

'Sorry,' Jane says, through a wet sniffle, 'it's probably nothing. My mother is invincible. She's made of tungsten steel. When she gets inside the CT scan, it'll probably melt.'

Helen laughs but doesn't let go of her. It's Jane who finally pulls back and wipes her eyes.

'Wait there,' Helen says. 'Back in a mo.'

When she reappears, she's carrying a hot chocolate from the machine. It's so disgusting Jane almost laughs. 'How can it be so thick and yet so weak at the same time?' she wonders out loud.

'The water is too cold to melt the powder,' Helen says, taking a swig of her own, the way a cowboy might knock back a whiskey before slamming the tin cup down on the bar and asking to have his horse saddled up. 'Puts hairs on your chest.'

Jane's laughter is weaker than her drink, but it's better than crying. 'I'd better get back,' she says finally. She's stayed longer than she meant to. Suki will be waiting.

'Want me to come with you? I can get Kim to cover for me for half an hour,' Helen suggests.

'Best not. My sister is here . . .'

'I'm guessing from your face that's not a good thing?'

'It's a complicated thing,' Jane says.

'Ah, family dynamics. Always fun,' Helen says. 'I'll find you later. Here if needed.' She reaches out and touches Jane's arm lightly. Jane closes her eyes for a second, lets herself think about their perfect evening on the pier. Helen by her side. A shared bag of doughnuts, sugar on her lips. Then she thinks of Min at home, collapsed.

Jane makes Suki a horrible hot chocolate of her own. Grey with floating lumps of brown powder on top. Even when she stirs it, the lumps refuse to sink. It reminds Jane of a suspicious-looking curry the pair of them had tried in Laos. Neither of them would admit how much it burned going down.

'I *love* it,' Jane had said, eyes watering.

'Me too, don't finish it – I want more!' Suki said, sneezing.

Both of them had raced to the cockroach-infested loo that night, half laughing while clutching their stomachs. Took it in turns to wring out a tepid flannel for the other.

It was Jane's birthday the following day. Suki had forced her to get out of bed.

'Come on. Get up. We need to celebrate. You are nineteen!'

'I am four hundred and nineteen. Let me go back to dying,' Jane had croaked.

'Never!' Suki shouted enthusiastically, then retched as she poured the rest of their bottled water over Jane's head. Jane had finally got up and crawled into the shower.

Now Jane holds out the beige plastic cup to Suki. 'I made you a hot chocolate,' she says.

'Did you spit in it?' Suki says, frowning into the cup.

'No, I did not.'

'It looks rank.'

'My sincere apologies that it's not been passed through the bowels of a gold-tusked elephant first, or however it is you take your cocoa these days.'

'That's coffee,' Suki says, 'and it's a civet cat not an elephant.'

They fall into silence until Min is wheeled back, stirring but still asleep. The doctor arrives soon after.

'The results are back. It's gallstones, large ones. She'll need to have them removed via a laparoscopic cholecystectomy. Relatively simple to perform. Low risk of complications. She'll be fine.'

'Oh, thank God,' Jane says, and Suki closes her eyes briefly as if in prayer.

'You can both go home and get some rest,' the doctor says.

'I'm staying,' Suki says. As if it could make up for all the times she didn't.

When Frankie and Birdie arrive later in the morning, Jane goes out to Reception to meet them. She is stiff from a night spent sitting on a plastic chair. Suki had fallen asleep within minutes of the doctor leaving. She was exhausted, Jane realized and had dug her out a blanket from the supply cupboard. Helen had popped in with a coffee before she went off shift. Pressed a kiss to the crown of Jane's head.

'Morning, Mum,' Frankie says. 'You look tired. Did you sleep? I made you breakfast.' Frankie passes Jane a peanut-butter-and-honey bagel. Jane feels guilty for spending the night away from her, but Frankie doesn't seem to mind. Jane gives her shoulder a quick squeeze. She'd love to hold her girl, bury her nose behind Frankie's ear, where a row of moles are dotted like morse code that says, 'Don't touch me.'

'I'm off to work,' Birdie says, 'Frankie is just popping in to say hello and then she's on washing-up duty at the WRVS.'

Jane doesn't want Frankie to see Min like this. She remembers her dad in bed, how it had scarred her. But Min isn't dying, Jane reminds herself. She's going to be fine. Jane tries not to think about that missing button on her mother's blouse, the smeared glasses. Min is the toughest person Jane knows. The day after their dad died, Min took down all the curtains in the house and scrubbed them in the sink so vigorously that they had faded from red to pink. Then she went at the kitchen so hard the grout fell out from between the tiles.

'I've read up on Min's operation,' Frankie says, 'I know exactly what the surgeon will do. First they—'

'Jane, I'm so sorry I didn't come over last night,' Birdie interrupts. 'I—'

'Birdie, there was nothing you could have done,' Jane says gently.

'I could have been there for Frankie,' Birdie says, her voice full of tears. 'I should have been there.'

'It's okay, Birdie,' Frankie says. 'Ada was there.'

Was she? Jane didn't know that. She'd been and gone again by the time Jane arrived, like some sort of superhero.

'Come on, let's go and say hi to Min,' Birdie says.

Suki is hunched over her bed when they enter the ward, muttering under her breath. Jane edges closer, trying to be quiet.

'I'm sorry, Mum,' Suki is saying. 'I shouldn't have stayed away so long.'

Jane stops walking. She should let Suki have this moment. She should stop eavesdropping.

'I'm not even enjoying it. My job is too hard, and no one likes me,' Suki carries on, 'and I can't speak French for love nor money.'

Jane feels a pang of sympathy for her sister as she whispers her sad little confessions.

'Please wake up, Min. There's something I really need to tell you,' Suki says, 'and I'm so sorry I didn't do it sooner . . .'

Jane feels the hairs on the back of her neck prickle. She looks round and sees Birdie and Frankie are right behind her, listening in just as hard as she is.

'I really hope you'll understand,' Suki says, her voice breaking on a sob.

Don't do it. Don't you fucking do it, Suki, Jane thinks.

'Frankie, I think we should give Suki and Min—' Jane starts to say, but it's too late. Suki cannot be stopped.

'Jane isn't Frankie's mother, Min. I am.'

36

Ada

Ada is trapped in a dream. Wilbur has cancer. He comes to her using a pseudonym. She is expecting a Mr Jones but she gets Wilbur instead, pale and nervous. All that broadness, that quiet confidence gone. Hands that once looked as though they could crush bombs now hang gnarled and useless by his sides. 'How long have I got?' he asks her. His pupils are two black holes.

'Three months,' Ada finds herself saying. 'You have three months.' Wilbur nods and smiles, relief painting his face with grotesque colours, clown-like happiness. He grins so widely it splits his cheeks; he bleeds with joy. When he leaves, he is leaning on a stick that Ada did not see he had with him. Bits of him are left behind. Fingernails and strands of hair. Ada collects them in one of Connie's mugs. The phone rings as she is under the desk, reaching for a button from his shirt. A Polish number. A Polish person telling her that her mother is dead.

Ada wakes with a gasp in the semi-darkness, her heart pounding. She stumbles out of bed and blindly pulls on leggings and trainers. Runs all the way to Carats café and back without stopping. Doesn't look back once to see how far she has come. She has set too fast a pace. 'Slow down,' she hears her mother saying.

'Slow down,' she hears Lech chastise her, but Ada can't. She knows only how to keep going, how to be this person. She finally gets home, exhausted, strips off on her way to the shower, tilts her face up into the spray. Her big toenail is black, half lifted from its base. Ada bites her lip and pulls it off, relishing the pain. She bandages it, takes two painkillers and gets the bus into work. She shouldn't have run so hard. Her feet will be ruined for the race. Somewhere along the line the marathon has changed from being ridiculous to the most important thing in her life. So why make it even harder?

'Morning, Ada!'

'Hello, Connie. Hello, Birdie.'

Both of them look younger than Ada feels right now. Her toe throbs in her flat shoes. She has never worn trainers to work before. Connie and Birdie notice the lack of heels immediately.

'Are you okay, Ada?' Birdie asks.

'I'm fine,' Ada says, not meeting her eye. Ada cannot look at Birdie without seeing her in the garden, without thinking of Frankie's grandmother, Min. Without picturing her mother alone in the field, having slipped and fallen in her open-backed slippers. No one to come and help her, while the animals look on, bovine and useless.

'Just hungry,' Ada says. She eats a hot cross bun as she waits for her bacon roll. She cannot fill the hole inside her, sate her worry with food, but that won't stop her trying.

She pulls the collar of her leather jacket up against the breeze coming in from the open door. She doesn't normally wear it to work either – it's old and tatty, with a rip under the armpit and scuffed elbows. Her thumbs find the holes she's worn into the seams of the sleeves over the years. This is the jacket Ada wore when she first arrived in England, passport tucked inside the secret pocket. It has been a blanket, a pillow, an umbrella. Constant as sorrow, lucky as a black cat. It has been a friend. As she waits for Connie to deliver her roll, Ada looks over the sleeves, finds a tiny crescent of Ania's turquoise nail varnish, a smear of white paint from walking, drunkenly, into a freshly painted wall. Ada feels for the tiny badge pinned inside a rip in the lining. A silver eagle in flight with a gold laurel wreath in its bill. The Polish Air Force all wore them, and this one belonged to her grandfather. He, too, wanted to fly away.

Ada had noticed the jacket at the local market, hanging high up at the back of the stall. Her dad must have seen her looking because Ada knew, the second she came downstairs on her eighteenth birthday and saw the clumsily wrapped parcel, what it was. What he'd done. Ada still can't think of what he must have sold to pay for it. Though she's sent a hundred times what the jacket is worth back home to him, she will never be out of his debt.

'That'll be six pounds, please,' Birdie says, holding out her hand.

Ada tries to work out how long it's been since Birdie came to see her. Had Wilbur started working with her? She can't stop thinking of her life this way: before Wilbur, after Wilbur.

'Connie added an egg because she says you look pale,' Birdie says, handing over her change.

Connie, who Ada knows has thyroid cancer. Birdie, who

has months to live. Connie frying her an egg because she, the woman who has failed them, looks pale.

When she gets to her office, Wilbur isn't there. Ada tells herself she doesn't care. Hangs her jacket on the back of her chair. Puts on her white coat, but everything feels wrong. As though she's wearing it back to front and her insides are on the outside for everyone to see. The room is colder without Wilbur and disappointment numbs her fingers.

'You look tired. What have you been doing?'

'Morning, Denise,' Ada says flatly.

'Wilbur called. He's running late.'

Wilbur has Ada's number. He could have texted *her* to tell her. He could have texted her many times over the weekend, in fact. Ada's running shoes waited, like two puppies wanting a walk, hoping he'd make contact.

'Fine,' Ada says, getting up to fiddle with the radiator then sitting back down.

'And I've left my husband.'

'Okay.' Why is Wilbur running late? Did he spend the night somewhere? Is he feeling unwell? Why won't the *cholerny* radiator come on?

'Ada? I just told you I've left my husband. Is that all you're going to say?'

Ada looks up and sees that Denise is crying. That she looks awful. Her hair is tied back in a greasy knot and she's wearing crumpled clothes and fluffy sheepskin slippers. Ada's aching legs protest as she gets up again. 'Good for you. Sorry. He was a *kutas*.'

Denise is trembling, Ada realizes. Her whole body is shaking with the effort of being brave.

'Hug me then, you weird Polish robot,' Denise demands.

Ada puts her arms around Denise awkwardly, as though she's about to pick her up. This close, Ada can see her normally flawless makeup has been applied in a rush by an unsteady hand. The line of her foundation isn't blended. Ada wants to smooth it for her but doesn't. 'You did the right thing,' she says.

'I know I did,' Denise says, then bursts into a round of noisy tears. 'But I lent the thieving bastard all my savings. I paid for the TV, the washing-machine, the bed, all of it. He's got everything. I'll have to move back in with my mother. She's going to love saying I told you so.' More sobs, some incoherent swearing. 'Everybody told me not to,' she tells Ada, 'but I never bloody listen, do I?'

'Ada, you are so pig-headed,' her teachers used to admonish her. 'Ada, you always think you know best,' her father used to say. 'Ada, kindness is not a weakness,' Ania told her once, when she cried over a patient. 'Ada, have an egg. You look pale.' She thinks of her spare room, decked out with grey *huaga* furniture. A foam-topped mattress with the plastic still on.

'Can you drive?' she asks, letting go of Denise.

'Yes, why?' Denise says, blowing her nose.

'Hire a van. We're going to go and get your stuff after work, and then you will move in with me.'

'With you?' Denise says, as though Ada has just told her the moon is made of cheese. 'But I can't. I mean, I can, but I won't have any stuff. He won't let me take any of it.'

'Let me worry about that,' Ada says, thinking of Lech and Aleksey. 'Just go and sort out a van. *Now*,' she adds, seeing that Denise is about to cry again.

'Ada . . .' Denise says, looking awkward. 'I never, I mean . . .'

'It's fine, just go, and don't forget to blend your makeup!'

Denise backs out of the room, one hand on her face, rubbing frantically. 'But, why?' she asks by the door. 'Why are you doing this for me?'

'Because that is what we do.'

Wilbur arrives mid-morning, bearing a mug of coffee. 'Sorry I'm late,' he says.

'It's fine,' Ada replies stiffly, turning briefly from the filing cabinet she's been sorting through. She has imagined him in many places doing many things since she arrived at work, and none of them has made her feel very happy.

'So I hear you have a new flatmate,' Wilbur says, going over to the radiator. Ada has managed to make it hiss but not heat up.

'Her husband is a *kutas*,' Ada says. 'I'm going to enjoy telling him as much.'

'You're not going over there alone, are you?' Wilbur says. 'Not that I don't think you can handle yourself. You could kill a man with your frown alone but—'

'I'll be fine,' Ada says, and Wilbur's eyebrows crease. 'I'm taking back-up just in case,' she adds.

'Do you need some extra back-up?' Wilbur asks, flexing his biceps.

'No,' Ada says. Yes, Ada thinks. I'd like to do a trust fall backwards into your chest.

'Very nice of you,' Wilbur says, 'letting her live with you.'

'Well, she's my—' Ada breaks off, not sure what she was going to say.

'I see,' Wilbur says, as he twists the valve on the heating pipe. The radiator glugs into reluctant submission.

'And what about me? What am I to you, Ada?'

His smile pins her to the wall. Makes her feel transparent. Is he joking? Ada is a kid again, toeing her way on to the recently iced-over lake. Excitement mixed with trepidation. Will it hold her, or will it give way? 'I . . .' she starts, 'you—'

'Booked it!' Denise declares, flinging open the door and cracking the moment in two. 'I can pick the van up at six p.m. Is that still okay?' She has applied a thick layer of red lipstick, fluffed up her hair, sprayed on something sweet with a heavy hand.

'Fine,' Ada says, feeling disappointed at the interruption though she's not sure why.

'Anyway,' Wilbur says, when Denise has gone, 'I got you a coffee.' He places it carefully on the desk. Ada thanks him without looking at it, then turns back to the filing cabinet.

The afternoon spirals away. Patients and phone calls and chasing up results. When she finally gets back from a departmental meeting, Wilbur has already gone. Sitting down heavily, toe sore, Ada spots the coffee she forgot to drink. Then she notices what is written on the mug.

'I want to do with you, what spring does with the cherry trees' is written in Wilbur's neat handwriting across one side. Underneath, he has written 'by Pablo Neruda', then crossed it out and put *Wilbur Smith*.

'Are you ready, Ada?' Denise asks, poking her head around the door. She's reapplied her makeup again since lunch, Ada notices. It's caked on now, blusher streaked across her cheeks like war paint. 'It's time to go.'

37

Birdie

SEEING MIN BROWN SLEEPING in a hospital bed, in any bed, feels odd. It does not go with the image of the grandmother that Frankie had painted for her. It's as though death came for Birdie, then got confused, seeing Min wielding that giant suitcase up Jane and Frankie's garden path. I'm the one you're here for, Birdie wants to say. Leave her alone. She thinks about how she hid behind her curtain when she saw the ambulance. Shameful, utterly shameful. Rose would not have hidden; Princess Margaret would not have hidden either. She'd have strutted out and aimed a gun at Death, challenged it to a duel.

Birdie sits down on the little plastic visitor's chair. She's tired today. It was a long shift, and her painkillers are wearing off. Min looks so peaceful, all tucked up, a sleeping dormouse. Birdie has to fight the sudden urge to pull back the thin blue cover and slide in, like a little fish finger. To ding the bell and ask for the strong stuff.

'Hello, Min Brown, I'm Birdie Greenwing,' she says, patting Min's hand awkwardly, 'Jane and Frankie's next-door neighbour.'

Min is smaller than Birdie imagined. Tiny but sturdy, like a West Highland terrier. She is also, Birdie notices, as she peers closer, clearly awake. Rose's eyelashes used to flutter like that when she was pretending to be asleep. 'Min,' Birdie says, louder.

A woman in the bed next to them snorts in response, while Min's left eyelid merely twitches.

'It's Birdie Greenwing . . . from next door.'

'Jane?' Min murmurs.

'No, *Birdie*. Jane is . . .' Birdie trails off, wondering how long she's been awake, what she heard, '. . . getting some food.' The last time Birdie saw Jane, she was chasing after Frankie, who'd turned and run out of the ward after Suki's shocking confession.

Min lets out a sigh that turns into a groan.

'How are you?' Birdie asks.

'Dreadful,' Min whispers, eyes still closed. 'It's the end for me, I can tell.'

'Horsefeathers,' Birdie says.

Min's eyes open wider. 'What?' she says, no longer whispering.

'It's not the end,' Birdie says.

'How do you know?' Min croaks. 'You've no idea of the pain I'm in.'

Birdie smiles like a crocodile. 'Oh, I do, trust me. More than you could know.'

'Who the bleddy hell do you think you are?' Min splutters, fully awake now, cheeks pinking up as if she's just eaten a hot pepper.

'I told you, I'm Birdie Greenwing, Frankie's neighbour.'

'You're a bleddy nosy parker is what you are. A rude, interfering old boot. Now sling your hook before I ring for the nurse.'

Birdie almost laughs. 'That's more like it,' she says. 'Now you fit your description. You'll be up and about in no time.'

'You heard what the doctor said. I need an *operation*!' Min says. 'I could die.'

'So you *were* awake the whole time. Thought so. You're not going to die, Min,' Birdie says, smiling.

'Stop smiling at me. Who do you think you are? Mystic bleddy Meg?' Min says angrily, moving to sit up, before groaning and falling back against the pillows.

'I'm still Birdie,' Birdie says, 'and you are trying to push to the front of the queue.'

'What?' Min's eyebrows go up.

'The queue. I'm ahead of you. I'm the one dying, Min. Properly, none of this stomach-ache nonsense.'

Min frowns, her facial muscles struggling to keep up with the conversation.

'Cancer,' Birdie says, pointing to her breast, as if Min had asked her where she got her lipstick from.

'Does Frankie know?'

'Yes. Well, I think so. Jane has told her, but I've not mentioned it.'

There is a silence, in which two softer women might have exchanged polite platitudes. Sorry about your gallstones. Sorry about your cancer. Not Min and Birdie, however. They're sitting there like two boiled eggs, eyeing one another suspiciously, wondering who will crack first.

'She likes you, my Frankie,' Min says accusingly, as if Birdie had caught cancer on purpose.

'I know, selfish of me,' Birdie says.

'Humph,' Min says. 'She thinks she's tough, like her mother.' Min pauses, frowns, then says, 'But they aren't. None of my girls are.'

'I know, which is why they need you,' Birdie says.

'They don't. They all left me.'

'Well, can you blame them?' Birdie asks. 'I've only just met you and you've insulted me three times.'

Min glares at her, eyes bright and blue. Mouth opening and closing like a codfish's.

'Get up, Min,' Birdie says. 'Your daughters need you. All you have is a case of the lonelies. I know it well, believe me. It's a pig of a virus, but it won't kill you. You've just had too much time on your own. Too much time to think. Nothing ages you like heartache.'

Min stiffens in annoyed denial but Birdie places a restraining hand on her arm. 'Listen to me, Min. It's true. When my husband and sister died, I had nothing. They were my whole life. I just hung about like a bad smell, waiting to die. Now that it's too late, I realize how wasteful that was.' Birdie looks down at her beautiful pinny, brushes off a cake crumb.

'Well,' Min says, 'the devil makes work for idle hands and all that.'

Birdie almost laughs. Min's attitude makes it easier for Birdie to carry on. To say what she came here to say. 'I didn't think I deserved to be happy, after they died,' Birdie says, 'because of what happened to them.'

'Which was?' Min asks. She's more interested than cross now, and has found the remote control for the bed. She's rising up slowly in small jerks.

Birdie takes a deep breath. She's never told anyone this part before and has to coax the words out. They hover on her tongue, shy toddlers hiding behind their mother's legs. 'I killed them. My Arthur and Rose. I killed them.'

'You bleddy what?' Min roars. 'How?'

'Well, it was a Friday,' Birdie starts.

'What's that got to do with it?' Min says.

'I'm trying to tell you,' Birdie says. 'It's not easy.'

Birdie shuts her eyes, takes herself back. Rewinds to the right part. She'd been fighting a cold and was losing. Her nose was sore, her throat was raw, and a brass band seemed to have taken up residence in her brain. All she wanted to do was go back to bed, but Rose had a nurse's appointment at the surgery. She was just coming out of the other side of a flare-up, a bad one. She'd had to have steroids that stopped her being able to sleep, painkillers that hurt her stomach.

'I wasn't feeling well,' Birdie murmurs.

'Well, how did that kill your husband and sister?' Min demands.

Birdie is not sure which bits she's saying out loud, and which are stuck in her head.

'Are you okay, Birdie?' Rose had asked, seeing Birdie searching in the medicine cabinet.

'Fine, just a head cold,' Birdie had said.

'You don't look fine,' Rose said. 'Go back to bed, I'll cancel my appointment.'

'Nonsense.'

'Go on.'

'No!'

'Go!'

'No!'

Arthur had come to see what was going on. He agreed with Rose. 'Birdie, you look grey. Get back to bed, I'll take Rose.' Normally Birdie would have argued, insisted that she was okay, that she could manage. Rose was *her* responsibility, but on that day, just for once, Birdie let Arthur take up the reins. As soon as she heard the car pull out of the drive, she'd slipped into her comfiest nightgown, and got back into bed with her hot-water bottle and a Georgette Heyer.

When she'd woken, the room was dark. Birdie had rolled over to check the time on Arthur's bedside clock and realized she'd been asleep for hours. She assumed that Arthur and Rose were in the living room, being quiet so as not to wake her. Birdie pictured them, sitting there like a pair of bookends so Birdie could sleep. The pair of sillies. It was only a cold! She was already feeling much better.

'I'd slept for so long. Rose's appointment would have finished hours before,' Birdie says.

But when she went looking for them, all the rooms were empty. The house was cold and silent, and all the lights were off. Birdie had stood by the living-room window, ears pricked for the sound of Arthur's car. Each time a set of headlights went past, her heart skipped a beat, but none stopped outside. No slam of the car door, no beep of the alarm. No click of Rose's stick on the drive, of Arthur jangling the loose change in his pockets. Hours went by, but Birdie didn't move an inch. The stars appeared, but Arthur and Rose stayed hidden.

'At nine p.m. a police car pulled up.'

Two men got out, quietly closing doors, and made their

way up her path. One spotted Birdie, hidden under her net curtain like a bride, and looked down at his boots.

The doorbell was loud in the silence. Birdie had to force her feet to move.

'Mrs Greenwing?' They took off their helmets and tucked them under their arms in a well-practised move.

Birdie had felt her knees turn to water. 'No . . .' she'd said, clutching at her dressing-gown.

'Please can we come in?'

'No,' Birdie said again, even as she moved aside, some part of her knowing what was coming. Had known since she woke up to an empty house.

'Is there somewhere we can sit down?' one asked kindly.

'Would you like a cup of tea?' said the other. 'Are you alone? Can we call anyone for you?'

'Sit down, Birdie, you're shaking,' Min says now, taking her arm. Birdie hadn't even realized she'd stood up.

Birdie's legs had been shaking back then too, so much that she'd had to be helped into a chair. She could hear her cupboard doors opening, the familiar sound of her kettle being put on. It could have been Arthur in there, or Rose. But it wasn't. It was a man wearing black and white, muttering into a radio, while his partner told her that he was very sorry. He was very sorry indeed.

The mug was hot, the tea too pale. She remembers that bit so vividly. How Birdie had looked at Arthur's empty chair, Rose's half-read book. They couldn't be gone. It was impossible.

'Birdie.'

Min is saying something, but Birdie can't hear her. She is

back in the morgue, where she'd been driven by the police. Ivy and her neighbours had stood on their doorsteps and watched her being taken away.

It was so cold in there. Birdie has never forgotten the smell, the starched white sheets. She would have given anything for them to be two strangers, but she recognized her sister's little finger, the same as her own. When she looked down at Rose, she was looking at herself. It should have been her on the metal trolley, a tag round her ankle. She'd stumbled on to Arthur. There was a gash down his face, cracking his profile in two. Birdie had slid to the floor, a puppet who'd had her strings cut.

'Are you bleddy listening, Birdie? You didn't kill them. No more than I killed Tom by making him put up the Christmas lights,' Min is saying.

'Why? Did he fall off the ladder?' Birdie asks, confused. She's back in the ward, in the present again. Min is peering at her. There is a tissue in Birdie's hand that wasn't there before.

'No, but he could have done. You can't take credit for accidents, Birdie.'

'It was my fault. I should have been there,' Birdie argues. 'I would've seen the car coming the other way.'

'It wasn't.' Min has found some antibacterial wipes in the bedside table and is giving the chair arms a going-over. 'And you don't know that.'

'I promised Rose I'd never leave her,' Birdie says.

'People leave people. That's life, you stubborn dollop,' Min says.

'I am not a dollop!' Birdie says crossly. The conversation is running away with her. Her legs ache from trying to keep up.

'Tom promised me in sickness and in health for as long as we *both* should live. Well, I'm still living,' Min says with a wave of her arm, 'and he left me. He bleddy left me. My Tom . . .' Min punches at her chest, wipes angry tears from her eyes. 'Well,' she says, 'well.' She takes a deep breath and adjusts the cuffs of her nightgown.

It makes no sense. Birdie's brain is swimming in water. Her eyes are blurred. Every thought she's ever had has been handed to her upside down.

'Sit down on the bed,' Min offers, 'you look very tired. And a bit green.'

Birdie finds herself stumbling towards it, sinking gratefully on to the raised mattress. She is so exhausted, and Min is saying it's not her fault, it's really not, and the pain in her back is insisting that she notices it, like Audrey when she wants something. 'Just for a moment, then,' Birdie says.

38

Jane

'FRANKIE, I KNOW YOU'RE in there.' Jane is in the patients' toilets. She can see Frankie's feet under the cubicle door.

'Is *she* with you?' Frankie says.

'Who? Suki?'

'Yes.'

The door slams.

'Not any more,' Jane says, as Suki leaves.

Frankie comes out slowly. Her hair is a mess, and her face is tight and angry.

'Frankie, I'm so sorry,' Jane says.

'Is she going to take me away?'

'What?' Jane asks.

'Suki. Has she come to take me away from you?' Frankie repeats.

'No, of course not, never. She's here to see Min,' Jane says.

'Suki is not my mother. I don't care what she says. *You* are. It's not just a noun. It's also a verb.'

Jane frowns. 'What do you mean?'

'Being a mother, it's something you do, not just something you are. I am *your* daughter. You belong to me. You mother *me*.'

The words are a hot cattle brand, sizzling themselves into Jane's heart, confirming everything she has ever believed. They belong to one another.

'I won't leave you. I won't go,' Frankie says, fists clenched as if preparing for a fight. As if Suki is going to come in and try to drag her away.

'No one is asking you to, I promise. You're not going anywhere, and neither am I,' Jane says, hovering a hand over Frankie's, but not touching her. Letting Frankie decide what to do next.

Frankie grabs it, squeezes hard. 'You are my mother. My only mother ever,' Frankie declares, as if they are exchanging vows.

Frankie's black-and-white thinking, often a difficult landscape to navigate, is suddenly blessedly simple. Jane had always worried that the truth would destroy their relationship. She should have known Frankie better than that. 'And you are my daughter, Frankie, ever and always.'

Suki is not there when they get back to the ward. Neither is Birdie. Jane is grateful they have made themselves scarce. That it's just the three of them again, Jane, Frankie and Min, except Min is not normally in bed, sucking an ice cube.

'Nil by mouth until after the operation,' Min tells Frankie. Jane realizes her mother is rather enjoying all the fuss.

'After you've been knocked out by the anaesthetic, the surgeon will make four small incisions in your belly,' Frankie says. 'Then they'll insert a flexible tube that contains a light and a tiny video camera inside you.'

'Well, I hope they bleddy clean it first,' Min says.

'Then they'll get a scalpel and—'

'Perhaps tell her the rest afterwards?' Jane interrupts.

'Fine,' Frankie sighs. 'Did you hear about Suki being my mother?' she says, as though informing Min it has just started raining.

'I did,' Min says calmly, sucking hard at the ice, like she does with her toffees.

'It's a lie. Mum is my mum, not Suki.'

Min and Jane look at one another. Jane was expecting to see anger on her mother's face, like when Suki dropped Min's favourite vase, 'the irreplaceable family heirloom', but Min is not angry, she's hurt. Jane's stomach drops like she's on a roller-coaster.

'Okay,' Min says, looking away from Jane and back to Frankie. 'Pass me another ice cube.'

'And you are still my grandmother,' Frankie says, trying to navigate her new world. To make sure the corners are still in the same place.

'Well, of course I bleddy am. Did you think I was going to turn into Widow bleddy Twankey all of a sudden?'

When the surgical team come to prep Min, Frankie has a lot of questions about the tools they'll use to slice her up. Min has a lot of questions about how naked she will be and rules about where they are not allowed to look at.

'Okay, Mrs Brown,' the surgeon says. 'I promise to keep my eyes closed the whole time.'

'Cheeky beggar,' Min says, but she's doing the little smile she does after a sherry, or when she's witnessed her neighbour arguing with her husband.

'Can I have her gall bladder?' Frankie asks the surgeon.

'Well, we're going to keep that bit inside your grandmother, all being well,' he says, smiling.

'Can I have the stones, then?'

'The gallstones?' Jane asks.

'What on earth for?' Min asks.

'My specimen collection,' Frankie says.

'No problem,' the surgeon says easily. 'Want me to shine them up for you? Make a nice bracelet.'

'Yes. Yes, I would, please.'

Frankie's behaviour is so oddly normal, Jane could almost forget that a bomb had just been dropped on her world. 'What else is in your specimen collection, Frankie?' Jane asks.

'Some teeth, mostly mine. A couple of headlice . . . I found this dead mouse in the garden a while ago . . .'

'I've changed my mind. I don't want to know.'

'We're going to have a very big talk when I get back,' Min says to Jane, and Suki, who has reappeared, and is looking somewhat sheepish.

'*If* I come back, that is,' Min calls dramatically, as she is wheeled away, blue stockings on her feet, which she demanded Jane put on (she slapped the nurse's hand away when he tried and called him a deviant).

'Bye, Min, see you in about an hour,' Jane says.

'We'll be right here,' Suki says.

The silence Min leaves them in is an awkward one. Suki keeps casting glances at Frankie, quick and greedy, like hen pecks. Is she trying to spot traces of herself, of Frankie's dad? They don't even have a photo of him. He was there and gone in a flash, hence Frankie's middle name (which Min will never *ever* know about). There was no way to trace him, even if they'd wanted to, which they'd agreed they never would. Or has that changed too now?

'I want to go and see Birdie,' Frankie says.

'She's in the WRVS,' Suki says quickly. 'Would you like me to take you to her?'

'No.'

'Frankie . . .' Jane sighs.

'Fine,' Frankie says. 'You can take me to Birdie, but you are still not my mother.'

'Fine,' Suki says back.

Jane tidies the space round Min's bed, falling into the comforting routine of wiping the side-table and under the chairs. Suki reappears as Jane is folding Min's clothes.

'Frankie says to go and collect her as soon as Min gets out of surgery,' Suki says, 'and also that I'm not very nice.' She adds this very matter-of-factly, as if it's a known truth.

Jane's instinct is to defend her sister, but she stops herself. 'Why did you do it?' she asks instead, refolding Min's beige cardigan.

'I don't know,' Suki replies, after a long moment. 'I thought she was going to die.'

'I told you her vitals were good. I told you she'd be okay.' *But of course you didn't believe me. I'm only a nurse. I'm just your silly little sister, what would I know?*

'I'm sorry, Jane. I wasn't thinking.'

Jane can't turn around to look at her yet and there is nothing left to fold. The cubicle is clean, but Jane takes another wipe and starts again anyway. As if this conversation, the last twenty-four hours, is something she can erase.

'I mean, how could you be so selfish?' Jane says to Min's shoes, tucked under the chair.

'Maybe I wanted her to think I'd done something amazing with my life,' Suki says, 'like you.'

'But Min thinks everything you do is amazing. You are the big Brown success story.'

'That makes me sound like a large poo,' Suki says.

'Well, you are,' Jane says.

They almost smile at one another, but don't.

'Every time someone at work gets pregnant, they ask me when I'm going to settle down. If I want children of my own,' Suki says, stroking the buttons on Min's blouse.

Jane feels a jolt of fear. Could Frankie be right? Has Suki come to take her away?

'I say no, but it's a lie, isn't it? I already have a child.'

No, you haven't. She's mine. 'But you said you never wanted children. You said you were not born to be a mother,' Jane says. *Don't take her away from me. Please. Anything but Frankie.*

'I don't. I'm not. But also I am. It's not easy, giving up a baby,' Suki says quietly, 'justifying it to myself every time I see a child the age mine would be. The age mine is.'

'I know. I was there. It's not easy to raise one either,' Jane replies. 'We said we'd never let it change us, though!' She lets the tears come. Lets the words she's been holding in all this time pour out of her. 'You said it would still be you and me. What changed?'

'Nothing. *I*'m still the same,' Suki says hotly.

'No, you are not. *I* am,' Jane replies.

'No, you're not. The second you held Frankie, you disappeared. I wanted *my sister*, Jane. Not updates on Frankie or photos of her asleep. I know it's a fucking awful thing to say. It's not that I don't care. I did, and I do. But she was always yours. Your daughter. I was shut out the second I passed her to you. I disappeared in plain sight. I still needed my sister, but you were gone. You turned into a mother instead.'

'I needed you too, Suki,' Jane says. 'I needed you to tell me I was doing a good job.' She mops at her face with her arm, wipes her snotty nose on her sleeve.

'Is that what you think? That you're not a good mother?' Suki says, half laughing, half crying. 'I've never, not even for a second, had a single doubt about you. Jane, you've done an amazing job. Frankie is . . . Well, there are no words for Frankie.'

'I thought you thought I was doing it wrong. Raising her wrong.'

'Why would you think that?'

'Min, in your ear, telling you how useless I am.'

'Min thinks the sun shines out your arse,' Suki replies flatly. 'Jane, I never doubted you. Never. I doubted myself.'

'What?' Jane says.

'Come on, you should know me better than that. Better than to buy into my bullshit.'

Suki entwines her fingers with Jane's. Their hands are exactly the same size. It is like holding her own, but better. It is like coming home. 'I missed you,' Suki says.

'I didn't miss you at all,' Jane says.

'Liar.'

'Cropped-trouser wearer.'

'Can we hug now?'

*

There is only one thing to do to make it up to their mother. Creep and crawl like earwigs. Pander and fawn. Turn on their dad's charm. When Min comes out of surgery, Jane and Suki are ready and waiting.

'Here she comes!'

'Oh, thank God you're okay!'

'We've been so worried!'

Min eyes them with sleepy suspicion.

'Wow! You look *amazing*,' Jane says.

'Ten years younger.'

'Where are your gallstones?' Frankie asks.

'Look, we've got you some bits. Walnut Whips and a lovely thick dressing-gown,' Jane says.

Suki had been on a mad dash round Brighton, no expense spared. 'A nice new beige cardigan, a hot-water bottle,' Suki adds, laying out each item on the bed, 'memory-foam slippers.'

Min looks at them, but still says nothing.

'Some fruit, those peppermints you like. A hairbrush – hard bristles – carbolic soap.'

They look at one another and frown. Min is not biting.

'Would you like me to get you a cup of tea?' Suki asks.

'A foot rub?' Jane offers, desperate.

'I would like to know why you both lied to me,' Min says.

39

Ada

DENISE IS VERY LOUD. She sings in the shower. She leaves neon-coloured lace bras hanging from any available surface. She likes . . . stuff. Ada's sofa is covered with fluffy pink cushions that were *not* in the IKEA catalogue. Her glass dining table has a cloth on it, covered with tigers. There are scented candles everywhere, real ones. None of Ada's fake-flame nonsense. Piles of self-help books are stacked on the coffee-table. Real plants adorn every windowsill. A vase of flowers kicks out scent from the table in the hall. There is a framed photo of a dog that Ada has never seen before in her life on the mantelpiece.

Denise doesn't knock before she enters the bathroom or Ada's bedroom. She loves flinging open windows and curtains. And hoovering. And dusting. She brings Ada drinks that Ada never asked for, tries to do her washing for her.

'I can do it myself,' Ada says, wrestling her laundry basket back out of Denise's tight grasp.

'But I *want* to,' Denise says.

Denise wants a lot of things. She wants taco Tuesdays and pizza Fridays. She wants face packs and film nights on

Saturdays. She wants Ada to let her give her a makeover. To take Ada shopping for new clothes. Denise wants – really wants – to talk about Wilbur.

'I like her,' Lech says, when Ada takes Denise into the *Polski sklep*. 'Her long nails would be very useful for opening my boxes.'

'You sound like your son,' Ada says.

'She is beautiful, yes,' Aleksey says, as though someone had asked him, 'and exotic, but my loyalty lies with you, Ada. I will not have my head turned by her sweet scent, that long hair . . .' He sighs.

'She drinks like a Polish person,' Lech says approvingly, after Denise downs her third shot in as many minutes. 'Your husband is a *kutas*,' he tells her.

Denise giggles, then cries. Aleksey pats her on the back, assuring Ada it means nothing. He is just being nice.

'I've never had a cuddle from a nice man before,' Denise says, dabbing at her eyes, 'didn't know they existed.'

'They hide in Polish shops,' Ada says.

Denise wants Ada to invite Wilbur over. Ada and Wilbur are as good as married in Denise's mind.

'How are you still pro marriage after everything you went through?' Ada asks.

When Ada, Lech and Aleksey knocked on Denise's door, her husband Darren went from being confused, to patronizing, to angry very quickly.

'Who are you? I see. Denise said that, did she? Well, let me tell you something about Denise . . .' Darren's lip had curled unpleasantly.

'No, thank you,' Lech said. 'We just want her stuff.'

Darren was fine with it – 'Take it, load of shite' – until Lech unplugged the TV, turned to Aleksey and said, 'You get one end, I'll take the other.' That was when Ada saw the dents in the wall. Realized how much Denise had hidden under that thick makeup and confident smile.

Lech ignored his rants and raves and threats, whistling as he worked. 'Come on, Aleksey, washing-machine next.'

Ada went round with a bin bag, putting everything of any use into it, and all of Darren's work clothes while she was at it.

'How?' Denise said, when they got back to the van. 'How did you do it?'

Ada saw she'd been picking at the skin round her nails as she waited for them to return. Blood edged her cuticles like a row of fringes.

'Are you all okay?' Denise asked. 'Did he . . . I mean, was he . . .?'

'Do not worry about that poor excuse for a man,' Lech said.

Denise opens the front door. Signs up for the Neighbourhood Watch. Answers Ada's phone for her when she forgets to take it with her into the bathroom. 'Ada, it's your mum, I think?'

'Minka? Is everything okay?' Ada says, taking the phone. Her mum doesn't call for no reason.

'Ania tells me you are running some big race for charity. Why didn't you tell me, Ada?' Ada picks at a flake of paint on the wall, doesn't know what to say. 'Forty-two kilometres!' her mother exclaims.

'I'll finish it,' Ada says fiercely.

'We know you will.' Ada can hear her mother's smile.

'Will you come and watch me?' Ada asks suddenly, the words saying themselves without permission.

'Oh, Ada,' her mother says, 'you know we can't. The farm, and . . .'

'Of course,' she says. 'I understand.'

'Maybe you'll come back here soon. Your father has been rebuilding the main shed. He's put some new self-watering system down in the bottom field. He read about it in your magazine.'

'It's not my magazine,' Ada says.

'Tell your daughter to go out with Wilbur!' Denise shouts into the mouthpiece.

'Who is that?' Janina asks. 'What is she saying?'

'That is Denise,' Ada says, 'my flatmate, and my *sometimes* friend,' she adds. Denise beams, then wells up, and scuttles off to wash Ada's tea-towels.

'I'm pleased you've made some friends,' her mother says. 'Ania was worried about you.'

'Me? Why? What did she say?'

'She just said you sounded tired.'

'Well, I am training for a marathon,' Ada replies, hating the defensive tone in her voice. She wants to tell her mother that she misses her. That she tried to make her special bread. Tried to look after a neighbour along her street like she was brought up to do. She wants to tell her that she's so tired. Of trying. Of not getting it right. I want to come home, Ada longs to say, but I'm scared. Scared not to fit in there, the way I don't fit in here. Scared to see you looking older. Scared of everything.

'Maybe after the marathon,' Janina says. 'Your father would really love you to see the new barn roof.'

'Maybe,' Ada says.

'I'll come with you,' Denise says, when Ada has hung up. 'I've never been to Poland. Never been anywhere, actually. That prick didn't even take me on a honeymoon. We had one weekend in a caravan in Bournemouth. Rained the whole time. He went out to get some food, didn't come back till the morning.' Denise's lip wobbles again.

'If you stop crying, I will let you put makeup on me,' Ada says. Denise wipes her eyes and runs to her very heavy makeup box.

Ada's finger hovers over Wilbur's number. She's not seen him since the coffee-cup day. Maybe he's busy. He's probably busy. He might be in one of his meetings. Ada wants to text him, but saying what? 'Yes, please to doing to me what-spring-does-to-cherry-tree stuff. By the way, I've only had sex once and I was crap at it. Wait, that line is about sex, right? I'd be a mug for you.'

'Friday was his last day,' Denise says, peering over her shoulder to look at Ada's phone. 'He did tell you that.'

Did he?

'Stop being nosy,' Ada says, turning her phone away.

'He's gone to Haywards Heath hospital,' Denise carries on, as if Ada had asked. 'He's still going to come to badminton, though. And the quiz night. You really should come to the quiz night, Ada,' she adds kindly.

'I'm busy,' Ada snaps.

'You're not. I know you're not. I live with you now, remember? All you do is run, wash your white coat, and read medical books.'

A painfully accurate summary.

'Why don't you just call him?' Denise says, flicking on the

kettle, getting down two mugs. She makes it sound so easy. But there are things about Ada that Denise doesn't know. That Wilbur doesn't know. Ada thinks of her mother crying when she left, the weight of grief she'd left her father to deal with. The promises Ada had made to herself and the sacrifices she's made ever since to keep them. I do not deserve nice things, she thinks. I do not deserve that man.

'I don't want to call him,' she says, walking towards her bedroom.

'Liar!'

Ada shuts the door. Tries to read a medical journal, but can't concentrate, so goes out for a run instead.

40

Birdie

ONCE SHE GETS GOING, Min has rather a lot to say to Birdie. In fact, Birdie is given quite a dressing-down when she tells Min she plans to check into a palliative-care home.

'And leave my granddaughter high and dry, after all she's done for you?' Min says. 'That's gratitude, that is!'

'She has you, Min. I was merely a stand-in.'

'Oh, don't give me that old flannel. It won't wash.'

What would Princess Margaret say to Min? Birdie thinks. She wouldn't take this assault lying down. 'You have no right to talk to me this way,' Birdie says primly, patting her hair.

'And who, pray tell, do you think you are? The Queen of bleddy Sheba?' Min says.

'It's my life, my choice,' she says.

By this point, both of them are pink-cheeked.

A nurse comes over to tell them to pipe down. 'Other people in this ward are not feeling quite as chipper as you two,' she tells them sternly.

They sit sulking for a moment.

'I cared for my husband when he had cancer, you know,' Min says slowly.

Birdie looks at her.

'So I know a bit about it too, and I don't think you're on your last legs yet.'

'You know nothing about me,' Birdie says. 'You just told me you were going to die, and you only had gallstones. You're hardly an expert on such matters.'

'Look here, madam, do you want my help or not?' Min says.

'Your help?'

'Yes, my help. Want it or not?' Min says, glaring at her.

'With what?' Birdie says.

'Palliative care, of course,' Min says casually, 'see you safely over to the other side and all that.'

'But . . . why?' Birdie asks, heart pounding.

'Why not?' Min says. 'I've nothing better to do.' She sounds so like Frankie that Birdie wants to weep. Could it really be so easy? That all Birdie has to do is say yes? To admit that she'd like some help, please. That she's rather tired and very scared, and she doesn't want to die in some insipid bedroom in some magnolia care home. She wants to have a hand to hold when she goes.

'I'll need to think about it,' Birdie says.

'Oh, of course,' Min shoots back. 'I'm sure you've had lots of offers.'

Birdie almost laughs. Min almost smiles.

When visiting hours are over, Birdie goes down to the graveyard for the first time in eight years. She's never liked cemeteries. She didn't plan to come back here – at least, not alive – but this is where her feet have decided to take her. Birdie runs her hand along the pebbled wall, cold under her fingers, like a row of closed fists. She must have walked this path before, at Arthur and Rose's funeral, but she can't remember it. That day only appears to her in fragments. The cloying smell of flowers. The sight of the hearses. High heels on small stones. Throats clearing and orders of service being handed out. Did Birdie choose the photos on the front? She must have done.

It was freezing at the chapel – Birdie's fingers were white and numb. At one point, she had to be helped up. She thinks Arthur's golf friend, Burt, might have said some words, but all Birdie could hear was her own heart beating loudly inside her. It felt viscous, as though her ribcage had been cleaved open, the chambers and valves tugged, like an engine from a car. Birdie had tried to set Burt and Rose up once but it didn't go well. Rose had thrown her hat at him. Birdie had worn the same hat to bury Rose in. Everything was wrong, melting. She was a candle, dripping tears like hot wax.

When the curtains had drawn themselves round the ugly coffins and 'The Lark Ascending' was being piped through the tinny speakers, Birdie hadn't moved. She'd always popped back, one last time, to see if her sister had everything she needed before she went to sleep, to tuck her in, whisper goodnight. Birdie would have sat in that room all day, for the rest of her life, had the chaplain not come in to explain that another service was due to start. Someone else's sister, husband, best friend, son.

So Birdie had had to force her legs to walk her out into the sunshine. To stand and thank people for coming. To be kissed and hugged and told to be strong.

They had held the wake at the vicarage cottage. On the

walls, photos of children making salt dough and last year's hanging-basket winner smiled out at her. Birdie can't remember who organized the food. Cups of tea she didn't want were pressed into her cold hands. Rose's doctor brought her a sausage roll. For some reason, it made Birdie want to laugh. Grief numbed her, made her clumsy. Made her smile when she wanted to cry. Cry when she wanted to sleep.

After the funeral, everyone else went home to husbands and children. Birdie went home to lamps that would only be switched on by her. Curtains only she would draw. Beds only she would sleep in. Well, Ivy went home alone too, Birdie supposed, but the thought was of little comfort.

And now here is Birdie, back again. The graveyard is quiet, the ground soft under her feet. Her low heels sink into the mud. The smell brings back that camping trip with Arthur, and for a moment, Birdie falters, but then carries on.

Arthur and Rose have a small headstone each. When the funeral director asked Birdie what she wanted, it felt wrong to say she didn't want anything, as though she were being cheap, but she had no plans to come back and visit. They were not in the graveyard. They were gone. Birdie might as well have spoken to the post-box. She did, in fact, when letters for them still appeared. 'They are not here and left no forwarding address,' she told the envelopes as she put them back in the post-box.

It takes rather a lot of scrubbing at the granite with her hankie for their names to appear. Rose Clarke. Arthur Greenwing. Nothing else. Birdie had nothing else to say. How could she fit how she felt about her sister and her husband on to half a metre's worth of stone? And who were the words for anyway? Nosy strangers wandering past on a Sunday afternoon?

It is hard to talk to a piece of rock. Birdie tries to think of something to say as she kneels among the worms and angels. She thinks about the last time she saw her husband and her sister alive. The last thing she said to them. The last thing they said to her. 'Get to bed, Birdie, see you soon.'

Had she known what was going to happen, Birdie would have told them how much she loved them but, then, they already knew that. There is nothing new to say.

'See you soon, darlings.' Birdie thinks of them shifting over to make room for her.

Tights damp and back aching, Birdie gets up and goes inside the chapel. Into the smell of beeswax and old books. Her heels click across the uneven stone floor as she makes her way to the front pew, where she sits and bows her head. Thinks about what Min said. What she offered. *Do you want my help or not?*

If Birdie says yes, what comes next? Could she be cared for in her own home? Ask someone to pass her a drink or adjust her pillow without feeling guilty? Without feeling like she didn't deserve it. Could she ever stop thinking Rose's illness was her fault? Rose never had to ask for help. It was given unconditionally. Rose was an extension of Birdie. If Birdie had been the one who was ill, Rose would have looked after her. But Rose is not here, and Min is.

Do you want my help or not?

What would Princess Margaret say? Yes, of course! 'Yes, you can help me,' she'd say. 'Pass me that drink, light my cigarette. More gin in my tonic. Turn down the sun – it's too bright.'

'Yes,' Birdie says out loud. To no one but herself.

41

Jane

JANE AND SUKI HAD met Frankie's father in a bar in Laos. His name was Simon. He was on a gap year. He pronounced the word *bath* differently from them. Added an *r* that they didn't.

'Because it hasn't got an *r* in it,' Suki explained.

'You are a right laugh,' he'd said later on, three drinks in.

'That doesn't have an *r* in it either,' Suki had said.

'How about marry me? That has two,' Simon had said.

They had spent the night like this, arguing about accents, about the best line-up for a rock festival if you could bring people back from the dead. When the bar finally closed, Simon invited them to come and watch the sun come up while he played his guitar. As if he owned the land. In truth, he only invited Suki, but Jane went along too. Simon spent ten minutes trying to serenade Suki with a rearranged version of 'Sexual Healing', which Jane ruined by laughing, before he put his guitar away and asked Suki if she'd like to see something interesting behind the rocks.

'Careful it's not a crab,' Jane called, and watched as the sun rose like a loaf of pink bread in front of her, all alone.

Suki didn't notice for six weeks. She put the nausea and fatigue down to their diet and lack of sleep. Jane's periods had always been irregular. It was not till she told Suki that she needed to stock up on tampons that Suki realized.

'I can't be pregnant,' she told Jane. 'His name was *Simon*. The sex wasn't even any good.'

'I don't think it needs to be,' Jane told her, unwrapping a pregnancy test and handing it to her sister, who was squatting over the low toilet.

'There was nothing interesting behind those rocks,' Suki said. Then, 'Yuck, I just wee'd on my hand. Here.' She handed the dripping test to Jane.

'And now I have it on my hand,' Jane said. 'Excellent.'

'Deal with it – you're going to be a nurse,' Suki said, rolling her eyes and pulling up her knickers.

'And you are going to be a mum,' Jane said, minutes later, when the two lines turned pink.

Suki spent two days crying in the grotty hostel bed. Jane fetched fresh orange juice and bananas. 'You need it, the baby will need it.'

'Stop saying "baby",' Suki said.

'Sorry,' said Jane. 'The foetus? Crab? Which do you prefer?'

On the second evening, Jane managed to drag Suki out for dinner. They picked at some plain rice and drank flat lemonade.

'What am I going to do, Jane?' she asked, over and over again.

'I don't know,' Jane said. Suki was always the one with the answers, not her. 'What do you want to do?'

'Nothing,' Suki said. 'I don't want to do anything. I want to wake up and for it to have been a bad dream. I don't want to be pregnant. I don't want to have a baby and I don't want an abortion either. I just want to be a girl on her gap year.'

Back at the hostel, Jane lay beside Suki on the thin grey sheet, stroking her long hair back from her face as she cried. 'I don't want to talk about it any more either. Can we just pretend it's not happening? Just for a little bit?'

'Whatever you need,' Jane said, and for the next six weeks, neither of them mentioned it. They flew from Laos to Vietnam to Cambodia to Malaysia as planned. They walked part of the Ho Chi Minh trail. Spent a day at Angkor Wat. An evening on a riverboat watching the fireflies glowing between berembang trees on the Selangor river. The words 'baby', 'foetus' and 'crab' were not mentioned once, but Suki didn't drink alcohol at the bars, didn't scuba-dive or do anything that signs mentioning pregnancy forbade.

When Suki was twelve weeks pregnant, Jane woke her up with a bunch of flowers in a glass, a plate of toast and a plan. 'You don't have to have the baby, and you don't have to abort it either. I'll do it,' Jane said.

'What?' Suki mumbled, sitting up and rubbing her eyes. 'You'll have my crab for me?'

'Yes, I will. I'll have your crab, and you can go on and start your job like you planned.'

'But what about you?' Suki asked.

'I'll go back to Bristol like I planned, but instead of going straight into nursing, I'll take a couple of years off.'

'But where will you live? How will you cope?' Suki said.

'I'll move back home, live with Min,' Jane said, trying to sound happy about it. She'd planned to rent with some fellow nurses, do a couple of years in a Bristol hospital, then move on to another city. London maybe, or Brighton.

'I can't let you give up your life for me,' Suki said.

'Yes, you can.'

'Why?' Suki asked. 'Why would you do this?'

'Because you are my sister,' Jane said simply.

'Jane,' Suki said, tears sliding down her face, 'you have to know, if it were you in this situation, I wouldn't do it for you. I couldn't have a crab for you.'

It hurt Jane, Suki's honesty, but Jane had always known Suki would put herself first.

'I know you wouldn't,' Jane said, 'but I'm not you. I'm me. And I want to do this.'

They argued back and forth, stopped the conversation mid-sentence and didn't pick it up again for hours. Then Suki would say, 'But how?' or 'Whose name would be on the birth certificate?'

'Yours,' Jane said.

'Jane, I don't want to be a mother. Not now, not ever,' Suki said one night.

'I do, though,' Jane said, 'and who knows? Maybe this is my only chance.'

Jane wasn't lying. She did want to be a mother: caring for people was in her blood. She hadn't planned on having a baby right then, but babies and crabs come along when you least expect them.

From Malaysia, the sisters were due to go on to Singapore, Australia, New Zealand and then Fiji. Suki still hadn't decided what she was going to do, but they changed their flights, heading back to England via a safari in South Africa.

A week in Egypt to see the Pyramids and snorkel on top of the glassy sea. Finally, they stopped in Italy for pizza and ice cream, before landing in cold, wet Manchester on a Monday morning where everything was grey and everyone was miserable. It was like being in a black-and-white film. Their tans glowed unnaturally as they trundled along the filthy pavements, looking for a place to stay.

'I feel like Mary on her way to Bethlehem,' Suki said.

'Does that make me Joseph or the donkey?' Jane asked.

Suki was almost seven months pregnant by then. They'd still not officially made a plan, but Suki made a doctor's appointment and was told off for not being seen sooner. They went to the hospital hand in hand and came back with a tiny black-and-white photo of a baby. 'There's three of us,' Jane said in wonder.

'I can't look at it,' Suki said, passing it to Jane, then taking it back a moment later to look at it. 'It really does look like a crab.'

They rented a cheap bedsit above a kebab shop. It was like something out of a Pulp song. Jane got bar work in a noisy pub that played Britpop and served overcooked pasta. Suki tried to find a job, but she was big by then, and no one wanted to hire her. She spent her time walking round Manchester, reading books in the library, and eating iced buns. When Min called, they pretended to be abroad still, that the reception was bad.

'She can never know,' they had agreed. 'She'd kill us.'

'Promise never to tell.'

'Promise.'

*

When Suki went into labour three weeks early, they didn't even have a pack of nappies.

'This hurts!' Suki shouted at Jane. 'I don't want to do it any more!'

Jane rubbed her back, fed her ice chips. Told her to channel her pain. To imagine her vagina opening like a lotus flower.

'Stop talking,' Suki roared. 'My vagina is not a flower, it's a fucking forest fire!'

Frankie came out red and cross, just like a crab. The midwife wrapped her in a white towel that said, 'Property of Manchester Royal Infirmary', and placed her in Suki's arms. Suki fed her, a thin stream of colostrum, kissed her head, then handed her over to Jane and promptly fell asleep.

Jane sat in the chair by the window, sun coming through the blinds in perfect rectangles of light, a bundle of baby in her arms. Love hit her like a ten-ton truck. Frankie's eyelids, the curl of her lip when she screwed up her face. Her tiny little fists, punching out at nothing. She had Jane's feet, Suki's eyes, Min's frown, their dad's chin. Jane inspected every millimetre of her, pressed her nose into the crook of her flower-stem neck, laid her little finger in Frankie's tiny palm.

Jane didn't realize that Suki had woken up, that she'd been watching her.

'So,' Suki said, 'what are you going to name her? We can't keep calling her "the crab".'

Suki breastfed Frankie for ten weeks, then weaned her on to formula. During that time, they registered her name, Frankie Flash Brown, took her to be weighed and jabbed, poked at and prodded.

'Do you want to hold her while she does it?' Jane asked Suki, as the nurse filled the syringe.

'No,' Suki said. 'I'm the nice auntie. You're the evil mother. I'll cuddle her after and cheer her up.'

'I'm a mother,' Jane said in wonder.

The nurse, not understanding the situation, said, 'Have you only just realized?'

'Sort of,' Jane said.

'Come home with me,' Jane begged her, as they packed up to leave.

'I can't. I've already delayed my internship once,' Suki said. Plus Min would take one look at Suki and the game would be up. Her hair was falling out and her boobs were huge and leaking.

'Are you sure about this?' Suki asked, as they posted the key through the door of their horrible flat.

'I'm sure,' Jane replied. When she held Frankie, it was the most certain she'd ever felt about anything. Everything else would fall into place somehow.

Frankie was asleep in a sling on Jane's chest when Suki last saw her. 'Don't wake her,' Suki said. 'Just stay there, like you are.' She had bent down, kissed Jane's head and then Frankie's, whispered, 'Goodbye, little crab,' turned and walked away. Jane watched her go. Suki Brown, back in her old jeans, with a rucksack full of girly shoes. Jane's backpack was full of nappies, Babygros, formula and bottles. The train pulled away with a lurch, and it was just Jane and Frankie, Suki getting smaller and smaller behind them, until she disappeared from sight.

'Looks like we're really doing this, kiddo,' Jane whispered.

Every emotion possible had played out on Min's face when she'd opened the door, seen Jane, looked for Suki, then noticed the baby strapped to Jane's chest. Joy, fear, shock, confusion. Anger. Jane took a deep breath. 'Surprise!' she said weakly. 'I brought you back a souvenir.'

She waited for Min to roar at her, but Min was struck dumb. It was almost funny, the look on her face. 'Shut your mouth, Min, or you'll swallow flies. Here, will you please take your granddaughter? I really need a nap,' Jane said, holding out Frankie.

Min extended her arms automatically. When Jane placed Frankie in them, Min's hands shook, and her eyes were shining. 'Well, hello,' she said finally, fussing with the blanket, cradling Frankie's soft little head. 'Hello there, and who are you, eh?'

42

Ada

'Do you have everything you need?' Denise asks Ada, for the tenth time.

'Yes,' Ada says. Denise had taken Ada down to the registration point the night before to drop off her bag and collect her number. Ada can't look at her kit. She still doesn't feel ready, worries about bones breaking and sprains, about being knocked over, about getting cramp. What if someone collapses next to her? Does she stop to check on them or carry on?

Denise feeds her a bagel with peanut butter, shoves gels into her hand. Kisses her cheek and slaps her arse.

Ada sets off from Preston Park at 9.30 a.m. with hundreds of others to a brass band playing and half the city cheering them on. Her group snakes in and out of the Lanes, before heading out to Ovingdean along the seafront. And Ada feels fine. Good and strong as she passes twenty-five Supermen in various shapes and sizes. Eat my dust, she thinks as she overtakes them.

When she gets to the halfway point, Aleksey, Lech and Denise are standing front and centre wearing T-shirts that say, 'Run Ada Run'. She shakes her head at them, accepts the jelly beans Denise hands her, and carries on. It's on the way to the power station that her calves begin to burn. Her big toe has a heartbeat. Around her, people start to drop into a walk, to crouch, to fall. St John Ambulance members bring out stretchers. Runners lie by the side of the road, crumpled and broken. Ada thinks of Birdie and of Min, of her mother, and has to force her gaze forward, her legs to keep going. As she nears Carats café, she remembers her and Wilbur eating breakfast and wants to stop more than she's ever wanted anything in her life. But she doesn't. Come on, legs, she tells them, come on, Ada. You can do this.

By the time she's on her way back, past the beach huts, on the long straight towards Yellow Wave, Ada is running on empty. Her feet are bleeding and her legs feel wooden. Her arms ache – even her face hurts. She wants to stop. To let her legs give out. She wants to fail. Her calves are crying tears of lactic acid and breathing feels like inhaling glass.

And that's when he appears. Even among the hundreds of feet hitting the pavement on either side of her, Ada can tell it's Wilbur. That steady breath, the smell of cold mornings and wood fires.

'It took me twenty-two miles to find you,' he says, his voice even.

'You are very slow,' Ada grits out.

'I started at the very back,' Wilbur says, 'so I wouldn't miss you.'

He blew his chances to improve his personal best, for Ada. All that training. All that work. For her. A surge of adrenaline, like a fire coming back to life, sparks inside her. Her spine straightens, and her legs feel lighter. Her heart is a pair of bellows, blowing air into her lungs. 'Well, hurry up then,' she pants.

They finish hand in hand, Wilbur reaching for hers mere seconds before they cross the line, Ada linking her fingers in his, a long-buried sob climbing out of her throat, joy and pain, one and the same.

And then Denise, Aleksey and Lech are there, with their T-shirts now saying, 'Ada did it!'

Ada falls into Denise's arms, half crying, half laughing. 'Did you have a back-up T-shirt just in case?' she asks.

'Never even considered it,' Denise says. When Ada pulls away, Wilbur has gone. Lech wraps a tinfoil blanket around her and Aleksey passes her some gherkin juice. 'I'm not hung-over,' she tells him. 'Give me a bloody Mars Bar.'

'Just let me finish watching you eat that lucky, lucky banana first,' Aleksey says.

'God, you were amazing,' Denise tells her. 'You looked very angry the whole time, but you did it! You did it, Ada!'

'How do you feel?' Aleksey says.

Ada feels full and empty. Happy and sad. It's over, she did it. What next? 'Hungry,' she says, 'and a bit sick.'

Back at home, Ada sits in an ice bath, swearing, while Denise passes her rehydration drinks. 'Right, fuck this, I'm going to bed,' Ada says after five minutes.

'If you sleep, your legs will ache even worse,' Denise warns her, wrapping her in a towel.

'I don't care,' Ada says, hobbling towards her bedroom.

*

Denise wakes her four hours later with painkillers and a bowl of carbs.

'Get dressed,' Denise says. 'We're celebrating.'

Ada goes to say no, that she is busy. But then she thinks, Oh, fuck it, I'm really not.

'I may need some help getting dressed,' she says. 'My legs will not bend.'

Minutes later, she hobbles down the street in a skirt Denise has lent her, feeling like one of the newborn calves on the farm back at home. The bar Denise picks is full of people wearing marathon medals. The *Rocky* theme tune blasts out of the speakers. Kate Bush is running up that hill. When 'Sweet Caroline' comes on, the whole bar sings as one. Two beers in, Ada feels drunk. Lets Denise talk her into dancing. Aleksey has joined them and is attempting the robot. Ada's face hurts from laughing. 'I need to pee,' she tells Denise.

When she comes out of the Ladies, Wilbur is leaning against the opposite wall. He is wearing a black T-shirt and jeans. His hair is still wet. When he sees Ada, he smiles and it's suddenly hard to breathe.

'Hello,' he says. She waves at him like an idiot, is probably smiling like one too.

'So,' Wilbur says, 'here's the thing. In case you didn't get the message on the mug . . .' He pushes off the wall and steps closer towards Ada. She notices that he is not hobbling. 'I like you, Ada. And I think you like me too.' He is close, but not too close. Ada could easily walk past him if she wanted to. 'And you are not ready to admit it,' Wilbur continues.

Ada's smile falters slightly.

'But I am,' he carries on. 'So, I'll say it for both of us, for now.' He briefly touches her face, a large hand cupping her cheek. 'I really want to kiss you,' he says, and his Adam's apple bobs. 'Badly. But if I'm wrong, if that's not something you'd like, then I apologize for being so forward, and I'll never mention it again.'

Ada is frozen in place. A deer in headlights. Every muscle in her body throbs.

'But if it is,' Wilbur says, 'then please,' he holds out his hand, 'just come outside, right now, and leave with me.'

43

Birdie

BIRDIE'S MORPHINE PATCH IS running out. The pain is back, as big as a whale. Soon it will swallow Birdie whole. She fumbles in her bag for another. Connie notices and helps her find it. Brings her a cup of hot chocolate in a mug that says, 'Sorry I'm late. I didn't want to come.'

Birdie doesn't want to go. The day is almost over. Connie is wiping down the counters. A woman in pink is sweeping under the little tin tables. Crumbs and cupcake cases and dropped mini eggs being eaten up by her hungry little hippo broom. The Easter-egg hunt that morning was a huge success. Min oversaw it as though she were a prison guard. Her job (self-imposed) was to make sure no one got more eggs than she deemed fair. 'Go and cry to Jesus,' she'd told one child. 'Your tears won't work on me.'

Patients in their dressing-gowns had searched the bushes for chocolates. Kids ran from tree to tree, digging among the dirt and the dying daffodils. Frankie, who had hidden all the eggs personally, according to a plan she had spent hours devising, called, 'Cold, warmer, hot,' to the ones who struggled. The ones with plaster casts. The ones in wheelchairs.

The ones with tubes coming from their noses, with fluffy fuzz for hair. Patients stood in lines with their drips and their sticks in their tatty dressing-gowns, ID tags on their wrists like antisocial behaviour orders, as if they were a group of escaped convicts who had all stopped to watch. To say, 'There's one, over there!' and for a moment it was as though no one was ill at all.

Yes, Birdie had thought, watching Min use her stick to stop a child getting to an egg hanging on a low branch. Yes, I'll be okay with you. I'll be in safe hands.

She will not be going to a palliative-care home. She will be in her own bed with her dog and her bits around her, and Min, who is refusing payment. 'You were kind to Frankie,' she said, 'gave her that bed. That's payment enough.'

Min is going to spring-clean the bungalow. Give it a good going-over. Get it all nice and ready. Birdie is not sure Death cares about cobwebs, but Min insists. 'Just leave all the heavy work to me,' she said. All Birdie needs to do is breathe in and out until her lungs stop working. 'Don't you worry about anything,' Min said. 'I'll be right there with you.'

They are not twins, but they are the same age. They are not even friends, but they understand one another. Understand loneliness and pride and love and pain. At the end of the day, what else is there to know about someone?

After the egg hunt was over, and the dusty Easter Bunny with his big, dented head and stained knees had scared more children than he'd made smile, the nurses and porters came to collect everyone. To take them for scans and blood tests. To put them back into bed. 'That's enough excitement for you,' they said.

And then the pleasure garden was empty again, all pleasure gone, save for the odd tinfoil fragment dancing along the grass, catching the light. Shining like gold. Without it, Birdie would have wondered if the event had ever happened at all. She stood in the sun for a moment, let it warm her face, crown her thinning hair, make her momentarily a queen.

Back inside, day done, Birdie tots up the takings, mumbling sums out loud, counting on her fingers. Her till has trilled like a lark all day. Connie told her to take a break more than once, but Birdie was determined to see it through. Her last ever shift. Her last ever go on the spinning stool, where she has served doctors and surgeons and nurses, children and grandparents. She even served a criminal, handcuffed to a police officer. Rose would have squealed.

When there is nothing left to do, Birdie gets up and takes a last slow walk around. Down to the X-ray department, along to Phlebotomy. Up the stairs and into the chapel, empty save for two lit candles. She goes to her old Kingfisher ward, where people sleep with loose lips and gnarled fingers. Giant wordsearch books half completed, and knitting utterly abandoned. Hand cream on side-tables, beakers with lids on. The remains of meals that don't require much chewing. A dollop of mash, a puddle of gravy. The room smells of slow rot, of decomposition. These people are autumnal, turning to mulch. To dust, back to earth. In the gloom, their gold fillings and wedding rings twinkle like stars.

Birdie is pleased she never saw Arthur and Rose like this. She would not have liked to come and sit by these metal beds, trying to think of banal things to say. To peddle cheer like a one-woman Punch and Judy show. Pretend that everything was fine when it clearly wasn't.

Arthur and Rose approached death with their spines straight, their heads up. Rose was wearing her best green velvet hat. Arthur had his newspaper with him, folded just how he liked it. They made themselves comfortable before departure. Checked their wing-mirrors before heading off. Birdie didn't have to see Arthur shrinking, fading, like a painting that has been hung where the sun can hit it. She never had to witness him diminishing. Her husband opened a sticky jar of honey for Birdie on his last day on earth. Rose hung a new fat ball on the apple tree on her way out. Stopped to admire her roses, turned back to wave. They'd watched *Death on the Nile* the night before, devoured a box of chocolates, drunk too many rhubarb gins. Tomorrow she would wake up with a cold. Tomorrow Rose and Arthur would die. Perhaps the wheels had been set in motion long before Arthur offered to drive Rose to the doctor instead of Birdie. Maybe their final second was set, like a timer on the back of a clock, from the day they were born.

Birdie heads back to the stool for one last spin. She'll leave the cushion she brought for the next person. And the next and the next.

'And did you get what you wanted from this life even so?'

I did, Birdie thinks, looking down at the till. Remembering her typewriter and her work shoes and Arthur sweating as he put up the tent. She remembers Rose and her, swimming underwater. The Queen's coronation and the tears they cried. Thinks of Frankie putting on the kettle and talking about taxidermy. Of the first time Birdie popped on her WRVS pinny. Of the last time Arthur held her in his arms. Birdie runs her fingers over the buttons gently. 'Thank you,' she says to the cash machine. 'Please come back again soon.'

44

Jane

'I've been offered a transfer to the Australian office,' Suki says. They are sitting at Jane's table folding laundry. Suki wears very sexy underwear, Jane notices. She wonders what Min will think of it.

'Cool,' Jane forces herself to say. 'We never did get to go.'

They share a brief look that spans decades. Christmas Eve, the year they were convinced they were getting a dog and didn't. Measles and strawberry-shortbread cake and their dad's funeral and Min's rage. Period pains and a fifteen-hour bus journey next to a basket of live chickens in India. Simon and the sunset. The kebab shop in Manchester. The hospital room. The places they have seen together and the things they've seen alone.

'I might not take it,' Suki says. 'I've not decided.'

The fact that Suki has options stings Jane. But Jane picked Frankie, and she'd do it over and over again. Jane does not envy Suki her high-heeled shoes and her expensive face cream.

'You should know that some of the deadliest insects in the world live in Australia,' Frankie tells Suki, walking into the kitchen. 'Sixty-six venomous species. Not as many as Brazil, which has seventy-nine, or Mexico, which has eighty. The venom of the species is far worse, however. Taipan snakes, box jellyfish, funnel web spider. Stonefish . . .'

'Stop it, Frankie,' Min snaps, appearing from nowhere. 'You're making me itch. Go and fetch me a new Hoover bag. Suki Brown, are those your knickers?'

'No,' Suki says, trying to hide them.

'Yes,' Jane says.

'I raised you better than that!' Min says, gathering them up and dumping them in the bin.

'And now I will be going out and about knickerless. How is that better?' Suki says.

'You can wear mine,' Min snaps, walking out of the door. She has been busy cleaning Birdie's bungalow. She and Frankie are in seventh heaven de-cluttering.

'The muck on your blinds!' Min told Birdie happily. 'The state of your microwave!'

Min almost whistles as she digs piles of yellow newspapers and out-of-date tins from the back of Birdie's pantry. Frankie brings out jars coated in dust and cobwebs. She even carried out Birdie and Rose's mother's ashes, in a little brass urn, which she didn't tell anyone about until Min found it.

'Put that back at once!'

'But my specimen collection!'

'Don't you mention that dirty assortment to me, young lady.'

'Remember you've just had surgery,' Jane reminds her.

'Oh, pish,' Min says, 'I'm fine. Come on, Frankie. Let's tackle the loft! Lord knows what we'll find. Remember that house near us in Bristol?'

It had been, quite possibly, the best day of Min's life.

Britain's Biggest Hoarders had filmed a live show in their city and Jane had arranged to take her and Frankie. They had stood for five hours, watching Pat and Janet carry boxes of urine-soaked bedsheets and rotting food to a skip. Frankie made notes, took photos. Min, armed with Stardrops and Marigolds, asked to join in but was refused. She did meet Pat, though, which made her day.

'I'd like to thank you for all the pleasure you've brought me over the years,' Min said.

'That's very kind,' Pat said. 'Would you like my autograph?'

'No,' Min said, confused. 'Why would I?'

Jane's phone beeps with a text from Helen, asking if she wants to come for dinner. Jane doesn't know how to tell Suki about Helen. What to tell Helen about Suki. She feels like a book that has been dropped, pages scattered all over the place.

'Girlfriend?' Suki says, peering over her shoulder.

'No,' Jane says, closing the messaging app and putting the phone down. 'Yes. I don't know.' She wants to tell Suki about their one and only date on the pier, but Suki still feels so far away. As teenagers they'd pore over the agony-aunt pages in magazines, shrieking with laughter as they imagined Min answering their dilemmas.

'Cut his hands off,' Suki said. 'That'll stop him.'

'A good bath in Stardrops, and they'll soon drop off,' Jane said.

'Leave enough space between the two of you for the Holy Spirit, and you'll have nothing to worry about.'

They'd howled until Min came up, rolled up the magazine, hit them both on the head with it, then tossed it into the fire.

'Do you have a boyfriend?' Jane asks Suki.

'I don't know,' Suki says, frowning. 'I thought so, but then it turns out someone else thought so too.'

'Oh,' Jane says.

Suki shrugs but the movement is forced. 'I didn't like him much anyway,' she adds.

'Of course,' Jane agrees. 'Me neither. He sounds horrible.'

'He was,' Suki says. 'He wore shoes without socks, so I could never have introduced him to Min. He had a technical vest from an outdoor-clothing shop that he put on at work in protest about the air-con.'

'Even worse than my Crocs!' Jane says.

Suki laughs. 'When I told him, drunkenly, that I was named after a pussy cat, he sang Tom Jones to me in bed.'

'Oh dear,' Jane says.

'That's not the worst part,' Suki says, her voice thick with tears. 'The worst part is that I loved him. I bloody fucking loved him and I was just his bit of fun at the office.'

'Bastard,' Jane says, stroking her sister's hair.

'And I really wanted to call you,' Suki says, expensive makeup running down her cheeks, 'but I didn't know how.'

'I wanted to call you too. All the time. But all you ever sent were emojis.'

'I'm sorry. I don't even like emojis.' Suki sniffs.

When Min and Frankie get home from another long day of de-cluttering, Jane and Suki are on the sofa in pyjamas under a duvet. *Dirty Dancing* is on with the volume up and they are singing.

'Oh, no, not this,' Min says. 'Filthy bleddy ballet. You two always used to watch it. Don't look, Frankie. Your eyes will bleed.'

Frankie looks at her mum and her aunt, wedged together side by side on the sagging sofa. 'You look better like that,' she says to Suki, who has a green face-pack on and her hair in a bun on the top of her head. 'You look happy,' she says to them both.

The sisters camp in the living room. Stay up all night long, breaking down the wall they have built between them, brick by brick.

'I thought you thought I was a bad mother,' Jane says.

'No, I'm the bad mother. I gave away my crab.'

'Is that what you really think?' Jane says. 'That you're bad?'

'I think I did the right thing for me, and when I saw Frankie in your arms, I knew you were doing the right thing for you. Giving Frankie up was hard but giving you up was harder. Maybe that makes me a bad mother.'

'I think it makes you honest,' Jane says. 'It makes you brave.'

'What would you do if I took a job closer to you all?' Suki asks.

'Make you take Min to the chiropodist,' Jane says automatically, 'and for her mammogram, which she demands they perform without touching her breasts at any stage.'

'Amazing,' Suki says.

'I'd be really happy,' Jane says.

Min gets up at seven a.m. to go to Birdie's, headscarf tied on double tight.

'Good idea. Hair thieves are rife in Brighton,' Suki tells her.

'You can laugh now,' Min says, 'but you and me are going knicker-shopping later.'

'Can't wait,' Suki says.

'Call in sick,' Suki says, when Min has left.

'I can't,' Jane says, skin prickling at the idea of it.

'Go on,' Suki says, passing Jane her phone. 'Live a little, just for once. Quick, take it. It's ringing!'

'What do you mean you're not coming in?' Sadie says.

'I'm . . . unwell,' Jane says, her heart thumping.

'Well, you'll have to find someone to cover your shift,' Sadie says.

Jane feels herself go red, tears gather in the corners of her eyes, and a knot of nerves forms at the back of her throat. 'No,' she whispers.

'Pardon?' Sadie says.

'I said no. That's not my job, it's yours.' Jane slams the phone down and turns to Suki.

'Well done,' Suki says drily. 'You sure told her.'

'Oh, sod off,' Jane says, smiling. She said no to someone, and nothing bad happened. She didn't people-please and she's still alive.

'So, shall we go and get those matching tattoos we planned in India?' Suki suggests.

'I think we're a bit too old for butterflies at the base of the spine. Plus Min would kill us.'

'True,' Suki says.

'Hey, Frankie,' Jane says, 'want to bunk off for the day?'

Frankie's eyes are huge in her face. 'And go to the Booth Museum again?'

45

Ada

Ada doesn't realize where she's going until she gets to Birdie's house. It's been a long time since she's listened to her heart and not her head. She is wearing Wilbur's jumper. It is too big for her. It is perfect. For the first time since coming to England, Ada isn't cold. She pushes open the gate, marches up the gravel path.

'Who are you?' says Min. 'You'd best not be from the bleddy Neighbourhood Watch. I'm about done with that nosy, interfering—'

'My name is Ada. I'm Birdie's neighbour.' This information alone doesn't seem to satisfy Min, who makes no move to open the door. 'And I'm a doctor,' she adds.

Min looks at her suspiciously. 'Have we met before?'

Ada thinks about saying yes. About telling her she was there when Min collapsed in front of her granddaughter. That she was the one who had felt for a pulse. 'No, we've not met before,' Ada says. 'Is Birdie in?'

'Well, of course she's in. Where do you think she is? Out doing the bleddy can-can?'

Ada has to swallow a smile as she walks down the hallway. 'Shoes off!' Min cries, from behind her. 'I've just hoovered.'

Birdie is in the living room, propped up on the sofa with a thousand pillows, covered in piles of blankets. Ada is used to seeing cancer take a bite out of a person, but it still shocks her. How ill Birdie suddenly looks. How small, how thin.

'Hello, Birdie,' Ada says. 'I brought you some more of my bread.' She sets the heavy loaf down on the side-table.

'Ada,' Birdie says happily, her eyes morphine blue, 'how nice of you, come in. Sit down. Audrey, say hello to the nice doctor who saved my life.'

Ada pauses, freezes on the spot. Birdie must be confused. Maybe it's the morphine. Ada didn't save Birdie's life: she did the opposite. She read out her death sentence. 'You did,' Birdie says, as if she can read Ada's mind. 'You saved me that day in the garden. Because of you, I got to know Frankie and Jane. I got to work at the WRVS with Connie. I met Min. You gave me a life, Ada, after eight years of death. Thank you.'

Ada wants to argue, wants to say that she is wrong. That Ada doesn't see it that way. It was all Birdie and Frankie and Min. That she is not the hero. 'You are welcome,' she says instead.

Min brings her in a cup of tea and a slice of lemon polenta cake. She eyes the dark brown loaf as though Ada has brought a cowpat with her. 'You are too thin. You need some meat on your bones,' Min says, passing her a fork. 'Well, go on then, eat.'

Min is like a female Lech. For one second, Ada imagines them together, taking over the world.

'Something funny about my cake?' Min asks, eyebrows raised.

'No,' Ada says, taking another bite, 'no, not at all.'

'I'll take this,' Min says, picking up the loaf the way you would a dirty nappy.

'So,' Birdie says, 'you know everything about me, Ada. Tell me a bit about yourself.'

'Nothing to tell,' Ada says automatically.

'Well, tell me about Poland, then,' Birdie says, 'I always wanted to visit. Me and Rose planned to go to Kraków for the Christmas market. One has a fairytale theme, am I right?'

'Yes, in Wrocław,' Ada says. She and Ania went once. Ada finds herself describing the square, with its fairy forest, gnome rides and mulled-wine stands. The festive cakes and pretzels. The chocolate-covered fruit. 'Roasted nuts and smoked cheese. Grilled sausages and hot chocolate as thick as cream.'

'Mmm,' Birdie says, licking her dry lips.

Ada and Ania walked round eating for two days, stamping their cold feet in the snow. Buying tiny wooden toys for their mothers' Christmas trees.

'It sounds like you miss your friend,' Birdie says, closing her eyes.

'I do,' Ada says. Admits, at last, 'And I miss my mother.'

'When did you last see her?' Birdie asks. Her voice slowing down like a tape-player running out of battery, slurring its way into sleep.

'A long time ago,' Ada says quietly, looking at Birdie's face, translucent in the light. It is as if she's already fading away. Ada wants to shut the windows, draw the blinds. Trap Birdie here in this room, in this world. Life doesn't work like that, though, and it's not Birdie whom Ada is really thinking about.

'Too long ago,' Ada says.

'Well, book a bleddy flight, then,' Min says. 'It's not hard. My daughters flew around the world when they were nineteen and twenty and one of them was pregnant at the time. If they can do that, I'm sure you can manage to get to bleddy Poland. Didn't you just run a marathon?'

Ada hadn't even heard her come back in. Min makes it sound like her daughters were the pilots. Her voice is dipped in pride, glazed in love. Ada misses being talked about like that. Loved like that. 'I will,' she says. 'I'll do it now.'

46

Birdie

WHEN BIRDIE SLEEPS, ARTHUR and Rose appear, asking her how long she's going to be. Arthur has the engine running, beeps the horn once. Rose is by the front door, clearing her throat loudly.

'Hurry up and get in the car, Birdie,' Rose calls.

'I can't find my bee brooch,' Birdie mutters.

Birdie still doesn't want to go, but she knows there's no avoiding it. She can feel them in the bungalow, fingers reaching in to claim her. Swore she caught a glimpse of Arthur out of the corner of her eye when she woke up the other day, and that Rose was in the kitchen, sitting on the stool, binoculars glued to her eyes, when Birdie went to fetch a glass of water. Min scared her off, scared them both, by roaring, 'And what do you bleddy think you're doing, getting out of bed?'

Min's hands are a constant blur of action. They make bowls of custard, ice cream, porridge, stewed apple. They clean and dust and clap and flap. Birdie likes to watch Min going round her bungalow, wiping and tutting and polishing. If Stardrops and Vim could stop death, Birdie would be safe. She could put her pinny back on. Get on the bus, have her ticket punched.

Hold the bar as it lurched round corners. Smile at her fellow passengers. She'd be able to ding the bell, thank the driver, who'd smile at her pinny. *I'm a WRVS volunteer. What's your superpower?* Mind how you go, love, he'd say.

But Birdie isn't going anywhere now. Min's superpower is her determination. Her unshakeable belief that she is in control of everything, even the woodlice who live under the floorboards. Min knows about them, and they are there by permission only. One false move and they are out! Min runs on staunch principles and long-held grudges, which she airs like laundry. 'My wedding cake was as dry as a plop in the desert. Tina Street made it. Should have known she'd try to ruin it. She always had her eye on my Tom.'

Min will never burn out. Min is a marvel, but even she can't stop the pain. It is a constant thing, like lugging round a wardrobe. Sometimes Birdie wants to open its doors and climb inside.

'Time for more jollop,' Min says, which is what she calls morphine. Then Min sits in the chair next to Birdie's bed, and knits furiously as Birdie drifts between the sky and the sea. She is here and not here. In the background, Min talks. 'Lovely hands, my Tom had on him, first thing I noticed. Clean white nails, starched white collar. Suki was named after a lovely white fluffy pussy cat I once knew. Jane was named after Marilyn Monroe. Not her stage name, her real name, Norma Jane.' Min stops to sip at tea. It's Norma Jeane, Birdie thinks, or maybe says. Min carries on regardless. 'That Ivy stopped by the house again this morning, asking questions. Neighbourhood Watch, my elbow. I know a nosy parker when I see one and I told her as much. She's a weed, creeping round and over everything. Not knowing where she's not wanted.'

In the background the washing-machine buzzes, the radio plays.

'And madam here,' which is how Min refers to Audrey, 'has had her walk and done her *business* and had a long hot bath. She was growing potatoes out of her ears!' Min lifts Audrey up on to the bed. The dog sniffs at Birdie's papery skin. Gives a long sigh at whatever she detects there.

Death, Birdie thinks, it's here in this room. It's hiding behind the curtain like Rose used to do. Birdie wishes she could press rewind. See herself walking backwards, out of the bed, out of the door, the film moving faster and faster until Rose appears in the shot and further back still. Her mother, their little flat. The broken window, her and Rose sitting up on the roof, swinging their legs over the ledge. What will we be when we grow up? Will we get married? Not me, never. I am going to be a jockey. I am going to find Dad and live in the royal palace. I am going to be Princess Margaret's personal shopper.

Min carries on, bemoaning the seagulls. The price of fish. How clothes pegs are not what they used to be. Jane and Suki, keeping secrets. Frankie in trouble again for telling someone the truth about their painting. 'Doing the girl a favour, stop her wasting her time. We can't all be bleddy Picasso.'

Time, time, time, Birdie thinks. That's all it comes down to in the end. She wishes she had more of it. That she'd not wasted what she had. She wants to tell Min not to squander hers on things that do not matter. Arguing with bin men and getting cross about the new toothpaste lids. Picking up dropped leaves in the garden, only for the wind to blow and scatter more. Ironing tea-towels and hoovering behind the sofa.

Birdie wasted hers looking at old photographs, walking her dog with her head down, re-watching films to which she already knew the ending. Dancing with ghosts after one too many gins. We honour the dead by living, Birdie realizes. We grieve by getting up, carrying on, walking wounded as we may be. We love by letting go. Birdie opens her fingers as much as she can, splays them out on the blanket. But Min's time is her own to spend. She is currently wasting it on a cardigan for Birdie that she will never wear.

'Be done soon. Lovely wool this one. Soft and warm, but not too pricy. Almost there, just got to finish the sleeves. Add the buttons. I got brown. You can't go wrong with brown.' Click, click, click, go her needles. 'Not long now, almost there.'

When Birdie closes her eyes, Arthur and Rose smile out at her from behind her lids, like two cameo brooches. Everything is pink. Everything is warm.

'Oh, I like this one,' Min says, turning up the radio. 'They used to have such nice smart haircuts.'

'Here Comes the Sun' plays, drifting into the room like smoke. Paul McCartney tells Birdie that it's all right. She can hear fingers strumming the guitar, plucking at notes, pulling her in, placing a smile on her face. It's over now, the long cold winter. The sun is coming. It's all right, Birdie, it's all right.

47

Jane

'WELL,' HELEN SAYS, 'THAT'S some story.'

They are at one of the bars tucked into the wall behind the seafront. It's warm enough to sit outside. Beer shines like amber in the sun. Jane looks at the merry-go-round, gold and pink and yellow and green. Stationary horses and roaring dragons. Thinks how they are waiting to move. Waiting to be lit up. Jane knows how they feel. She's been at a standstill for a long time. Hoping for a green light. For someone to give her permission to be herself.

Jane tells Helen her story as if she's unpacking a bag she's been carrying for miles. For all of her life. Each sentence leaves her lighter. She tells Helen about the weekend in Brighton. The girl she'd kissed in a dark corner. The way she'd felt on fire. She tells Helen about her dad, about Min's anger. About her travels. Simon's poor attempt to serenade her sister. How lonely Jane was, sitting on the beach, an empty space next to her where a lover should have been. An empty space she has felt beside her all her life. She tells Helen about ice cream in Italy and the Pyramids in Egypt. About the first time she held Frankie. She talks and talks, gulping at her beer. Apologizing and being told to carry on, to say more.

'But what about you?' Jane says. Jane wants to walk along the avenues of Helen's mind. Stop by the lampposts of her life and bathe in the glow. Jane wants to ask Helen if she'd like children of her own. She wants to know how many other women Helen has sat across a table from like this, holding hands like this. Kissed sweetly on the waltzers. Jane wants to tell Helen she's not got much experience with this sort of thing. A few fumbles, tripping over her own feet in the dark. Soft hands and silk and nervous giggling. Nothing more.

But Jane is not going to be that version of herself any more. The one who apologizes for who she is and who she isn't. She's not going to say sorry for being plain Jane boiled potato. All this time she's had the key to herself and now she's finally been unlocked. The Book of Jane can fuck right off. Jane will write her own future, thank you very much.

'So, what is Suki going to do?' Helen asks. 'Stay or go?'

'I don't know,' Jane says, picking the label from the bottle in front of her. Once, she'd have prayed that Suki would choose her, to be near her. To like her more than anyone, anything else. Not any more. Suki and Jane will always be sisters. They will always have the past they shared. It cannot be erased or undone. Sibling love can stretch to the far corners of the globe without snapping, and it will always ping back.

'And you, Jane. What do you want to do with the rest of your life?' Helen says, studying her with a half-smile.

Everything, Jane thinks. I want to go Interrailing across a cold country. I want you in the tiny bed next to me. I want to hold your hand when the plane takes off. I want to fall in love with you and jump from a cliff. Hold my nose, shut my eyes, and dive in.

'How about a turn on the merry-go-round?' Jane says.

They walk along the promenade hand in hand. Time, for now, is theirs. They have nowhere to be. Suki and Frankie are at the cinema, having discovered they share a love for films. Well, for going to see them and then moaning about how awful they were. How factually incorrect and implausible.

Suki is getting to know Frankie. Frankie is slowly letting her. They circle one another like two dogs meeting for the first time. Wary, interested, shy. Sometimes Frankie will forget she doesn't like Suki and bring out her specimen collection. Suki has offered to take her to the taxidermy museum in Tring. 'Every animal you can think of. Dead as a dodo. I think they have a dodo there too actually,' Suki said.

'And we'd come straight back home after? You wouldn't take me away?' Frankie asked, frowning.

'I'll be glad to be rid of you,' Suki promised.

Suki is clumsy with Frankie, awkward. Tries too hard to be cool. It's quite fun to witness, actually.

'Shut up, Jane. Stop laughing. It doesn't come naturally to me, this maternal stuff. Not like it did for you.' Jane remembers Suki breastfeeding, wincing when Frankie latched on, sighing with relief when it was done. Jane taking her back, warm and sleepy.

'Give yourself a break,' Jane said. 'You're better than you think.'

Min is with Birdie. Jane's mother's ailments have all miraculously cleared up. No dropsy. No milk leg, housemaid's knee or tennis elbow. No quinsy or scurvy or whatever it was she used to ring Jane about.

'I'm fine,' Min said, when Jane suggested she slow down. 'In rude health. When have you ever known me to be otherwise?'

Jane offered to help with Birdie, but Min refused. The Macmillan nurses and she have it all covered between them. 'Birdie doesn't want you there for the messy bits,' Min said, almost smugly. 'She knows none of it fazes me.'

'None of it fazes me either,' Jane said. 'I am a nurse.'

'But she doesn't want you there,' Min said. 'She wants me. So, buzz off.'

Once, one of Jane's patients pulled out their IV line when Jane told them a visitor was coming to see them. 'You need that drip. That's your antibiotics,' Jane had said in alarm, seeing a stain of red bloom in the crook of their elbow. 'What are you doing?' she'd asked.

'Trying to die quickly, before they get here,' her patient said. 'I don't want them to see me like this.'

Dying on your own terms is a lot like living on them. Jane still wonders about her dad, if he coughed that day so Jane would hear him, would go in. If he was trying to say goodbye as he held her hand over his on the glass. Did he want to see her one last time, or was it just a cough? Jane will never know. She leaves Birdie to Min.

'So, my place?' Helen asks, eyes bright. She has her lipstick on and, yes, it's for Jane. It's all for Jane. The ironed shirt and the quiet scent of her perfume.

'One day,' Helen told her, 'you bit into this orange . . . and I was gone. I thought I was going to die.'

Jane laughs, shocked and delighted.

'There is nothing plain about you,' Helen tells her, 'nothing average or dull at all.'

Is there anything nicer in life than to be noticed? Jane thinks. To be admired, quietly without agenda, for exactly who you are?

'I dig your big weird feet,' Helen tells her, when they get back to her house. 'Stop hiding them away in your mum's socks.'

In the second before Helen kisses her, Jane thinks of Suki, sends up a little prayer that one day her sister will get to feel like Jane does now. Helen undresses Jane with all the lights on. Peels away her layers. Exposes the baby hairs on her face, the skin tags on her spine. The stretch marks inside her thighs and scars from mosquito bites. The green bruises on her shins from banging into hospital beds. The dry skin on her elbows. The soft scoop of her belly, melting over her bikini line. Helen studies it all. Her slightly larger left breast, the dimples on her bottom, the beginnings of cellulite on her upper arms. All of it out on display, to be kissed and petted by Helen, remarked on for its beauty, and Jane has never felt more seen, prettier. More like herself.

48

Ada

ADA SLEEPS ON THE train and reads on the plane, but every line is about cherry trees. About the night they shared. That kiss outside the bar. About sleeping in the safety of Wilbur's arms. She imagines Wilbur in the seat next to her. Them getting drunk on quince-flavoured vodka shots, eating little hoof potatoes in paper cups from a takeaway vendor in the middle of winter. Something hot in a cold country. What would her father think of him? Would Ada's horses eat apple slices out of his open palm?

The plane lands with a jolt. Around her, people jump up to grab bags from the overhead lockers. Ada stays in her seat until the plane is empty. She wants to see her mother badly, but at the same time, she is petrified. What if she looks older? What if she's cut off her long plait? And her father, does he walk with a stoop now? Can he still chop wood? These are the thoughts Ada could keep at bay in Brighton. But here, as she makes her way down the steps from the plane, Polish air hitting her cheeks, there is no hiding from them.

Jan Paderewski Airport is tiny. It smells of strong coffee and vinegary sauerkraut from the little café in the corner. Ada buys *kabanosy* sausages from duty-free, the cherry liqueur her father likes. Waits an hour for a bus that goes sort of near her village.

When she finally gets off, Ada heads straight to the baker for her mother's favourite biscuits.

'Ada?'

'Pani Szymanska?'

The old woman comes round from behind the counter to cup Ada's cold face in her oven-hot hands. 'Look at you, little Ada, back from England at last.' Ada's cheeks are pressed together firmly, her lips squished into a pout. 'Too thin,' Mrs Szymanska says, studying her, 'too tired. Too long away.'

She drops a swift kiss on Ada's head, then goes back round the counter and whips out a paper bag. In goes rye bread, two kaiser rolls, a sand cake. Proper Polish food, no showy flowers. Ada's jeans have holes in them. Her hair is tied up in a loose knot. 'And two *drożdżówki*. I have not forgotten your favourite, little Ada.' Pani Szymanska twists the edges of the white paper bag containing the rose doughnuts and hands it over.

'How much do I owe you?' Ada asks, realizing she has been counting in English.

The old lady snatches a small note from Ada's hand and tells her to run along and see her mother.

It starts to drizzle on the way. A thin rain, cold and full of needles. Ada had forgotten how hard Poland can be. In her mind, the light was always golden. She zips up her jacket, swaps her bags from one hand to the other and hoists her rucksack higher on her back.

It's a long walk. She could have called her father. He would have come and got her, borrowed a car, driven his tractor, but

Ada wants to make her own way. She has run a marathon. This is nothing to her, and also, everything. Every tree is familiar, every curve and dip and bend and branch. The fields bow and dip around her. Absorb her back into her homeland.

The children are just getting back from school as Ada reaches her street. She listens greedily to their fast Polish tongues. She may count in English, but she dreams in *Polski*. She always will. The old wooden front door of her house is open when she approaches, and Janina appears on the step, just as she used to when Ada was a schoolchild, waiting for her daughter. Her plait is still there, long, and silver now. Draped over one shoulder like a scarf. Ada's mother's cheeks are red from the oven. Her apron is white with flour.

Ada drops the bags at her feet, shrugs off the rucksack and runs. 'Minka!'

'Adrianna?'

Ada cannot speak for a moment. All she can do is let herself be held in her mother's arms, surround herself with the smell of bread and lemons and home. 'You were waiting! Did you know I was coming?' she asks, when they finally let go of one another.

'No, little Ada,' her mother says. 'I just hoped.'

Ada sleeps in her childhood bed for sixteen hours straight after two helpings of her mother's *bigos*, followed by blueberry *pierogi* with sour cream. When she wakes, she knows exactly where she is before she opens her eyes. Home. No IKEA side-tables, no blackout blinds. No paintings of places that Ada has never been to. The sun lights up the same old fractures in the same old walls. Ada used to feel like she was inside an eggshell about to crack open. Dreamed of flying out of the window and into her real life. Now she lies on her back in a happy star shape, her smile a crescent moon.

She is not treated like a guest this time. Her mother brings her tea without milk. Ada thinks of Wilbur's coffee cup, of his kiss. Her face in his palm. The way he paused to smile at her, his laugh as he collapsed next to her on the bed. Ada thinks of the date they have planned when she gets back. She wonders where he will take her. Ada has eaten in restaurants with open kitchens, seen men and women in white aprons chopping herbs so fast their fingers were a blur, pulling pizzas out of ovens with pretentious shovels. None of them had the finesse of her mother, moving around her small kitchen. It's in the way she rubs the flour and butter, how she tips her head to listen to the dough. How she tucks the loaf under her arm to slice it. Her fingers are as soft as babies' feet but can pluck dumplings out of boiling oil. It is like watching an orchestra: the pans are the strings section, Janina the conductor with her wooden spoon baton.

Ada sits in the old armchair drinking tea and watching, feet tucked up beneath her. When her father returns that evening, smelling of cattle and hay, it is to a feast. To a table covered with food, the kitchen steamed up, Janina's cheeks two pink balls of candyfloss, Ada, tipsy, filling shot glasses.

'What's all this?' he asks, hanging up his hat, coming to kiss his wife and daughter.

'It's nothing,' Janina says.

It's everything, Ada thinks. And when her parents have gone to bed, Ada creeps round their small house, touching small things. Her mother's spoons and the tiny salt pot Ada made at school as a child. Nothing has changed here. Her mother looks well, her father stronger than when she left. She will get up at five thirty, head out with him to the farm. She will not be an oncologist, a marathon runner, a coward. She will be a daughter.

When the morning work is done, Ada suggests that they go to the market. Her mother leaps up to get the wicker basket she keeps in the pantry. Ada thinks how many times it must have escorted her in place of her daughter. Today she tucks her mother's arm in hers. Doesn't interrupt as Janina fills her in on the life of every person along their street.

Ada is kissed, pinched, held, chastised, complimented, twirled round. 'Where have you been, little Ada?' everyone asks. 'What kept you away so long?'

'Stop, stop,' her mother says, dragging Ada away.

Ada doesn't let herself assess her mother's friends for early signs of cancer, and if she did, she wouldn't find any. This tiny village is frozen. People are covered with a fine dusting of flour, of their past, protecting them like sun cream.

They buy meat and cheese, fruit and tea. They walk down to the old railway line, where Ada used to go when she needed to escape. The tracks end abruptly, turning into brown fields that lead nowhere. Ada used to dream of rebuilding the line, of bursting through the forest, out to the other side of the country, to a place where it was okay to want to be more than a wife and mother. Now she looks at them from a different angle. From the other side of the green grass.

At home, she wears her mother's old cardigan and the wellies that live by the back door for traipsing up the lane. She sleeps for hours at a time. Her mother fills her room with flowers, her bath with rosemary and lavender oil. Her father kills a chicken. Her mother makes a cheesecake. Every day is Christmas Eve. Ada's cheeks are no longer blades. She lets her hair hang loose. Lets her mother brush it and plait it and trim the ends with the scissors held together by string that are older than Ada herself.

She phones Ania and they go to the park. Ada hefts up little Alina and puts her in the swing. The weight of her, too heavy and too light at the same time.

'*Wróciłeś do domu*, you came home,' Ania says.

Ada pushes Alina carefully, her little-girly feet pumping like pistons in their scuffed leather shoes.

'Higher! Higher! I want to fly,' Alina says.

Ada pushes the swing harder, pushes out her little confession. 'I had an abortion, six weeks after we moved to Brighton, Ania.'

'On your own? Why didn't you tell me?' Ania says.

Ada closes her eyes and lets the memories come . . .

'Ada, how are you settling in?'

She had still been in the hospital, recovering from the procedure when she took the call from her mother. 'Fine, good.'

'I've been worried about you. We've not heard from you in a couple of days. Are you ill? Can I send you anything?'

Ada had been waiting to be discharged. She had a thick pad between her thighs.

'I miss you already, Ada. We've never been apart so long.'

All her mother had ever wanted was another child. Ada could have given her one. Janina would have done everything for her daughter. The sleepless nights, the nappies and the colic, walks with the pram to the river. She would have treasured every single second, but Ada never gave her that chance because it was not her mother's choice.

'I thought you'd try to talk me out of it,' Ada says.

'Why? Because I told you I'd always wanted to get married and have babies?' Ania asks.

'Yes,' Ada says.

'Ada, that was my path, not yours.'

Ada looks at Ania's baby, sleeping in the pram, at Alina in the swing, still so little, so vulnerable. Ada's baby would have been almost eight by now, skipping along the wild banks, picking flowers. Buckled shoes, bruised knees. Or maybe not.

Ada has always understood absolution. When her patients decide to stop treatment, no matter who they are leaving behind. The young mother, the adored father. The teenager in love. Even if there are still options, other things to try.

'I can't do it,' some people say to her. 'I just can't do it any more.'

'Then we stop,' Ada always says.

If love could be bottled, if the strength to do for others what they cannot do for themselves could be plucked and pickled and tapped into veins, maybe no one would die of cancer. Maybe Ada could have kept her child, with her mother's devotion fuelling her. But, like her patients, it was her body. It was her choice. It will always be her choice.

'I did the right thing for me,' Ada says, 'but maybe I didn't mean all of it. The no-marriage part, for example.'

'Shit the bed, Ada,' Ania says, an English expression she learned and loves. 'You haven't fallen in love, have you?'

'Fuck off,' Ada says, then grins so hard it hurts.

Ania laughs, pulls a bottle of milk from under the pram

and passes it to Kasienka, who grabs at it with chubby hands and starts sucking furiously.

'But seriously. All those patients you have cared for,' Ania says, 'all the hours, the things you sacrificed to try to make a difference. You have given up everything for others, for strangers. That is love too, Ada. You are a mother, in your own way.'

Ada thinks of the tattoo she got the week before she left Poland for Brighton: 'Never again believe in the benevolence of God.' Has Ada been getting it wrong all this time? Maybe benevolence is the only thing to believe in when there is nothing else left. For all Ada has seen of cancer, of loss, she has seen more of kindness.

When she gets home, she walks straight into her mother's arms and cries. Her mother does not ask why, or what the tears are for, and Ada doesn't tell her. She will never tell her. Truth be told, Ada does not know who she is crying for. Janina simply holds her daughter, wipes her cheeks dry with the handkerchief that has been waiting up her sleeve all these years, just in case.

49

Goodbye Birdie Greenwing

BIRDIE DIED ON A Sunday afternoon, Min by her side, holding her hand. The room did not grow colder. There was no death rattle, like there had been with Tom. Min never told Jane that part. How he was still trying to say sorry for leaving her with his last breath.

Birdie died with a soft smile on her face. Her ugly, bulky dog resting a paw on her heart. Birdie died wearing her sister's green velvet hat and her conker-brown shoes. 'I want to look my best when I go,' she'd told Min, 'for when they see me again.'

Min had understood immediately, rushed to iron Birdie's silk blouse and the skirt that once flirted with her knees when the breeze blew. 'Arthur will hardly recognize you,' Min said, pulling the covers back up gently.

Birdie died thinking about royal velvet pillows and Frankie's shorthand. She died thinking about Audrey's wagging stumpy tail when they'd first met. She died remembering the time a slightly drunk Rose had opened the door, naked, to Ivy, then said, 'Watch this,' and wiggled her arthritic bottom at her. She died on an old bed, washed clean by a new friend. Birdie died at two o'clock, which was when she, Arthur and Rose would have a gin and tonic. They called it an aperitif, but no meal ever followed. A bowl of olives and some fancy biscuits with cheese perhaps. Birdie died to the sound of ice clinking as it landed in her favourite tumbler. To the fizz of a lemon as it slid in, like a lady lowering herself discreetly into a pool. She died to the tinkling bell of her wedding ring against a glass of champagne. She died to the sound of Arthur and Rose, toasting her name.

Min cried, privately and painfully, then rallied. Wiped her tears on her apron, folded Birdie's hands on her stomach and patted her hair into place before the ambulance came. She had stayed with Birdie, as she'd promised she would. Birdie Greenwing did not die alone. When it is Min's turn to go, she knows Jane and Suki will be there to do the same for her.

Frankie took the news more or less as Min thought she would. She talked about Birdie's body going into rigor mortis. 'That's the stiffening of the body muscles due to chemical changes in their myofibrils,' she said.

'I see.'

'Hopefully, I'll be an embalmer by the time you die, Min,' Frankie said. 'It's the job of a lifetime,' she told Suki.

'Literally,' Suki replied.

Frankie explained the whole process to Min. 'First I'll wash your dead body in disinfectant.'

'Good start,' Min said. 'I like Stardrops. Value for money.'

'Then, I'll glue your eyes shut and secure your jaw with wires. I can make it into whatever position you like.'

'Always leave them laughing,' Suki said.

'Then I'll insert a big needle into one of your veins, drain your blood and replace it with formaldehyde-based chemicals before cutting open your abdomen, puncturing your organs, draining all your gas—'

'I don't have gas!'

'Are you sure you're okay about Birdie?' Jane asked her.

'We're all going to die, Mum,' Frankie said. 'You should know that, being a nurse.'

To Min's chagrin, Birdie had left all of the arrangements to Frankie, which is why they are all wearing head-to-toe mourning black for the funeral.

'It's what Birdie wanted,' Frankie says.

'It's what *you* wanted,' Min comments.

'It's the same thing,' Frankie replies, and maybe she is right. The group receive more than one odd look as they walk to the church in floor-length velvet skirts and gloves the colour of midnight.

Frankie follows the coffin very slowly, a heavy lace veil over her face, waving a stick of cloying incense.

Birdie's coffin is a simple affair. It took some persuading for Frankie to agree to a closed casket. She had spent a long time in the chapel of rest with Birdie.

'Is your daughter all right?' the funeral director asked Jane, when they went in for the second time.

'She's perfect,' Suki had snapped. Jane wanted to read Frankie's eulogy before she read it aloud, but Suki assured her that she'd looked over it and it was fine. 'Great, actually.'

As the last note of the funeral dirge plays out, Frankie stands completely still at the front of the chapel, her eyes coolly assessing the room. 'I don't like many people,' she says, in her serious voice. 'I don't like people who stand too close to me. I don't like people who have bits in their teeth. I don't like people who touch my hair. I don't like people who tell me to stop talking.'

Jane shares a look with Min. Helen tries to remain serious, nodding as Frankie says, 'I don't like people who eat bananas. I don't like people who breathe loudly . . .'

'I don't either,' Ada says to Wilbur.

'I don't like my teacher and his lessons that are factually incorrect. I don't like people who are scared of spiders. I don't like people who think knock-knock jokes are funny.'

'Knock-knock jokes are brilliant,' Wilbur whispers.

Min looks at her watch.

'I don't like people who talk loudly on the phone. I don't like people who chew gum. I don't like people who say "know what I mean" all the time.'

Min tuts.

'I don't like people who hurry me,' Frankie says, glaring at Min. There is a long pause and then Frankie finally adds, 'But I liked Birdie.'

What more is there to say?

'Nailed it,' Suki says, clapping. 'Bloody nailed it.'

Ada and Wilbur join in. Frankie gets a standing ovation, which she receives with a frown.

Birdie will be buried with Rose and Arthur. Min has polished their graves, cut the lawn, planted a heather bush, made the place ready to receive a new housemate.

They hold the wake at the WRVS café. A small group of black-clad people in the middle of all its rainbow bunting and cherry-topped cupcakes. 'Like a murder of crows,' Helen comments.

'An unkindness of ravens,' Frankie replies.

'A kettle of hawks,' Helen offers. Frankie looks impressed.

Connie hands out mug after mug of tea. 'I don't do funerals myself,' she'd said, when Jane invited her to the ceremony. 'If I said yes to one, I'd have to say yes to them all, and then I'd be going to so many funerals I'd have to give up my volunteer work!'

They decide to eat outside in the pleasure garden. Cucumber sandwiches, cheese straws. Mini sausages and slivers of quiche. Scones with blackberry jam.

'Birdie wanted it to feel like a picnic,' Frankie says. 'Slow down, Ada. Leave some ham for Audrey, my dog. My dog that I own called Audrey.'

Min shoos away the seagulls, tells them they were not invited. Makes people use napkins and proper knives. Wilbur passes Ada another sandwich. She pours him some tea.

'It should not feel so nice,' Jane says, buttering a second scone, the sun warm on her back. 'I should feel sadder than this.'

'Birdie didn't want you to feel sad,' Frankie says. 'She told me she'd spent enough time feeling sad for all of us twice over.'

At that, Jane's lip wobbles.

'"Life – there's no getting out of it alive,"' Suki reads from her mug.

'My mug is dirty,' Min notices. 'Needs a good soak with some soda crystals.'

'Well, there's a job going if you want one,' Connie says. 'Just lost my last volunteer.'

Jane watches her mother consider it. 'Min. I don't think you—'

'Free lunch included,' Connie interrupts, 'and any pastries too stale to sell the next day.'

Min has not officially said she isn't going back to Bristol, but Birdie left Min her bungalow, and Min has just got it how she likes it. Jane doesn't want her mother to move in next door but, also, she does. Because it's Min. Min, who asked Helen what her intentions were with her daughter. If they were using protection. 'You can get dirty doing anything,' Min told Jane.

'There will always be a bedroom for you, Suki,' Min told her, 'and I expect to find you in it, often, no matter where you go off to next.'

'Yes, Min,' Suki said. 'Am I allowed to bring boys back to stay over?'

'No, you are not,' Min said.

'You'll just have to go behind a rock again,' Jane told her.

'What did you just say?' Min hissed.

'Nothing,' Jane and Suki said as one.

Epilogue

BRIGHTON IS AN ADVENT calendar. All the doors have been opened except these last few.

At number six, Min is washing up, happy hands scrubbing the traces of dinner off the plates. Her WRVS pinny is clean and pressed for the next day. She has already reorganized the canteen and replaced all the dirty, *dirty* mugs with plain blue ones. Next stop, world domination.

At number eight, Jane and Helen are in the living room, planning an Interrailing trip. Suki is on loudspeaker, saying she'll meet them in Berlin. Frankie is out walking Audrey. They have found a different school for Frankie, one in which she is encouraged to be herself instead of being compared unfavourably to everyone else. Where being neuro-diverse is seen as a superpower. She has even – almost – made a friend her own age.

At number twenty-two, Ada is reading a medical journal, scanning for the latest developments. Wilbur is sitting next to her, reading over her shoulder. Their white coats are tossed over the old sheepskin-covered armchair that Ada found in the Lanes and Wilbur carried home. The IKEA furniture is slowly being replaced with something that feels more real.

And above the Polish shop, Aleksey is making Denise his famous sausage stew while Lech sleeps in front of the TV, the sound turned down low.

Outside, the moon is pinned in place, held up by the stars. Underneath a purple sky, everyone is okay. Everyone is exactly where they should be.

Thank-yous

I am incredibly lucky to come from a long line of difficult women. Women who refused to stay at home. Women who only eat tomatoes they have grown themselves. Women who still go on exercise bikes well into their nineties. Women who ignore well-meaning waitresses who call them 'love'. Women who won't get out of bed until they have had a cup of Earl Grey tea and finished the cryptic crossword. Women who would buy an expensive plant but never spend money on lip balm or face creams. Women who steal cuttings from other people's front gardens. Women who scorn rubber gloves and lean on garden forks with bits of dead leaves in their hair. Women who answer back and read books and do as they please. I am determined to keep this tradition going as I raise my own witches.

It takes a village to write a book. I could not have done this without Kirsty Dunseath, who has been my champion, sender of dog photos, cheerleader, editor, and fairy godmother through book two. Thank you. Big love to Alison Barrow, Milly Reid and everyone at Doubleday who has helped get Birdie on the breeze.

Thank you, mother of mine, for taking me to libraries and not being scared of spiders and climbing on horses without a saddle and talking to plants and still trying to cook dinner even though you have lost all the skin on your fingers. For arriving at school pick-up with horse nuts in your pocket and straw in your hair and not giving a single shit. I salute you.

To my south-east book group, thank you for letting me hang, listening to me stress out, and recommending amazing books. Tilly, if you like it, I buy it. Jules, thank you for the cinnamon-bun recommendation and for always keeping it real. I am not good at being friends with women, and I've never had a gang-a-lang, but Clair, Sara, Kath, Alisha, Raye – you have made me feel a part of something I've always wanted. Sara, thank you for your manifesting. Don't listen to people who call it delulu.

Alisha – thank you so much for your early review and all the love when I needed it most. Gaming truck party soon, please.

Thank you, Wayne Kelly, Steve Watson, Sarah Bonner, Alex Thornbur, Jodie Matthews, Helen Trevorrow, Andrew Dell, Nick Barrington, Sammy Berry (for the early read and love). Thank you, Helen Paris, for being Helen Paris. Thank you, Agata Tobolewska and Ania Kierczyńska, for all your meticulous research and answering my questions about Poland. Any mistakes are mine. Thank you, Jenny Williams, for everything, the cheese toasties and homemade cake and Bliss's costume and loose-leaf tea and for rescuing Olive. There is a line in a poem by Marilyn Hacker that goes like this: 'What your mother left undone, women who are not your mother may do,' and when I read it, I think of you. Thank you, Kerri, kisses to Cathal. Annie Mead, thanks for your nursing information and for nursing me. Thank you, Sonali Kaushik, for your insight into the female body. Thank you, Mara, Shirley and Dawn, for being the sisters I never had. Dawn, I miss you every time I do a jigsaw. Paxton, thanks for teaching me cards. Let's play again real soon. Thank you, Nula and Pam.

Thank you, Alex Fox, for getting me and all my weird crap and crazy family and making me feel seen. I wish I were your neighbour.

Thank you, Helen Gambarota, for being so genuine and warm and kind. The second I saw your face I knew you were beautiful inside and out.

Thank you, Aunt Pat, for the wonderful letters and your very strong opinions and the homework and book recommendations.

Thank you, Anne and Annie, Sophie and Molly. Proud to be related to you. Kiss to Alwynne on the other side (the shorthand bit was for you). Thank you, Jennifer Newton, for being kind, strong and beautiful all the way through (we walk the same line). Thank you, Linsey Waters, Toni Harding, Heather Howard, and Shelley Frostick, for being inspirational women.

Thank you, Janina (Karczmarek) Zielińska and Magda Zielińska (Kuzemko). We carry your name on in our children.

Thank you, Grace, Daisy and Bliss for your wisdom and kindness and capacity for joy. Thank you for trusting me with your secrets and your concerns. For making me a mother. Sorry about being so loud and embarrassing. I promise I'll never stop.

Thank you, Fleur, for your faith and friendship. I waited a long time to find you. Kisses to Biba and Em.

Last but never least, thank you, James Waller, for coaching girls' football. For learning how to plait hair and for always trying to be better at everything you do. For cheerleading all things pink with utter dedication and devotion. For seeing autism as a superpower. For believing in me when I don't.

This book is to all women everywhere. I incite these dedicatees to rebellion!

ERICKA WALLER lives in Brighton with her husband, three daughters and dogs. Previously, she worked as a blogger and columnist. Her first novel, *Dog Days,* was widely praised by authors and reviewers alike. *Goodbye Birdie Greenwing* is her second novel.

Twitter/X: @erickawaller1
Instagram: @erickawaller1
Website: www.erickawaller.com